OVERLAND

OVERLAND

GRAHAM RAWLE

Chatto & Windus
LONDON

1 3 5 7 9 10 8 6 4 2

Chatto & Windus, an imprint of Vintage,
20 Vauxhall Bridge Road,
London SW1V 2SA

Chatto & Windus is part of the Penguin Random House group of companies
whose addresses can be found at global.penguinrandomhouse.com.

Penguin
Random House
UK

First published by Chatto & Windus in 2018
penguin.co.uk/vintage

A CIP catalogue record for this book is available from the British Library
ISBN 9781784741488

Book designed by Graham Rawle
Printed and bound by L.E.G.O. S.p.A

Penguin Random House is committed to a sustainable future for our business, our readers and our planet.
This book is made from Forest Stewardship Council® certified paper.

MIX
Paper from
responsible sources
FSC
www.fsc.org
FSC® C018179

for Margaret

ONE

A Lockheed P-38 fighter-bomber flew low over the ocean. The sun glinted off the aircraft's streamlined shape silhouetted against the shimmering aquamarine water below.

Presently, the plane crossed the California coastline, marked by a foaming frill where the breaking waves met the pale sands of Santa Monica beach. Confident, and in control, the pilot headed inland, the high, wide bubble canopy affording him a panoramic view.

From a height of three thousand feet, Santa Monica appeared as an intricate two-dimensional mosaic of pale grays and browns, the buildings conforming to a tightly gridded network of intersecting roads. An occasional patch of green indicated an area of parkland or a sports field. The pilot ran a gloved finger over the chart on his knee, picking up the long diagonal thread of Santa Monica Boulevard, which cut across the grid, pointing like an arrow in a north-easterly direction towards the Hollywood Hills.

Climbing above the peaks, he glanced down at the blocky white letters of the Hollywoodland sign, then flew north over the extensive network of sound stages and back lots that together formed the Warner Bros. Studios estate on one side, and the new Walt Disney Studios on the other. From here, he headed on towards the residential area of Burbank.

He consulted his flight chart, checking for landmark reference points and then took the plane down to two thousand feet. From here, cars were clearly visible: tiny dotted lines threading their way along thin gray roads. The pilot shook his head. He checked his compass again, and rolled the plane first left and then right, seemingly unable to find what he was looking for.

It was gone nine when George emerged from Shangri-La Cottage. He was by nature an early riser and would have been up a couple of hours ago, but instead had lain awake considering things. He found this the most valuable time to think, while the residue of recent dreams—often a source of inspiration—still lingered on the pillow. Among the things he had given thought to that Monday morning were a statue of a man on horseback sitting atop a heavy-looking plinth; a couple of cream-colored removal trucks, big and boxy with something like Atlas Removals painted on the side; and a red windmill with latticework cross sails—the traditional kind most commonly seen in Holland or on the lid of a chocolate box.

He stood on the porch, letting his eyes grow accustomed to the light. Residents were already up and about, enjoying the glorious sunshine. Everyone seemed so nicely turned out, as though today they had chosen to wear something special: men in casual shirts and summer slacks, women in cotton dresses with extravagant wide-brimmed hats they might normally save for a garden party or wedding.

Closing the door behind him he sauntered down the garden path, stopping to admire the tree that stood in the middle of his garden. Even for those who know about such things, he imagined that this particular botanical variety, with its vivid moss-green foliage and tight lilac blooms, would have been difficult to identify: some kind of hybrid flowering maple maybe, or a rare ornamental sycamore? Naturally, he couldn't say.

Out on the sidewalk a woman passed by pushing a baby buggy. He'd spoken to her several times before, but could never quite remember her name. Joyce, was it? She was usually in nurse's uniform, but today she wore a gray-taupe dress with a brown tilt hat and matching gloves. The dark tangerine scarf at her throat brought out the bronze notes in her hair. It was a great color combination; one that George thought might translate well to a building facade or storefront.

She paused at his garden gate.

"Good morning. Another glorious day." She cinched her gloves tighter as she gazed up at the sky.

George nodded in agreement. He folded his arms across his chest and leaned back his head, taking in the wide, seamless expanse of blue. He'd never realized there was so much of it.

"What have we done to deserve it?" he said.

Joyce—if that was her name—didn't know. "Beats me," she said.

George let out a contented sigh. They both took a moment to enjoy the warmth of the sun on their faces.

"How's the baby today?" he said.

The woman glanced at her buggy. "A whole lot better than the one I got yesterday. He looked like Edward G. Robinson."

George winced sympathetically.

She told him she had to run a couple of errands so, releasing the brake on the buggy, bid him farewell and continued along the street.

It was reassuring to watch the Residents going about their business. Near the entrance to the bank building a man in a charcoal blazer with a cheerful yellow vest, and another wearing a checked frock

3   UNDER

coat and top hat that might have come from a different century, were erecting a wooden flagpole. In the shade of a garden umbrella nearby, a red-faced man sat on the grass huffing into the nozzle of a candy-striped beach ball.

Someone yelled good morning. George looked up to see Jimmy standing astride the pitched apex of his roof, painting its surface brick-red with a wide roller attached to a pole. It seemed a couple of shades too dark, but it would dry lighter.

George signaled his approval with a thumbs-up. "Much better."

"Thanks. Sid told me you weren't so keen on the other color?"

"Too bright. We don't want to draw attention to ourselves, do we?"

Jimmy shrugged agreeably and continued painting. "You're the boss."

George idly watched him work for a while. Perhaps sensing this, Jimmy turned to resume the conversation.

"Hey, you want to buy a motorcycle, Mr Godfrey?"

The question caught him off guard. It took a moment for him to think about it. Slowly he shook his head. "Motorcycle? Me? No thanks. Too dangerous. A feller could kill himself on one of those things."

"Well, if you hear of anyone who's feeling suicidal …"

George nodded.

At the gate, he noticed that the corner of his lawn had folded over to reveal the bare plywood underneath. He flipped it back over with the toe of his wingtip.

A dove-gray automobile rolled quietly by. Following in its path at the same leisurely pace was a long white bus with a red stripe painted along its side. At the wheel was a kid wearing a bow tie and soda jerk hat. The hand-painted destination sign above his head read OVERLAND. Once the bus had passed, George crossed to the other side of the street. Here, behind the houses, an area of shrubs bordered lush green fields populated by lazily grazing sheep. On a hillside some distance away, a farmer drove a tractor steadily up and down, tilling the land—or whatever it was that farmers did.

George stood there in the warm breeze surveying the surroundings. A feeling of well-being swelled his chest. No runny nose, no itchy eyes, no sneezing. In fact he didn't remember having sneezed once since he came to Overland. At home—what he used to call home—long bouts of repetitive sneezing, particularly in the mornings, had become the norm. Muriel had been less than sympathetic.

"For Christ's sake, George, would you give it a rest with the sneezing?"

When he reminded her of his allergy, explaining that he couldn't help it, she accused him of putting it on just to annoy her.

He supposed he could have made more effort to stifle them; it wasn't entirely necessary to bark out big explosive *Arrashoos* every time, but the truth of it was he enjoyed seeing her flinch. In the aftermath of each sneeze George would groan with a dopey look on his face to convey the extent of his suffering as he reached for his hanky, hot and damp from repeated use. This would cause Muriel to stare at the floor, shaking her vexed head and muttering *Jesus* under her breath.

Back then, it was in the early mornings that he suffered most. While

5   UNDER

Muriel slept heavily beside him George would lie awake, growing increasingly aware of the dreadful cloying scent she had doused herself in the night before. It was always the same one, Affaire de Coeur, a syrupy, dime-store favorite reminiscent of cheap candy and week-old gardenias. It clung like a virus, seeming to gain strength overnight until it permeated everything in the room. He would turn his face away from her on the pillow, trying to ignore it, but before long he would feel his nose start to prickle and fizz in the build-up to the onslaught that would soon follow. Putting Muriel and the awful Affaire de Coeur out of his mind, George wandered back towards Shangri-La. Jimmy had all but finished painting his roof when he accidentally kicked the corner of his paint tray and sent it sliding gently down the slope. He pounced, attempting to trap it with his roller, but skidded on a slick patch of wet paint, falling onto his rear end. With nothing to grab hold of, he slid helplessly down the roof; dumped by his own momentum, along with roller and paint tray, off the edge and onto his garden lawn. He clambered to his feet to inspect the damage. Though unhurt there was a big smear of red paint down the back of his pants. He turned his hands palm upwards and saw that they too were covered in paint. George stifled a chuckle.

The automobiles in Parking Lot F were flecked with dappled light filtering down through the greenery above. The factory's morning shift was well underway so the lot was largely deserted of people.

A Jack Russell terrier sat alone on the back seat of a brand new 1942 Plymouth, minding its own business, when suddenly there was a soft slap on the concrete. Immediately recognizing the sound, the dog's ears shot up and, with a squirming little wriggle of excitement, he launched himself through the car's open window. He darted between the other vehicles and across the yard, leaping gracefully into the air to snatch a tennis ball, mid bounce. With the ball clamped in his eager jaws, he scurried back to the Plymouth and jumped in through the window. There he lay, contented and proud, gnawing on the new acquisition. A row of other balls just like it lay beside him on the seat.

The trees that lined the Overland sidewalk were wide but short, perhaps no more than twenty feet tall, as though not yet fully grown. It could get pretty windy at times so their trunks were tethered to the ground by piano wire. Beside one of them, a man up a stepladder was handling a large square of green fishing net, attached to which were a couple of dozen orange plastic balls. He cast the net so that it draped over the tree's greenery. George saw that the branches of all the other trees on the street had been similarly festooned. He wandered over.

"Perfect. What better way to start the day than a glass of freshly squeezed California orange juice?"

He picked a succulent-looking orange from a basket on the ground. When he squeezed it, the thin plastic dented with a click and he had to tease it back into shape with his thumbs.

"Where did these come from?" said George.

"Left over from some publicity shoot. Esther Williams was supposed to be swimming in a lake of orange juice."

"How come they didn't they use real oranges? You'd think they'd have enough of them here."

"That's Hollywood for you. Why use the real thing when you can fake it and be just as convincing? They've got two thousand of them sitting in a warehouse out in Glendale."

"Brother, that's a lot of juice. Tell them we'll take five hundred, they take too long to hang. Nice touch though. Cheers the place up."

"Is anyone really going to see these, Mr Godfrey?"

"You never know, Walter. Attention to detail. That's the key." Across the street, a fire hydrant spouted not water but smoke.

TWO

In a run-down suburb of Los Angeles—shabby houses with peeling paint—where sprawling middle-aged women sit out on the front stoop and grubby kids run loose, a youth leaned over the rail of an apartment building fire escape, spitting onto the passers-by below. The sun beat down, but this neighborhood looked exhausted by it, slumped into a state of fatigue. Somewhere overhead, ignored by the locals, was the steady, rasping drone of an airplane.

In the front yard of a once smart Victorian family house, a wooden sign on a post had been hammered into a scratchy patch of dry lawn: *The Rosary Hall Residence.* Below it, in smaller letters: *Hospitality—Friendliness—Just Like Home.*

Queenie struggled awkwardly on high heels carrying two bulky suitcases, with a tartan purse slung over her shoulder, a vanity case tucked under one arm and a ratty fur coat under the other. Halfway down the front path she dumped her luggage on the ground and stomped determinedly back towards the house. Before she got there, the sour-faced Mrs Snaith appeared in the open doorway and slung out her portfolio with as much force as she could muster. Queenie made a lunge for it, hoping to catch it before it fell, but she was too late; it landed smack on its spine and split open, sending its contents skidding across the path.

The front door slammed shut and Queenie was left alone—furious and humiliated. Becoming aware of passers-by on the street who had witnessed the commotion, she picked on a middle-aged bluenose in a business suit and stared him down.

"What's eating you, pal?"

The man sheepishly bowed his head and continued on his way.

Queenie stooped to gather her scattered belongings: eight-by-ten glossy portraits of herself in a range of poses—demure, dramatic, cheesecake. At the window of the house behind her, Mrs Snaith looked on for a moment before propping up a sign against the glass: *Vacancy. Furnished room for rent.*

Queenie dusted herself off, picked up her bags and strode out onto the street. She glared bitterly back at the Rosary Hall Residence.

Just like home.

In another part of town, a spacious kitchen with clean, tidy surfaces boasted a modern Magic Chef gas range in off-white with matching cupboards set against cheerful floral wallpaper. On the kitchen table was a cardboard box sealed with gummed strip, stamped and labeled for mailing. The recipient, Mrs Ishi, stood over it, her eyes sparkling with quiet anticipation. She fetched a short knife from her kitchen drawer and carefully sliced through the tape. Lifting the flaps and

folding them back against the sides of the box, she revealed two dozen neatly packed cans of sardines. She nodded, pleased at the sight, and ran her hand over the top layer.

Watching with interest from the edge of the sink was a green conure parakeet.

"Oh, no," it said. "What's this?" The bird's voice was small and scratchy as if down the line of a long-distance telephone call.

"It's fish," explained Mrs Ishi.

The bird studied the cans carefully as if considering this before asking again, "What's this?"

"It's fish," said Mrs Ishi.

The bird began bobbing its head rhythmically as if counting the cans then paused before repeating the question a third time.

"It's fish," said Mrs Ishi patiently. She stroked the feathers of the conure's chest with the back of her forefinger, which seemed to break the loop of inquiry. She then opened the wall cupboard.

Inside, stacked in neat rows like a food-mart display, were several dozen identical cans.

The bird gave a high, swooping whistle.

In the women's accessories section of a small department store shoppers milled about, inspecting the goods. Two ladies were trying on hats, while at the cosmetics counter an attentive salesgirl assisted a customer in choosing the right lipstick.

The store manager, Mr De Silva, a middle-aged man with a flower in his buttonhole, stood behind a glass-topped counter bearing a display stand of perfumes. Facing him was Kay, perfectly turned out in a smart gray suit with a matching pillbox hat, looking a little like an air stewardess.

"I don't understand, Mr De Silva. When I spoke to you on the telephone yesterday you told me the job was practically mine, that an interview would be a mere formality."

"Yes, but that was before …"

"Before you saw me?"

Mr De Silva looked away. He tapped at some paperwork on the counter with his pen. "On the phone you said your surname was Ashborough."

"Ashborough? No, I didn't. It's not Ashborough, it's Nashimura."

"Well it sounded like Ashborough when you said it. That's what I have written down here."

"Well, I'm sorry, Mr De Silva, you were mistaken."

"Apparently so. Very much so," He set down his pen. "Nashimura? The name is er … Japanese, isn't it?"

"Irish, actually."

Mr De Silva looked up, regarding her blankly. "Irish?" He quickly realized she was being perverse.

A nosy customer who had been eavesdropping sidled up to an adjacent counter on the pretext of inspecting the goods on display. The woman looked Kay up and down. She lifted a perfume bottle and brought its glass stopper to her nose. Wrinkling her nose in

distaste, she set the bottle firmly back down. She shuddered, fanning the air in front of her face while uttering a sound expressing her repugnance. Mr De Silva clocked it; he wanted Kay out of his store. He smiled obsequiously at the customer and waited until she had wandered out of earshot. He lowered his voice discreetly to resume their conversation.

"Look. I have nothing personally against your people, but it is my understanding that families of your … er … origin, Miss Nashimura, are to be relocated in the very near future so even if I were to offer you the position, within a couple of weeks you'd be sent away to your new home, wherever that is, and frankly, I'd be back to square one looking for a new sales assistant."

"I was born right here in California. So were my parents. We've never even been to Japan. I'm as American as you are, Mr De Silva, so I very much doubt that I'll be relocated anywhere."

Mr De Silva did not agree, but was reluctant to prolong the debate; a florid-faced woman at a nearby display stand was inspecting a tin of face powder. He turned his attention to her with an unctuous smile.

"Ah yes, madam. The new Cashmere Bouquet: nature's aid to loveliness. Perfect for the cream rose complexion."

After the interview, Kay headed through the busy shopping streets in West Hollywood, replaying the conversation over in her head. Among the thriving businesses on Wilshire Boulevard, she noticed that Yamamoto's Invisible Shoe Repair had boarded up its windows. Scrawled on one of the wood panels were the words *Closed for good*—to which someone else had added an extra *Good!* A little further along, Salzman's Family Restaurant informed its customers that they were *Famous for Steaks, Seafood, Real Spaghetti and Sandwiches*. It also assured them, as if as further testimony to the quality of their food, that they were *Not Hiring Japs*.

Next door was a camera store, outside which stood an Asian woman with three big looping curls set stiffly on top of her head. She wore a button on the lapel of her dress that said *I am Chinese, not Japanese*. Their eyes met for a second before the woman looked guiltily away, presumably afraid that Kay might be better positioned than most to see through her deception.

THREE

The long shadow cast by the Overland Church steeple pointed like a compass needle towards a tennis court, which overlooked the gently sloping green pasture of a nearby farm. Two Residents in tennis whites sat, ankles crossed, on the ground with their backs against a wall, leisurely sunning themselves and chatting.

George was coming from the shower block when he happened to spot them and decided to go over.

"What gives? Why aren't you playing?"

"We lost all our balls," the man whined. "Every time they go out of play at that end, they roll down the slope and drop over the edge. We must have lost a dozen balls down there. Now we're left without a single one."

George was cheerfully cajoling. "That's no excuse. You can pretend."

"Pretend?"

"Sure. Swing your racquets, run around a little. You know what a game of tennis looks like. No one's going to notice if there's a ball or not."

"Kinda pointless, isn't it? Playing tennis without a ball?"

George sighed inwardly. "This isn't a recreational park, created for your amusement. You've got a job to do."

The tennis players turned up their noses at the idea, but George wouldn't be defeated. "Come on. Snap to it. Let's see some fancy rallying. Show us what you can do."

Reluctantly, the couple hauled themselves to their feet and took their positions either side of the net. The man got things going with an apathetically mimed serve. The woman, feeling self-conscious, couldn't bring herself to join in the charade.

George tut-tutted as the imaginary ball bounced past her. "That was a gift. You could have gotten that one easy. Fifteen love."

Play continued. This time, the woman returned the serve with a languid backhand volley. Her opponent countered with a cross-court forehand, and so they went on, stepping from side to side and swinging their rackets through the air. As the rally progressed, their mimed strokes became increasingly athletic and graceful. The players realized that without the ball to spoil things, they were able to execute each shot faultlessly. They quickly became match-perfect professionals.

"That's the idea. Keep it moving."

Finally, the "ball" went out of play.

"Excellent. Fifteen all."

The man still had a gripe to air. "If you had put a fence round the edge, we'd still have a real ball to play with."

"Ah, quit bellyaching. This is a good test of your acting skills. As

15   UNDER

a matter of fact, I think I like it better without a ball. You're much more convincing as tennis players."

The woman registered the jibe just as she was poised to serve. She took out her annoyance on the make-believe ball and with a powerful swipe aimed it straight at George. He "saw" it coming and dodged smartly to the side. He gave her a look, pretending to feel affronted; she glared back with playful defiance. Stepping towards the edge, he peered down the slope to where the ball would have landed. He turned back to face them, wagging a reproachful finger.

"See? That's why you keep losing your balls." George turned to the man. "You gotta teach Babe Ruth here a little self-control."

Over at the visitors parking lot, Jimmy kick-started his motorcycle. Using his feet to maneuver it, he carefully eased the chugging machine towards the exit

        where a series of

            descending ramps

                and transitional platforms

           of varying lengths and gradients

        zig-zagged a path

     to the—

—ground. At the far end of the final slope was a border fence and gate where a young soldier raised a red-and-white-striped rising-arm barrier to let him through.

As the bike picked up speed, Jimmy noticed that to his left, several tanker trucks were parked haphazardly on a wide area of tarmac. A giant hose hung from one of them like an elephant's trunk, its end supported by a man in coveralls who guided the nozzle as it spewed green paint all over the ground. Other men were walking up and down spreading the liquid with big wide brooms and squeegees.

George was at the bus stop, checking his watch. A Roman centurion on a red bicycle sailed leisurely by, raising his hand in greeting. George returned his salute.

Up on the hill next to the church was the tennis court where the game he had just instigated was hotting up. The play itself was silent, but he could just make out the players calling out the score. He turned to watch them for a moment, then noticed the bus approaching. It didn't make the scheduled stop, as buses are supposed to do, but George was unfazed; he ran alongside it, opened the door and leapt inside. The driver's seat was vacant, but he chose to sit in one of the passenger seats, settling down to enjoy the journey.

The bus ran, like all the other vehicles, on a track like on a scenic railway or a fairground ride, its route predetermined by the metal rail on which it traveled and its speed regulated by the mechanism that drove it. It was a two-way street so vehicles were approaching from the opposite direction, always perfectly in line, yet randomly spaced so that groups of vehicles might move together to simulate natural traffic flow. George watched as cars, taxis and trucks idled by, punctuated by the occasional motorcycle and dummy rider.

The traffic ahead curved to the right—past the library, past Kaiser's corner drugstore, where two men with ladders were fitting smart new green awnings over the windows. George's heart sank a little; they were supposed to be red, not green. How had they managed to get it so wrong? He wondered if the new Vanguard color chart was to blame and took out the concertina-folded sheet from his breast pocket to inspect it.

In an attempt to make their color range sound more exotic, they had named their colors with reference to faraway places: Zanzibar Storm, Oxford, Havana, Belgian Mist. He'd never visited any of these places, and he suspected that his painters hadn't either. Without the swatches they'd be clueless to guess which hues these names represented. Color names, in George's view, depended on a shared point of reference: charcoal, peach, blood, buttercup—most people would be familiar with the inherent colors of these things. But what was the predominant color in Oxford? Only the dons could be expected to know.

As for the awnings, the painters appeared to have mistaken Geneva (which was green) for Genoa (which, for some reason, was red).

George didn't want to make the men feel bad about their mistake, but the green wasn't right. Kaiser's was based on the drugstore he knew as a boy and those awnings had always been red. He resolved to leave a note for them later.

The bus rolled along past other stores with sporadically populated parking lots. Nearer the Orpheum movie theater, clusters of Residents gathered to chat; some of them, including a pair of middle-aged twins dressed as banjo-playing minstrels, saw George on the bus and greeted him with a theatrical wave.

Catching sight of a military uniform George realized too late that he'd also been spotted by First Lieutenant Franks who was on the sidewalk, trying to catch his attention. The military presence in Overland was a niggling element that had the potential to curdle the cream. It was important to keep it at bay.

"Mr Godfrey!" The lieutenant started to trot alongside the bus to keep up. "Can I have a quick word about Major Lund's visit?"

George talked to him through the open window. "Sorry, Lieutenant. Can't stop now. I'm late for an important meeting."

"You haven't forgotten he's coming on Friday?" The lieutenant's voice shuddered in rhythm with his footfall. "The thing is, we've just heard that Colonel Wagner may also be visiting. It's very important that we make sure everything is in order."

"Look around you, Lieutenant. Everything's perfect. We're in Paradise."

"Yes, but—"

George turned a deaf ear and faced cheerfully ahead, relaxing back in his seat to resume his journey in peace. The lieutenant gave up the chase and was left stranded on the sidewalk.*

The bus passed a newly wooded area of parkland, its trees constructed from vertical wooden poles, each with an armature of cross-beam branches draped with netting and covered with painted burlap strips or dyed chicken feathers. Care had been taken to use a range of green shades and hues—deep emerald, celadon, fruity yellow-green, jade, mint, malachite, moss—according to their designated varieties. Further along, on a patch of open ground, a handful of men in workwear were using ropes to hoist the timber studwork frame that would form the gabled end wall of the new schoolhouse.

Very nice, thought George. He hoped one day to have children, though in hindsight it was just as well he and Muriel had never got round to it.

The sneezing put paid to the morning affections that had once played a part in their marriage, and for George this became something of a blessing. An enthusiastic yet demanding lover, Muriel always somehow made him feel that whatever he was doing, he wasn't quite doing it right. During what he came to think of as "the preliminaries" she often seemed irritated by his advances and once even repositioned his hand, with an impatient "Not there. There." It was the same way she dealt with Fuffy if he misbehaved; a firm jerk of his leash would bring him in line.

Muriel was skeptical of medical opinion, however sound, always thinking she knew better.

"Allergic? Baloney! Allergic to what, for instance?"

"Dr Kowalski said it could be anything in the home. Pet hair, dust mites. He actually suggested it might be your perfume."

She stared at him indignantly. "What's wrong with my perfume?"

"Nothing. It's lovely, but I may be allergic to it, that's all. And well, it *is* quite strong."

Dr Kowalski had not in fact mentioned perfume at all in his list of possible triggers for his symptoms; this was more George's diagnosis. Muriel suspected as much.

"No one else has a problem with it, George. I've had many compliments about my perfume. Other people can't get enough of it."

"I don't doubt that."

Muriel caught the snide edge to his remark.

"It's just you, George. You're peculiar."

*MEANWHILE *At a news kiosk at Sepulveda and 11th, a string of true detective mags dangled by their corners from a string above the vendor's head. Lust, violence, revenge and greed seemed to be the major motivators of the crimes within. Other magazine covers:* Fighting fit with Barbara Stanwyk; on the road with Dorothy Lamour; behind the scenes with Claudette Colbert. Stabbed 78 times by her jealous lover. Grow your own mushrooms. Build muscles in just 3 weeks and be a REAL he-man. *A stack of newspapers announced the latest war news from the pacific:* Bataan Collapses.

At the next bend he jumped down from the moving bus and continued on foot. In the town-square gardens the ground was covered by lengths of rough undyed burlap. A man wearing a metal backpack tank with a hose attached was spraying the area in a wide sweeping motion, transforming it into a luxuriant green lawn.

George headed for an adjacent building that had a painted sign over the door. The Overland Diner wasn't a fancy place, but it was cosy; popular with the Residents—somewhere they could hang out and chat over coffee. Outside tables with cheerful umbrellas gave the establishment a Continental feel, like the "Gay Paree" cafes George had seen in pictures. At one table a man reading a newspaper sat with a woman holding a shopping basket.

She looked up. "Morning, Mr Godfrey."

The man felt the need to justify their presence. "We're on our break."

"I didn't say a thing."

"We're allowed a break: fifteen minutes in the morning."

George laughed, halting the argument with outstretched hands. "I know. I know. Please. Relax. Enjoy your breakfast."

A Negro man, elegantly dressed in a splendid check suit and bowtie was perched on the edge of a barrel of plastic flowers at the diner entrance. George touched his shoulder warmly. "Hey, Tommy."

"How's it going, Mr Godfrey?"

"I think we're getting there."

"Did you do anything nice and relaxing at the weekend?"

"Sure did. There's still a lot more work to do, but hey, you know. A guy's gotta take a little time off now and again, hasn't he, sit back and enjoy the fruits of his labor? I mean … even God took Sunday off."

"You got that right. Good for you to get out of town."

"Oh, I didn't leave town. I stayed right here in Overland."

"Really?"

"Sure. Why not? It's beautiful here. Travel is very overrated."

"What did you do?"

"Well, I had the place to myself so I sat around, enjoying the scenery. Did a little fishing down by the lake."

Tommy chuckled, shaking his head. "I'm guessing you didn't catch nothing?"

"Not yet, Tommy. But I'm hopeful."

"Well, let me know when you do."

George nodded. "You bet."

Inside the Overland Diner was distinctly less Continental: a long tiled counter with a row of stools in front of it. It was kitted out with the usual stuff: a cash register, napkin dispensers, sugar shakers. A few of the Overland Residents sat at the counter drinking coffee or reading newspapers; other customers occupied the tables and chairs. Some had lunch pails in front of them and were busy eating.

A woman in her sixties wearing a little cardboard hat stood beside a big metal coffee urn and a tray of donuts.

"Morning, Effie." George approached the counter, studying the extensive list of "breakfast suggestions" on the painted menu board behind her. "Now then. What will it be today? My, my. It all looks

23   UNDER

so good. Hot meatloaf platter? The blue plate special? Pork chops? Hmm. No, bacon and eggs, I think. Yes. Two eggs over easy."

Effie distractedly straightened her uniform. "Uh-huh."

"Not too easy mind."

Effie nodded, humoring him. "Uh-huh."

"And … let's see … how about some buttermilk pancakes? Are the pancakes specially light and fluffy?"

"Pancakes are off today. Sorry."

"Oh. Well, that's OK. I'll just—"

"Oh, and you know what? We're all out of bacon too."

"Gee. No bacon, huh? How about the—"

"Uh-uh. Chickens stopped laying. Must have gotten spooked or something."

"Oh, that's too bad. Poor things."

She stared back at him for a moment before pointing to the tray on the counter. "I've got donuts," she said brightly.

"Ah. Donuts! Now why didn't I think of that?"

"And coffee?"

"Perfect."

The guy sitting at the next stool glanced up from his own coffee, snorting a little chuckle. He enjoyed this daily routine as much as George did.

George took a donut while Effie poured coffee into a paper cup.

"You oughta eat something proper once in a while," she said.

"I would if you ever had anything else on offer."

"Can't live on donuts. No good for your digestion. You need to keep yourself regular."

"I'm here three times a day, Eff. Can't get more regular than that."

"Hm. Smart Alec. How about an apple?"

"Apple?"

"Sure," she said. "An apple a day keeps the doctor away."

He checked the counter. "I didn't know you had apples."

"I don't. This is one I brought from home."

She ducked below the counter, reappearing holding a shiny red apple.

"Take it. You'll feel the benefit."

"Apple, huh? OK, Effie. You win."

George tossed it up into the air, letting it land with a satisfying slap in his palm. He studied the apple, admiring its bright color.

"I was thinking of putting in an apple orchard behind the library. You think that would look nice—the red against the green of the leaves?"

Effie rolled her eyes.

"You know," he said, "Delacroix loved using red and green."

"Della who?"

"Never mind."

Effie's attention lingered absently on the apple; it was the perfect opportunity for George to practice his sleight of hand. He pretended to snatch it from his open palm while secretly retaining it in the original hand. He showed her his empty hand with a *hey presto* flourish. He'd gotten pretty good at this maneuver, but Effie must

have glimpsed the apple in his hidden hand. She pointed at it with a discerning finger. Palming such a large object was hard—unlike a coin or matchbook, which could be easily ditched in a pocket or up a sleeve.

Muriel had never been keen on the art of illusion and misdirection. When he was first practising the basic coin vanish he had tried to use her as his audience. Having deftly made the pass, he would offer both fists for her to guess which of them contained the coin, but she would never play along. She thought magic was 'silly'. By her reckoning, the coin was bound to be in one hand or the other and she frankly didn't care which.

He had once seen an amazing trick performed by a magician hired to mingle with guests at one of the MGM parties. With dazzling dexterity, he had vanished a coin from George's open palm without ever touching it. George neither saw nor felt it go. The magician turned over both of his own hands and tugged back his sleeves one by one to show that the coin was not hidden there. It was the most astonishing thing George had ever seen. Even Muriel was impressed.

Keen to know the secret, George asked him to perform the trick again so that he might take a closer look, but he wasn't prepared to do that. *I bet you're using some kind of magnet, aren't you?* George had suggested. There was no evidence of any such device, but it was the only explanation he could think of.

The magician shook his head slowly, dismissing George's pitiful line of inquiry.

" I haven't got the coin," he said. "You saw. I didn't even touch it."
"Where did it go then?"
"That's just it. It didn't go anywhere."
George was perplexed.
The magician explained. "You're thinking of it all wrong. I didn't make the coin disappear; I merely made it so that you can't see it anymore. It's still there in your hand."

It was obviously just a line of patter that went with the trick, but the idea stayed with George for days. From time to time he would find himself fingering the palm of his hand, trying to detect some trace of the vanished coin.

Though only a short walk from the busy town center, the area surrounding Overland Lake was a secluded haven of calm. George sat enjoying the view from one of the grassy slopes. He inhaled deeply as the fresh breeze cooled his face. For a brief second he thought he caught a whiff of Muriel's perfume. He had assumed the Overland air had eradicated his clothes of it completely, but somehow it seemed to linger. He sniffed his sleeve. Nothing. Perhaps he was imagining it.

George took off his sports coat, folding it neatly and placing it on the ground behind him for a pillow. Satisfied, he lay down and closed his eyes.

A deep, thrumming drone, at first reassuringly hypnotic, began to pervade the peace. The sound built in intensity to a reverberating roar until the huge dark form of a B-17 bomber suddenly burst through

the horizon, like a monster emerging from the depths of the earth. The plane climbed, banking to its left, away from the lake, the sound from its engines opening into a thick, throaty snarl before gradually fading to nothing.

George sat up, troubled, not by the plane but by something lumpy his head had detected in the improvised pillow. Rummaging through the folds of the fabric for the pocket opening, he produced the apple that Effie had given him. Again he went through the motions of the illusion, trying to figure how he could more convincingly hide it. He would have to practice more in front of a mirror.

He pulled a switchblade from his pants pocket, pressed the button to release the blade and prepared to cut himself a slice, but as the knife made contact, the apple slipped from his grasp and tumbled towards the lake. Once it reached the water's edge there was nothing to stop it. George scrambled to his feet, but he was too late. He looked on helplessly as the apple rolled across the smooth rubber-coated surface of the lake, heading towards the drainage aperture at its center where it was sucked into a spiraling rotation of ever decreasing circles before finally disappearing from view.

FOUR

Inside a vast factory building, the busy commotion of the construction industry was underway. Some parts were taking a familiar shape—a wing or a section of fuselage—but the majority of the work was carried out on vital but unidentifiable components of a yet-to-be assembled aircraft. Many of the workers were women—dressed in industrial workwear with their hair bundled up in headscarves, some wore thick leather-rimmed safety goggles. Crane operators high in the rafters hoisted sections of skeletal framework over assembly lines of punch presses, lathes, sheet-metal-forming benches. The din was relentless—clanking, popping, screeching drills, buzzing grinders and hissing hydraulics.

One young woman had squeezed herself into the cramped space inside the shell of a half-completed aircraft wing. Another woman shot rivets through the skin of the wing while she held her bucking bar to flatten out the tail on the inside.

It was grueling work, but everyone seemed motivated, not just to meet their targets but to exceed them. It was a scene that could have been created for a recruitment propaganda film, but here the workers' commitment was genuine. A banner stretched high above them reflected their determined spirit: *Production—Let's step it up!*

Through the factory came a small truck loaded with machine parts, driven by a skinny guy wearing a cap with a long peak like a mallard's bill. He weaved his way between the production lines, spinning his wheel to turn a tight corner into the yard outside. Bathed in a cool blue light filtered from above was a row of parked trucks and forklifts. The driver tootled past them, the contents of his trailer rattling and shaking as the rear wheels shimmied on the uneven ground. He turned sharply again and disappeared round the corner of the building.

There was a moment of stillness before, out of nowhere, something dropped from high above and exploded with a sudden smack on the ground. Like an asteroid striking an uninhabited part of the earth's surface, there was no one around to witness the event. The missile was, or at least had until that moment been, an apple. Collision with earth had pulverized its flesh into a pale yellow pulp. As evidence there were scattered seeds and shiny red fragments of skin, its juices still fizzing from the impact.

FIVE

Queenie had bagged herself a window seat halfway along the bus. Above her on the luggage rack were the two suitcases, her fur coat and portfolio, the latter now held together with a makeshift luggage strap made from a dress belt. On the vacant seat beside her sat her Royal Stewart tartan box purse with a cut-steel clasp and rope-leather handles. It looked like something for transporting small consignments of Scottish shortbread.

A magazine lay open across her knees at a feature charting Myrna Loy's rise to stardom. Inspired by the star's success story, Queenie unconsciously nodded with quiet determination.

Queenie had modeled her look on a variety of film stars. Her hair was styled the way Betty Grable might wear it: swept up and perched on top of her head in a neatly coiffed nest of curls. Her lips were full and slick with crimson—influenced by Hedy Lamarr—her eyelashes were darkly mascaraed and she had Garbo-esque eyebrows penciled in high, arched wings. Her skirt, cinched by a wasp-waist patent leather belt, was worn with a white blouse—perky and neat with puffed short sleeves and a low-fronted flounce of frills.

She touched her hair and ran her finger over her front teeth to check for lipstick. Taking a powder compact from her bag, she flipped open the mirrored lid and held it in front of her, checking first her lips and teeth and then, turning her head this way and that, took in the rest of her face for a general survey. She deftly snapped the lid shut and returned the compact to her bag with the practiced hand of someone who carried out this inspection routine a hundred times a day.

A man in the seat opposite was ogling her. She attempted to curb his enthusiasm with a dismissive glance, but it didn't take. He removed his hat and laid it on the vacant seat beside him. Leaning a little in her direction, he gestured at the magazine she was reading.

"You in the movie business?"

Queenie didn't look up. "I'm working on it."

"Are you a movie actress?"

"No, I'm a welder, but like I said, I'm working on it."

"You? A welder? Don't make me laugh."

She replied dully: "OK. I'll try not to."

With that, she coolly flicked over a page in her magazine and returned her attention to it. The man was left high and dry.

On a long, straight road, Kay stood at a bus stop, peering into the distance in anticipation of the bus's arrival. Up ahead a young man was nailing a piece of paper to a telegraph pole. She watched distractedly. He put the hammer back into his shoulder bag and mounted

* **MEANWHILE** *In the garden of a bungalow on Overland Main Street two limp shirts pegged by their cuffs to a washing line swayed in the breeze like lazy trapeze artists.*

a motorcycle parked at the roadside. The engine growled into life and the bike dawdled towards her, the rider's feet hovering above the surface of the road, like training wheels. The bike slowed again, drawing into the curb beside her.

The man wore thick denim work pants and an open-neck shirt, sleeves rolled high on his tanned, sinewy arms. He dismounted and flipped the kickstand, then approached the telegraph pole beside Kay, pulling his hammer and a flyer from his bag. She stepped aside to allow him clear access to the pole and they exchanged courteous smiles as strangers sometimes do. He grabbed a handful of tacks from his back pocket and quickly secured the flyer. She noticed the seat of his pants was stained with red paint. He returned to his motorcycle, kicked the starter and coasted along to his next port of call.

Curious, Kay stepped forward to take a look. The flyer announced the sale of a motorcycle, a 1936 Harley Davidson EL—presumably the one he had been riding. Her eye was drawn to the poster displayed above it, this one bigger, sturdier and more emphatic in its proclamation. Heavy block type set the tone: *Instructions to All Persons of Japanese Ancestry.*

She had, of course, seen the sign before. It had been posted at various locations across the city and for the past month the announcement had regularly appeared in all the local newspapers. She edged uneasily closer, in the futile hope of discovering some overlooked loophole, some detail that would make her exempt. She

anxiously skimmed over the paragraph outlining the exclusion area, her eyes flitting between sections of text.

The Civil Control Station is equipped to assist the Japanese population … provide temporary residence elsewhere … transport persons and a limited amount of clothing and equipment to their new residence … Evacuees must carry with them on departure for the Assembly Center … bedding and linens (no mattress) for each member of the family … Toilet articles … No pets of any kind … No personal items and no household goods … All persons of Japanese ancestry, whether citizens or non-citizens, will be evacuated from the above area by twelve o'clock noon, Sunday, May 10th, 1942 … Instructions Must Be Observed … The head of the family, or the person in whose name most of the property is held, and each individual living alone, will report to the Civil Control Station to receive further instructions. This must be done between 8:00 a.m. and 5:00 p.m. on Tuesday, May 5th, 1942.

Her stomach churned. The 5th was tomorrow.*

The bus pulled up, so she stopped reading and stood in line. She would pretend, she decided, that she hadn't seen the notice.

The door opened and a couple of other passengers boarded. Climbing onto the platform steps after them, she heard the cheerful driver greeting each of them with a hearty "thanking you ma'am," and "thanking you, sir" as they paid their fares. But when Kay put her coin in the slot, the driver said nothing. He threw the bus into gear and pulled away.

Though crowded, there were several vacant aisle seats, all occupied by shopping bags, parcels or coats. Kay hovered near one or two of them, hoping that the passengers would reclaim their belongings and give her a place to sit, but all of them ignored her, and the belongings stayed put. Queenie looked up distractedly for a moment and then returned her attention to a feature on why girls fall in love with Robert Taylor. The chatty man in the seat opposite betrayed a chink of weakness by glancing nervously at Kay. Quick to spot the possible opening, she homed in on him.

"Excuse me. May I sit here?"

He stared straight ahead, suddenly deaf to her words. She became more insistent.

"Excuse me. Your hat. Would you mind moving it?"

The man sitting in the aisle seat in front of Queenie was more forthright.

"There's a sign here." He jabbed at it aggressively with his finger.

She'd seen the sign before—a personal message to "her people," presumably erected by the driver. She didn't need to look.

"There *are* no seats at the back of the bus."

"Then either stand, or get off and walk."

Queenie took an interest in what had been going on and piped up.

"Hey, sister. Over here." She moved the tartan purse onto her knees. Kay quickly slipped in beside her. She turned to her savior, hoping to make some connection, but Queenie was already back with her nose in her magazine.

"Thanks. I only asked him to—"

Without looking up, Queenie cut her short. "Save it. I heard what you said."

After a pause, Kay tried again. "Actually, I'm an American citizen."

Queenie was still reading. "Congratulations."

The bus continued on its journey. Kay glanced at Queenie's magazine. Something caught her interest and she cocked her head a little to read the article over-the-shoulder style. Queenie turned her head to challenge her with an inquiring look. Caught in the act, Kay stared purposefully at the back of the head belonging to the rude passenger in front of her. The wrinkles on his neck suggested a man in his sixties, yet he boasted a surprisingly youthful head of hair. She studied the damp and wispy graying hair at the nape of his neck and compared this with the luxurious thatch of shiny chestnut hair that met it halfway up.

Queenie had been following Kay's studious gaze and now their eyes met. Queenie raised her expressive brows and wiggled her scalp back and forth so that her hair seemed to move of its own accord. Kay tittered shyly and her response made Queenie chuckle.

Queenie glanced out of the window to see where she was, checked herself in the compact mirror once more and then, as the bus slowed, gathered up her belongings and pulled herself to her feet. Kay stepped nimbly aside to let her pass.

As she moved into the aisle, Queenie raised her elbow and deliberately lurched towards the aggressive man, dragging her handbag

clumsily over his hairpiece as she passed. The man collapsed forward in his seat, trying to avoid the assault, but it was too late; the toupee had shifted forward on his head. Queenie followed up with her elbow for good measure.

"Oh. Pardon me, sir. So sorry."

The man, flustered and red-faced, quickly adjusted his wig.

Queenie smiled sweetly. "My bag, it caught on the … So sorry. I hope I didn't—"

The fuming man waved her away.

She glanced at Kay and wiggled her scalp once more before moving off down the aisle. Kay slipped back into the seat. Delighting in the man's humiliation, she watched him nervously fingering the back of his head.

Sliding closer to the window she looked out at the street, suddenly realizing that this too was her stop. She jumped up as the bus pulled in to the curb. Queenie was first to exit as the doors opened, followed by a handful of other passengers who went their separate ways. When Kay alighted, Queenie was already a couple of houses ahead of her. Kay followed at a discreet distance, but Queenie quickly became aware of the footsteps behind her keeping in synch with her own. She turned to confront her stalker.

"What's the big idea?"

"Big idea?"

"You following me?"

"Following you? No. I'm merely going the same way."

"To where, for instance?"

"Lakewood Drive."

"You don't say. That's quite a coincidence. Who lives on Lakewood Drive that you'd know?"

"I do."

Queenie was not buying it. "Oh really?"

"Yes, really. You want a hand with your bags?"

"I can manage."

Queenie struggled on, but the bags were heavy and cumbersome and Kay was forced to slow her pace to maintain a respectable distance. Queenie turned again, embarrassed to think how inelegant she must have looked.

"I'm on my way to see about a room," said Queenie. "Crestwood House. Lakewood and Seventh Avenue. You heading that way?"

Two minutes later, Queenie and Kay were walking side by side. Kay was carrying the two suitcases; Queenie, strolling more leisurely now, managed her tartan purse and portfolio, her coat draped casually over one arm like a catwalk model. She turned to Kay. "I'm Queenie, by the way."

"Kay." She might have offered her hand had she not been burdened with Queenie's luggage.

"What are you, a desk clerk in some fancy hotel?" said Queenie.

"No. Why?"

"The uniform."

Kay looked down at her suit. "It's not a uniform. I don't have a job

right now. No one's hiring—"

"Japs?"

"I'm actually American, but my face—"

"Is not."

"I have a driver's license too, but still no one will give me a job."

"What about Chinese? Are folks hiring them?"

"In theory. China is an American ally. They hate the Japanese more than Americans."

"Well. Say you're Chinese. Who's gonna know?"

"There *is* a difference."

Queenie was unconvinced. "Not as far as Americans are concerned. You can get buttons; I've seen people wearing them."

Kay shook her head dismissively. "I couldn't do that."

They continued for a while until Queenie decided to share some insider knowledge: "Olivia de Havilland was born in Tokyo. So was her sister, Joan Fontaine. But they've got normal faces. You know what I mean. American."

Kay nodded, letting it slide; she was used to this kind of talk.

"Maybe you could get work as an extra. They often do movies that need orientals. Like in *The Good Earth*. There were crowds of Chinese in that. Of course they use white folk to play the main parts, but you could be a peasant or something."

"Thanks, but I'm not Chinese."

"It's all the same. As a matter of fact, they're shooting something Chinese at Paramount. I was reading about it. Alan Ladd—he's pretty dishy—and Loretta Young. She's OK, I guess—if you don't mind the cob up her butt—though she doesn't look very Chinese to me. But they've got real Chinese in it too. There's what's-her-name from the Charlie Chan movies. Iris Wong. You don't hear much about her in the magazines. I guess she keeps herself to herself, being Chinese."

They were on Lakewood now. Queenie looked around at the houses, imagining herself in the new neighborhood.

"So where were *you* born?" said Kay.

Queenie's face soured a little. "Wisconsin."

"Is it nice there?"

"It's OK, I guess. If you like cheese."

"Is Queenie your real name?"

"Actually it's Victoria, but keep a lid on it."

Kay was amused. "Victoria? Like Queen Victoria? Oh—Queenie. I get it."

Queenie rolled her eyes. "Chalk up one for your side."

Kay was out in her front yard—kind of coincidentally on purpose—when ten minutes later Queenie came trudging back along the street.

"No luck?"

Queenie was seething. "Goddamn room was already taken when I got there. I only called about it this morning."

"Where will you go?"

"Beats me. Keep looking, I guess."

Kay had an idea. "Wait there."

Queenie dumped her bags. Hot and uncomfortable, she sat on a

low wall and lit a cigarette, blowing a big exhausted sigh of smoke into the air.

After a while, Kay appeared at the doorway with an older Japanese woman. She smiled and nodded respectfully, her hands neatly clasped over her midriff. Queenie stood and bowed awkwardly, unsure of the protocol. Kay introduced them.

"This is Mrs Ishi. She says you can stay here."

Mrs Ishi nodded. "Nice room on second floor."

"She doesn't normally rent to non-Japanese. I told her of your kindness."

Queenie frowned. "Kindness?"

"On the bus. That man."

"Oh, I wasn't being kind." Queenie realized she might be shooting herself in the foot. "Not really, I mean. That guy was a jerk. Begging your pardon, Mrs …"

Kay repeated the name. "Ishi."

Mrs Ishi smiled warmly. "You have a job?"

"Sure," said Queenie.

Kay was curious. "What do you do?"

"Well, at the moment I'm doing shift work at the Lockheed plant—you know, doing my bit for Uncle Sam while the men are overseas fighting the … er … Germans. But that's not my main career. Actually I'm an actress. Just getting started in the movie business. Doing pretty good too, so far. I'm an accomplished dancer and I sing a little."

"Would I have seen you in anything? I don't go to the movies much."

"*Anne of Windy Poplars, He Married His Wife, Diamond Frontier.* Just crowd scenes. I'm still waiting for my big break, but that could come any day. When opportunity comes knocking it doesn't call ahead to make an appointment. No sir. You've gotta be ready and waiting with your hat and coat on. As a matter of fact, I have an important audition tomorrow. I switched to the early shift at the factory specially."

"That's wonderful. What part are you going for?"

"Well, it's just a general casting, but it's at Warner Brothers so, you know, they're one of the biggest. Bette Davis, John Garfield, Bogart, Ann Sheridan, Barbara Stanwyck. Some of the best. Warners don't do as many musicals as, say, MGM, but they could be very good for me. Ida Lupino is a contract player there too. Some say we look rather alike, but I've gone blonder now so I don't really see it. Not enough to cause conflict of interests anyway."

Kay smiled weakly. She didn't know who Ida Lupino was any more than Mrs Ishi did.

"So. How much? For the room?"

Kay and Mrs Ishi looked at each other, as if trying to communicate a price telepathically.

Kay wanted to get an idea of the going rate: "How much was the other place?"

"Er, seven dollars a week. No, wait. Six dollars. That was it."

Kay spotted Queenie's ruse, but let it go. She and Mrs Ishi looked at each other again. Kay spoke to her loudly and clearly, like she might be deaf. "Six dollars a week, Mrs Ishi? Is that OK?"

Mrs Ishi nodded. "Six dollars? OK."

The deal was struck; Queenie was pleased. "Well, all right. Let's take a look at it."

Mrs Ishi smiled. "You are friend of Kay. Kay very good girl."

Kay decided to answer on her new friend's behalf. "Oh I'm sure Queenie is a very good girl too, Mrs Ishi."

Kay's eyes met with Queenie's and they both stifled a chuckle.

Mrs Ishi stood in the doorway to welcome her new tenant into her home. Kay helped her in with her luggage and the door closed.

That night, Kay lay in bed listening to Queenie unpacking in the next room: the shuffle of fabric, the metallic click of hangers on the wardrobe rail, the jangle of her bracelets, the scrape of her high heels on the wooden floor. From time to time Queenie would sing a bluesy phrase from a popular song. *My mama done tol' me*. Each time, she would hum the next line so whatever her mama done tol' her remained a mystery.

It was somehow thrilling to have Queenie under the same roof, with her factory job and blossoming career in motion pictures. Her future looked rosy, full of promise. Now that people of Japanese descent were being banished from American society, Kay didn't hold out much hope for her own future. Kay's face was her passport to rejection, enforced segregation and incarceration, yet Queenie's presence seemed to carry with it new hope for her too, even if it meant renouncing her national ancestry to become a Chinese peasant.

As she pondered this, Kay's gaze fell on the calendar that hung on the wall beside her bed. It had been there since she first came to live at Mrs Ishi's nine years ago after her parents died. Mr Cochran, the nice old man from next door, had brought it round on her first day there; his idea of a remedy for (what was then referred to as) her recent trauma.

"That, young lady," he had said, holding the picture up for her to see, "is a little piece of heaven on earth. How would you like to live there, huh?"

It was a promotional wall calendar issued by the Taylor & Goodman Engineering and Manufacturing Company. Mr Cochran no longer had any use for it—it was two years old and all the months except December had been torn off—but he thought she might enjoy looking at the picture.

He was right.

The depicted scene, cheerfully unrelated to the manufacturing world of power-transmission machinery, was entitled *When Evening Shadows Fall*. The painting featured a picture-book lakeside cottage nestling amongst dense, verdant woodland. Above the treetops, soft cerulean skies were suffused with the burnt tangerine, pink and gold of a setting sun. In the foreground a profusion of foxgloves lolled like drunks among the ferns.

She studied the picture for hours like a detective scrutinizing a piece of evidence: the wisp of blue-gray smoke from the chimney stack promising comforting warmth from the fire within; the little rowboat moored to the jetty; the two rocking chairs out on the

porch, and the pair of young deer taking a moment from drinking at the water's edge to look up at the cottage like prospective home-owners admiring a piece of sought-after real estate.

That summer, determined to escape her grief, she spent much of her time daydreaming about boys. Older boys—men practically. She wasn't interested in anyone at school, or in the film stars her friends doted on; she just wanted that perfect someone with whom she could have a deeply loving relationship, fired by the kind of exhilarating passion described in the romantic stories she had been reading of late. Books from the local library with titles like *Homeward to my Love*, *Stranger at Newhaven* and *Meant for Each Other* described the physical thrill of being swept up in the dizzying embrace of a tall, tousle-haired Stranger-at-Newhaven type, whose brooding determination belied, as it so often did, a sentient vulnerability. She would lie awake at night fine-tuning the details of their romance, running the carefully constructed scenario like a movie in her head.

The library-book men had names like Raith, Kyall or Trent, but she preferred something more regular: a Joe or a Bill. Her fantasy never included anyone else; she and Joe might have been the last two people on earth.

They lived together in the lakeside cottage; it was the perfect home for them. He was the artistic type, naturally: a carpenter or a sculptor—someone "good with his hands." There was a vague notion of domesticity—her stirring something delicious with a big spoon while he was out on the jetty, fishing or repairing his rowboat—but most of her reverie centered around the long romantic walks she imagined they would take together through the surrounding countryside, the topography of which would require him, at various points in the journey, to scoop her up and lift her over a fence or hedgerow. She adored it when he picked her up: feeling his one strong arm around her back, the other tucked under the crook of her knees. She would wrap her arms around his neck and nuzzle into his collar, enamored by the nearness of him. She so enjoyed these moments that their progress became increasingly hampered by invented obstacles: streams, fallen trees or jagged rocks presented themselves to obstruct their path at every turn. At each one, Joe would insist on carrying her to safety.

Her daydreams seldom ventured beyond kissing, cuddling and being carried in the arms of a strong man (preferably all at once); it was all she wanted, though in the most amorous moments of her fantasy, when a clumsy stumble from a log brought Joe rushing to her side, gently lifting her ankle to remove her shoe and cradling her foot in his strong hand to assess the damage—*a nasty sprain, I'm going to have to carry you*—she would look at his handsomely shaped head, his broad shoulders, the tanned perfection of his rugged cheek and, feeling herself to be the most beautiful girl in the world, beautiful just for him, her thoughts would veer towards a daringly intoxicating moment back at the cottage as he carried her across the threshold.

SIX

On the north side of a pasture of grazing sheep, a wide, low smokestack protruded from the ground emitting gray smoke, which was dissipated by the gentle Overland breeze. George and First Lieutenant Franks stood at the gate, mid-conversation. The lieutenant shook his head.

"You can't expect us to take a plane up for a joyride just so you can have a look around. Do you know how much it costs to—"

"I realize that. But I need to see it from the air."

"You have photographs. Extensive aerial reconnaissance."

"Yes, Lieutenant. But it's not the same thing."

"I can assure you, Mr Godfrey, that the photographs you're being given show exactly what an airplane sees."

"How can they? They're two-dimensional images. They only show me what the camera sees, not what the pilot sees; it's not the same thing. The real world is three-dimensional. Besides, everything you give me is black and white. I have no idea how the colors I'm using appear to the eye from a distance."

"All air reconnaissance pictures are black and white. Nobody sees it in color. This isn't *Gone With the Wind*."

"The pilot must see it in color. He's not viewing it as a black and white photograph. I need to know how it looks to him. If I could just see it for myself."

"I don't think that's going to be possible, Mr Godfrey. Sorry, but you're a civilian. There are certain military protocols to be observed. Besides, we're through here. Mission accomplished."

Jimmy had pitched up during the exchange. Not wanting to interrupt, he hung back. His lurking presence was nevertheless a distraction. George decided to deal with it.

"Did you want something, Jimmy?"

"Can I have a word, Mr Godfrey?"

"Can it wait, Jimmy? I'm just talking to Lieutenant Franks."

The lieutenant saw his opportunity to escape George's badgering. "No, no. I don't want to get in your way. Listen, Mr Godfrey. You've done a great job. I'm sure that after Major Lund and the colonel's visit, we'll get everything signed off. It's time to move on to new ventures." He looked at his watch. "I'd better get over to the airfield."

The lieutenant patted George on the shoulder and headed off down the street. George was left feeling hollow, troubled by the idea of "moving on," but tried to shake himself out of it.*

"Yes, Jimmy. What is it?"

"I'm worried about these sheep."

"Really? How so?"

"They haven't moved in days."

"Are you sure?"

*__MEANWHILE__ *DiMaggio crushes Giants. Why Linda Darnell left home. War fashions for feminine safety. Horrors of Jap torture in the Philippines. Fifty hilarious pages of comedy. Shirley Temple grows up.*

"Positive. I've been keeping an eye on them."

"Damn it. They're supposed to move."

"Well, that's what I figured."

"This is exactly the kind of thing that could catch us with our pants down."

Jimmy nodded in agreement.

George shook his head. "Jeez. How am I expected to think about new ventures when there are things like this to deal with?"

He straddled the fence and stepped into the field.

Jimmy was concerned that he might be partly to blame. "I would have done something, but the signs say not to stray from the paths and we were told never to …"

"No, you're OK, Jimmy. You did the right thing. Besides, it's not your job, handling livestock."

"I don't mind lending a hand."

"You sure? All right. Thanks. All of the grazing pastures should be OK to walk on, but tread carefully. You don't want to fall through a hole and end up in the bowels of hell, do you?"

"No, sir, I do not."

George lifted up one of the sheep and carried it a dozen paces before setting it down again. Most of the sheep were posed head down in a grazing position; those without legs were deemed "sitting." George picked up another and repositioned it a few yards away, facing in a different direction.

Jimmy held a sheep under each arm. "Where do you want these?"

"Anywhere. Just move them around. It's OK if you put them in groups sometimes. They tend to do that, apparently."

Together, they set about repositioning sheep. From time to time George would call out a suggestion: *Bring those two over here by the fence. How about we scatter that group in the corner? Try turning those two to face the road.* Each time, Jimmy complied, eager to please. After a while, the job seemed complete and the two men stood contemplating the new arrangement.*

"What about the other pastures, Mr Godfrey? Do you want me to take care of them?"

"It's a lot of work, Jimmy."

"No trouble. I'd like to feel like I'm doing something useful here."

"Are you sure you want to take this on? You'd need to do it twice a day—morning and afternoon. Weekends too."

"No problem. I get here early. I could do it before any of the Residents are up and about."

"Well, OK. You've got yourself a new job title: Shepherd."

"Thanks, Mr Godfrey."

He shook George's hand enthusiastically. George had not been expecting such gratitude.

"Welcome to the fold."

"Did you make these sheep, Mr Godfrey?"

"Not me personally, but somebody did. These are from the props department at Paramount. They made hundreds of them for some big movie, set on a sheep farm."

* **MEANWHILE** *Are you late? End Delay Worry. American Periodic Relief Compound Double-Strength Tablets safely end periodic delays and worries. Relieves most stubborn cases. No pain. New discovery. Easily taken. Solves women's most perplexing problem. Women everywhere are receiving joyful relief and peace of mind from this scientific formula compounded from USP ingredients in an up-to-date laboratory of graduate pharmacists. Usually relieves when all others fail. Don't be discouraged. End worry at once. Send $2.00 for double-strength standard-size package and full directions. Mailed same day, special delivery, in plain wrapper.*

"Why don't they use real sheep?"

"Because you can't control them. Real sheep move around by themselves. Plays havoc with continuity."

"What's continuity?"

"Well, say John Wayne is talking on screen and in the background there's a field of sheep. The big guy's got a long speech, see, but he forgets his lines halfway through. Most actors can't remember much more than their own name and address. So he takes a look at his script, learns the next few lines, and picks up where he left off. Later, the editor splices the two bits of film together and makes it look like one take. Trouble is, while John Wayne's eyeballing his script, the sheep have got bored—like everyone else working on the movie—and decided to wander off. So now the two bits of film are joined together and everything looks pretty smooth, except that halfway through, the sheep in the background suddenly vanish. One minute they're there and then poof—they're gone. The continuity is broken, see? Now with these sheep, you don't get that problem."

"How come you know all this, Mr G?"

"I'm an art director in motion pictures."

"No kidding. What are you doing here then?"

"My expertise was required. Most of the guys here are from MGM or Warners: set builders, carpenters, painters, props men."

"But you're the boss, right?"

"I guess so. We all got commissioned for this job."

"So now you're working for Lockheed instead. That's quite a switch. Two different worlds."

"Oh, they're not so different. Warner Brothers' studios are about the same size as the Lockheed plant. They're both factories. Same number of employees, give or take. Everybody working together to manufacture their product. Lockheed, at its most productive, puts out one B-24 bomber a week, plus a number of smaller planes and parts; Warners put out one A-class feature plus a number of B movies and shorts. Some of those take off and fly; some of them get shot down—either by the public or sabotaged by the critics. They crash and burn. Sometimes the star manages to parachute to safety and their career survives; other times they go down with the plane and are never heard from again."

"I never thought of it that way," said Jimmy.

"You know, it beats me why a star would want to take a chance on piloting the plane. Hundreds of people work on that big heap of tin and any one of them could have screwed up. And the beauty of it is, you don't get to find out about it until you're twenty thousand feet up in the air."

"I guess you have to have a little faith in other people."

Though innocently pitched, it was quite a leveling comment. It made George seem cynical and rather callous. He stared thoughtfully at Jimmy for a moment.

"Aren't you from one of the studios?" he said.

"No. I live local," said Jimmy. "I heard there was some part-time work going so I came along and got myself hired."

"How come you haven't been drafted?"

"I enlisted. I've already completed my basic training. I volunteered for Parachute Training; I'm waiting to hear if I've been accepted. I'm just working here until I get word."

"Parachute? Well, well. Bit of a daredevil, huh?"

"I guess. My brother's already out there in the Philippines. Defending the Bataan Peninsular against the Japs. How about you, sir? You going overseas?"

"No, I'm serving my country by creating this beautiful scenery. Seems I'm better with a paintbrush than I am with a rifle."

"I'm sure all this is considered important war work. Building Overland, making it seem so …" He looked down at the sheep-shaped bundles of wool. "… lifelike."

Jimmy's comment sounded patronizing. George responded spikily.

"It is, as a matter of fact. Very important. Overland isn't only protecting the lives of the workforce below, but also the production of hundreds of planes that will defend our Pacific Fleet."

Jimmy nodded in eager agreement and George quickly mellowed.

"Well. Good luck. I'm sure you'll do great. If there's one thing the army needs, it's good shepherds."

"Good training for rounding up Jap prisoners," said Jimmy.

George smiled uneasily.

The Lockheed P-38 was at 2,000 feet. The panorama was clear to the horizon where a light haze softened the distant peaks of the Verdugo mountains, lending them a bluish tint. The pilot dipped his wing a little to take in more of the city below him. Long, straight roads, sun-bleached houses with terracotta roofs, sporadically populated by bushy green trees. He consulted his charts.

Japanese Americans were waiting patiently in line outside a flat-fronted public building. Most of them looked like professionals: proudly turned out women, businessmen in suits and hats. Keeping the group in check was a US Army corporal—garrison cap, field jacket, khaki pants with canvas leggings—who patrolled the line like a sheepdog mustering his flock. Those at the front of the line faced a second soldier armed with a rifle and who stood rigidly "at ease" at the building's gated entrance through which the Japanese were slowly being checked and filtered by officials.
  Across the street, Mrs Ishi hurried furtively by.

In Overland, a daisy chain of loudspeakers connected by draping wires had been haphazardly rigged throughout the town. Some hung in clusters from trees like giant mechanical flowers; others appeared as single speakers attached to buildings. They bore their original light blue paint and were scarred and battered from wear. They began to play a series of chimes, *Bing bong-a-bing bong*, rather like an over-amplified musical box—a sound more commonly used to hail the arrival of an ice-cream truck. The head-jarringly cheerful phrase had been looped to repeat every few seconds.

The Overland Residents responded by sliding diligently into their assigned roles. In contrast to the visible sharpening of activities, a group of hikers stood on a nearby corner, chewing the fat. One of them glanced nonchalantly up at the skies then resumed his conversation.

George too looked up and spotted a plane soaring overhead. On high alert, he dashed over to them, yelling, "Plane!"

One of the hikers reassured him. "It's OK. It's one of ours."

"How do you know?"

"It's a P-38. You can spot it a mile off by the forked tail."

"What about the pilot? Is he one of ours?"

"What?"

"Can you see the pilot? From here? Is it someone you know?"

"No, of course I can't see the pilot."

"Then how can you tell who's flying it?"

"Well it's not going to be a Jap, is it—in a P-38?"

"So if you were a Japanese pilot flying over enemy soil, trying not to get shot down, what plane would you want to be in? A Zero? A Kawasaki? Or might you choose something a little less conspicuous? A Lockheed P-38, perhaps?"

"They can't do that."

"Can't they? Why not?"

"Well, that's not fair, is it?"

"Not fair?"

"Pretending to be something you're not."

"No, pal. It's not fair, but it's what people do."

SEVEN

A tall perimeter fence surrounded numerous vast buildings with blank high-sided walls and arched corrugated steel roofs. They looked like aircraft hangars but they weren't. A billboard outside proclaimed that this was the home of *Warner Bros. Studios. The world's greatest entertainment is produced in this studio! Warner Bros. lead the field!*

Inside the studio gates, in the middle of an expanse of open ground sat a long trailer-type building. A man with slicked-back hair wearing a fancy sleeveless pullover looked out through the open top half of a stable door. On the lower half was a hand-painted sign: *Casting Dept. Mr McKintyre.* Leading up to the door was a long line of hopeful extras, bit players and stand-ins. Some were in costume, but most wore everyday clothes. Several of them carried small suitcases, looking like refugees, shabby and desperate. Old hands at the "extras" game had brought tiny folding seats.

At the very end of the line Queenie looked at her watch and shuffled her feet impatiently. She wore a pair of red satin shorts with crossed bib straps over a white short-sleeved blouse. On her feet were classic dance shoes with a blocky heel, tied with a ribbon bow.

A group of gaily-dressed Apache Indians—Caucasian males painted with what looked like Bosco chocolate syrup—strolled past, smoking cigarettes. A couple of them lifted their sunglasses to ogle Queenie's clean-limbed figure. One of them responded by slapping his mouth and emitting the high oscillating *woowoowoo* battle cry that Hollywood would have us believe is characteristic of "his people."

A man drove by on a tractor; a youth in a droopy wool cap straddled the front, riding it like a horse.

Queenie glumly waited. Up ahead she noticed a woman in her forties with her skirt hitched up to reveal shapeless bruised legs. She sat on the asphalt, cracking walnuts with the heel of her grubby tap shoe.

The waiting line did not appear to be moving.

One girl had a chubby-legged baby perched on her forearm. Not the smartest accessory to bring with you to a casting. It put Queenie in mind of her own little problem, which she'd been trying to ignore, hoping against hope that it would resolve itself.

In the movie magazines the only babies ever talked about belonged to "old guard" actresses like Norma Shearer with their happy homes and doting husbands. For them, family life was "simply the most important thing in the world." At the end of each day's filming they would rush home to spend precious time with their darling children. As for movie stars with a baby born out of wedlock, well, if there were any, they were keeping it pretty hush-hush. According to one of Queenie's fellow extras on *Anne of Windy Poplars,* if an up-and-coming contract player did get herself into trouble she would be sent by the studio to

see a "special" doctor who could make the problem go away—all on the QT and no questions asked. Those kind of doctors cost money, lots of money, but stars under contract were valuable commodities so it figured that a studio would want to protect its investment. Extras, bit players and chorus girls, on the other hand, were a dime a dozen so were offered no such remedy. Queenie sighed heavily. If she couldn't get a break now, what chance did she have if her "little problem" turned out to be the real thing? She was praying it was a false alarm, as had been the case once before, but she had to face the possibility that this time she really was in a jam. What then? What kind of parts would she be good for six months or a year down the line? Heavily pregnant flapper doing the Charleston? Postnatally depressed cigarette girl pushing a baby buggy round a nightclub?

Gradually Queenie became aware of another line forming nearby, this one heading in the opposite direction towards a different building. She feigned nonchalance, but her eyes were drawn to the livelier group. These candidates were all young women, aspiring hoofers dressed in a variety of rehearsal costumes: jaunty gym suits; short dresses and ankle socks; culottes and halter tops; ballet leotards and tights. With their bold make-up and cute hairdos, these girls already looked like screen starlets. They laughed and chattered, flexing and stretching, while others limbered up with a few shuffling steps. Two blonde girls in matching jersey-knit playsuits were going through a syncopated duet, their heavy silver tap shoes clattering on the asphalt as they punched out the routine. The style was meat-and-potatoes Ruby Keeler: solid

steps, stabs, shuffles and skids accented by snappy claps and hand gestures. Queenie was impressed. She quickly decided that this is where the action was, instinctively migrating towards the new group. By comparison, the folks in her line looked like a bunch of deadbeats.

She approached what she thought was the end of the line only to find that it dog-legged around a corner, a trail of girls snaking back towards the studio gates and out onto the street. Her heart sank. She turned to a girl in the line.

"What's the audition for anyway?"

The girl shrugged. "Must be something big—a musical or something."

Another girl chipped in. "I heard it was a Busby Berkeley sequence."

Queenie perked up. "Really? That could be a big break for some lucky girl—if she were to get a close-up."

Buoyed by this promising news, Queenie followed the train of girls, mentally pitching herself against the competition as she passed. Some gave her the up-and-down. She was about to join the end of the line when first one then another new girl stepped in before her. Queenie moved further towards the rear, but each time, a girl seemed to appear from nowhere to get there first, squeezing her out like in a game of musical chairs.

Finally, she took a place in the line, but now she found herself on the wrong side of the studio perimeter fence feeling shut out, her goal no longer in clear sight.

A scrawny dough-faced Henry with his pants hitched a little too high sauntered along the line, unashamedly checking out the talent.

The clipboard he was holding indicated that this was his job and he was authorized to do so. He picked out one or two of the prettier girls for closer inspection.

"What's your name, toots? Carol? Turn around, Carol. Let me see how far you can bend."

The girl touched her toes, her shorts rode up and the kid got an eyeful.

"Hold it like that." The young man whistled and adjusted the crotch in his pants. "Carol, huh? How old are you?"

"Fifteen."

"Holy catfish. Put it away." He covered his eyes to the temptation.

Further down the line he spotted a lithesome lovely wearing a military style brass-buttoned tunic in powder-blue satin with a matching peaked cap. Army regulations regarding pants had been ignored in favor of bare legs and high heels. The kid looked her up and down.

"Nice epaulettes, doll face. How about you and me getting together for a little drill practice?"

The girl, evidently more experienced than he had thought, rolled her eyes. "Take a hike, shorty."

Undaunted, the "talent scout" strolled on until he came to Queenie, clearly liking what he saw.

"How about you, sister? You play the flute?"

Queenie missed the reference.

"Flute? No, but I sing a little."

"No. The *flute*. Do you play? I can get you straight in to see Mr Michaels if you do."

She frowned quizzically. The kid's cheek bulged out a couple of times, poked from inside with his tongue.

The penny dropped.

"Oh."

"You catch my drift?"

She did, but pretended not to.

"I think so. You're looking for a flute player."

"You got it."

"I'm a quick learner and I'm very musical."

"You looked like you might be. Just the kind of girl Mr Michaels is looking for."

Queenie gushed. "I am?"

The young man beckoned her with a crooked finger. "Follow me."

As Queenie passed her competitors on her way to the front of the line, the girls eyed her with disdain; they all knew what tune she'd soon be playing. One or two murmurs of "Whore." But Queenie held her head high, apparently considering it an honor—as if Fred Astaire himself had chosen her for his new partner.

In a spacious rehearsal room, with a polished wooden floor and one mirrored wall, stood a line of leggy young women in an assortment of costumes, all bright smiles and perky bobbed hair. Queenie had earned her place among them—enduring a furtive bout of rub-and-tug fumbling with the junior talent scout in a store closet—but she put the sordid encounter out of her mind. She looked radiant, full of hope.

The choreographer, a tubby twinkle-toes in shirtsleeves, nodded to a bald man playing an upright piano who started up a lively dance number. On the choreographer's count, the girls began a recently rehearsed basic tap routine. After eight bars they formed an advancing chain that snaked past the piano, one arm doing windmills while the other rested on the hip of the girl in front. At first glance, all the girls seemed on a par, each worthy of a place in any chorus line. The choreographer looked on, satisfied, but as the dancers passed by, his attention was drawn to Queenie, who was towards the back of the group. With her pretty face and engaging smile, she certainly looked the part, but while her arms seemed to be in unison with the others, he quickly spotted woeful inconsistencies in her footwork. Where the other girls, more experienced or more talented perhaps, fell easily into the prescribed step-step-kick-shuffle-step pattern, Queenie's scant approximation of it seemed based on little more than a determination to "keep things moving." The choreographer leaned forward and touched her shoulder. She ignored him and blithely carried on, still beaming, until he tapped her shoulder more firmly and pulled her from the line. The girls behind her quickly closed the gap and the line continued gaily around the room. Queenie bowed her head and slumped her shoulders; she knew the game was up. The young talent scout watched her go, smugly chuckling to himself at the outcome.

Kay was leaning over the banister when Queenie let herself in through the front door. Queenie, still wearing her red shorts and dance shoes, wearily climbed the stairs.

"How did it go?"

Queenie looked up at the sound of Kay's voice. "I've had better days," she said.

"No luck?"

"Nah. I got in to see an important choreographer, but I was a little off my game. Things on my mind."

Kay was intrigued yet reluctant to pry. Queenie joined Kay on the landing. Seeing her friend's look of concern, she decided to share. She let out a long sigh before speaking.

"Between you, me, and the grand piano, I'm still waiting for my Aunt Flo to visit."

Kay looked dubious. "Oh. I'm not sure Mrs Ishi is very keen on us having visitors."

"Not that kind of visitor, dope. You know … Aunt Flo? … From Redding? … Comes to stay for a few days once a month?" Queenie stressed the words to make sure that Kay had caught on. "Except mine hasn't turned up and I'm starting to get worried. She's never normally this late."

"Oh dear."

"Oh dear is right. I don't know what the heck I'm going to do if she doesn't show up soon."

There was a pause while Kay considered this.

"Do you think we should call the police?"

EIGHT

George was down at the Overland Diner waiting to be served when he became aware of a Resident in painting coveralls leaning against the counter reading a newspaper.

"'Bout time huh?" he said.

"What?"

The man held up the newspaper. The headline read *Expulsion of all Japs in California near.*

George frowned. "Do they mean civilians?"

"Anyone with even a drop of Japanese blood. Sayonara."

"Why are they doing that?"

"Are you crazy? 'Cos of Pearl Harbor, you dope. Don't you read the papers?"

"Are they sending them back to Japan?"

"Uh-uh. Concentration camps. Stick 'em out in the middle of nowhere, throw a big barbed-wire fence around 'em."

"That seems rather …"

"Extreme?" The man shrugged. "War's war. What are you gonna do? Nobody wants one of them crazy Kamikazes dropping in for supper."

George ruminated on this. "No, that could be awkward."

He picked up his coffee and donut to leave. On his way out, he noticed that many of the Overland diners were reading newspapers. One word seemed to dominate many of the front pages: Bataan. Wasn't that where Jimmy had said his brother was stationed? He had no idea where Bataan was, but the headlines gave some hint of developing events there: *Japanese Forces Take Bataan. Bataan falls! 36,800 US troops trapped. 15 Generals among war prisoners.*

Outside, crossing the square, a young man was carrying a wide roll of fabric on his shoulder. George trotted after him, trying not to spill his coffee.*

"Harry, tell Mr Beckman on the gate I don't want any of the workers bringing in newspapers from outside."

Harry took the roll from his shoulder and stood it upright, draping his arm around it like it was a high-school sweetheart. "Gee, boss. The fellers like to take a look at the paper during their lunch break … find out what's going on in the world."

"Well, not me. I don't want to know what's going on out there. I don't want to hear a goddamn thing about it. Tell them that while they're here in Overland they should keep their mind on the job. No newspapers."

"Hmm. I don't know if the men will go for that."

"Well then we'll print our own newspaper. Local news. News of what's going on in Overland."

"You're serious, right?"

*__MEANWHILE__ *In a dark corner of the factory a man in bulky jacket and gloves, wearing a thick leather smoke hood, was stoking the glowing embers of a forge with a long-handled trowel. The mask's dark goggling eyeholes gave him a demonic look as he lifted and sifted the bright, hot coals. It was reminiscent of a scene from Dante's Inferno.*

"Sure. Why not?"

"Because nothing's going on in Overland; there's nothing to write about. Besides, everybody finishes at the end of the week. There'll be nobody here to read it."

"What are you talking about?"

"The Overland project. Friday's our last day. The carpenters, construction crew, the painters, prop-makers, sparks, lighting guys—we're all heading back to our regular jobs. Back to the studios, back to construction sites."

"What, everybody? There's still so much to do."

"That's the way it goes. Contracts end. No more pay. Everyone goes home to momma."

"Where's your loyalty? Don't you care about the success of the project?"

"Major Lund's orders. He says we're through here. You should check your contract too, boss. The major said you were being moved out to Seattle."

"I'm not *being moved out* anywhere. I'm in charge around here, not Major Lund. Overland is my project and I say what goes on in this town. Get it?"

George felt embarrassed by his own haughtiness.

"Whatever you say, Mr Godfrey." Harry's tone carried a patronizing edge.

"And tell Mr Beckman, from now on, no newspapers. We'll be printing our own."

Harry pretended to make a mental note. "No newspapers. Check. We'll be printing our own … Even though there will be no one here."

George responded testily. "The Residents will still be here. I'm sure they'll be interested to read about what's going on in their town."

"Oh, sure they will. Stop press: *Overland Resident to embark on leisurely walk … Local woman forgets to hang out laundry*. Bro-ther. Hold the front page."

This sort of thing used to happen at the studios too; someone on the crew would repeatedly do or say things that exposed and undermined the verisimilitude of whatever fiction George had created, seemingly unable to accept that this was simply another kind of reality. It wasn't meant maliciously, but it was annoying just the same. Yes, George *knew* that the mountains were a painted backdrop and that the castle was made from papier mâché, but it didn't help the actors, director, or anyone one else involved in telling the story, to be constantly reminded of it.

While at MGM, much of George's day was spent in the various work shops, figuring out design and production details, but he was happiest wandering round the various sound stages and backlots. That was where the sets really came to life. He preferred them just prior to shooting, before the crew cluttered the area and spoiled the illusion with their camera cranes, lighting equipment and dolly track—when each set was still a blank canvas onto which any number of stories could be painted.

Though it was a modified version of reality, in most cases he saw it as an improvement. He'd never been to Bali, had no idea even where it was, but he couldn't imagine that the beaches there would be any more exotic than the one created for Dorothy Lamour in *Aloma of the South Seas*. He'd never been to New York either, but thanks to his familiarity with the Brownstone District on MGM's Lot Two he felt au fait enough with the area to know where he might get his pants pressed or buy a good steak dinner.

The studio backlots were so vast, some of them sprawling over more than sixty acres, that once you were in the midst of them the perimeter fences fell away into the distance; there was nowhere else to go but to some other reality.

Once, when he'd run out of cigarettes, he intuitively headed for a tobacco shop in the French district only to be reminded that this particular store was "facade only" and had no interior. Some did, but he could never remember which.

Stray dogs and cats roamed the streets or dozed in the shade of buildings; birds perched on branches. They couldn't tell, and didn't care, whether the trees or houses were real.

Employees involved in the Andy Hardy series of pictures spent years working day in, day out on the elaborate New England street set that stood permanently on Lot Two, representing Andy's fictional hometown of Carvel. And though it was a confection rather than a reflection of the American way of life, they came to know and love the neighborhood better than their own. Carvel was a real nice town; who wouldn't want to live there? Its inhabitants were always generous and tolerant, whereas in the world outside the studio gates most people turned out to be selfish and morally corrupt.

When George had worked on the snow scenes for *The Mortal Storm*, they covered the entire area of Stage Fifteen with 300 tons of white dolomite and gypsum. Falling snow made from goose feathers and shaved paper pulp added to the effect. During the course of the day, he began to notice that the crew working on set were wearing

sweaters and coats. It was maybe eighty degrees, yet folks were all wrapped up because they felt cold. That's what happens—your eyes see snow and send a signal to your brain that it's midwinter; suddenly your teeth start chattering and you're putting on mittens.

He loved how convincingly this sense of place could be created. On a typical day he might eat breakfast in a Mexican bordello, take a mid-morning nap aboard a pirate galleon and then later enjoy a fried chicken lunch on the ice-capped summit of Mount Everest. When the working day was over, instead of going straight home he would take a stroll through Dickensian London or sit and smoke cigarettes on the surface of the moon.

The Lockheed Aircraft plant sprawled over a hundred acres, bigger even than MGM's Lot Three. There were seventeen hangars, some longer than a city block, and dozens of other major buildings, parking lots, manufacturing plants and factories. Without its Overland shell, the plant was like a bullseye painted on the Burbank townscape; strategically, it was one giant self-advertising target.

The aerial footage of the unconcealed Lockheed factory, taken before George made it disappear, had been shown to him at his initial meeting with Major Lund at an airbase in Glendale, where they had sat side by side in a small screening room along with a number of other military men. Nobody spoke; the only sound was the whirr of the projector and the quiet chatter of the film running through it. George felt very much the outsider: the only one not in uniform, watching a film that he assumed all the others had seen before.

All this was clearly leading up to something big, but nobody had yet mentioned exactly what they wanted him to do. It was as if they were shy about putting it to him too directly. Major Lund finally came out with it.

The proposal was to design and fabricate a three-dimensional town covering the entire Lockheed factory plant that from the air would look like an ordinary residential neighbourhood—concealing, and therefore protecting, the factory below from Japanese air attack. It was a huge area to cover, Major Lund realized, but considering the capabilities of the movie studio art departments and the lengths they went to …

Apparently, the major had witnessed this himself on official visits to Warner Brothers and MGM. He had been particularly impressed with aerial photographs of art director Lyle Wheeler's spectacular city of Atlanta set for David O. Selznick's *Gone With the Wind*, constructed on RKO's "back forty" in Culver City. Why, suggested the major, couldn't they build a simpler, more modest version on top of the Lockheed plant? A large area of camouflage netting, some trees and a few houses dotted about. He stressed that the fake town would only ever be seen in extreme long shot, certainly no closer than a thousand feet, so there would be no need for any great level of detail. With a large enough workforce to overcome the logistics of covering such a vast area, he felt sure this would be achievable.

George was already picturing it.

An entire town, like Andy Hardy's Carvel, except that this would be his own design—and with no cameras, lights and microphone booms to compromise the reality. It would be far grander in scale than any movie set ever built and he, George Godfrey, would be its creator. Overland would be the greatest achievement of his career.

Without giving it a second thought, he agreed to take on the mission.

NINE

The man who came to Jimmy's house to buy his motorcycle was called Wilf or Whiff; Jimmy didn't quite catch the name because he had a few missing teeth that affected the way he spoke. He was a bear of a guy with a thick, woolly beard and a black eyepatch like a pirate. When they shook on the deal, the man's hand felt thick and crusty like it was covered in barnacles. Jimmy half expected to be paid in gold doubloons or pieces of eight. Instead, the man counted out bills onto his hand. In exchange, Jimmy handed over the owner's title and a key on a fob.

The man brought the document close to his good eye, squinting to read the words. Satisfied, he folded it in half and stuffed it into his inside pocket. He reached for the handlebars, swung his leg over and mounted the motorcycle, settling himself into the saddle. Jimmy stepped back and put his hands in his pockets, distancing himself.

"Don't forget, the headlight needs adjusting," he said.

"No big deal. I won't be riding it at night." The pirate tapped his eyepatch with the tip of his index finger. "Makes judging distances a problem," he explained. "I don't see so good in the dark."

Kay was folding laundry and setting it in neat piles on the bed while Queenie sat at her dresser mirror titivating her hair.

"What kind of work do you do ... at that factory?"

Queenie took a moment to consider her three-quarter profile before answering. "Lockheed? They build airplanes. They're taking on a lot of women to do the men's jobs while they're overseas fighting."

"What kind of jobs?"

"Welding, riveting—manual labor."

"Women do that?"

"Sure they do. Why not? We're twice as tough and ten times twice as smart as any man."

"Welding? I don't think I could do that."

"Sure you could. All the girls do it. Nothing to it. They're crying out for workers to increase production. Taking just about anyone who can make a fist. Good pay too."

"You think *I* could get a job there?"

Queenie was forced to backpedal. "Oh, I don't know about that, sweetie. No one's hiring Japanese now. *You* know that. Especially not Lockheed. High risk of sabotage. A factory making fighter planes and bombers isn't going to risk having a Jap spying on them and telling what's-his-name old Hirohito all our military secrets. There *is* a war on. And strictly speaking, Lotus Blossom, you are the enemy."

"Why would I spy on Americans? I *am* an American—and as patriotic as you are."

"They're not going to see it that way. Take a look in the mirror."

She did. Her Asian face stared glumly back at her.

"Besides, I thought all you lot were being packed off to concentration camps. How come you haven't been sent away?"

"I was supposed to register at some assembly center yesterday. I didn't go."

"Will they be looking for you?"

Kay shrugged. "I don't know. I guess. May tenth is the final deadline for exclusion of all Japanese. By then everyone is supposed to be in a camp."

"May tenth? That's soon. What day is that?"

"Sunday, I think," said Kay.

Queenie studied the calendar above Kay's bed, running her finger along the rows of numbers. "May tenth is a Saturday. Wait, this says December." She took a closer look "What's this? Nineteen thirty-two? Holy Toledo. You're a bit behind the times, aren't you, sweetie?"

"It's an old one," explained Kay. "I only have it because of the picture."

Queenie took a good look at the lakeside cottage scene. She didn't get it. She turned to Kay with a quizzical look.

"It's from the man next door," said Kay.

"*The Man Next Door?*" Queenie said it like it was the title of a movie she had not yet seen, supposing that the lake picture might be a still from it. She had no idea what Kay was on about.

"And anyway," said Kay, "why is it only Japanese people? What about the Germans or Italians? How come they're not being imprisoned? America is at war with them too."

"That's different."

"Is it? Why?"

"Well, I guess because …"

"Because Germans and Italians don't look foreign? Because they don't have flat noses and slanting eyes?"

"Don't chew me out. I didn't make the rules."

"Well, I don't know who did. I'm an American citizen, but they're saying that anyone with even one-sixteenth Japanese ancestry has to go be evacuated. That's saying that if you have just one Japanese great-great grandparent, you're Japanese."

"I guess they want to be sure. In case there's, you know, spies."

"So they lock *all* the Japanese up? Just in case?"

Queenie shrugged. Like she said, she didn't make the rules.

"So there are no Japanese workers at your factory?"

"There are a few orientals," said Queenie. "I don't know what they are. Chinese, probably. Chinese are allowed, apparently."

"Do you think maybe I could say I was Chinese—like you said? You know, an American citizen, but with Chinese ancestry instead of Japanese?"

"I guess."

"Are they hiring Chinese?"

"I don't know. We could try. Better still, we make you look American. Then you don't have to worry about it."

Five minutes later, the makeover was underway. Kay sat in front of the

* **MEANWHILE** *George was on a ladder trying to hang an old checker racing flag over the library entrance. The pole was in place, protruding diagonally from the facade, but the flag itself was not yet unfurled. In storage, the fabric had been wrapped around the pole and tied with string. George fiddled with the knot, but couldn't undo it. He reached into one of his pants pockets and then the other to locate his pocketknife. It wasn't there. He checked both back pockets, his shirt pocket. Damn. He must have lost it. He'd had that knife for years.*

mirror wearing sunglasses; her hair was pulled up and stowed under a green wide-brimmed hat. Queenie assessed her protégée's look.

"Let's get you out of that suit and into something a bit more eye-catching. We need to dazzle the personnel officer."

"What's wrong with it?"

"It's too … chaste. Haven't you got something with a bit more oomph?"

"Not really. I don't tend to go for garish colors."

Queenie went to the closet. Kay took off her suit and stood in her slip, re-evaluating her look in the mirror.

"Are you sure these sunglasses don't just make me look like a spy?"

"Well, maybe. But at least you look like an American spy."

Queenie turned, holding a dress aloft on a hanger. It was a three-quarter sleeve summer dress with a gaudy red, white and pink flower motif on a swirling leaf-green background. She tucked the hanger under Kay's chin, draping the dress down her front to check the effect.

"This'll take his mind off your great-grandparents."

"Thanks, Queenie, but it's not really my style."

"Phoo. Your style? You haven't got a style. That's your problem. You'll look a million dollars, trust me. When he sees you in this, he won't care whether you're Chinese, Japanese, Hercules or antifreeze."

Kay looked doubtful.

"Anyway," Queenie went on, "once they see an American name on your Social Security card, you'll be home free. What *is* your surname?"

"Nashimura."

"Oh, Jesus."

Queenie was huddled over Kay's Social Security card. Holding a razor blade at right angles she scraped lightly back and forth over Kay's surname. Little by little the letters faded from dark to pale gray and eventually began to vanish completely as the surface of the card was scraped away. Queenie lifted the card to her lips and blew hard at the fine dust on the surface. She held it up for Kay to inspect.*

Mr Westermann set Kay's card down on the desk next to him, adjusting his glasses on his nose as he typed the details from it onto an employee registration card. In the space next to *Surname*, he typed N-A-S-H, stabbing at the keys with one forefinger while holding down the shift key with the other. Kay's date of birth was entered next. He looked up at her for further information.

Kay stood formally across from his desk looking as obligingly deferential as her sunglasses would allow. She looked like a film star traveling incognito: the disguise made her doubly conspicuous. The wide-brimmed hat and the vivid colors of Queenie's flowery dress seemed jarringly out of place amidst the factory's dreary grayness. Queenie, for once more appropriately dressed in the muted hues of her workwear, perched on the edge of Mr Westermann's desk, from which vantage point she hoped to provide the necessary diversions. Mr Westermann seemed resolutely unimpeachable.

"Birthplace?"

Kay answered. "San Bernardino."

He typed it into the appropriate space.

Queenie added helpful clarification. "San Bernardino, California."

In the box marked *State or Country* Mr Westermann typed "CA." He hit the keys a little sharply, suggesting that this was not the first "helpful" comment from the applicant's chaperone.

"Light bothering your eyes, Miss Nash?" He delivered the question without looking up.

"No, I …" She nervously removed the sunglasses and folded them in her hand. Queenie winced.

Mr Westermann finally glanced up at her, and then looked down again at the card. There was a tense moment before he spoke again.

"Height?"

Kay was surprised by the question. "Height? Oh. Five three."

Mr Westermann cleared his throat. "Any Japanese ancestry?"

Queenie jumped in. "Good Lord, no. She's as American as apple strudel—aren't you, Kay?"

Mr Westermann glanced at Queenie dismissively, addressing Kay. "Well, you've obviously got some kind of oriental blood in you."

Queenie overplayed her surprise. "Have you, Kay?"

"A little. My great-grandfather was Chinese."

"Chinese? Oh, well that's OK, isn't it, Mr Westermann? China's on the same side as us—against the Japs."

"I'll need some proof. A birth certificate—with the nationality of your parents. Bring it with you tomorrow."

While Mr Westermann looked down at the typewriter keys the two women exchanged glances. Kay's perturbed expression signaled her distress. Queenie closed her eyes and jiggled her head, shrugging off the problem.

"You know, Mr Westermann, you have nice eyes. Do you really need to wear those glasses?"

Mr Westermann was wise to Queenie's ploy. "Only when I want to see things clearly." He looked down at his form, then back at Queenie. "You don't really need to be here, Miss Meyer. I'm sure Miss Nash can provide all the information I need."

"Oh, sure. I was just here to give the kid a little moral support. Well, I'll see you later, Kay. Good day, Mr Westermann."

Later, when Kay descended the iron staircase from the offices, Queenie was waiting for her.

"Everything go OK?"

"No thanks to you. He didn't suspect a thing until you started chipping in with your apple strudel and all that hooey about his glasses." She did a silly cooing imitation. "*Oh, Mr Westermann, you have such beautiful eyes!* I thought you were supposed to be a great actress."

"Well thank *you*. I stuck my neck out for you."

"Yeah, well. I just hope you know how to forge a Chinese birth certificate," said Kay.

"What does a Chinese birth certificate look like?"

"How should I know?"

"Well, if you don't know, chances are he won't either."

TEN

Kay's instructor was a short guy wearing a cap whose peak pointed straight up in the air. Instead of the full arc welder's helmet mask that she and the other trainees had been given, he made do with a visor with a handle attached to the chin, which he waved casually in front of his face like a nonchalant guest at a masquerade ball. On the first day, he picked her out of the group to take part in his demonstration, clamping an electrode into a grip holder and pressing it into her clumsily gloved hand. Flipping a switch on a piece of apparatus behind him, he guided her hand into position. She hunched over, peering closely through the small window of dark glass in her mask, to strike the electrode along the join as she had been taught. After a few attempts, the arc was established and the electrode tip burst into a fizzing, sparking crackle of dazzling blue light.

Once her weld was completed, the arc was broken and the light flash died away, leaving the area in darkness. She couldn't see a thing. The instructor switched off the current and tilted back the heavy mask on top of Kay's head so that she could review her handiwork. The other apprentices were gazing blindly at the now dark spot, their faces still encased in protective facemasks; they looked like curious visitors from another planet. The instructor leaned in to inspect Kay's weld and nodded his approval. She beamed with pride.

Queenie was assigned as her mentor and helped teach her what she needed to do. Once she got the hang of it, the work was pretty repetitive; she gradually gathered confidence and began to speed up her production output. She was a welder now. Who'd have thought she could ever do that?

At the 8 p.m. shift changeover, Queenie and Kay headed out from the locker room in their street clothes. Queenie playfully shoulder-barged Kay out of the way, skipping ahead.

"Come on, I'll buy you a beer to celebrate your first day."

Kay quickened her pace to catch up. "You sound like a man."

"Why the hell shouldn't I? I work like a man."

"Where would we go?"

"Clancy's."

"Clancy's is rough. It's a man's bar. They drink hard liquor and spit."

"Well then, my dear, we shall drink hard liquor and spit."

They linked arms and headed for the exit.

Several hours later, Kay and Queenie emerged from Clancy's, arms still linked. The girls were in high spirits: a little raucous and unsteady on their feet.

Kay should not have risked disobeying the curfew. For several weeks now, persons of Japanese ancestry were forbidden from being out between 8 p.m. and 6 a.m. She had not dared to break

the law. Public Proclamation No. 3 also stated that *at all other times all such persons shall only be at their place of residence or employment or traveling between those places or within a distance of not more than five miles from their place of residence.* But Queenie wasn't having any of it. She insisted that those rules didn't apply to Kay because her ancestors were Chinese, not Japanese. As far as Queenie was concerned, Kay's nationality change was complete. Or, at least, nearly complete. They were still one birth certificate away. Kay had managed to stall Mr Westermann before starting work that morning with a solemn promise to bring the required document with her the next day.

They had already gone half a block past the Hong Fu Chinese restaurant when Queenie doubled back, leaving Kay on the sidewalk.

At a table near the door, an elderly Chinese gentleman with chopsticks teased wriggling noodles from a bowl into his mouth. Above him, framed on the wall, was some kind of official-looking document. It had a gold crested motif at the top, and a pale blue decorative border surrounding neat rows of Chinese characters in various weights and sizes. Amongst the calligraphy was a long number, and in the corner a red rubber-stamped emblem. It could have been anything: a menu, a school swimming diploma, a manufacturer's warranty for a fridge-freezer, but it was unmistakeably Chinese.

Focused on his food, the diner remained oblivious as Queenie sidled over and gently removed the certificate from the wall above his head.

The next morning Queenie was standing in front of Mrs Ishi's hall mirror teasing her hair, contemplating possible new styles. As she did this, she made shuffling jitterbug steps, singing her own accompaniment to a song playing on the radio.

Hold tight, hold tight, hold tight, hold tight
Fodo-de-yacka saki
Want some seafood Mama
Shrimps and rice they're very nice
I like oysters, lobsters too
I like my tasty butterfish—foo
When I come home late at night
I get my favorite dish, fish!
Hold tight—

Mrs Ishi had appeared from the kitchen. "You like fish?"

Queenie contained her dance to a gentle sway. "Oh, morning, Mrs Ishi."

"You like fish?"

"Huh?"

"You want some seafood, Mama?"

"Oh, it's just a song, Mrs Ishi."

"You like?"

"Fish? Sure. I like it well enough."

"Eat plenty fish."

Queenie nodded, unsure whether it was a question or a command.

* **MEANWHILE** *On Fairview Avenue a middle-aged woman in a cloche hat lay on her side, painting white lines along the center of the road. Fifty yards ahead, a driveway led down to the Rest Haven Motel, a simple L-shape structure created from two boxcars set at adjacent angles. Painted along their duck-egg blue walls was a row of dark square windows with white frames. The upper section of each window had a horizontal panel of green; these were of varying widths to suggest roller blinds pulled to different heights. Parked outside on the forecourt were five red fairground bumper cars. At the building's rear, two men were rolling out a length of cobblestone footpath to the (not yet functioning) European-style three-tier fountain. Across the street, a billboard ad for Christie's Premium Soda Crackers urged the Overland Residents to "Beware of imitation!"*

Mrs Ishi bowed, offering something in both hands. Queenie looked down and saw a small can with a key attached to its lid. It had a red label with Japanese writing, and an illustration of a leaping silver fish with a startled look in its eye.

"Oh, no. I couldn't. Thanks, but …"

"Fish very good. Good for health."

"But it's yours. I can't."

"No problem. Look."

She beckoned Queenie into the kitchen where Mrs Ishi's pet bird, Mr Green, edged from side to side as it watched her guardedly through the bars of its cage. Queenie ignored it, turning her attention to Mrs Ishi as she opened the wall cupboard to reveal her stash.

"For you. One every day," she said, squeezing Queenie's hand.

"Gee, thanks, Mrs Ishi." Queenie was somewhat taken aback by this gesture. Vaguely aware of some cultural protocol she had picked up in the movies, she accepted the can with both hands, mimicking Mrs Ishi's bow. Mrs Ishi seemed pleased with the exchange.

"Every day. You eat fish. You live long."

"You don't say. OK … swell. Thanks."

Mr Green let out a high, cackling laugh.

The factory bus edged forward with the steady flow of morning traffic on North Hollywood Way. Taking a right at a set of stop lights, it headed along a side street past some small stores and businesses until it made a hard left and, with a wide swinging turn, dipped down a concrete incline towards the entrance to an underground parking lot. A soldier at the checkpoint scrutinized the driver's particulars before raising the barrier arm to let the bus through. Once below ground level, the bus advanced slowly along a dimly lit subterranean corridor.

Kay and Queenie sat together at the back of the bus, their bright spirits unaffected by the tunnel's pervading gloom.

"What's the story with Mrs Ishi-with-the-Fishy?" Queenie produced the sardine can from her purse and wiggled it teasingly in front of Kay's nose.

Kay laughed. "Oh, she gives me one of those every day. Her brother-in-law is an importer. She's building quite a stockpile."

"I saw. Have you ever tried them?"

"Sure."

Queenie squirmed. "And?"

"They're good."

Queenie shuddered. "Urgh. I couldn't eat sardines. Slimy little things. You don't know where they've been."

Truth was, she couldn't hold down much of anything in the mornings without feeling queasy. Just the thought of sardines made her nauseous.*

The road eventually began to climb again and the bus resurfaced from the tunnel into Lockheed's Parking Lot D where it swung into the curb to let the workers off. As she and Queenie stepped out into the diffused sunlight, Kay tilted back her head to gaze up at the huge expanse of netting that stretched between the hangar roofs high

above them. Supported by a series of tensioned wires, it stretched over the entire parking lot like a giant safety net. Long strips of dyed hemp had been laboriously woven through it to create a lacy green and brown patchwork resembling some ancient threadbare quilt.

"Why do they go to all this trouble to hide the factory?" said Kay.

"Aerial attack, stupid."

"Yes, I know that, but wouldn't the enemy only have to look at a map of the area to find the Lockheed plant? I mean, you can buy one in any store and the factory must be clearly marked."

"Not anymore. In wartime all the old maps are withdrawn and destroyed in case the enemy gets their mitts on them. They switch them with nice new ones with all the important military installations removed: army bases, shipyards, munitions factories—all made to disappear. Poof!"

"Wouldn't that be just as obvious—a big gap where the factory used to be?"

"Well it's not like they just leave a blank white space on the map, you dope. They draw it all again, but instead of showing the factory they add fields and houses so it blends right in with the surrounding area. No one would know it was ever there."

"So, according to the new version, we don't actually exist?"

Queenie nodded. "You and I, Lotus Blossom, are officially off the map."

ELEVEN

An army command car was parked on the edge of a wide area of green asphalt. Major Lund and First Lieutenant Franks were sitting in it, looking upwards to the sky. The lieutenant focused his binoculars on the plane passing overhead.

The major squinted, shielding his eyes from the sun. "Is that him?"

The lieutenant continued to track the plane through his binoculars. "Must be."

"Well where the hell's he going?"

A corporal emerged from a nearby building and trotted over to them. The officers returned his salute.

"Excuse me sir. Message from Colonel Wagner. He won't be landing here sir."

The major watched as the plane flew further into the distance. "Won't be landing? We arranged a meeting here at—"

"The colonel sends his apologies sir. He regrets that he is unable to locate the runway."

"Unable to locate the runway? You're kidding me."

"No, sir."

"That's priceless." He began to laugh. "You hear that, Lieutenant? Colonel Wagner can't find us."

The lieutenant started to laugh too.

The corporal was awaiting further instructions. "Should I send a reply sir?"

"Yes, Corporal."

The corporal dug a notebook and pencil from his breast pocket, ready to take down the message.

"Just say—*We're over here!*"

"Do you know what's funny, Mr Godfrey?" said Jimmy.

George was on his way to the lake when Jimmy caught up with him. "Do I know what's funny? No. Tell me. I like a good laugh."

Jimmy continued as they walked. "Well, you know when I said I'd take care of the sheep, you gave me my new job title—shepherd?"

"Uh-huh."

"Well guess what my surname is?"

George shrugged.

"Shepherd!"

"No kidding? Did that connection only just occur to you?"

"No, I was going to say something at the time, I just—"

"So, you're a Shepherd, huh? Well that's how you would have gotten the name. Your great-grandfather or your great-great-great-grandfather must have been a shepherd, tending his flock, just like you. He'd be proud to see you carrying on the family tradition … though your technique might surprise him."

"But get this. You know the guy who drives the tractor?"

"Howard?"

"Yeah. Do you know what *his* last name is?"

George shook his head.

"Farmer!"

"Seriously? Wow. That *is* funny."

"I know! Howard Farmer the farmer and Jimmy Shepherd the shepherd. Pretty neat, huh? I've been looking at the list of Residents on the work rota." He took a pencil and a folded sheet of paper from his shirt pocket. "There's a Dorothy Cook who does general housewife activity … shopping, hanging out laundry and stuff. I figured you could put her in the diner as a cook. She'd replace Effie—whose surname turns out to be Driver—and Effie could have a job driving one of the buses."

"Excellent. We could have a town based on the medieval system of occupational surnames where your name tells other folks what job you do. Hey. Maybe I could get my ex-wife a job here. Muriel Cheats-on-her-spouse."

There was a moment before Jimmy decided this was a gag and laughed. He failed to notice the bitter note in George's voice.

"Of course it doesn't work with *your* surname, Mr Godfrey." Jimmy thought it over for a moment. "Unless we shorten it to God."

"God?"

"Sure. That would work, what with you being in charge of all creation."

George rocked his head from side to side, mulling the suggestion over before nodding his approval.

Jimmy studied his list. "We're out of luck with some of the names, especially the foreign ones … Rodriguez, Gustafsson, Schumacher."

"Schumacher is a shoemaker, surely?"

"Oh, yeah. I guess."

"I'm not sure we need a shoemaker in Overland just yet, but you could be onto something. Let me know how it pans out. In the meantime, tell the new kid, Danny Cleans-out-latrines, he's got the job."

Jimmy chuckled. "OK. I'll tell him … Oh, Mr Godfrey, I almost

forgot." He delved into his pants pocket, and pulled out a knife. "Your switchblade. I found it on the grass by the lake. I've been using it; I hope you don't mind."

"No Jimmy, I don't mind."

"It's a swell knife. The military issue ones like these to paratroopers, once you've made your qualifying jumps. The retractable blade means you only need one hand to use it. Very handy if you land in a tree or river and need to cut yourself out of your lines and harness."

"Well then you'd better keep hold of it so you can practice. Get the jump on the other guys."

"Really?" Jimmy offered it back to him, giving George the chance to change his mind. "But you might need it."

George waved his hand dismissively, like it was nothing.

Jimmy looked down at the switchblade. "Thanks. I'll make sure you get it back before I leave for special training."

George shook his head. "Keep it. It's a gift. Maybe it'll be like a good-luck charm."

They had reached the turning for the lake. George raised his hand as a parting wave and headed down Lakeside Steps.

Jimmy was beaming. He called after him. "Gee, thanks, Mr Godfrey."

Left on the sidewalk, Jimmy weighed the knife in his hand, enjoying its comforting solidness. He thumbed the button that released the blade (as he had done a hundred times since it had been in his possession) then retracted it before slipping it back into his pocket.

A trolley car bound for George Street approached, moving steadily along the track. Jimmy trotted alongside and jumped aboard.

First Lieutenant Franks and Major Lund were on the move in their command car, the lieutenant at the wheel. They approached a roadblock with a manually operated rising arm barrier painted in red and white stripes like a candy cane. Attached to it was a sign: *US Army. Restricted Area. Road Ahead Closed. Designated Cars Only. By Order of US Army.* A youthful-looking army private, who had been sitting on an upturned crate, grabbed his rifle and jumped to his feet. He raised the barrier, allowing the major's car to proceed. The private saluted smartly as the car passed; the major responded with a half-hearted hand gesture. He checked behind him in the side mirror and saw the private replacing the barrier and sitting down again.

"And that's our security?"

"He was told to expect us, sir. No unauthorized vehicles would be allowed to get this far anyway. We've got the whole area cordoned off."

The major let it go.

The road took a sharp bend between some hedgerows fabricated from painted burlap. Presently, the Lockheed factory came into view, though it was no longer recognizable as such; its shape had been skillfully transformed with wide, irregular patches of green, black and brown, interspersed with stippled areas of realistic-looking vegetation. Amongst it, set at varying heights from the ground, were the simple painted shapes of houses and buildings, white with red-brown colored roofs, and black shadows giving the illusion of three-dimensionality.

91   UNDER

The effect was evidently designed to be viewed from above, and from here it was difficult to make out what it was all supposed to be.

The road merged into a wooden ramp that climbed steeply to the flat roof of an adjoining building. Here it leveled out and then turned about-face, climbing steeply again up the sloping roof of the main building. Eventually the car made it to the flat surface where a sign greeted them: *Welcome to Overland. Please drive carefully* and then below it, *No vehicles beyond this point.*

The lieutenant parked alongside a row of other cars; the two men got out and wandered over to the perimeter fence to look out. There were sloping pastures intersected by neat, fence-lined walkways and clusters of evergreens. A meandering road with the occasional ply-wood car parked at its curb served a row of white bungalows, each with its own spacious garden. On a road running perpendicular to it, there was a gas station and a bank building, outside which, somewhat incongruously, was a putting green where a school bus driver and an Egyptian pharaoh smoking a cigar were tapping golf balls towards a flag sticking out of the ground. The community was moderately populated with shoppers, trades folk, cyclists and assorted pedestrians. The major took in the scene.

"Jesus. This is incredible."

The lieutenant was obviously excited by the prospect of showing the major around. "This is the only section of road we can drive on. The other roads aren't strong enough to take the weight of a real car. We'll park here and take the trolley car up to Shangri-La Cottage—that's just a nickname they give to the site office."

"Trolley car?"

"Mr Godfrey will meet us there. The model's there too so you can see the additional plans he has for the runway. It's pretty ingenious. I think you'll be amazed, sir."

The major seemed unable to get past the idea of public transport. "Trolley car?"

"Takes us right to his door, sir. He's got a whole traffic system working off a network of electric track. Most if it comes from fair-ground scenic railways. They just modify the mechanism and remodel the vehicles by adding new lightweight carcasses—instead of little carriages they've got full-sized automobiles, trucks and buses. Should be along any minute now."

"What in sweet Jesus … ? Who authorized all this?"

"Well, you did sir. You said—"

"I didn't say anything about …" he struggled to find the words to describe the transport system "… this. And where have all these people come from?"

"They're the Residents, sir."

"Residents?"

"They come up from the factory after their shift or on their lunch break. Mr Godfrey feels it's important to populate Overland with real people to bring the town to life."

"Residents? What are you talking about, Residents? Are they being paid extra to do this?"

"No, sir. All volunteers. They like it up here. Mr Godfrey has built quite a community."

"Community? Why the hell …? I don't like this, Lieutenant. I don't like this at all. This is supposed to be highly secret."

"No one else knows about it, sir. The Residents have all been through strict security checks."

Disgruntled, the major was shaking his head as, round the corner of George Street, came one of the red and white Overland trolley cars.

"Here she comes. Right on time." The lieutenant hailed its arrival like an enthusiastic commuter.

The major stared, incredulous. "I'm not taking any goddamn kiddie car ride."

"It's much quicker, sir. It's a long walk otherwise."

"Oh, for Christ's sake."

"Just hang onto the rail, sir. It'll set off again in a few—"

The car started to move again. The major reluctantly stepped aboard.

George was sitting by the edge of the lake, his fishing rod in his hand. As on most days no one was around to disturb him. Though the lakeside area was locally considered one of the town's foremost beauty spots, the Residents respectfully kept their distance. They seemed to regard it as George's own private place, especially now that he had moved into the waterside cottage, and were loath to intrude. And while George liked to think of Overland as belonging to *all* the Residents, he was grateful for the chance to spend time alone there.

The cottage interior had been coming along nicely. Here, he was able to make his own decorating and furnishing choices, which in his "underworld" home had always been blighted by Muriel's gimcrack aesthetic. For her, a home was not a home without goggle-eyed ceramic chipmunks, flamingos in top hats and cutesy swollen-faced children. It wasn't until shortly before their marriage, when they began decorating the apartment they'd rented, that he first became aware of her poor taste. By then it was too late; he was committed to matrimony and he wrongly imagined that once they'd settled into it he would be able to educate her, persuade her to defer to him as a professional and learn to trust his artistic judgement over her own. It didn't happen.

According to Muriel everything he suggested was stuffy, boring or just plain wrong. *Don't you know* anything *about home decor, George?* Her face soured at his suggestion of ivory, pale ochre and oatmeal soft furnishings; dark lacquered furniture featuring elegantly designed Blanc de Chine porcelain pieces; subtle garland-print wallpaper, and magnificent Greek key motif doors in light maple like the ones he'd designed for the city apartment set of *The Women*. He tried to explain how the classic simplicity would maximize the space in their small apartment, but Muriel would have none of it.

"It's boring, George. Bland. Everything's the same. Beige, beige, beige. I need more color, more vibrancy, more excitement."

Naturally, she'd got what she wanted in the end.

Over on George Street, the trolley car trundled along. The major took in the rows of houses, noting how each of their chimney tops was billowing smoke.

"What's with the smoke, Lieutenant? Californian residences burning coal fires in the middle of spring?"

"You'd be surprised how many do, sir."

"Even so. Was it really necessary to go to all this trouble?"

"No trouble, sir. The chimneys on the houses provide a plausible outlet for the emissions generated in the factory. We have to monitor levels, of course; we don't want it to look like the burning of Atlanta. Lockheed produces a great deal of smoke and steam which has to be vented somewhere. It's less noticeable if we break it down into as many outlets as possible. Mr Godfrey has found a solution that also adds a level of credibility to the residential buildings. Smoke equals movement, and movement equals reality."

Irked by the lieutenant's fawning enthusiasm the major muttered the words to himself with cynical disdain: "Movement equals reality."

Down at the lake, George stood up to recast his line, flashing the rod and flicking the line out towards the center of the lake. The float went skittering across the surface of the canvas tarpaulin. Dissatisfied with his cast, he reeled in the line and tried again. This was all new to him; he'd only recently taken an interest in the sport. This one went farther, but as the float landed on the surface it sank into a small hole in the tarp and fell straight through. The line paid out from George's reel.

First Lieutenant Franks knocked loudly on the door of George's house. No answer. He opened the door and put his head inside. "Mr Godfrey! Hello? Mr Godfrey."

The major made a show of looking at his watch. He stood with his hands on his hips, clearly frustrated.

"I don't have all day, Lieutenant."

"He said he'd be here, sir. He's usually …"

The lieutenant went check the rear of the house. The vexed major stared up at the Shangri-La Cottage sign, shaking his head.

Jimmy had been on the same bus as the two military men, keeping his distance, but curious to know where they were going. They got off at the same stop and he saw them heading for Shangri-La. He'd fetched a broom and was now sweeping his front garden path so that he could covertly observe their movements next door. The lieutenant spotted him and called out.

"Hey, son. Do you know where Mr Godfrey is?"

"Yes, sir. He's down by the lake, doing a bit of fishing."

The major was not sure he had heard right. "Fishing?"

"Well … pretending."

"Pretending? To fish?" The major was quietly fuming.

Jimmy was innocently accommodating. "Was he expecting you?"

The lieutenant upped his game to fall in line with the major's outrage. "He most certainly was. And he's keeping the major waiting."

"Oh. Should I go tell him you're here?"

Major Lund sighed with frustration. "Go with him, Lieutenant. Bring him back here. Pronto."

TWELVE

The factory yard was canopied by a vast turquoise tarpaulin that stretched between the roofs of two hangar buildings. A few feet below its surface an inspection gantry was supported by a pair of portable scaffolding towers. Sunlight filtering through the semi-opaque surface of the tarp lent a strange blueish tint to the area below, making it look a little like it was under water.

Kay had temporarily freed herself from the upper half of her coveralls, which she now wore hanging down from her waist. She and Queenie wandered out into the yard and joined a group of women from Section D sitting on the ground with their backs against the high outside wall of one of the buildings. Stenciled on the concrete above them was a large number *80* and the words *Keep Clear*. On the other side of the yard were a couple of lean-to work sheds, some caged carts full of scrap metal, and an assorted row of trucks and forklifts.

The women were dressed for the workplace: dungarees with sturdy shoes, hair tied up with hairnets or headscarves, shirtsleeves rolled high on their greasy arms. They looked heroic and tough. All had open lunch pails and were eating sandwiches, drinking from thermoses or soda cans as they chattered loudly. It was only Kay's second day, but already she'd been accepted among them. This would not have happened had Queenie not held such sway with the group. She had stuck by her, making it clear that Kay was her friend and by association should be considered one of the gang. Some of the women were chary of Kay's "Chinese" ethnicity, as they were of anyone foreign, but kept their prejudices to themselves.

Unseen, high above them, a fishing float broke through a small hole in the surface of the tarp and began its slow descent.

At the lakeside, George, bemused, watched the reel of his rod spinning round.

On his way from the factory hangar, Donaldson, the Section D foreman, passed through the yard and saw the untidy straggle of girls littering the foot of the wall.

"What are you lot doing out here again? You know there's a perfectly good canteen."

"Too far. All those tunnels. By the time we get ourselves over there and get served, it's time to start back again. Besides, we like it here."

Donaldson shook his head and continued towards the canteen.

Kay had taken Mrs Ishi's tin of sardines from her bag.

"Would anyone care for a sardine if I open them?"

Queenie turned up her nose. "Peoria. No thanks. Put them away."

Sour faces. There were no other takers.

Something red and white entered Kay's peripheral vision. Unable to identify exactly what it was, she watched, somewhat mesmerized by its steady descent. The mysterious object seemed to hover like a hummingbird. One by one, the girls looked up, curious to see what she was looking at. Eventually it settled, just a foot or two from Kay's eye level, as though the sole purpose of its journey had been to come face to face with her.

Queenie was first to identify it.

"It's a fishing bobber with a hook. Where the hell did that come from?"

"Must be some schmuck on the roof," suggested one woman.

"What do you think he was hoping to catch down here?"

Queenie was ahead of them. She had made a grab for Kay's shoulder purse and was rummaging through it.

Kay looked a little ruffled. "What are you doing?"

She didn't answer; Kay would see soon enough.

Grabbing the bobber and bringing it towards her, Queenie attached the sardine tin by hooking it through the head of the key attached to the lid. She gave the line a couple of yanks before releasing it.

George, rod in hand, was puzzled to feel the pull on his line. He began to reel it in.

The girls cracked up laughing as the sardine can began its determined climb towards the canopy overhead. The light intermittently caught its silvery surface as it twirled gently on the line.

George continued to wind the reel until the can appeared through the hole and slithered towards him along the surface of the lake and was finally lifted into the air. Unable to understand how this had happened, he brought it in, swinging the line towards him and grabbing the catch on the end of it. He stared at the hooked sardines, turning the can over in his hand.

Later, when the other women had packed up their lunch things and returned to work, Kay lagged behind, looking up at the tarpaulin.

"Where do you think that fishing hook came from?"

Queenie was already heading back. "Beats me. Come on. We're late."

"All that way, and it ended up right there in front of my face. It was as if it was intended just for me. Don't you think that's strange?"

Queenie pretended to give the question careful thought before answering. "Er. No."

"What do you think goes on up there?"

"Nothing. They're putting up some kind of camouflage I think. Somebody must be up there working on it."

"With a fishing rod?"

Queenie shrugged, incurious. "Come on."

"I have to take a powder. I'll be there in a minute."

"Donaldson will have your ass if you're late back."

Kay waved her away and Queenie left her to it, stepping into the relative darkness of the hangar.

Inside, Donaldson pulled Queenie to one side. When he asked her where Kay was, she feigned ignorance, shrugging herself from his clutch and returning to her bench.

He went out to where the girls had previously been eating lunch, but none of his workforce were there now. He headed back to the hangar, failing to spot Kay who had climbed the scaffolding tower to the overhead gantry and was now standing on the crosswalk immediately under the surface of the turquoise tarpaulin.

George was napping. An insect buzzing around his face partially stirred him, but he gradually closed his eyes again to enjoy the lazy stillness of his surroundings. From the roadway at the top of the hill, soft music from the Overland speaker system floated gently on the breeze.

Kay found she was able to touch the tarp canvas above her head. Up close she could see that it was formed from a series of strips, each about twenty feet wide, fastened together along their edges. A hole the size of a ship's porthole had been cut into the fabric. The unfiltered sunlight, glowing golden in contrast to the cool aquamarine, punched through the opening and shone directly onto Kay's face like a theater spotlight. Above her, she could see clouds scudding across the sky.

Keen to see more, she stepped up onto the crossbar of the safety rail. Bringing her outstretched arms together above her head like a diver, she pushed herself up through the hole until—

—she emerged, as far as her middle, into the empyrean blue yonder.

Beneath the surface, her lower half—dirty overalls and work boots—
carried all the grimy evidence of her existence in the netherworld;

above it, her upper half felt cleansed and unburdened, like an ethereal spirit of the divine waters, or something poetic like that—a woman clearly divided between two worlds.

Romantic music rose and faded on the veer of the wind. With her fingertips resting lightly on the surface of the tarp, she looked slowly around her, taking in her first view of Overland.

Immediately in front of her, set against lush woodland undergrowth, was a handsome red-roofed cabin. A cute pink rowboat with a red stripe painted along its side was moored to a wooden post where the gentle grassy slopes met the edge of the blue tarpaulin. Looking across the rippled expanse of blue, she began to realize that she had surfaced in the middle of what was supposed to be a lake.

Despite this puzzling note of inauthenticity, she felt an immediate connection with the place, something she couldn't quite put her finger on. Then it came to her, as though the words had appeared like a picture caption. "When Evening Shadows Fall." It was, as old Mr Cochran had said, a little piece of heaven on earth.

George slowly stirred back to consciousness, breathing deeply to bring himself fully awake. As his eyes floated open, he was seized by a growing sense of Kay's presence. He sat up suddenly and found himself facing a vision of loveliness, a mysterious Lady of the Lake rising from the waters like a goddess from mythology. The light reflecting off the lake's shiny surface brought a soft glow to her exquisite features. George was captivated. Overland's piped music swelled in his head: "You Stepped Out Of a Dream" played by the Glenn Miller Orchestra. He continued to stare, afraid to move lest she should disappear.

When Kay finally caught sight of him, she was a little taken aback; she had assumed she was alone. The lakeside scene on her calendar had been unpopulated and, though it was irrational, she had not expected to see anyone here either. She couldn't quite figure out where the stranger had come from—why hadn't she spotted him until now? How long had he been watching her? She couldn't help but observe that he was tousle-haired, ruggedly lean and unassumingly handsome, and that he fitted perfectly into the picture.

A voice from the underworld, heard only by Kay, broke the spell.

"Hey. You. What are you doing up there?"

George watched as the vision raised her arms and slipped noiselessly below the surface of the water like a synchronized swimmer from a Busby Berkeley sequence. He instinctively held his breath in anticipation of her resurfacing, but the enchantress remained submerged and George, lungs burning, was finally forced to let out his breath with a spluttering cough.

On the top road, Jimmy and the lieutenant were approaching the slopes to the lake.

"So how come you haven't enlisted?"

"I have, sir," said Jimmy. "Completed my basic training. Waiting for my Duty Assignment. I volunteered for the five hundred and ninth Parachute Infantry Regiment, Second Battalion. I'm just helping out here until I start my special training. Assuming I'm accepted, that is."

"Not everyone is. Still, you look like you've got what it takes."

"Thank you sir."

"So you're ready to see some action, huh?"

"My brother is already out in the Philippines so I'm pretty keen to get out there after him."

"Where is he based?"

"Bataan Peninsular."

The lieutenant winced. "Ooh. That's tough. Have you heard from him?"

"Not recently. Why?"

"I'm sure he'll make it out of there just fine."

Jimmy frowned, unsure what the lieutenant meant.

They rounded the corner of a bungalow and looked down the slope to see George gazing into the lake. He seemed transfixed by some vision, yet there was nothing there.

The lieutenant called out. "Mr Godfrey!"

George turned. He was still dazed, uncertain whether what he had just seen was real.

"Meeting with Major Lund!" The lieutenant tapped his wristwatch impatiently. "He's waiting."

George checked his own watch. He nodded slowly, bringing himself back to normality.

Donaldson was up on the gantry. Kay stepped down from the rail and, wanting to avoid the confrontation, began to make her way back down to the factory floor. Donaldson grabbed her wrist.

"I said, what were you doing up there?"

"Nothing." Kay pulled her arm free.

"That's a restricted area. You're not allowed to be up here. What were you doing?"

"Nothing. I was just curious."

"You're not paid to be curious."

"I was on my lunch break."

"And you decided to poke your nose in?"

"No. I—"

"How did you get a job here anyhow? You look like a Jap to me. Show me your identity card."

She produced it from the breast pocket of her coveralls. Donaldson studied it.

"You sure you're not Japanese?"

"No, I've never even been abroad."

"Your family, then. They must be Japanese."

"No, they're American. Like me."

"You're not an American," he sneered, handing back the card.

"There's some Chinese ancestry on my mother's side, that's all," said Kay feebly.

"What did you see? Up there. What did you see?"

"Nothing."

"You'd better not have done. And if you did see something, you'd better keep your trap shut about it. I could give you the boot for this."

"I'm sorry. I didn't see anything. I promise."

"Get your butt down there."

She headed along the gantry towards the scaffolding tower; Donaldson followed.

Down on the factory floor, Queenie watched as Kay entered Section D and headed back to her bench. Donaldson followed at a distance, eyeing her suspiciously. Kay kept her head down and tried not to draw further attention to herself, but Queenie could sense that something had gone on between them.

"What happened? You in trouble?"

"Tell you later."

They both got back to work. Queenie, curious to know the full story, sneaked a sly glance at Kay, but Kay already had her welding helmet on and her visor pulled down, and was giving nothing away.

THIRTEEN

The major and first lieutenant were in Shangri-La Cottage standing beside the scale model of Overland. With their hands clasped respectfully behind their backs, they bowed dutifully to view the miniature construction, like awkward visitors at an exhibition of Etruscan artifacts. George, the reluctant curator who regards the public's presence as an intrusion, looked on uneasily.

The lieutenant had identified their present position, pointing, for the major's benefit, to the exact house they were in, its roof no bigger than a matchbook. Shangri-La Cottage, and even the street on which it sat, was only a tiny part of a much larger model. George had built an entire town including houses, commercial buildings, roads, vehicles, fields and woodland, crafted in miniature with painstaking consideration. Another set designer, an architect or professional model-maker would have recognized the scale as 1:144, often thought-provokingly described as the scale of a dollhouse made for a dollhouse. George's fourteen-feet-square tabletop model represented Overland's one hundred acres.

"Congratulations, Mr Godfrey. Wonderful job. The lieutenant here's been giving me a tour. Your attention to detail is quite something. I'm not entirely sure how much of that detail is essential to the mission, but nevertheless …"

Lieutenant Franks took up the slack. "Colonel Wagner saw the post-camouflage reconnaissance photos taken last week. For a week now they've had a bunch of planes flying over taking pictures. He was so impressed, he wanted to see it up close for himself so he took a P-38 up and flew over the area. He was totally fooled—couldn't tell what was real and what wasn't. From the air this entire area looks like any other suburb of Los Angeles. He was planning to land here, but he couldn't even find the runway—the one thing we thought would be too difficult to hide. He was at a thousand feet with it right there in front of him. Couldn't see a darned thing."

"As a matter of fact, you've presented us with quite a problem, Mr Godfrey," said the major. "As you are probably already aware, every plane manufactured here has to undergo a number of flight tests at altitude before it can be put into service. The pilots responsible for these tests have learned to negotiate the camouflage-painted runway when they're taking off, but when they return, they just can't find it. So they end up having to land at Clover Field fifteen miles away."

The lieutenant nodded affably. "What goes up must come down."

George felt unable to humor them. They were so full of themselves.

"Despite what we tell them is a runway," said the major, getting into his stride, "the optical illusion is so strong, every instinct in them as pilots tells them that it's not safe to land there. So we need to devise a

system of ground markers that the pilots can recognize—but we can talk about that later. For the moment, I think we should congratulate ourselves on the success of the project …"

George looked up. "*Our*selves?"

The major plowed on. "… Time to wrap things up here and move on to the next site where we can make use of the lessons we've learned here at Lockheed. Your motion-picture studio, Mr Godfrey, has agreed to loan you to us for just a little while longer—six weeks to be exact—so we'd like to get you up to Seattle to start laying plans for the Douglas factory. Now, the plant there is—"

"Just a minute, Major, I can't go to Seattle. There's a lot more work to do here. Besides, the success of Overland relies on constant maintenance. There's the road system, keeping the vehicles moving …"

"Fine. We'll get a couple of kids to keep an eye on that."

A couple of kids? George was insulted. The major clearly had no idea what was involved in the day-to-day running of the town.

"There are a hundred other things that need to be done here. Things I need to oversee."

"For instance?"

George picked one example: "The parked cars outside the houses. We move them out during the day and put them back late afternoon to suggest that the man of the house is driving to work and returning home at the end of the day."

"You really do that?" The major touched one of the tiny cars on the model to see if it was glued down. It wasn't.

"Of course. It's important to create a living, breathing community. We also need to move the sheep around. There are three fields of them."

"You move the sheep around? You're kidding. Why?"

"I would have thought that was obvious. An enemy plane photographs the farm from the air—"

"He's just taking a snapshot. He can't tell if the sheep are moving."

"No, but if he comes back the next day and photographs it again, when he compares the two pictures he's going to notice that the pattern of white dots is identical, suggesting that the sheep are in exactly the same position. A farm with sheep that don't move? He's going to know right away that they're phony. That means our whole cover is blown."

"Yes, well, we might be being just a little overcautious here. They're not flying over every day, Mr Godfrey. Between you and me, we don't know that a Jap plane has ever flown over this area. This is what you might call a precautionary measure—being one step ahead of the enemy. Don't you think it would be better to wait until *after* a plane sighting before rearranging the livestock?"

"I was told that comparative referencing would be used."

"Well, yes, but if features like grazing sheep require this level of maintenance, maybe they're an unnecessary detail."

"Perhaps I'm the best judge of what is necessary. You tell me that Overland is a success. An entire aircraft plant housing twenty-five thousand employees and a strip of tarmac three hundred feet wide and nearly a mile long—all made to completely disappear into the surrounding landscape. How do you think I was able to hide it so

115   UNDER

convincingly, Major? With what you call unnecessary details."

The lieutenant stepped in. "Now let's not get overexcited here. We're just saying that—"

George was indignant. "This is the level of detail that would normally be required by a director for a long shot in order to make the scenery seem convincing. I normally go that bit further with certain areas, just in case a closer shot may be required. I find it saves time."

The stillness of the air in the low-ceilinged room was oppressive. Both George and the major were becoming fractious, annoyed by each other's querulous self-importance.

"Well there won't be any close-ups, will there," said the major testily, "because our cameraman is a little guy who's going to be seeing this, not as a tourist strolling around town, but from a goddamn Zero flying overhead at three thousand feet. He's hardly going to notice flowers in gardens, oranges on trees or the price of a baby's bonnet in a goddamn store window."

Before George could respond, the major snatched up a handful of air-recon photos. "Look! Look at the photographs." He thrust one under George's nose. "This is taken at fifteen hundred feet. See the roads? See the houses? See the trees and hedges? Just about … maybe." He took another photograph. "This is five hundred feet, the lowest any air reconnaissance is ever going to fly without running into power lines and church steeples. At this height, you might see a car moving along a highway, you may even see a person waving a big red flag, but I assure you, Mr Godfrey, no Japanese air-recon photo is going to show

the stripes on the tie you're wearing or the goddamn house number painted on your front door. The level of detail you have introduced is a waste of government money and time—time you and your workforce could be spending on other strategic military buildings."

George was feeling bullied. "I'm used to doing things properly."

"Street signs, Mr Godfrey? Who in hell is going to read street signs?"

"They're more for the benefit of the Residents. Gives them a sense of place. The success of this operation depends on the psychological aspect. If the Residents don't believe Overland is real, how can you expect the enemy to believe in it?"

"*Believe in it?*"

It was the inclusion of the word "in"; that's where George went wrong. "Believe *in* it"—like the tooth fairy or Santa Claus. He should simply have said "believe it." The major was all over it.

"What the hell are you talking about? Who are we building this place for, Peter goddamn Pan?"

"I was hired because of my expertise in this area, Major. Kindly allow me to get on with my job."

"No, Mr Godfrey. You were hired because of *my* expertise in this area. I am the country's leading authority on military and industrial camouflage and it was my decision to recruit you."

There was a moment while the major's remark settled. George had been put in his place.

"You are working for the United States Army and now that this

117   UNDER

project is complete, you are being transferred to a new location."

"That's just not possible. Overland is far from complete. There are many details yet to attend to."

"Are these details for our benefit or for yours?"

"What are you saying?" George felt flustered; the major had him on the ropes.

"That's it, isn't it, Mr Godfrey? You've created your own little world here. Got everything just how you want it. This goes beyond camouflage. You put up street signs because you want a proper address, because you need to make it feel like home. Perhaps you have no other home to go to."

"What do you mean?"

The major shook his head, shrugging off his insinuation.

George was humiliated, but refused to be baited. "We have some major elements still missing."

"What else can this place possibly need?"

"All kinds of things. A boating pond. A windmill …" George pointed to the miniature he had made for the model.

"A windmill, Mr Godfrey? You haven't forgotten, I hope, that this is supposed to be downtown Burbank, California, not Amsterdam, Holland. The idea is to blend into the landscape. A Dutch windmill is going to stick out like a turd on a wedding cake. Maybe you need to spend a little more time on terra firma … take a look at the real world."

"I just thought a windmill would add character." He immediately regretted his feeble justification. The major was quick to pounce on it.

"Add character? This isn't a tourist attraction, Mr Godfrey. A windmill is a landmark and it's an anomaly—exactly what we're trying to avoid. Think about it. It's a tower with a big easy-to-identify cross on top of it. It might also interest you to know that sheep farms are relatively uncommon in California."

"I realize that, but we had a hundred and fifty sheep available to us from the prop department at Warner Brothers and with the timescale and budgetary constraints, it seemed—"

"And if they'd had a couple of dozen elephants and the Leaning Tower of Pisa, I suppose you'd have taken those too?"

"Now you're being ridiculous."

"Is that so? A boating pond? You don't consider that ridiculous?"

"We need it … for the children."

The moment of madness hung in the air. George realized he had gone too far. He started to backpedal. "If you'll just let me—"

"You're through here, Mr Godfrey. You are under the directive of the United States Army and your services are required elsewhere. I thank you for your time, but as of today, Project Overland is terminated."

Minutes later, George was heading along George Street towards the lake. He was seething. A passer-by asked him how he was enjoying the weather, but he was too distracted to think about it.

It was Major Lund's dig about not having a home to go to that so enraged him. Where had he got that from? It wasn't true anyway; George still had the apartment—although he had to admit he no longer thought of it as home.

Even before Muriel left him, he was spending less and less time there. Increasingly tight production schedules at the studio meant more nights working late. At least that's what he told her. Even on days when he was able to quit work at a reasonable hour he would find an excuse to stay behind. As the studio working day began its slow fade to black, George would wander the backlot streets, from Chicago's South Side to the boulevards of Paris, simply enjoying the scenery.

Meanwhile, left alone at home, Muriel had begun to explore new avenues of her own.

The boss of the Skateland Roller Rink, where she worked the afternoon shift selling snacks from a concession stand, had offered her free skating lessons after work. His name was Gus Moretti. George had met him once when dropping Muriel off at the rink on his way to the studio. He was showily chivalrous, the oh-so-gallant hand-kissing type that likes to be regarded as a "ladies' man." He was wearing a tight red shirt, all puffed up with bumptious vanity like a frigatebird with mating on his mind. A pencil moustache hovered like a pair of migrating eyebrows over his upper lip. The tightly crimped wave in his hair was doused in oil and plastered down as flat as it would go. He informed George that Muriel was a naturally gifted roller skater—was George not aware of this? George was not. And now he was being reprimanded for failing to recognize his wife's potential to be shunted around on wheels.

Though they were not wearing skates at the time, Gus offered to demonstrate their latest move. Without waiting for a reply, he positioned himself behind Muriel, cinching her waist with stubby pork wiener fingers. She seemed to know what was coming. He bobbed down on his knees and suddenly sprung up again, lifting her up so that she was sitting on his right shoulder. George regarded this as something of a liberty, but Gus seemed to think that he was perfectly within his rights. Muriel was all for it; she crossed her ankles and brought her toes to a dainty point, her arms held out to her sides, palms presented upwards to emphasize the gracefulness of their pose.

George smiled wanly, unsure how to react. Later, when he was driving along the freeway, he imagined Gus practicing his lifting technique at home with a hundred-pound sack of Purina Dog Chow.

Still, George was niggled by self-doubt. Movie stars like Douglas Fairbanks Jr and Humphrey Bogart carried women all the time—women who had fainted or been injured, women too feeble to walk on their own. In the Tarzan films, Maureen O'Sullivan seldom got anywhere under her own steam; Johnny Weissmuller insisted on conveying her everywhere she went. It was second nature to Johnny; he made it look easy—that broad chest of his—but George had never carried a woman before, and certainly had never attempted to carry Muriel for fear that he would be unable to perform adequately.

In Shangri-La Cottage, the two military men lingered in the aftermath of George's indignant departure. The major took off his cap, fanning himself with it before replacing it on his head. He stood surveying the model landscape.

"Jesus H. Christ, Lieutenant. What the hell has this guy been doing? Look at this thing. He's got orchards, a library, a tennis court …"

"I know, sir. It's quite remarkable."

Spontaneously, they both started snickering. It was a side of the major that Lieutenant Franks had never seen and both were a little embarrassed by their juvenile outburst. It somehow made them laugh all the more.

"Do we feel, Lieutenant, that in the creation of this make-believe world, Mr Godfrey might have lost a few of his marbles?"

The lieutenant brought his laughter under control. "Well, sir, he certainly has gone beyond the call."

"Jesus, Lieutenant. The guy needs help. Best thing for him, and everybody else, is to remove him from this site—get him up to Seattle. Who knows, maybe they've got some good couch doctors up there."

"Yes, sir."

"You can tell the *Residents* they no longer reside here." He bent over George's model. "Christ, what a nut. Look at these. What are they? Sheep? And what are these?"

The Lieutenant leaned in to study the model more closely. "Um. Not sure, sir. Cauliflowers?"

That set them off giggling again. The major's wheezing laugh brought on a coughing fit; he struggled to control it, wiping a tear from his eye. "Oh lord." He put his hand to his mouth and studied the model, gently shaking his head. "How does he photograph this thing?"

The lieutenant pointed up to the ceiling. "From up there, sir. He climbs up on the roof and pokes his camera down the chimney."

More laughter.

"The amazing thing is, sir, he's even built what's underneath us. The model is in two parts. Overland is just the top layer. The whole thing lifts off like a lid."

"Really? How?"

"If you just grab that side, sir."

The major took hold of one edge; the lieutenant took the other.

"After three …"

The lid was lifted.

FOURTEEN

While they were in the midst of it, right there on the factory floor, for the majority of workers there was no sense of anything beyond Lockheed, beyond even their own section. Only the privileged few were aware of Overland. For the rest, the hangar walls and the roof above them disappeared into darkness beyond a labyrinth of cranes, jigs and heavy machinery. Even if it were possible for the workers to see far enough to identify the parameters of their world, there was never time enough to look up. Day merged seamlessly into night with no let-up in production. Like a colony of fiercely patriotic worker ants, each of them concentrated on the job to which they had been assigned. The part they turned or the section they welded was a small but critical component in building an aircraft that could help win the war. Morale among the workers was generally high, but ironically it wasn't the successes that brought it all home to them; it was the failures.

That morning, news had reached Section D that one of the planes they had been working on, the Lockheed XP-49, a variation on the P-38, crashed during its test flight over Glendale. Following a successful eighteen-minute appraisal of its low-speed handling characteristics, Lockheed test pilot Eric "Mac" MacDonald lost both port and starboard ailerons as well as a section of the lower wing surface while performing a dive of 350 mph at 2,300 rpm. MacDonald bailed, but his chest struck the forked tail structure as he exited the fighter, either killing him outright or rendering him unconscious, as he made no effort to deploy his parachute. The aircraft span to starboard and crashed just outside the airfield perimeter. Though no one said it, many of the workers wondered if the fault had developed as a result of some minor error they had made: a misaligned wing strut, an incorrectly wired altimeter or a seized aileron cable. The young test pilot, whom many of them had known, left behind a wife and one-year-old daughter.

In the wing assembly section, Queenie skulked over to a woman with dyed red hair who was checking for fractures in the wing frame with a tiny flashlight.

"Have you got it?"

The redhead looked round furtively. "Not here." She nodded towards the women's restroom.

A few minutes later, Queenie was at the sink as the redhead entered. She handed Queenie a small label-less medicine bottle of black liquid.

"It's not for me; it's for a friend," explained Queenie.

The redhead nodded knowingly. "Yeah, right."

Queenie shook the bottle, holding it up to the light. "It looks disgusting. What's in it?"

"Search me."

"But it works?"

"So I've been told. Takes about six hours to take effect. I've never used it myself."

Queenie echoed the knowing nod. "Yeah, right."

She handed over a ten-dollar bill. The woman pocketed it and headed towards the door. Queenie turned the bottle over, looking for some guidance.

"Are you supposed to take it all at once?"

"I don't think it makes much difference."

Later, as Queenie approached her workbench, she could see Kay wearing her welding mask visor flipped up on the top of her head while she inspected a recently welded seam. She took a small hammer with a pointed end and chipped away at the slag residue before removing the piece from the vice. Satisfied, she tossed it into a bin full of similar joints and prepared to repeat the process. She looked as though she had been doing this for years rather than a couple of days.

She caught sight of Queenie.

"Where've you been?"

Queenie was noncommittal: she widened her eyes and poked out her tongue, wagging it playfully from side to side.

"You can't keep any secrets from me," said Kay.

"What do you mean?"

"You've been eating licorice."

"What?"

Kay laughed. "Your tongue—it's black."

At the shift changeover, they were standing in line to board one of the half-dozen special buses that were waiting to transport the factory workers away from the plant. Queenie was quizzing Kay.

"What do you mean, on top of the factory?"

"What I said: on top of the factory."

"On the roof?"

"I guess so. On the roof. And between the roofs. It's hard to see what they've done. For instance, that blue tarp over the yard is actually supposed to be a lake. I don't know how they've done it, but there's a whole town up there."

"A town? How can there be?"

"There were trees and fields with houses and cars in the distance."

"That can't be just camouflage. Must be something else."

"And there was a lovely lakeside cabin. Except none of it looked quite real. Like scenery in a theater."

"You mean like a movie set? You think they're shooting a movie up there?"

This had not occurred to Kay. "I don't know. Maybe."

Queenie snapped her fingers. "I'll bet that's it. It's a movie set. It must be. They always try to keep it secret to keep the fans away—and to avoid having all the locals hanging around and getting in the way of a shot. That must be why no one's allowed up there."

"I didn't see a camera."

*MEANWHILE *In Overland, two women were dragging a plywood car onto the driveway of 2301 Lake Street. The car had spent the day out of sight under some trees while the supposed owner would have been out at work, but now it was around the time a nine-to-fiver would be returning to the bosom of his family, the car needed to be visible once again.*

"Did you see any actors?"

"I saw one man. He was fishing by the lake."

"Ah. The guy with the fishhook. Was he famous? A movie star?"

"I'm not sure. I don't go to the movies much. He was rather handsome."

"You're hopeless. It could have been Cary Grant or someone."

"I don't think it was Cary Grant, but I couldn't say for sure."

"Did he say anything? Did he say—" Queenie slipped into a bad Cary Grant impersonation "—I love you my dearest darling; I love you with all my heart—?"

"Not exactly, but he stared at me for the longest time. It was like there was this … connection between us."

"Connection? Between you and Cary Grant? Are you kidding? You're hardly his type. Maybe whoever you saw was one of the extras—that's what they call actors who don't have a speaking part—"

"I know what an extra is."

"—Except sometimes extras get to say a line or two and then there's a chance the director or a big studio producer will see them and give them a screen test and make them famous. That's how Lana Turner got her break. She was just one of the gals in the chorus, or a passer-by on the street, pushing a baby buggy or something."

"Pushing a baby buggy?"

"Yes. That's the kind of thing extras do—push baby buggies or sell flowers from a market stall. You never know what you'll be asked to do from one day to the next. One minute you're a diner at a medieval banquet in a conical hat, the next you're running screaming from an erupting volcano. But you've only got to catch a producer's eye and you can be on the fast track to a starring role in a major motion picture. If I could get myself up there as an extra, I'd have a good chance of landing myself a speaking part. I could make good money too."

"What about your factory work, doing something for the war effort?"

"Oh, phooey to that! Someone else can do my shift."

"That's not very patriotic."

Queenie yielded to a compromise. "All right already, so I'll go on tour and entertain the troops like Marlene Dietrich or the Andrews Sisters."

"What are *you* going to do to entertain the troops?"

"I'll do a medley of my hits."

"What hits?"

"Well, I haven't had any yet, have I? Give me a break."

Kay raised her palms in surrender.

"But first I gotta get myself up there," said Queenie.

"Well you can't go up through the lake; they've removed the scaffolding and gantry."

"There must be another way," she said, balling her fist determinedly. It could have been Scarlett O'Hara in her finest screen moment.*

They were maybe ten minutes into their journey, sitting side by side on the crowded factory bus.

"Hot milk's good for an upset stomach," said Kay. "I'll make you some when we get home."

Queenie winced and shook her head. She was suffering. She turned sideways in her seat and drew her knees up to her chest, burying her face in the hem of her skirt. She groaned.

"Not far now."

"Oh Jesus. I have to get off."

"Just sit quietly …"

Queenie spoke more urgently now. "I have to get off." She called out to the driver, pushing past Kay and heading down the aisle like an anxious bride. "Stop the bus, stop the bus! I gotta get off."

She headed quickly for the door; Kay followed close behind, her hand resting reassuringly on Queenie's back. The driver was reluctant to pull up at an unscheduled stop until Queenie demonstrated the urgency by vomiting thick black bile into her cupped hand. That did it. Within seconds the bus had swerved into the curb and the doors were flung open. Queenie lurched out and spewed the remaining contents of her stomach onto the grass verge. The driver watched before pulling smartly away.

Kay looked on with sympathy, tinged with revulsion. She handed Queenie a hanky. Queenie straightened, wiping her mouth and swallowing hard.

"How much licorice did you eat?"

"It's not licorice, you dope. It's something else. Something I took."

"Something you took?"

"A potion."

"What kind of potion?"

"Some useless quack remedy. Supposed to, you know, get rid of something."

"Constipation?"

"No, you goofball. A baby."

"A baby? What baby?"

"The baby I'm going to have—unless I can do something about it."

Despite his reluctance to face the reality of it, George had been well aware of the imminent termination of Project Overland. Yet he somehow imagined that when the construction guys, the carpenters, decorators and painters returned to their regular jobs at the studios, he would remain there to manage things. The army would pack up and ship out, or whatever it is they do, and finally leave him and the Residents in peace. There were still jobs to do, but nothing so urgent that it couldn't wait awhile. Of course when fall came he would need to change the color palette of all the trees and bushes, but that was a long way off.

He remembered how Major Lund had criticized his plans to build a Dutch windmill in Overland, saying it would "stick out like a turd on a wedding cake." Now he thought about it, he recalled seeing just such a windmill on San Fernando Road not a mile from the Lockheed factory. In fact, there was a chain of Van de Kamp bakeries dotted across the city, each one styled as a sixteenth-century Dutch windmill. There were probably more windmills in Los Angeles than there were in Holland. He wished he'd used this as a comeback to Lund's argument at the time. LA was full of whimsical, out-of-place architecture of all kinds, far odder than anything he had designed for Overland. Surely he had seen the famous hat-shaped Brown Derby, the Wilshire Coffee Pot with a giant coffee pot on top of the building, or the Pup hamburger joint whose edifice was a giant concrete bulldog smoking a pipe. There were buildings shaped like pianos, ice-cream cones, zeppelins, cameras and boots. Down there, a tepee, an igloo and a sixty-feet donut might sit comfortably together on the same block. Nothing stuck out as unusual. A turd on a wedding cake would fit right in amongst them.

He'd get round to the windmill in good time. The Residents would help. They took great pride in their town and were only too glad to pick up a paintbrush, a hammer or a shovel to help improve the look of the place.

Besides, Seattle was out of the question because he needed to find the girl from the lake. The only way he could do that was to wait in Overland until she appeared again. He had no idea when that might be, but he simply had to be there. He knew it was foolish, they had never even spoken, but he'd never been so sure of anyone in his life.*

Up on North Ridge, George found his Negro friend Tommy relaxing on a bench overlooking a sloping pasture known locally as Lost Hammer Hill.

"Hey, Tommy. You seen an oriental-looking girl hanging around?"

"Around Overland?" Tommy shook his head. "Uh-uh. Why?"

"She just appeared, er, out of the blue earlier and I haven't seen her since."

"You think maybe she's a Japanese spy?" said Tommy.

"Spy? No, I wasn't thinking that."

"Can't be a Resident. She wouldn't pass the security checks. Where d'you see her? Maybe she came up the ramp."

"No, she came up out of the lake."

"Out of the lake? You mean through a hole in the tarp? How'd she do that?"

* **MEANWHILE** *Going on Vacation? For a perfect vacation free from cares and worries about your furniture investigate our storage facilities. A few cents a week will safely store a surprising amount of home furnishings with this old and reliable storage firm. We offer you an outstanding service that merits your convenience. Lyon Removal & Storage Co., 210 N. Beuna Vista, Burbank.*

Forced to close! Prices smashed on entire stock. Silks, woolens, accessories. Must be sold! Many lines half price and less. Hurry as this sale is to last only a few more days. Yamato Silks "A Reliable Place To Shop."

"Don't know. I was fishing and, well … Suddenly she was there, looking at me."

Tommy laughed. "Man, you really *did* catch something!"

"She was beautiful, Tommy. She looked like Botticelli's Venus, or one of those other ones—Aphrodite or someone like that."

"Didn't you ask her who she was?"

"No, I didn't speak to her."

"But you assumed she must be a Resident?"

"I didn't assume anything."

"I'll check the roster for Japanese names … see if she's from the factory. It could be a big security risk. In the meantime we should plug that hole."

"No! The lake may be her only way to get up here."

"Ah. You want to catch her so you can interrogate her?"

"No. I don't want to interrogate her; I want to meet her."

Tommy looked puzzled. "… A Jap?"

"She may not be Japanese. She could be Chinese or Korean or something. She could be from Bali."

"Where's Bali?" said Tommy.

"I don't know. Someplace in the Far East, I think. She could be an exotic Malaysian princess or something."

"An exotic princess with her head poking through a dirty old tarp?"

George balked at the description. Tommy noted his reaction.

"Oh I get it. You got the hots for her. Cute figure?"

George was embarrassed. "I've only seen her from the waist up. The rest of her was hidden below the water."

"That sounds a little fishy. There could be anything going on down there. Hey. Maybe she's a mermaid."

Tommy was making fun of him, but he played along. He didn't want to appear too desperate. "I hadn't thought of that."

"I'll bet that's it. Was she trying to lure you to your death?"

"Hmm. I don't think so. She didn't say anything."

"They don't say nothing, mermaids."

"They don't, huh?"

"Uh-uh. Mermaids can't speak."

"Well that would explain the silent treatment."

"At least I don't think they can. If she does say something and she mentions anything about a watery grave, tell her you're not interested."

George pretended to make a mental note. "Watery grave. Not interested. Check."

FIFTEEN

There were a couple of payphones mounted on the wall outside the factory offices. Queenie was at one of them, speaking secretively into the mouthpiece.

"Is that Dr Young?"

"Who's this?"

"I was told you might be able to help me. A friend, Connie, gave me your number."

There was a moment's pause. "How long since your last period?"

"Ten weeks. Nearly eleven."

"It'll be fifty dollars."

"Fifty? I was told forty."

"You're over ten weeks. Makes it more risky. I have to charge more."

"Fifty dollars?"

"That's the price. Call again when you have the money."

Queenie slowly hung up, despondent. She didn't even have the forty and had no way to get it. She'd made the call in the hope of some kind of IOU arrangement. She stood there, weighing up her remaining options. Find a guy and get hitched? Who would marry a girl having another man's baby? Go back home to the parents—if they'd have her? The shame would probably kill her mother. Why bust her crockery? Besides, that would be the end of Queenie Meyer, movie star; she'd never get out of that town again.

She'd heard about girls attempting to terminate their own pregnancies—knitting needles, coat hangers and suchlike—but she was too squeamish to consider that sort of thing as anything but a last resort.

What if she were to keep the baby and make up some story about being a war widow? She knew at least one girl who had done that. She had told everyone that her husband was an army officer who had been heroically killed in action. In truth she had never been married. The child had been the outcome of a brief union with a schools inspector who had claimed to be a freelance talent scout. On hearing the "joyous news" he had threatened to pull her tongue out if she ever named him as the father.

Queenie's own experience had been little better. After a brief show of loyalty—*Stick with me, baby, you'll come in on the tide*—the father-to-be was off like a prom dress. *Arrivederci, sweetheart. Don't call me; I'll call you.*

The offices were made up from a row of windowed cubicles that overlooked the factory from a fifty-feet-high gantry running along one end of the hangar wall. As Queenie headed for the staircase leading back down to the factory floor, she caught sight of a woman in bib overalls carrying a lunch pail who was climbing another staircase,

one that Queenie had never noticed before. It extended from one end of the office gantry all the way up into the gloomy darkness beyond the factory lights towards the roof. She watched the woman's ascent with growing curiosity.

At the top of this second staircase was a small platform and immediately above it a trapdoor accessed via a short vertical ladder. The woman climbed up rung by rung, flipped open the hatch and, after first setting her lunch pail outside, nimbly hoisted herself up through the opening. Swinging her legs out of sight, she closed the trapdoor behind her. Queenie continued to stare, but the trapdoor remained closed. She glanced round; none of the other workers appeared to have seen any of this.

Queenie approached one of the office secretaries, a woman in her thirties. As someone working high above the factory floor, she was in the privileged position of wearing her hair down. She leaned over the rail, smoking a cigarette while idly taking in the industrious activity on the factory floor below.

"Where does that staircase go to?" Queenie pointed with her thumb to indicate the one she had been watching.

The secretary glanced over her shoulder. "Up to the roof. There's a skylight thing you can get through."

"Where was that woman going?"

The secretary shrugged. "Dunno. I've seen a few of them going up there. Some of them come and go several times a day. Not just on their lunch break either."

"Playing hooky, you think? How come the boss lets them go? He must know what they're up to."

"Oh, he knows all right. He's the one who's sending them."

"What are they doing up there?"

"Beats me. Maybe they're making camouflage netting or something—like that stuff they got hanging over the parking lots. Camouflage is considered *classified military information*—national security. Threading bits of green wool through chicken wire. Big deal. Whatever they're up to, I think the girls only do it because it gets them out of the factory. Probably working on their suntans."

Queenie nodded. She was pretty sure there was more than camouflage and suntans on offer—someone was secretly making a movie up there. From what Kay had told her, there could be no other explanation. If she could get up there, she felt sure that with her looks she might be able to get herself cast. If she landed a small speaking part, in a day or two she might earn the fifty dollars she so desperately needed. Kay could cover for her at the factory and nobody would be any the wiser. Problem solved. Queenie had it all figured, but kept her cards close to her chest. No point in letting everyone in on it.

"Sounds like a cushy number," said Queenie. "Have you ever tried to get up there?"

"Not permitted. Unless you have special security clearance. The girls who go up there are sworn to secrecy; they're not allowed to tell."

"Tell what?"

"I don't know. They're not allowed to tell."

* **MEANWHILE** *A couple strolled arm in arm along Baker Street. The street sign mounted to one of the telegraph poles had originally featured in* The Adventures of Sherlock Holmes *and had been "rescued" by a 20th Century Fox employee who had kept it as a souvenir and had subsequently donated it to the head of Overland town planning: George Godfrey.*

The secretary looked at her watch, dropped her cigarette and ground it out with the toe of her shoe before heading back to her office.

Queenie ventured to the far end of the gantry. Sitting alone at a table perpendicular to the foot of the mystery staircase was an old boy in a sports coat smoking a pipe. He had only one arm; the empty sleeve of his jacket had been squarely folded at the elbow and the cuff attached to his shoulder with a safety pin. Strung across the stair handrails was a chain from which hung a small sign prohibiting unauthorized personnel. On the table in front of him lay a clipboard bearing a list of names and signatures. Queenie hung back, watching surreptitiously.*

After a few moments, a woman in overalls approached the table, showing the man her identity card along with something small that she took from her bib pocket. Satisfied, he spun the clipboard round to face her and she signed her name in the appropriate column. The man rose, clamping his pipe between his teeth, and unhooked one end of the chain to let the woman through. She then climbed the stairs, her booted footsteps clanging on the iron treads.

By the end of the day, Queenie had gathered enough information from various people in the factory to figure out how it worked. According to what they knew, access to the roof was restricted to people who had undergone special security vetting. To bypass that, she would need to show her ID card and some kind of official badge or pin (that she didn't have and couldn't get) to the one-armed man—who, as keeper of the pearly gates, had apparently been dubbed St Peter. He would then check her name against the list on the day's roster. If her name wasn't on it, she wouldn't be allowed up.

Queenie mulled this over. "And who makes out the roster?"

The woman Queenie had been quizzing was a gossipy busybody who worked in the drafting department. The woman pointed to a spotty kid in one of the offices typing away on his typewriter. "He does."

Queenie studied the kid; he looked about sixteen—barely in long pants. "Think I could get him to add my name to the list? I wouldn't mind working outdoors."

The woman was dismissive. "Uh-huh. Strictly forbidden."

"Surely he could be persuaded to bend the rules a little?"

"Not that one. He's incorruptible. Like a little Honest Abe Lincoln."

Perhaps sensing that he was being talked about, the young Abe looked up and saw Queenie eyeing him flirtatiously. She touched her throat and looked away coyly. The young man stared back at his typewriter, his face sizzling. She could practically see the steam coming off of him.

Queenie smiled smugly. "No one's incorruptible," she said.

The next day Queenie stood at the pearly gates like the start of some old gag. St Peter ran his finger down the list, finding her name, which had been added at the bottom. He checked his watch and, in the column headed *Time in*, wrote the relevant numbers, his one arm working overtime juggling pen, wristwatch, clipboard, ID card and pipe.

"Where's your pin?" he said.

She was expecting this—the one part she had been unable to resolve. She began to squirm. "My pin? Oh, do you know what? I think I must have left it behind."

"You'll have to go and get it," he said.

"I can't. It's … at home."

"Sorry. But I can't let you through without the pin."

"I know. I feel so stupid. You must think me an awful idiot. And now I'm going to be in such trouble—and on my first day too." She pouted a little.

St Peter stared at her for a minute before yielding to her wheedling charm. He stood to unhook the little chain for her.

"Go on. Make sure you bring it next time."

Queenie touched his empty sleeve. "Thanks. You're a dear."

Queenie emerged through the hatch. Climbing to her feet, she lowered the trapdoor behind her. She found herself, not on an open flat roof as she had envisioned, but inside a large barn-like structure. Having crossed the threshold, Queenie was having a hard time getting the picture squared; this was not what she had expected at all.

She seemed to be in some kind of storage facility like a lost property office. There was a row of gray metal lockers and roughly made shelving units containing rows of suitcases, wicker picnic baskets and carefully folded fabric. An umbrella stand with various umbrellas, parasols and tennis rackets stood between a lawnmower and a couple of old wrought-iron park benches, stacked one atop the other. On the opposite wall was a bicycle stand with a few bicycles in it, and an evenly spaced row of assorted baby carriages, parked like auto-mobiles in a used-car lot. Edging closer, she saw that the first three buggies each contained baby dolls of differing types and makes, all swaddled in white blankets. The fourth, she noted uneasily, contained a battered old ventriloquist's dummy. The little man stared back at her, his grotesque features frozen in apparent surprise: eyebrows raised and mechanical jaw dropped open in a stupefied grin. The "baby" in buggy five was even less lifelike: a yellow casaba melon with the cartoon face of Emperor Hirohito crudely painted on it, characterized by thick black eyebrows over thin slits for eyes, round spectacles, a tight chevron moustache and a choking mouthful of ludicrously large teeth.

A woman in a nurse's uniform swished back a curtain and stepped out from a changing cubicle at the far end of the room. It startled Queenie; she had assumed she was alone there. The nurse straightened her belt and checked her cap in the mirror on the wall. It was then she saw Queenie watching her.

"Oh, sorry, hon. Have you been waiting for me?"

"No, I …"

"It's all yours. Here. Let me get this out of your way."

The woman stepped back inside the cubicle and removed a pair of greasy blue coveralls from the rail. She took something small and shiny from a pocket before hanging them up in one of the lockers.

"You're new, aren't you?"

Queenie nodded hesitantly.

The shiny object turned out to be a black enamel pin with the word *Resident* in white letters. Queenie watched the woman pin it above the left breast pocket of her uniform.

"Are you on your way in … or on your way out?"

Queenie was unsure how to answer. "Um. Out, I guess."

The woman looked at herself wistfully in a full-length mirror.

"I always wanted to be a nurse. When I was a little girl I used to bandage my teddy bear, give him medicine. When my dad got sick and took to his bed I was quite pleased because I thought I could make him better, but of course it was no use."

Queenie nodded sympathetically, but the woman had already shifted gear.

"I had a go at playing tennis yesterday, but I was tuckered out after

139   UNDER

five minutes. And I've done something to my shoulder. So it's back to being nursemaid today."

She grabbed at one of the buggies and began to back it out of the line when she suddenly saw the baby inside—the vent doll—and changed her mind. "Oh, Jeez. I can't look at that ugly bastard all afternoon."

She inspected the contents of the other buggies, picked one and wheeled it past Queenie.

"Get the door for me would you, hon?"

"Yeah, sure."

Queenie had not yet noticed the door behind her. A big sign on it read *Residents Only. No workwear.* Underneath it, a smaller sign: *You are now entering Overland. Are you wearing your Resident pin?* And a third: *Cameras strictly prohibited.* She lifted the crude latch and swung open the heavy door. Dazzling sunlight filled the room, making her squint. The nurse stepped out into the midday sun, pushing her buggy. Intrigued, Queenie peered out after her.

Although logically she knew that this must be on top of the aircraft factory, everything before her was telling her otherwise. Up here was a regular downtown street just like any other, with houses, stores, automobiles and people milling about. She had opened a door to another world.*

A man on a motorcycle sailed slowly by—apparently freewheeling, as his vehicle produced absolutely no sound. Queenie pushed the door further ajar, hoping to see more, but felt resistance from the other side. A man wearing a burgundy doorman's uniform with a double row of brass buttons blocked her view.

"No workwear, miss. You gotta get changed first."

He pressed the door gently but firmly towards her until it was shut again, leaving Queenie in comparative darkness.

Exploring further, she pulled back the curtain on one of the other cubicles and saw another pair of denim coveralls hanging on a hook. Below them was a pair of work shoes stained with oil and grease.

There were several free-standing metal clothing rails—the kind one might find in a department store—from which hung a variety of costumes. Queenie skimmed through them and saw that some had labels, not from the manufacturer, but from film studios. A gray long-sleeved dress with a wide, lace collar had a label with the Metro-Goldwyn-Mayer trademark in green embroidered script. Beneath it, handwritten in inked block capitals, OLIVIA DE HAVILLAND. There were several labels from Warner Bros. Pictures—mostly allocated to names she didn't recognize, but one, sewn inside the collar of a man's tailcoat, bore the name James Cagney. Queenie pulled it from the rail to study the label more closely. The production number was given as 363, the date, 11/13/41. She held the accompanying pants up to her waist and kicked out one leg; even on her, they ran a little short. Further along the rail, she found another Warner Bros. label, this time showing the name E. Flynn with the word *doubles* faintly stamped under it. One of the baby carriages, she noticed, also carried a label that revealed its origin. *Property Department. C/11 Baby Buggy 1934.* Queenie was excited.

* **MEANWHILE** *In a report to President Franklin Roosevelt, General John L. DeWitt, commanding officer of the Western Defense Command, argued that although no cases of sabotage by Japanese Americans had yet been reported, "the very fact that no sabotage has taken place to date is a disturbing and confirming indication that such action will be taken."*

General DeWitt's justification for the broad-scale removal of Japanese on the Pacific coast is to thwart espionage and military sabotage. Newborn babies, young children, the elderly, the infirm, the handicapped, the mentally ill, children in orphanages, and even children adopted by Caucasian parents are not exempt. "They are a dangerous element," DeWitt told Congress. "There is no way to determine their loyalty."

She gingerly tried the door again, intrigued by what might be going on outside. No sign of any headline stars. Instead, through a gap an inch or two wide, she spotted the doorman a little way off chatting to a man with a wheelbarrow. She closed the door and returned to the clothes rail, scooting hangers of clothes along it. Picking out a drum majorette uniform—short white skirt and red jacket with gold braid frogging down the front and chunky fringed epaulettes at the shoulders—she held it up against herself, checking the size.

Five minutes later she was out on the sidewalk, her outfit now complete with white mid-calf tasseled boots, and topped off with a tall peaked cap that had a bushy plume of white feathers attached to its front. The hat was a little on the large side; she nudged the peak up her brow to allow her to see more freely. She was feeling rather conspicuous, but since no one seemed to be paying her any attention she began to wander along the street, taking in her new surroundings.

The trees were clearly artificial, like ones she had seen used on other movie sets, but shorter than normal, as were the telegraph poles and street lamps. Close up, she noticed that the grass verges lining the street were nothing more than strips of green canvas; the cobblestones were smooth underfoot, the stones painted onto the flat surface of the road.

A sprightly old man in golfing attire passed by carrying a golf bag.

"Good morning. Great day for a game."

"You said it."

"Do you play?"

"Um. No, not really. But I'm a quick learner."

"A lot of women do these days, you know."

"I know."

"Well. Keep twirling."

"I will." Queenie found herself saluting him.

She looked back at the barn-like prop room from which she had just emerged and saw that it had the exterior of a movie theater with big red cut-out letters spelling out "Orpheum" mounted on top of the marquee. The movie purportedly playing was *Sullivan's Travels*, starring Joel McCrea and "on-the-take" Veronica Lake, a film Queenie had not seen on account of Joel McCrea being, in her opinion, nothing to write home about.

She wandered to the corner to explore more of the goofy-looking town. There was a mailbox, a news kiosk, a park with a garden of colorful flowers and shrubs. A drugstore, Kaiser's, had green awnings to shade the windows; she noticed a handwritten sign pinned to the fabric: *Red, not green. Please adjust.* A woman standing stiffly in the doorway—white dress, shoes and hat—turned out to be a window display mannequin.

Though this was largely in keeping with other film sets she had been on, Queenie was puzzled by the level of activity. Rather than standing round waiting for the director's call of "action," the extras and bit players here seemed to have come up with background business of their own. Everyone was doing something. It was as though she had blundered into the middle of a well-rehearsed scene that was in full swing—yet nobody seemed to mind.

143   UNDER

A man on the sidewalk picked up a clock the size of a bass drum. He rested it on his shoulder with the side of his face pressed against the dial as though listening to check whether it was still ticking. Queenie wasn't sure if he was an actor or part of the crew.

"If you're looking for a marching band they went thataway," the man said, catching sight of her in his peripheral vision.

She dutifully acknowledged the quip.

"Could you steady that stepladder for me, sweetheart?"

"Sure. You need a hand?"

"I got it. Just make sure the ladder don't slip."

He stepped blindly onto the first step, gingerly negotiating the other steps by feel until he had climbed to the right height. With a burst of extra effort he hoisted the clock aloft so that the hooks on top of it fitted onto the hanging bracket that extended from the building. Once it was in place, he climbed down from the ladder and stepped back to admire it.

Queenie checked her watch. "It's ten after twelve, not seven fifteen."

"That don't matter. The clocks on public buildings often tell the wrong time."

"What *is* this place?"

"This is the new library."

"No. I mean this whole area. Where are we?"

"Overland, of course. Are you a new Resident?"

"Er, no. I …"

"Where did you come from?"

"I'm just visiting. Is this like a movie set or something?"

"Didn't anyone explain it to you?"

"Er. Not really."

An enthusiastic woman in glasses and a big hat stepped up, holding a clipboard.

"I don't think we have your vote yet, do we? Regarding the flowerbeds in the town square. Red or yellow?"

"Excuse me?"

"We're voting on what color flowers to have."

"Oh, I see."

"You must have your say. As a Resident."

"Well, I'm not really … er … sure. Yellow, I guess."

"Yellow? Excellent choice." The woman made a note.

The clock man, clearly a partisan of the reds, shook his head slowly from side to side at Queenie's careless betrayal.

Jimmy was sitting on a park bench near the half-built schoolhouse, whittling a piece of wood with his new knife, when he first caught sight of Queenie in her majorette uniform. She appeared not to have seen him so he was able to observe her as she walked along Main Street, twirling her baton with limited success. When she came to the junction with Lake Street, she reviewed all her options before making a decision to turn left into it.

Jimmy continued to watch her until she was out of sight.

SIXTEEN

Queenie approached a woman who was window shopping at Jennings Grocery and Delicatessen, checking out the display of bottles and cans.

"Hey, sister. You got a script I could take a look at?"

The woman turned, distracted by Queenie's costume, her eyes transfixed by the bobbing feather in her cap. "A script?"

Queenie noticed she wore a Resident lapel pin, just like the nurse. "You're one of the Residents, right?"

The woman nodded. "Uh-huh."

"A non-speaking role, I assume."

"What of it?"

"Doesn't anyone have a script?"

"No. We just get told what Mr Godfrey wants us to do."

"Who's Mr Godfrey?"

"He's the boss. He's running the show."

"Oh, like the director? Which one is he?"

"He's usually around someplace. Probably down by the lake."

Queenie took this in. "I don't see any cameras. When do they start filming?"

"Nobody knows. That's why we're supposed to be performing all the time, just in case."

"Do you think they might be filming now?"

The woman shrugged her shoulders. "Could be."

Queenie touched her hair and affected a false smile, looking nervously about her for where the camera might be.

"Peas and carrots, peas and carrots, peas and carrots."

The woman frowned. "What?"

Queenie lowered her voice, speaking out of the side of her mouth. "Peas and carrots. Background conversation. What are we supposed to be doing?"

"Relax. We're just incidental pedestrians. You don't have to worry too much until you hear the chimes playing over the speaker system. That's when you're supposed to jump to it."

"Action!"

"Right."

"So what's your part in this?"

"Huh?"

"What's your bit of *action* when the chimes sound?"

"Oh, it varies. I often picnic with friends. Today I'm window shopping."

"What's the day rate?"

"Day rate?"

"Pay. What are you getting—to be a Resident?"

The woman shook her head. "Nothing. It's volunteer work."

147   UNDER

"Volunteer work? You're kidding me. What is this, the Red Cross or something?"

"We do it because we enjoy it."

"Are there any bit parts up for grabs?"

"They're all bit parts, sweetie."

"I mean like a speaking part. Something bigger. Something with the promise of either a career or a paycheck at the end of it."

"Uh-uh. There aren't any speaking parts."

To Queenie this made no sense. "What about Errol Flynn and Olivia de Havilland?"

The shopper smiled weakly. "What about them?"

"Have any of the Residents been given close-ups?"

"It doesn't work like that, dear. There *are* no close-ups."

"Yeah? Well, we'll see about that."

George was sitting on a wall, drawing in his notebook when Queenie pitched up.

"You seen this Mr Godfrey around?"

George looked her up and down. He was about to volunteer his identity, but decided to keep it under his hat for a while. "Who's looking for him?"

"I'm Queenie Meyer. I want to ask him about a speaking part."

"Let me guess. You want to be a movie star."

"I've been doing some work as an extra, but I really want to—"

"Yeah? Well so do half the girls in America. Hundreds of them arrive in Hollywood every day hoping to become movie stars. What do you think you've got that's so special?"

Queenie was affronted. "Thanks very much."

"A pretty face, a nice figure? The studios have got cover-girl beauties lining up from here to Poughkeepsie."

"What's in Poughkeepsie?"

"Nothin'. Just a whole load of cute-looking potatoes like you."

George smiled to himself. He was rather enjoying playing the hard-bitten movie producer. He could really have used a fat cigar to chew on, maybe bitten off the end and spat it out on the ground. *Why, you dames are all the same.*

Queenie was undeterred. "Oh, I know all about potatoes. I read the film magazines. I know there's stiff competition. But I'm different. I can act. And I can sing and dance too."

He folded his arms. "Really? Well now tell me. Where did you gain your acting experience?"

"High school. I was told I was pretty good too. Don't pull a face. I was."

"I believe you, but it's Mr Godfrey you've got to convince."

"Well, don't think I won't."

"I haven't seen you before, have I? Are you a new Resident?"

Queenie hesitated.

"You're not supposed to be here if you're not a Resident."

"Oh … but I am."

"You've been checked?"

UNDER

"Oh sure."

"Where's your Resident's pin?"

Queenie touched her tunic. "Oh, no … I must have dropped it."

A young man passed by, providing Queenie with a welcome diversion. He greeted George cheerily: "Afternoon, Mr Godfrey. Beautiful day."

"Hey, Bob," George answered sheepishly, aware that his cover was blown.

Queenie nodded, acknowledging that she'd been duped. "Swell place you got here."

George ignored the sarcasm. "Yeah. Something, isn't it?"

"So you're the director."

"Artistic director."

"Oh. Artistic director. Pardon me. Do you work for one of the big studios?"

"MGM. Before that I was at Warner Brothers. Right now I'm kind of on leave of absence."

"Me too. I should really be getting back."

"To Warner's?"

"No, not Warner's."

"Back where then?"

"Well where do you think?"

"I don't know. MGM?"

"No. I work at the aircraft plant."

"You don't say. Which one?"

She stalled, worried that she had broken some Residents' taboo about mentioning the factory. Then she figured he was goofing with her so she answered.

"The Lockheed plant."

"Oh. Is that near here?"

"Yes. It's very near. You should come visit sometime—see what it's like in the real world."

"Oh, I don't know about that. I like it here. This world feels real enough to me. Sun shines all day long, beautiful scenery …"

"There *is* a war on, you know."

"War? Oh yeah, yeah. War. I did hear something about that. I figured it was none of my business."

"The war is everybody's business." There was a serious note to her voice; George's flippancy had backfired.

Queenie took a moment to survey the town.

"So this is all your idea? This scenery."

"Uh-huh."

"Why does it look like this?"

"Like what?"

"The trees for a start—they're too short."

"How tall should they be?"

"I don't know. Tree height, I guess."

George looked along the row of trees as if considering the idea.

"And what's with the houses? There's no upstairs."

"Don't need an upstairs."

151   UNDER

"Who built all this anyway?"

"I did."

"On your own?"

"I had my team of elves helping me."

"How far does it extend, this place of yours? I can't see where it joins the real town."

"It doesn't join."

"You built everything?"

"Everything."

"Those mountains. The entire state of California. The whole world perhaps? Hey, you're not God are you? Your face is awful familiar."

George was amused. He wanted to tell her that according to Jimmy's new naming system he actually was, but it would have taken too long to explain.

"You can't see where it joins because Overland is as real as any other place."

"Overland. Is that what you call this place? Cute. Well, it doesn't look real."

"Ah. That's because you're not seeing it from the right perspective."

Queenie was unconvinced. "Yeah, that must be it."

"I thought you wanted to be part of my phony little world."

"Maybe."

"Is this how you talk to your prospective employers? I bet you never get further than the studio gates."

She had no comeback; George's remark was a little too close to the truth. "So can you help me or not?" she said.

"What do you want me to do?"

"Let me be one of the Residents."

"Well, isn't that why you're here?"

"I don't want just a walk-on part; I want to show that I can act—say some lines."

"Go ahead. Say some lines."

"Swell. What do I have to say?"

"Say whatever you like. No one will hear you."

"Why not?"

"Sound is not a matter for consideration in the world I have created."

"A silent movie? You gotta be kidding. Nobody goes to see silent movies anymore. It's bound to be a big flop."

"What makes you think this is a movie?"

"You've got scenery, you've got costumes, you've got props, and you've got Errol Flynn, Olivia de Havilland and James Cagney."

George overplayed looking taken aback. "Is that who I've got? Wow. That's quite a line-up. You seem to know a lot about it."

"I've got eyes."

"Really?"

"Yep. And they see things pretty clearly."

George smiled wryly, happy to let her believe what she wanted. She was annoyingly pushy, but there was something about her he liked.

They strolled together down Main Street. Queenie was quietly taking it all in—the stores, the houses, the trees. It was as if the

153   UNDER

individual scenic elements were gradually coming together in her mind and for a moment she seemed to relate to the place as a whole, to see the bigger picture.

"Wow. You've got everything here."

George looked proudly about, as though seeing Overland through her eyes.

"Yep. It's all here. We've got a library, a church, a diner …"

"A diner?"

"Sure. Want to grab a donut?"

"I ought to get back."

"So what do you do there?" said George. "Secretary or something?"

"No, I'm a welder."

"A welder?"

"Yeah. Welding. You know—a big electric sizzle that joins bits of metal together."

"Men's work?"

"Not anymore. Women are doing the men's jobs now. Didn't you know? All the men have enlisted; they want to fight for their country. Well, most of them do."

He caught the jibe. "Oh, I like to think I'm doing my bit."

"Really? But no uniform?"

"Uniform doesn't prove anything. *You're* in uniform and I bet you've never led a marching band."

"What makes you so sure?"

"Can you really twirl that thing?"

"That would surprise you, wouldn't it?"

"Can you?"

Queenie answered reluctantly. "No."

"Why are you dressed like that anyway?"

Lost for an answer, it suddenly struck her as funny and she laughed. "I don't know."

George laughed too. For the first time Queenie's guard was down and he found it endearing.

"I thought I'd choose something that shows off my legs," she said. "Most people say they're my best feature."

George glanced at Queenie's legs. She immediately responded by posing like a model, one foot in front of the other.

"What do you think? Can you use a pair of legs like this?"

George shook his head. "No, thanks. I've already got a pair of my own. They'd only get in the way when I run."

Down on the factory floor, Donaldson was interrogating Kay.

Kay adopted an air of innocence. "I don't know where she is. I told you, she had a lousy headache so she went to Sick Bay for some aspirin."

"I've just come from Sick Bay. She ain't there."

"Maybe she went for a walk to get some fresh air."

"What are you givin' me with the 'fresh air'? You think I'm some kind of chump? I've just about had it with you two. First one, then the other. You barely do one job between you. You better buck your ideas up, the both of you, or you're gonna be out on your cabooses. Savvy?"

Queenie followed behind George along a narrow sloping walkway, just wide enough for one. The path was lined along each side by a makeshift handrail supported by a series of vertical wooden posts. A sign at the top of the path read, *Do not stray from the walkway. The netting will not support your weight.* Queenie leaned over the rail, peering down. Signposts such as this prompted her to return to her old, doggedly inquiring self, dismantling the broader Overland picture to scrutinize its individual components.

"Is this just netting? What's underneath this bit then?"

"Nothing."

"Nothing? There must be something."

"It doesn't matter what's underneath."

"How high up are we?"

"We're on top of the world."

"No, I mean in feet and inches."

"You're not a very aesthetic person are you? I bet when you look at a beautiful painting you want to know how much the canvas cost. Your sort always want to take a look round the back of the magician's cabinet to see how it's done."

"I already did. There's a secret panel in the back."

"Now why would you want to know that? Can't you see what you're doing? You're spoiling a beautiful illusion for yourself." *

George was both amused and irritated by the new visitor—the way she asked all the wrong questions, her refusal to see things from the correct perspective. Perhaps every visitor was like this at first, looking at Overland for what it wasn't rather than what it was. He couldn't honestly remember; the other Residents had been coming here for long enough to settle into what he considered the appropriate way of thinking. There may have been early niggling questions about the "pointless" street signs or the need for the laundry on the washing lines to be hung up and taken down again every day, but most succumbed to the Overland ethos surprisingly quickly. A handful of the construction workers had been difficult in the beginning: talking about baseball games and news stories from the outside; others complaining about the unavailability of hot food and wanting to know every last detail about the plumbing arrangements. They didn't stay. Some had felt the need to offer criticism, like those square-thinking army blockheads deeming certain architectural features or botanical embellishments as "unnecessary detail," as if it were their right to make such decisions. Some folks, George realized, would never "get it." They wouldn't make the grade in Overland and they shouldn't try to be a part of it. Queenie, he thought, just might eventually get it. Her motives for wanting to be a Resident were at present shallow and self-serving, but he could tell from the way she sometimes looked at things that one day she would understand what Overland was all about.

They had reached Lake Street and were walking up towards the lake itself.

"All I'm saying," she said, "is when a guy's wearing a toupee, you can always see the edge where it joins. That's what gives it away."

* **MEANWHILE** *At the .22 caliber Automatic Rifle Range across the street from the Star Loan Office, where a sign invited the public to learn to shoot like a marksman, a woman in a green plaid coat entered, paid her 25c for seven shots, and with the first of them shot herself in the face. While speculating on the difficulty she would have had reaching the trigger from this position, police noticed that she had removed one of her shoes and concluded that she must have used her toe.*

George disagreed. "If it's a good hairpiece there is no edge to see; it blends right in."

"Trust me. I can always spot the edge."

"On a bad toupee … sure, that's a cinch. But if it's a good one, you don't even know it's there … because all you're seeing is hair."

Queenie scoffed. "I've never been fooled yet."

"You don't think so? How about Fred Astaire or Bing Crosby?"

"Bing Crosby doesn't wear a toop."

"Doesn't he?"

"You're just making that up."

"How would you know?"

"I just know. I'd be able to spot the point of transition."

"Well, you're wasting your time looking for the point of transition here. It's so perfectly merged that even I can't tell where Overland ends and the rest of the world begins. Sometimes I go home at night only to find that I'm still in Overland, that I haven't been anywhere at all—I've just been hanging out in a different part of town."

"You're crazy."

"OK. Go ahead." George threw out his hands. "Show me where the edge is."

"That's different."

"No it isn't. Overland is just one giant toupee sitting on the ugly balding head of Burbank, California. And let me tell you, a toupee is a tricky one to pull off. Making it look like real hair is easy; the difficult part is making it look like the *other* real hair. That's the secret: blending the boundaries. Everyone's looking for that telltale edge."

She looked around her, shaking her head. She touched the burlap foliage of a bush. With her toe she scooted back the corner of some green netting that formed a grass verge.

"It doesn't look too convincing."

"That, Miss Meyer, is because you're standing right among the follicles. You can't see the wood for the trees."

"Huh?"

"You're too close. You see this from a few hundred feet away—it looks exactly like the rest of California. You'd never spot the difference."

Queenie spluttered a derisive chuckle. "I think I would."

"Go ahead then. Where does it join?"

Queenie pointed. "There behind that row of trees … where the ground changes color."

"Wrong."

"You seriously believe these trees look real?"

"It depends where you are when you're looking at them. They're not designed for close-up scrutiny; these are strictly long-shot. What about those trees behind the barn? Do they look real to you or fake?"

Queenie answered hesitantly. "I guess …"

"Who do you think made them, me or God?"

Queenie squinted into the distance. "I can't tell the difference from here," she said.

They walked for a while.

"Did you see the lake yet?" said George.

159   UNDER

"No, but I heard about it. It's not a real lake though, is it?"

"Sure it's real."

"With water in it?"

"What else are we going to put in a lake? Chicken soup?"

They dodged the slow-moving traffic to cross the street and stood at the fence looking down at the blue tarp.

Queenie let out a little snort. "Er, sorry to disappoint you, maestro, but that ain't real water."

George ignored her remark. "You know I'm beginning to think that lake is enchanted."

"Enchanted?"

"Enchanted. Like in a fairy tale."

She rolled her eyes. "Gimme a break."

"No, no. I'm deadly serious. The other day, there was this—I don't know how to describe her—Lady of the Lake. She came out of the water. It was like a vision. I thought I must be dreaming."

"Maybe you *were* dreaming—or drunk."

"No, she was real."

"Well, then she must have been a factory worker, someone poking her nose in for a look-see."

"Factory worker? No, she was beautiful."

Queenie flounced. "Excuse me. *I'm* a factory worker."

"She was different. Sort of ethereal."

"*Ethereal?* What does ethereal look like when it's at home?"

George looked upwards, trying to summon the right words. "Soft, delicate features ... porcelain complexion ... with flowing dark hair. Like an exotic Eastern goddess ... full of oriental mystery."

Suddenly it dawned on her. "Oriental? Wait a minute. You mean like a Jap?"

"Nothing so specific, just like a tropical lotus blossom of loveliness."

"Lotus blossom?" She smiled drolly. "Tell me, you hadn't by any chance been doing a little fishing that day—in your 'lake'? You didn't manage to catch any sardines—of the canned variety?"

"Yes, as a matter of fact ... I wondered if there might be a connection."

"Well, well, well. So you're Cary Grant? You could have fooled me."

"Do you know her?"

"Sure. She's this Jap girl, oh, pardon me, 'person of Japanese ancestry' who lives in my building. We work in the same section in the factory. She's no Eastern goddess; she's a welder."

"A welder?" George found this hard to imagine. "Are you sure?"

"Sure I'm sure."

"What's her name?"

"Kay."

"Kay." He savored the name for a moment. "K-a-y?"

"Yeah. Yak spelled backwards."

"Bring her up here next time you come. I want to meet her properly."

"She can't come up here. She's not a Resident ... like I am. If you want to meet her you're gonna have to go down there ... into the underworld."

George shook his head dismissively. "Can't do that."

"Why not?"

"I just can't. I can't go down there."

"What's up? Wanted by the law?"

"No, nothing like that. It's just that …"

"What?"

George unhooked the Resident's pin from his own lapel and handed it to Queenie.

"Here. Give her this. Then bring her up here with you next time."

Queenie studied the coveted pin now lying in her palm. She had been wondering how she might get hold of one.

"Well I guess I could give it to her. Won't you be needing it?"

He shook his head. "Not so long as I stay here in Overland."

"You're going to live up here permanently?"

He shrugged nonchalantly. "It suits me to be here."

Queenie looked down at the enamel pin, jiggling it around on the flat of her upturned palm. Slowly, her fingers closed around it.

163　　　UNDER

SEVENTEEN

Howard Farmer was driving his tractor steadily back and forth along the rows of crops in his field. No one in Overland except George, and presumably Howard himself, knew what the crops were supposed to be, or what he was supposed to be doing to them, but this is what he did, day in, day out.

The tractor trundled steadily from one end of the field to the other, looping about-face to continue back in the other direction—the agricultural equivalent of knitting. It provided a reassuring visual constant in the Overland community, seeming at once both leisurely and industrious.

Queenie was on her way up to Overland. Today she had come ready for business and was carrying her portfolio. She really needed that fifty dollars.

She was at the top of the stairs, about to climb the ladder to the trapdoor, when she saw Kay coming up behind her. Alarmed, she stepped down onto the platform, quickly scanning the factory to make sure they were not being watched.

"What the heck are you doing here?" Queenie hissed. "How did you get past the guard?"

"He left his post. A call of nature, I think; I saw him heading for the restroom."

"Left his post? You're kidding. So you just walked straight up here?"

Kay shrugged. "No one was looking so I—"

"Do you realize how much trouble I've been to?"

"I thought I'd come with you. To Overland." Kay was carrying her lunch pail, like she was planning a countryside picnic.

"I can't take you up there, Kay. I'm not really supposed to be there myself. If I'm with you, people are going to start asking questions. You have to be what they call a Resident. They've got tight security."

Kay looked crestfallen.

Queenie touched the pin on her blouse guiltily. "Maybe we can get you on the list. But for now you'd better go back down before you get into trouble."

"If you see the fisherman," said Kay, "would you give him a message from me?"

"The fisherman? You mean your Cary Grant guy?"

She nodded, a little bashful. Queenie was quick to pick up on it.

"Oh, it's like that, is it? Eyes meeting across a blue lagoon."

"It's silly. I just …"

"His name's Mr Godfrey … and I don't think he's much of a fisherman." She looked at Kay's face and could see that she was smitten. "OK. Where's the message?"

"Oh. I don't know. Say hello, I guess."

"That's it? Hello?" She was expecting a note, something written down. "OK. I'll tell him. Now scram before Donaldson sees you."

As Queenie began to climb the ladder, Kay made her way down again. But as she neared the foot of the staircase, she saw that the one-armed man had returned to his post; there was no way to get back past him without him seeing her. She froze, feeling exposed and vulnerable. With nowhere on the staircase to hide, she was trapped in limbo, unable to move either up or down.

Below her on the factory floor, Kay could just make out Donaldson; two soldiers with clipboards were approaching him. She watched anxiously. They looked like military police. One of them said something to Donaldson, but he couldn't hear above the racket of the heavy factory machinery. He cupped his ear and leaned in. One of the soldiers pointed to something on his clipboard. Donaldson nodded and quickly scanned the factory floor. Identifying his target, he pointed out two Asian women working side by side at a bench on a panel-forming production line. One of the soldiers approached,

and beckoned them to accompany him. The women seemed to know what it was all about; there was a look of resignation at being caught. As the soldier led them across the factory floor Donaldson turned away, distancing himself from his treachery.

Queenie emerged from the Orpheum movie theater in a stately-looking nineteenth-century silk dress edged with lace. According to its label the dress had been made for Deanna Durbin. Underneath her name was the word *Countess*. It was a little fussy for Queenie's taste, but its wide, full skirt skimmed over any inconsistencies of form. She'd had her eye on a cute cowgirl outfit—a Western style satin shirt with shimmering silk fringes—but found that in the tight skirt that went with it her tummy stuck out like she'd bust her girdle after an all-you-can-eat buffet. In truth the new bulge was barely noticeable, but this outward physical reminder of the baby's growing presence, compounded by morning sickness, was creeping her out. She *had* to find the dough to pay Dr Young.

Overland seemed a little quieter today; there were fewer extras on the streets. She wondered if they were filming on another part of the set. Or perhaps, with it being so sunny, they had found a place in the shade to rest and cool off. She approached an older man with a kind face—he was maybe in his sixties—wearing a gaily colored leisure shirt and a little pork pie hat perched high on his pink head.

"Hey, mister. You seen Mr Godfrey?" she said.

"Mr Godfrey? Last I saw of him he was up by the church talking to Jimmy."

"Who's Jimmy?"

"Jimmy Shepherd. Jimmy's Mr Godfrey's Man Friday."

"How would I get there from here?"

"Go along Main Street, past the library towards the intersection.

You'll see the clock on your right. Then take a right at Kaiser's. I mean left. Onto Fortune Way."

Queenie was trying to get the directions straight in her head. "Up this street, past the library and then at Kaiser's I turn left? What's Kaiser's?"

"Wait, I'll come with you. I need to take the dog for a walk anyway. I'll be right back."

The man nipped inside one of the houses and reappeared a few moments later with his dog, which turned out to be a push-along toy on wheels. Actually, it was more lifelike than a toy—most likely a dead pet reincarnated by a taxidermist, in which case the wheels were an odd choice. The dog, a Jack Russell, white with brown patches, had a slightly bewildered expression, as indeed it might, considering how things had turned out for the poor mutt.

"This is Chummy," said the man.

Queenie was a little taken aback. "Oh, he's … cute."

Chummy had a nice red collar, attached to which was a leash that was rigid like a yardstick, enabling his owner to push the dog along ahead of him. The three of them set off along Main Street.

"You had him long?"

"I found him in the prop room last week. I sort of adopted him … gave him a new home. Chummy's the name of the dog we had when I was a kid."

"It suits him."

"Did you ever have a dog?"

169   UNDER

Queenie shook her head. "No. I wanted one, but my dad was dead against it."

"You can hold Chummy's leash if you like."

"Nah. You go ahead. I'll wait till he gets to know me better."

They continued up the hill, Queenie taking in the rows of houses with their smoking chimneys and broad front porches. Each sat squarely within its own generous plot of land, bordered by tidy green hedges and flowering shrubs. They had red roofs and white walls with windows that looked little more than dark squares painted onto the siding. To her eye, the proportions of the buildings seemed slightly off; they were wide but unusually squat, like regular two-story houses that had been trodden into the landscape by a flat-footed giant. All the homes on the street had been built in this modern, low-profile style.

As far as film sets went, she regarded this as a particularly pleasing one. While it was not, in her opinion, always altogether convincing, this Mr Godfrey had managed to create the kind of neighborhood regular folks would be proud to live in, where people only ever saw the good in you. The atmosphere seemed to have rubbed off on the extras who, rather than constantly bellyaching about the long hours waiting around as they usually did, seemed to be enjoying every minute of their time here, whiling away the day.

They turned the corner into Fortune Way. The man was explaining how things worked.

"There's nothing to it. All you have to do is act like you're one of the locals."

Queenie nodded. "And I'm acting all the time?"

"In a manner of speaking. It comes naturally after you've been doing it a while. You become part of the community."

"So you and I, we're acting now. Just shooting the breeze, chatting about this and that. You're doing what you do … what do you do?"

"I'm a carpenter."

"Oh, so you're part of the crew? Or do you mean you're playing the part of a carpenter?"

"It's the same thing, isn't it?"

She frowned, a little confused. "I guess. So you're in this thing too."

He furrowed his brow. "We're all in it. Everyone here plays a part."

She nodded slowly, taking the idea on board. "OK. I get it."

She didn't, not quite. But she felt she was beginning to.

Playing their parts up ahead were a group of young women in summer dresses who had organized an impromptu picnic in one of the fields. Some sat or knelt on the plaid picnic blanket they had spread out on the grass, chatting convivially as they helped themselves to tasty prepared treats from a wicker hamper, while others played a spirited game of catch with an inflatable yellow beach ball. Queenie thought she recognized one or two of the women from the factory locker room, but here they seemed different—not just more feminine, but looking fresh and invigorated by their surroundings.

Caught by a sudden gust of wind the ball floated out of play and was carried over the fence where it bounced on the ground beside Queenie. The women stood smiling, waiting for her to return it. She

realized she was being invited into their world.

She went to fetch the ball and prepared to throw it back, but feeling the airy lightness of the ball and the force of the breeze blowing against her, decided that more force might be needed to get it back to them. She opted for a drop-kick technique she had seen practiced at football games, swinging her leg back for maximum power before making the connection. As the point of her shoe made contact with the ball there was a dull popping sound and her toe speared its way into the center of the ball. Suddenly deflated by the impact, the ball no longer looked like a ball but something more akin to a swimming cap, dangling off the end of her foot. She shook it off and skimmed it back to them over the fence. It landed flatly on the grass like a dinner plate.

"Sorry. Don't know quite what happened there. Must have been a fault in the plastic."

Having burst both their physical and metaphorical balloon of contentment, she expected to be ostracized by the group, but the women seemed warmly forgiving.

"That's OK. We were just about through with our game anyway. Why don't you join us? We have plenty to eat," said one closest to her.

"Thanks. That's swell of you. Maybe later. Right now I'm on my way to see someone."

The woman smiled. "Sure. Anytime."

As they continued strolling up the hill, Queenie's dog-owning companion decided it was time to introduce himself.

"You can call me Doc."

"Doc? Are you a real doctor?"

"No, I'm not a real doctor. It's just a name. What's yours?"

"Queenie."

"And are you a real queen?"

She smiled amiably, shaking her head. "I'm not a real countess either. I found this costume on the clothes rail in the … you know … movie theater."

"Oh, sure. I know how that goes. You see something nice, you put it on."

"I really wanted something to show off my legs. They're my best feature." She raised her skirt to show him.

"I don't agree," he said, looking down at them.

"You don't?" Queenie was a little affronted; everyone told her she had good legs.

"Uh-uh. I'd say your best feature is—" Doc raised an index finger to make his point "—your personality." He nodded sagely, letting the wisdom of his remark settle.

Queenie considered this. "My personality, huh? Well what do you know about that?"

As they arrived at a church with a tall spire, a woman approached them on the sidewalk from the other direction. She too was pushing a dog on wheels, this one a white Scottish terrier in need of a shampoo and set. The two dogs seemed drawn to each other, nuzzling nose to nose and gazing blindly into each other's eyes. Their owners looked

on like proud parents.

"They seem to be getting along," the woman said.

Doc agreed. "They do!"

"Dido and I were just heading to the park. Would you and …"

"Chummy."

"… Chummy care to join us?"

"Why, thank you. We'd be delighted." Doc turned to Queenie. "Your Majesty, it's been a pleasure. I don't see Mr Godfrey, but that's Jimmy sitting over there on the wall."

Queenie glanced at him then turned back to her companion. "Thanks, Doc. See you around."

In the factory office, one of the Japanese women tried appealing to the soldiers.

"I am an American citizen. Look. Here's my identity card."

She shoved it under the nose of one of them, but he brushed it aside like a stubborn infant refusing to be fed. Another soldier herded her back in line.

A military police sergeant sat behind a desk checking names on a list. He made an impatient stab at pronouncing the Japanese names as if they had been invented deliberately to annoy him. Each attempt carried with it the added suggestion that he thought the names sounded stupid: *Foo-ji-wara, Tacka-hashy, Yamma-goochy.* When her name was called, the woman in question protested.

"I'm not Japanese; I'm Chinese. American actually, but my parents are Chinese."

"Yamaguchi? That ain't a Chinese name."

He had a little US Army issue book, *How To Spot A Jap,* as a guide. He held up the open book for her to see. It showed exaggerated cartoon sketches of the perceived facial differences for comparison—Chinese (C) on one side, Japanese (J) on the other. The accompanying caption stated that *C is dull bronze in color, while J is lighter—more on the lemon-yellow side. C's eyes are set like any European's or American's, but have a marked squint. J has eyes slanted towards his nose. Look at their profiles and teeth. C usually has evenly set choppers; J has buck teeth. The Chinese smiles easily; the Jap expects to be shot ... and is very unhappy about the whole thing.*

The sergeant pointed first at the Chinese face—"That ain't you" —and then at the Japanese face: "That's you." He set down the book. Case dismissed.

The sergeant made his announcement to the group. "Anyone with any Japanese ancestry, any Japanese blood at all, must be sent to a relocation center. You all saw the signs, read the notices in the newspapers. You were ordered to register at a relocation center on May fifth. Deadline for evacuation of *all* Japanese was May tenth. That, in case you didn't know, was yesterday. You ignored the instructions, so now you're being taken straight to one of the concentration camps. You have been classified as disloyals. You especially have been privy to sensitive military information here at this factory. You are therefore regarded as high-risk prisoners. You will not be permitted to take any personal belongings with you."

Jimmy was taking a breather from tending his flock. He sat astride the churchyard wall, watching Howard Farmer's unfaltering progress. Feeling pleasantly fatigued from working in the hot sunshine, Jimmy was stripped to the waist using his balled-up shirt to mop his brow and neck.

Queenie approached via the narrow path that ran alongside the church.

"Phew. Finally. I found you."

Jimmy turned. Despite the rather different look the countess dress gave her he recognized her as the drum majorette he'd seen the day before. Surprised and rather thrilled to think that she might have been looking for him, he got to his feet, a little self-conscious.

Her eyes fleetingly took in his physique. Aware of her glance, he quickly put on his shirt, buttoning it with modest haste.

"I'm Queenie." She thrust out her hand for him to shake.

He took it, nodding in greeting. "Jimmy."

"Someone said you were Mr Godfrey's assistant."

Jimmy tucked in his shirttails. "Unofficially, I guess."

"You make any of the decisions?"

"Of course. Overland is run on egalitarian principles."

"What kind of principles?"

"Egalitarian."

"Oh, OK. Would you care to see my pictures?"

"Pictures? Of what?"

"Of me. My portfolio." She opened up the folder, and set it down on the top of the wall for him to see. "I'm getting some more up-to-date ones taken soon. I don't like my hair in these. It's blonder now, see?" She turned her head and smoothed the hair at her temple. "This photographer, Lex Foreman, took them. He's semi-professional right now, but they're pretty good I think. His aim was to showcase my versatility as well as my looks. Sure, I want to play glamorous leading women—who doesn't? But casting directors need to be able to see I'm not just a one-trick pony. Like, for instance, you probably look at me and immediately think showgirl, socialite, girl about town. In short, a good-time girl. But I don't always need to be having a good time."

"No?"

"No. I'm perfectly happy to be slaughtered in my home by a tribe of marauding savages, or persecuted for my political beliefs by Basil Rathbone. And I'm just as comfortable being a barefoot native dying of some awful disease as I am being a straight-laced lady scientist discovering the cure for it. I don't even mind being the daughter of a Welsh coal miner, like Maureen O'Hara in *How Green Was My Valley*, though between you and me, I can't imagine anything more dreary. If you tell me the kind of part you'd want me to play, I can perhaps show you what I can do."

"Well, actually …"

She turned the pages. "Here's me looking sultry. You like that one?"

"It's very nice, but—"

"Of course, I have a whole stack of cheesecake poses. That was the deal with Lex: he'd do my portraits free if I did some, you know,

177   UNDER

glamor-type pictures. They're just pin-up shots, nothing indecent. I thought, well, it's not as though pictures like that won't come in handy. I've done a little glamor work, but I see myself more as a serious actress. I can sing too. How about I give you one of each? That way you get an idea of my range."

She quickly assembled a sample of pictures and pressed them into Jimmy's hand. He looked down, accepting them reluctantly.

"If you're looking to play the part of a Resident here, all you've got to do is act natural," he said.

"Well, you've said it there, haven't you? Act natural. That's the hardest thing in the world for an actress to do. There's nothing guaranteed to make you feel more self-conscious than being told to act natural. When I was at high school our drama teacher, Mr Estler, used to yell at me to relax. In those days, I used to get a little stage fright; I'm over that now, of course. He'd get right in my face and yell RE-LAX!!!"

She lunged toward Jimmy and screamed the word inches from his face. Jimmy recoiled, visibly shaken by the outburst. He swallowed hard in an attempt to regain his composure. Queenie backed off, noting his nervousness.

"See what I mean? Pretty difficult to relax now, isn't it?"

On the staircase, Kay too was feeling far from relaxed. She watched the military presence uneasily as the "Js" were led out across the factory floor towards the exit; she knew exactly what was going down. On his way out, the sergeant nodded thanks to Donaldson and was about to leave when Donaldson grabbed his arm. He pointed to the clipboard and spoke conspiratorially into the sergeant's ear, gesturing in the direction of the welding bench where she and Queenie worked. With neither of them at their stations the sergeant's eyes had no specific point of focus, but he seemed to understand what was being said. The soldiers headed towards the bench to investigate further as Donaldson's searching gaze scoured the factory for the missing pair—or rather, Kay suspected, for her. She knew her number was up. Somebody must have checked up on her nationality, or identified the Chinese "birth certificate" as phony-baloney. Or it could simply have been that Donaldson wanted to get rid of her to satisfy some personal beef because he just didn't like her face.

Being up on the staircase had so far kept Kay out of the line of fire. She remained motionless in an attempt to blend into her surroundings, but Donaldson always seemed to have other senses in play; she knew it was only a matter of time before he would radar in on her.

Kay looked up in desperate search of salvation. She had no choice other than to head upwards.

EIGHTEEN

Kay's chosen outfit, or at least the one suggested to her by one of the Overland Residents, was a sky-blue skirt with black velvet bodice laced at the front over a white puff-sleeved blouse. In her hair, a long blue ribbon. White knee socks and shiny black pumps added to the look. It was a costume that might be appropriate for a peasant girl in a musical chorus, all swaying hips and a tra-la-la, or even a serving wench in ye olde tavern, but one that became the perfect emblem of innocence when worn by the eponymous character in a fairy-tale adventure: Snow White, Alice in Wonderland or Goldilocks. A girl in such a costume was almost certain to discover a special new world where animals could talk, dance, tell the time or be called upon to perform household chores.

As Kay stepped out into the daylight, a passing man reminded her that she was not wearing her Resident's pin. Having seen Queenie's she knew to what he was referring. She thanked him and told him that she would put it on momentarily, digging into her skirt pocket as if she was about to produce it.

As she headed cautiously along the main street she saw that Overland, the part of the film set beyond the lake that Queenie had described to her, was far bigger and more elaborate than she had expected. While much of it seemed make-believe and obviously fabricated—the colors too clean and bright, the vehicle and building designs too charmingly simple—the place seemed to have a genuine soul, the people in it part of a community.

She passed a house from which she could hear the sound of someone sawing wood: in out, in out, like the rasping breathing of an asthmatic dog after a long run. She spotted the blade of the saw intermittently protruding from a thin slit in the blank front wall and watched the back and forth movement until the blade had sawn a complete square, whereupon the cut piece fell with the clatter onto the front lawn, creating a window hole through which the occupant could now be seen: a young man with the saw in his hand. He waved a casual hello and Kay waved back. She felt sure she had seen him somewhere before—the young man on the motorbike at the bus stop? Was that him? She turned her head and moved quickly along in case he recognized her, even though, like the other people on the streets, he didn't seem particularly curious about who she was or how she had got there.

It was a pleasant town. Passers-by smiled; men respectfully raised their hats and bid her good afternoon; they didn't do that in the real world. Cars and trucks rolled quietly by, some with drivers, some without. From the speaker system, cheerful music—"I Know Why (And So Do You)" by Glenn Miller and his Orchestra—drifted

through the streets. Lulled by the pervading air of tranquility, she had to remind herself that she was a prisoner on the run and that even though she could see no police or military presence, the soldiers in the factory might soon realize where she had gone and make their way up there to look for her. She needed a place to hide. She had hoped to find Queenie so that she could tell her what had happened and seek her advice, but so far she was nowhere to be seen.

She came to an intersection with a sign pointing left *To the Lake*.

When she found the spot, she stood on the top road looking down across the valley. It looked different from up here, but she soon identified the stretched tarpaulin lake with the little hole in the middle from which she had first seen Overland just a few days earlier.

The lakeside cabin was there with the pink rowboat moored up beside it, just as picture perfect as she remembered it. It seemed like a haven, serene and secure—the ideal place for a fugitive to hide. No sign of the fisherman; the smoking chimney might have suggested that he was inside the cabin, though somehow she sensed that he was not.

She took the steps down and followed the path to the cabin where she knocked on the door. Behind her, the surface of the lake billowed slightly with a soft flapping sound, presumably lifted by an updraft of air. It rose and then gently fell again as if letting out a contented sigh. When there was no answer to her knock, Kay turned the doorknob and tentatively opened the door. She tried a feeble *Hello* to announce herself, just in case, but there was no reply.

The cabin had no interior walls; it was all one room and it had been furnished in a quaint country-cottage style. There was a rich smell of fresh timber from which the cabin had been built. A gentle breeze entered through the open windows, fluttering the pretty curtains. Kay stepped inside, her eyes adjusting to the subdued interior light.

In the middle of the room, a lumber floor with a green two-seater couch faced a pink tiled fireplace. In the grate was a bundle of blackened logs cast from some sort of resin. She noticed that there was an electric cord attached to them with a little inline torpedo switch. She clicked the button and the fire came immediately to life with blazing red coals and fluttering amber flames. By shifting the grate a little from the fireplace, she was able to see behind the scenes, observing that the illusion was generated by an orange light bulb surrounded by a rotating sleeve of red and yellow tinted plastic. She found the effect enchanting and imagined how cosy it would be at night to curl up on the couch and gaze into the fiery glow.

On a small table covered by a gingham cloth sat a little vase of plastic flowers and a bowl of wax fruit. There was a solid rocking chair and beside it, an old storage trunk on top of which was a globe and a wind-up phonograph with a few records in sleeves. The recording already on the player was "The Very Thought of You" sung by Al Bowlly.

Kay was certain that this was the home of the fisherman. Its contents provided clues from which she could form a picture of the man he was and the things he valued. It was her way of getting to know him.

The flowers and the choice of music told her that he was sensitive, romantic and caring, while the globe indicated both intelligence and an adventurous spirit. The rocking chair and the wood-burning fire, albeit fake, suggested someone who was at heart a home-loving traditionalist—solid, dependable and relaxed. And as she assumed that he had built the cabin himself, she surmised that he must be strong and capable—good with his hands.

Slightly more difficult to assimilate into her profile of him was the life-size stuffed deer—an unexpected decorative choice—which stood looking out of the window as though, like Kay, it might be fearful of being hunted down in the outside world.

Her fisherman was clearly well read; one wall was largely taken up by a library of handsome leather-bound volumes in oxblood and bottle green. She took a closer look and noticed that though the spines had various decorative gold-tooled patterning, none of the books had titles. She selected one to check its contents and found that they weren't real books at all; they were merely the spines of books attached to wooden panels. In fact, she realized, the whole interior seemed to be decorated from a props department, yet it seemed no less appealing for all its artificiality.

Kay was hungry. She flipped open the lid of her lunch pail and unwrapped the cheese sandwich that Mrs Ishi had prepared for her that morning. As she ate, she made herself at home, wandering around the room and gathering more evidence about the man who lived there. A shelf in the kitchen had an assorted display of empty storage jars. Her eye immediately fell upon an all-too-familiar can of Japanese sardines—the same one, she assumed, that Queenie had hooked onto his fishing line the other day when they'd been having lunch. Still unopened, the sardines appeared to be the only real food in the place. She took an identical can from her lunch pail and put it side by side on the shelf with the first one. Then she took her apple and set it in the fruit bowl atop the phony wax fruit.

Behind a folding screen, there was a wood-framed sleigh bed sporting a quilted comforter and plump pillows. It looked both real and extremely inviting.

Ten minutes later, Kay was lying in it, her shoes set neatly on the rug like bedroom slippers. She was pleasantly aware of the sound of birdsong from beyond the open window and the lilt of some distant romantic ballad carried on the drifting breeze.

What if the handsome fisherman were to return home and find her there? Would he be pleased or angry? She liked to think that he would be glad, but she realized that this might be wishful thinking. She was, after all, an intruder and one with the outward appearance of "the enemy."

Would he recognize her from her brief emergence from the lake, or would he be so startled to find a stranger in his home that he would take the hunting rifle she imagined he would be carrying and shoot her? No, he wouldn't do that. He just wouldn't.*

Blissfully untroubled, she closed her eyes and drifted. She was dozing rather than sleeping, wallowing in the comfort of the afternoon,

* **MEANWHILE** *Gold-rush days when eggs sold for $10 each may soon be duplicated—for strawberry eaters. This was indicated yesterday by Harry Oakley, district Farm Security Administration officer. Oakley pointed out that in Southern California Japanese farmers have grown more than 95 per cent of the strawberries. And unless white truck farmers move more quickly to replace evacuated Nipponese a strawberry shortage is in sight. Oakley announced that losses in the production of tomatoes, carrots, green peas and onions also are in view.*

no longer fearful of being caught. Here beside the lake it was almost as though something in the air was tranquilizing her, making her feel completely secure.

Outside, First Lieutenant Franks was taking a short cut from the woods along the pathway that ran past the cabin. He paused to pick up a pebble from the lake edge and skimmed it across the surface of the tarp, watching it bounce three or four times before it cracked against a section of fence on the other side. Satisfied, he headed up the steps to the street.

When Kay awoke, it was dark in the cabin. The flickering glow from the fire warmed the room. She must have been asleep for hours, yet she didn't remember giving in to the notion of proper slumber. She had no idea of the time, but when she got up to look through the rear window she could see the darkening sky tinged with burnt orange from the setting sun, and the distant glimmer of lights from the city. She wasn't sure whether they were part of the world outside or merely an illuminated feature on a backdrop, but the effect was so charming that she was incurious to know.

She checked the front window—no sign of activity; everything seemed quiet. She stepped out the door and saw the pretty string of lights bordering the lake. Who turned them on, she wondered? Perhaps they came on automatically when it got dark, like street lights. The evening breeze ruffled the feathery foliage of a nearby tree.

With the factory running on a continuous cycle of eight-hour shifts, she realized that Queenie would by now have gone home and a new team of shift workers would be in place. Surely the soldiers would have left too. They must not have figured out where she had gone or they would have come looking for her. She still didn't know how she was going to get past the one-armed man, but she knew she must go back down and figure out a way. Mrs Ishi would be worried—Queenie too, probably.

She climbed the steps and headed along Lake Street towards the Orpheum theater to find her way back down into the underworld.

Queenie was on the factory bus, the seat beside her empty. Having found no sign of Kay at her workbench, she had asked around the factory and learned about the military police's recent visit. No one had actually seen Kay among those arrested, but Queenie feared the worst. One girl said she saw a group of orientals being loaded on a truck with wire mesh fastened to the windows. No one knew where they had been taken.

Donaldson had been no help. Cold and aloof, he stood stiffly with his hands behind his back, his head held high. Unable to meet Queenie's eye directly, he scanned the space above her head as though carrying out some formal sweep of inspection that could be neither interrupted nor postponed. He was not prepared to discuss the matter, saying only that it was "classified information."

"That's no good," she had said. "I need to find her. She's my friend." Donaldson had simply shrugged and walked away.

So now she was heading home in the vain hope that Kay had somehow given them the slip and made her way back there. Queenie caught her own gray reflection staring glumly out of the bus window.

It was true; Kay was her friend. And she was genuinely worried about her. But, though she was ashamed to admit it, it was also true that one of the reasons for her concern was that Kay had recently agreed to lend her thirty dollars, a sizable chunk of the dough needed to persuade Dr Young to perform his magic vanishing trick. Kay had arranged to withdraw the cash from her savings the next morning and Queenie had booked an appointment with Dr Young in anticipation of having the necessary funds. With Kay now arrested and sent away to a camp, Queenie was well and truly up the creek.

Scraping together all of her own money, together with the few bucks she had managed to shake from the girls at work, had yielded little more than a third of the fee. She couldn't ask Mrs Ishi because she owed her rent, and Queenie's bright idea of asking Donaldson for an advance on her wages had recently been met with a derisive sneer. When, in desperation, she had ventured to suggest a personal loan, he had just laughed in her face.

"You've gotta be kidding, right?"

Queenie tried not to think selfishly, reminding herself that she was not the primary victim in Kay's crisis. Nevertheless, time was running out for her. The woman who gave her Dr Young's number had told her that he absolutely refused to terminate any pregnancy beyond twelve weeks. She had already lied a little, subtracting a week or two to stay within the specified limit, and now she was way over. If she didn't raise the money soon, it would be too late and she'd be stuck with the damn kid for life. It was hard to picture such a thing. Much like her own mother, Queenie didn't see herself as the motherly type.

Ginger Rogers had taken to it pretty well in *Bachelor Mother*. The baby wasn't actually hers; she just happened to find it on a doorstep. And now she was forced to deal with it. But despite the new responsibility, she managed to hold down a full-time job while carrying on a courtship with David Niven. How? By getting her kindly Jewish landlady to babysit. Maybe Queenie could get her own

kindly landlady, Mrs Ishi, to look after the kid while she pursued her career, making movies by day, while at night she'd be out on the town, dancing the night away with her handsome co-stars.

Who was she kidding? That was never going to happen; Queenie was stuffed, her career over before it had even begun. Twenty-two years old and her future was already behind her.

The funny thing was that while she was in Overland she didn't think that way. There, problems seemed to fade into the background, superseded by a vague yet reassuring notion that everything would somehow turn out fine. Really? Yes, she felt sure of it. A solution— she didn't know what exactly—would present itself and her little problem would vanish like a puff of acrid black smoke from the factory below, carried away on a gust of fresh Overland wind.

Now back in her coveralls, Kay cautiously approached the foot of the stairs. She saw that the one-armed man guarding the access point to the roof had been replaced by a man with two arms. He was up on his feet, deep in chin-wagging conversation with a fellow workmate, a white-haired man with thick glasses that looked like a pair of paperweights in a frame.

It seemed that security measures regarding people coming back down from Overland, rather than those going up, were more relaxed, which made sense—a nightclub doorman checks customers on their way in, not on their way out. The man glanced casually over his shoulder as Kay approached the foot of the stairs; barely seeming to notice her, he turned back to continue yapping. On the table was the clipboard with a list of employee names and numbers—hers naturally was not among them—along with times in and times out. She picked up the pen, unscrewed the cap and scribbled some numbers in one of the vacant spaces.

Kay crossed the factory floor towards the locker rooms. As she had anticipated, the evening shift was now in place: the same jobs being done by a duplicate workforce. There was another Donaldson, the alternative version shorter and with a thin moustache, doing the same job of section foreman, and, she presumed, another Queenie and another Kay. She looked across and saw two women at the station where she and Queenie usually worked—same coveralls, same welding helmets and doing the same jobs they did. The woman at her own bench was of similar build, and with her mask down could easily be mistaken for Kay. As she looked around her, she was struck by an odd sense of detachment, as though she were watching the movie version of her life in which all the characters, including herself, were being played by actors. The feeling was further compounded by the fact that no one was paying her any attention, as though she was no longer a part of this world and therefore could not be seen.

But her invisibility was short-lived. As she entered the locker room to change out of her coveralls she heard a voice behind her.

"Nashimura?"

She turned to see the two military policemen standing at the door.

NINETEEN

Queenie was out pushing one of the baby buggies. Today she was feeling uncharacteristically dowdy in a plain loose-fitting housedress. Not quite maternity-wear, but heading in that general direction.

While all the other Overland Residents were going about their daily business looking relaxed and cheerful, Queenie was tense and distracted. She saw Doc sitting under the library clock. He stood and graciously tipped his hat.

"Ah, good morning, miss. I didn't recognize you without your ballgown."

She put on a cheery smile. "Hi Doc. How's Chummy today?"

Chummy appeared to be fixated on something further down the street. Doc steered the little dog round to greet her. She bent and obligingly patted his head.

Doc took in her chosen ensemble. "Well, what have we today? The proud young mother? Quite a different look."

She glanced down at her dress. "I don't know what I was thinking. It's not really me, is it?"

Doc weighed up the overall effect. "Hm. I don't know. I think motherhood rather suits you." He peeked into the buggy and saw the doll lying there. "What's the little feller's name?"

Queenie didn't want to get into this.

"Say, Doc. You haven't seen a Japanese girl, have you? Chinese, I mean."

"In Overland?"

"She's my friend from the factory. She didn't come home last night."

He winced regretfully. "I heard they were putting them all into concentration camps."

Queenie felt guilty. "Yes, I heard that too. I thought maybe she got away … came up here to hide."

He shook his head. "I haven't seen any orientals."

"Her landlady is really worried."

"Did you ask Ray, the doorman at the Orpheum? He probably would have seen her if she'd come up here."

She nodded. "I've asked everybody. I guess they must have caught her. I don't have any idea where they might have taken her. What am I supposed to do now?"

Doc was full of sympathy, but could offer no solution.

A short ladder leaned against the little flat-roofed porch over the front door of Shangri-La Cottage. Jimmy had climbed up there and it was from this vantage point that he spotted Queenie approaching. By the look on her face, he guessed she'd had no luck finding the friend she had asked him about earlier that morning. He watched

191   UNDER

as she parked her baby buggy out on the sidewalk and walked down the garden path towards him. He was still having a hard time getting used to her conservative young-mother image.

She asked him what he was up to. He explained that he was getting a bit of practice in before he started his parachute training. Queenie listened distractedly to his enthusiastic explanations about altitudes, wind speeds and drop zones. Thinking he had her attention, he was now demonstrating the parachutist's correct position for landing.

"You've got to bend your knees when you hit the ground," he said. "And keep your knees and feet together. I got a book from the library so I can be one step ahead when I start training."

Queenie stood on the lawn looking up at him with her arms folded across her chest. "A book just to learn how to jump?"

"There's more to it than you think. A parachutist can hit the ground at tremendous speed. If you don't land correctly, you can easily bust a leg. We have to learn to do a forward or backward somersault as we land because the chute can pull you off balance if there's a strong crosswind. You've got to dishrag it before it can drag you." He liked using that phrase, dishrag it; it made him sound like an old hand.

Jimmy prepared to demonstrate the basic jump, his rigorous study immediately apparent as he posed, chin up, eyes forward with his arms straight in the air as if controlling the lines of his imaginary chute.

"What's that? A ballet position?"

Ignoring her, he launched himself from the roof and landed neatly, springing on his knees back into the upright position.

"And you had to read a whole book to learn how to do that?"

"Think you could do it?"

"It's a cinch. Stand aside."

"Better lose the heels unless you want a sprained ankle."

Queenie kicked off her shoes and climbed up the steps to the flat roof. She jumped without preparation. Landing heavily, she hit the ground with a jarring thud.

Jimmy winced. "Ooh. Jeez. You didn't bend your knees enough. You OK?"

"Sure. Let me try again."

"OK, but listen, you've got to keep your knees and feet together."

Queenie climbed determinedly up to the roof again, clearly not listening.

Jimmy looked up at her uneasily. "Maybe you shouldn't be doing this, you being a girl and all."

"Why not?"

"I don't know. It can be quite a jolt to your insides."

"Baloney."

Wilfully, she jumped again, but this time Jimmy caught her, breaking her fall.

"I can't let you do this; you're going to hurt yourself."

Queenie remained locked in Jimmy's embrace, but he could feel the tension in her, like a restrained animal taking stock of its options before deciding how to react. She suddenly flinched and broke free

from his arms, walking quickly away without meeting his eye. Jimmy was taken aback.

"Queenie! I didn't mean to … I was only trying to … protect you. Queenie!"

But Queenie wouldn't answer. She snatched up her abandoned shoes, and marched off down the street in her stocking feet, pushing the buggy ahead of her.

Jimmy stood, helpless and dejected, unsure what he had done to cause the upset. He watched as, a little further down the street, she paused to slip into her shoes, leaning awkwardly on a low wall to steady herself while she adjusted the heel straps with her forefinger. When she disappeared round the corner Jimmy followed, keeping his distance so as not to antagonize her further.

From the corner of Main Street, he watched her making her way along one of the walkways known as South Ridge to a tree-lined field where she stood on the upper slope looking out. She was rocking the buggy back and forth, as mothers often do to lull the infant into a state of slumber. But then something inside seemed to take hold. Even from so far away Jimmy sensed it, some tightening knot of frustration. Suddenly, she gave the handle a hefty shove, sending the buggy down the slope.

It rolled gently at first, gradually gathering momentum as it bounced unsteadily over the folds in the green turf. Queenie remained stock-still, watching the runaway carriage as it headed towards the edge of the field and finally disappeared silently from view over the edge.

She continued to stare for a moment and then dropped her head forward, burying her face in her outstretched palms. Jimmy could see she was terribly upset about something. Despite his apprehension about how she might react, he headed on over.

By the time he reached her, she was sitting on the grass, eyes blinkered, gazing despondently down at her feet.

"What gives?"

Queenie looked up and then turned away, unsure what Jimmy had seen.

"Oh, hi, Jimmy. Just taking a breather." She blew her nose on her handkerchief and tried to wipe the moisture from her mascara with her knuckle. "I must look a sight."

"I'm sorry if I said something …"

"Oh, no Jimmy. It's not you. I shouldn't have acted that way."

"Something bothering you?"

"Yeah, yeah. You could say that."

He sat down beside her, looking out across the hazy horizon ahead. "Feel like sharing?"

"You don't want to hear."

"Sure I do."

She shook her head slowly from side to side. "You don't, trust me."

"Try me."

She inhaled deeply, holding her breath for a moment before blurting it out. "My friend's in trouble. She needs an operation, but she's broke. I'm just sore because I can't help her."

"What kind of operation?"

"Oh. You know. Women's stuff."

"Oh."

"Sorry. Didn't mean to embarrass you."

"No, I … I'm not …" Jimmy's feigned nonchalance demonstrated just how embarrassed he was. "How much does she need, your friend?"

"Fifty dollars. She's got eighteen of it, maybe twenty. She gets paid in a couple of weeks, but she needs it right away."

"Another thirty? Thirty's not so much."

"It is to her."

"I could loan it to her."

"You?"

"Sure. Why not? I just sold my motorcycle. What with me going for my training and then probably overseas, I figured it would only sit around getting rusty."

He took a clip of folded bills from his pants pocket, peeled off three tens and offered them to her.

"But that's your dough."

"Nothing to spend it on in the army."

Queenie took the money, clutching it gratefully. "Oh, Jimmy. She'll pay you back. In a week or so. I promise."

"That's OK. Whenever."

"Whenever? That's it? No further questions?"

"If she needs help … I don't want you to be upset."

Queenie took a moment to consider Jimmy's kindness. Until then, she had not envisaged him as leading-man material, but his caring response to her crisis had been genuinely selfless. Now she was beginning to see him as a potential heart-throb, someone the fans might go for. He was not the obviously rugged type like Clark Gable, Robert Taylor or Tyrone Power; he was more the gangly-but-cute sort, like James Stewart in some of his early flicks: diffident, yet stalwart and morally resolute.

"You're a great guy, Jimmy."

He tried to shrug off the compliment, but she laid it right back at him.

"A really great guy. Someday you're going to make some nice girl very happy."

Jimmy smiled shyly. "Well, I'd better be getting back to my training. If you're OK."

"I am now. Thanks to you. Everything's going to be all right."

As he got up to leave, she pulled at his sleeve, bringing him closer, and planted a big grateful kiss on his lips. The gesture was meant to seem broad and playful, but Queenie found herself lingering in a moment of unexpected tenderness. She regarded him quizzically, trying to make sense of her emotions before letting him go. At the fence he turned to her.

"Oh, and don't worry about losing your baby. No one need know about it. I can get you a new one from Props."

UNDER

TWENTY

The following morning a group of Residents were waiting in line outside the Orpheum movie theater—familiar faces from the Overland community: Effie from the diner, Tommy in his splendid check suit, the twins, old Doc with his little dog Chummy.

Ray the doorman was keeping things in order, letting one or two at a time enter the building, when Jimmy pitched up. He checked the line, seeing how long it was.

"What's happening?" he said.

One of the Residents, a man wearing a check coat and a white homburg, answered. "We all got our marching orders. Courtesy of the United States Army."

"Where's everybody going?"

One of the twins answered. "Sent back down. All of us. Project Overland's been terminated."

"Terminated?"

"All Residents are surplus to requirements. They're closing the place down."

"They can't do that."

Another Resident, a woman on roller skates, piped up. "Where are we going to go now? We like coming here."

A big man in a battered straw hat and bib overalls echoed their frustration. "What's gonna happen to it all? I was halfway through building a paddling pool. Told to drop everything and get back down to the factory. No debate. Finito."

One of the tennis players joined in. "*We* were in the middle of a match. I'd just fought back from being two sets down to lead five four in the third. We were at deuce."

The big man was less sympathetic to these more personal concerns. He responded with mocking sarcasm. "Oh, that's too bad."

The tennis guy snapped back at him huffily. "Oh, screw you. And your paddling pool."

Ignoring the spat, Doc shook his head despondently. "I'm gonna miss this place." He lifted Chummy up, affectionately tucking him under his arm.

Jimmy was having a hard time catching up with the news. "Does Mr Godfrey know about this?"

"Haven't seen him around lately. I heard he was being sent to Seattle."

The line continued to shuffle forward, ushered by the doorman. What had at first looked like a line at a movie theater, now seemed more like some biblical expulsion of damned souls.

Down in the factory, the one-armed man was at the barrier. Several women crowded round his desk. He raised his hand, trying to fend off their questions and referring them to the hastily written sign that he had added to the chain guard on the staircase: *Closed until further notice. By Order, US Army*. The factory workers waiting to go up top were confused and disgruntled.

Above them, a straggle of expelled Residents slowly descended the staircase: the tennis players, no longer in tennis whites, no longer Residents, were back wearing their drab factory workwear; Doc, hardly recognizable without his multicolored shirts and his dog Chummy, now in greasy denim coveralls. Their vitality of spirit also seemed to have drained from them as they returned to face the drudgery of the world below.

The one-armed man unhooked the chain only long enough to let them through before clipping it smartly back in place. Residents could come down, but they could no longer go up. As they passed the one-armed man's table, each of them dropped their Resident pin into a little cardboard box.

Two workers crossing the yard outside the wing and fin assembly shop were unsettled to discover what looked like a midget lying face down on the asphalt. One of the workers approached, looming hesitantly over the lifeless figure. It became clear then that it was some kind of doll. He wore striped pants and a felt tailcoat and had glossy black hair painted neatly on his composite head, which was cracked open like an egg. The worker flopped the doll over with the toe of his boot. The caricature face gazed fixedly back at him with wild goggly eyes exaggerated by painted brows and lashes. An ugly dark fracture ran diagonally from the upper lip across one eye to the crown. The lower jaw was gone, leaving a horrific-looking gaping red throat. A thick piece of knotted string protruded from its gullet, which the startled little man looked as though he might have choked on.

The second worker looked around, trying to figure out where the doll had come from. When he looked up, he saw an upturned baby buggy entangled between a pair of tensioned wires fifty feet above them.

Jimmy was tending to some detail on the model in Shangri-La Cottage, when the major burst in.

"Hey, kid. Where's Godfrey?"

"Mr Godfrey's not here, sir."

"Well, where the hell is he? He was supposed to be in Seattle two days ago."

"Isn't he there? He set off on Saturday morning. He said he was starting work at the new plant on Monday."

"Well, he didn't show. He's not at his apartment. Nobody in the real world has seen him for weeks."

"That's a puzzler."

"He was so reluctant to leave his precious little town, I thought he might still be here."

"No, sir. I've been here since Saturday. Mr Godfrey hasn't been around."

"How come you're still here?"

"I'm about to do my special training, sir. Parachute Battalion. I'm just here for the next couple of days, tying up loose ends, making sure things are running smoothly."

"OK, son. If you see Godfrey, tell him to get his ass up to Seattle. And if he's made other plans, tell him this is a military operation. We can have him arrested for non-compliance."

"Arrested? Mr Godfrey didn't do anything wrong. He built this entire town for the war effort. Have you any idea how much work has gone into this—how much commitment?"

"Commitment, my ass. If he were so committed, he'd be in Seattle now, doing the job he was recruited to do. If you ask me, all this was just his way to dodge the draft." He looked at the model with a disparaging sneer. "Orange trees … riding round on a dumb kiddie car track. If he had his way, he'd be sitting here in Neverland with his thumb up his ass until the goddamn war is over."

"With all due respect sir, I think Mr Godfrey has got a little more dignity than that."

The major shook his head but decided to let the argument lie. He departed swiftly from the room, leaving Jimmy standing alone looking personally affronted by the attack on his boss.

There was a long pause before George's muffled voice could be heard from inside the closet.

"Has he gone?"

The major was walking back to his car, parked near the ramp. One of the Overland buses was passing by, but he refused to use it. Presently, he came upon a woman hanging her laundry on a clothesline.

"What are you doing?"

The woman turned, nettled by the accusatory tone. "What do you mean, what am I doing? I'm hanging out laundry."

"Why?"

"That's what I do. I hang it up; I take it down."

"Yes, but you're not supposed to be here now. Hasn't anyone told you? Project Overland has ended."

"But I'm a Resident."

"Not anymore. You're no longer needed. The project's terminated. You can go home."

She stared at him, bemused. "… But this *is* my home."

The major was stuck for words. Perhaps the woman was deranged, a basket case. He had neither the time nor the patience to reason with her. He spoke dismissively.

"Look. You can't stay here. No one can stay here. It's over."

Back in Shangri-La George was hunched over the model, his nose practically touching the buildings as he scrutinized one specific area with single-minded intent. Jimmy looked on, troubled by his boss's increasingly neurotic behavior.

George's point of focus was the ramp used by Major Lund and Lieutenant Franks to gain access to Overland. The model version of it was a wedge shape resembling something that might be used to prop open a door. George let out a soft, low growl like a hostile dog.

"This is the problem," he said, tapping the ramp with the tip of his craft knife. He teased the little triangle from the model baseboard, but it wouldn't budge. Finally he wrenched it free with brute force and held it aloft between forefinger and thumb. "We don't need it," he said. "We can get rid of it altogether." He tossed the ramp out of the window, then grinned at the simplicity of his solution.

Jimmy managed a feeble smile.

"It won't affect the Residents since they all come up through the Orpheum theater," George explained rationally.

Jimmy broached the subject gently. "Mr Godfrey, you do know that all the Residents have gone?"

"Gone? Gone where?"

"They've been sent back down to the factory. Permanently. Major Lund's orders."

"Really?" George sounded mistrustful of the information.

Jimmy assured him it was so. He was puzzled how his boss could have failed to notice the recent eviction. He gestured to the window, inviting him to see for himself. George moved closer to it to look out. He checked the street in both directions and saw that the place was deserted. George turned, seeming a little dazed.

"No Residents? Well that's ridiculous. How can Overland function as a proper community without Residents?"

203   UNDER

TWENTY-ONE

Despite Major Lund's decree to depopulate the Overland project, the next day the transport system was still running; the chain of passenger-less vehicles endlessly circling the town like an abandoned carnie ride.

A group of hikers, way up on the hillside, had perhaps not yet received the directive to leave, or had decided, like a handful of other Residents, to ignore it until pressure was brought to bear. Ray, the Orpheum doorman, had been appointed as agent in charge of chasing down the scattered few, and now spent his day roaming the ghost town like a vigilante. Once the last of the stragglers had been rounded up, he too would leave, closing the door behind him.

George, as yet undiscovered, stood at the lakeside staring at the little hole in the middle of the tarp, willing his beloved to resurface. After waiting for almost a week, spending endless hours gazing across the water, he discovered, frustratingly, that on the day that she did appear he had not been there to meet her.

It must have been on the following morning, Tuesday, as he lay in bed "considering things" while gazing distractedly around the room, when he had spotted the extra can of sardines sitting on the kitchen shelf. At first he thought it some kind of an optical illusion, the original sardines somehow reflected in a mirror, and had to get out of bed to check whether it was real. Sure enough there were two cans now instead of one. How had it got there? Later, he had found the apple.

Though he had not initially spotted either of these additions, the previous night he'd sensed that something was amiss; he just couldn't put his finger on it. And there was that lovely smell—in his bed. He had picked up the pillow and brought it to his face. Breathing in, he felt sure he could detect an unfamiliar perfume on the fabric, light and fragrant like some kind of sweet, exotic fruit. Figs? Passion fruit? Later he realized she must have been asleep in his bed. Traces of her dreams lingered on his pillow and now they were inside his head too.

At first he had taken this as a sign that she would visit again, but now he feared that she might have gone forever, never to return. Queenie's words echoed in his head. *If you want to meet her you're gonna have to go down there ... into the underworld.*

He had a growing urge to look down into the hole in the lake, to see if she was there. He edged to a spot where the branch of a tree overhung the water. Holding tight, he stepped gingerly up to the water's edge to test the surface with his toe. It felt reasonably firm so he dared to lean a little further out, allowing him to put more weight on the tarp, but when he felt it start to sag under his weight, he quickly stepped back onto the safety of dry land.

Jimmy, who had been given special dispensation to help "wrap things

up," was in the middle pasture rearranging his sheep. Through the Overland speaker system up on the street came the romantic melody of Artie Shaw and his Orchestra with Helen Forrest singing "Summer Souvenirs." He hummed along.

Interrupting the calm, he heard someone calling his name. It was Ray from the Orpheum. He was waving an envelope in the air and was about to climb the fence. Jimmy quickly set down his sheep and gestured for him to stop. Ray complied, stepping back down and staying on the road side of the fence. He shouted across, but Jimmy couldn't hear him properly.

"Wait there! I'll come over."

Jimmy approached the fence, distractedly checking his flock.

"This field's not safe underfoot if you're not used to it," he explained. Then he saw the envelope with his name written on it—no address. "What gives?"

"Gate guard on the ramp brought it up. Hand-delivered. Must be important, huh?"

Jimmy immediately recognized the writing.

"It's from my mom."

He opened up the envelope and found a telegram inside addressed to his mother. The paper had been folded back on itself so that only the address and the first line of the message were visible: *The Secretary of War desires me to express his deep regret …* Jimmy stuffed it back into the envelope without unfolding it.

Ray had evidently caught sight of the sender's address.

"Washington? Must be about where you're being stationed, huh? Where are you hoping for?"

Jimmy stared into the middle of nowhere, scratching his ear. "It's about something else."

"I got a buddy stationed in Bali—someplace like that. He says the women over there go bare-breasted—without a care in the world." Getting no reaction, Ray nodded, taking in the view. "It's nice up here. You're in a swell position. Pity everyone has to go back down. You'll be gone soon too?"

"Yeah. Well. I got work to do. Thanks for bringing the telegram, Ray."

"No big deal. I'll keep my fingers crossed."

"Huh?"

"Bali?" He mimed an implausibly curvaceous female, jiggling her imaginary bosoms.

Jimmy stared back vacantly, his mind elsewhere. He wandered over to his flock and continued to regroup his sheep until Ray was out of sight. Then he removed the telegram from its envelope again and unfolded it. The pasted strips of purple block capitals hovered before his eyes as though not properly glued to the paper. It was addressed to his mother so she must have decided to forward it on to him. He read it two or three times before he could make sense of the words.

THE SECRETARY OF WAR DESIRES ME TO EXPRESS HIS DEEP REGRET THAT YOUR SON PRIVATE FIRST CLASS CARL SHEPHERD WAS KILLED IN ACTION ON MAY 10 1942 IN PACIFIC AREA 15 LETTER FOLLOWS DUNLOP ACTING THE ADJUTANT GENERAL

207   UNDER

Jimmy's breathing became choked in a shallow space somewhere between inhaling and exhaling. He let his hand fall to his sides. The telegram fluttered in the breeze like a flag of surrender. He swallowed hard and took a couple of deep breaths, trying to quell the rising distress, but his emotions overwhelmed him. He felt faint. All at once, the ground beneath him dropped away and he felt himself plummet like a dead horse on a cut rope.

In reality it seemed he had chanced upon one of those gaps in the netting that until then he had been careful to avoid, for he now found that the lower part of his body had disappeared below the surface of the pasture as far as his armpits, the upper part of him saved only by his splayed arms. He repositioned his hands, using his elbows to try and gain sufficient leverage to haul himself back up through the hole, but it was no use; too much of his body had been lost to the world below for him to regain control of it.

Above the surface, with no one in sight to lend a hand, Jimmy desperately grappled for a firm handhold in the tight mesh of the netting. Over his shoulder he could make out the group of hikers climbing a path towards a hilltop ridge. He yelled for help, but they were just too far away; they seemed like those sketchy human figures added to a landscape painting merely to provide scale. At the ridge, they decided to take a break, removing their backpacks and scattering themselves on the ground in leisurely repose.

In the parking lot below, some of the factory workers had noticed the flailing legs dangling through the hole in the net that formed the canopy of vegetation overhead. They pointed and shouted, suddenly on high alert.

Down below, Jimmy's cries had escalated the urgency of the rescue operation. A fire truck was being maneuvered into position. One of the firefighters was frantically winding a big chrome wheel that extended the ladder into the air, while another controlled the angle and direction of its ascent. A man was already climbing the first section. Sure-footed and confident, he glanced up at the ladder ahead of him as he approached the distressed shepherd's dangling lower half.

Jimmy had found a seam in the netting, enabling him to get a firmer hand-hold, and was beginning to heave himself up when he heard the cries of someone beneath him.

"Hang on, pal. I'm nearly there."

Puzzled, Jimmy peered through the gaps in the netting and could just make out the helmeted head of his would-be rescuer.

The firefighter grabbed Jimmy around the thighs and began to pull him towards the safety of the ladder. "It's OK, buddy. I've got you."

Jimmy lost his grip on the netting and felt himself starting to slip.
He cried out.

"Let go. You're pulling me down. I'm trying to get back up."

"Let go! I'm trying to …"

"I've got you this side. Just let yourself drop. You'll be all right."

The professional firefighter is accustomed to victims in distress; he knows how they can be uncooperative and difficult. Just like a cat stuck up a tree, the minute the rescuer makes a grab for the poor animal, it will screech and scratch and wriggle and fight—do everything it can to get away. Survival instinct forces it to resist. It is scared and it doesn't understand that the firefighter means it no harm; that he's there to help. In situations like this, the rescuer must use a firm hand to take control, to overcome that resistance. The victim will thank him for it later.

A few fields away, Howard Farmer's tractor was still tootling steadily back and forth along the rows of crops in his field. Though Howard was no longer at the wheel, like the vehicles on Overland's main transportation system, the tractor kept rolling along. But after weeks of following the same regimented to-and-fro pattern, it now seemed to be deviating from its routine. Instead of turning round at the end of the row to continue back up the slope in the opposite direction as it usually did, the tractor kept on going down the slope towards the edge of the field where the ground gave way to a sheer drop to the factory yard below, and it showed no signs of stopping. Whether through a wilfully self-destructive act—a response, perhaps, to having been left driverless—or through some mechanical failure that had caused the vehicle to become disengaged from its track, the outcome now seemed inevitable. And with so few Residents remaining, there was no one to avert, or even to witness, the impending catastrophe.

As the tractor reached the furthest extent of the field, it toppled over the edge, quickly disappearing from view. And just like that, it was gone.

TWENTY-TWO

A series of fifty-feet-high watchtowers had been erected just beyond a five-strand barbed-wire perimeter fence on flat, barren ground. From the observation platform of one of them, a guard in American army uniform with an M1 rifle slung over his shoulder leaned out over the balustrade idly surveying the area through binoculars.

The main entrance gatehouse had a tiled pagoda-style roof. The decision to incorporate an architectural feature reminiscent of "the mother country" (a country most of them had never seen) was presumably the American government's attempt to convince the prisoners as they first entered the camp that they had arrived at a veritable home from home. Beside the gatehouse was a painted wooden sign sticking up out of a pile of rocks. In big letters it said *STOP*, then underneath: *Manzanar Internment Camp. No Admission except on official business. US Department of Justice.*

The camp extended over a vast area of open desert valley. Laid out in tightly regimented lines were seemingly endless rows of hastily constructed, tarpaper-covered wooden buildings like military barracks, each one twenty feet wide and a hundred feet long. Many were still under construction. Beyond them in the distance was the towering wall of the Sierra Nevada mountains, pale blue-gray powdered with snow and shrouded by a hazy cloud of dust.

Hanging from a piece of rope outside one of the buildings was a large piece of iron that had been bent into a triangle. A man struck it repeatedly with a club hammer, the dull clanging signaling lunchtime. The doors to one of the buildings were folded back; entry into it monitored by uniformed soldiers. Crowds of Japanese internees waited patiently in line.

Inside was barn-like with exposed timbers and no ceiling. A long chain of prisoners, each clutching a plate and a mug, waited to be served food by fellow internees in aprons and little white caps. The dish of the day was a handful of rice with a ladleful of something brown on top.

Accommodation in the barrack buildings was provided by basic iron-framed army cots with thin mattresses, lined up in long rows, little more than an arm's length apart. Those that were unoccupied came with a pillow on top of a folded blanket. Most were already claimed, with picture postcards and snapshots pinned to the bare plywood wall above the bed. Among the keepsakes brought from home were several American flags and, above one bed, portraits of George Washington, Abraham Lincoln and President Roosevelt.

On her first day at the camp, Kay had been sent to a hut designated for single women (i.e. those with no family). She approached one of the vacant beds to which a handwritten number on a slip of paper

was attached; she checked it against the raffle-ticket number she had been given. Hers, she noticed, was the only bed without a pillow.

The bed next to hers was at the end of the row with a wall on one side and a window above the head end. A Japanese woman was already well "settled in." She lay on her back, propped up by two pillows, her hands clasped behind her head and her eyes closed, a blanket wrapped loosely about her. She was wearing thick over-sized wool socks that had lost their shape. All the other clothing she had managed to bring with her hung on display from a series of clothesline strings suspended above her head, like a market stall. There were dishrags and underclothes, scarves, skirts, socks. Hanging from nails between the two beds was a hat with flowers on it, a drawstring toiletry bag and a cardigan. More things were piled on the cross-beams of the wall's studwork: an enamel plate propped up, a box of crackers, ointments, pills, photographs in frames—all of it encroaching on Kay's limited allocated space. But she had no possessions with which to counter the infringement.

By night the temperature dropped. Kay had been so cold the night before that she couldn't sleep. She lay fully dressed in her factory overalls—all the clothes she had—huddled under the thin blanket. Throughout the long night she listened to the low whistle of the wind, which intermittently threw grit and dust in hissing sheets against the outside walls of the hut, the sound brittle and dry like radio static.

She must have slept eventually because she awoke the next morning to the sound of someone sweeping the floor and found everything, including herself, covered in a fine layer of sand dust. It was everywhere: in her eyelashes, in her nostrils. When she scratched her scalp, she felt a gritty residue beneath her fingernails.

In one of the women's latrine blocks, she was among those waiting in line to use the facilities: a row of a dozen toilets which, like the beds, were an arm's length apart with no partitions between them. All were permanently occupied in strictly supervised rotation, each vacancy quickly taken up by the next user from the line.

Undercooked and unrefrigerated food had made diarrhea a pressing problem for many. A pair of middle-aged internees had volunteered to provide a modicum of privacy by holding up a bed sheet to form a curtain around one of the toilets. They stood with their arms raised, clutching the top of the makeshift canvas cubicle, heads discreetly turned to demonstrate their respectful detachment from the functions being carried out on the other side.

The indignity was too great for some to bear. Offered no such privacy, one elderly woman, her underwear around her ankles, was so racked with shame that she had put a pillowcase over her own bowed head like a prisoner awaiting execution.

Outside, Kay leaned against the wall of the latrine block, looking out over the barren landscape. There were no other buildings for miles: nothing but parched, open wilderness.

It was strange to see so many Japanese faces. Here Kay looked like everyone else; she should have fitted right in, yet she felt strangely alien, like an imposter.

It surprised her how compliant everyone was. They had been forced to relinquish their homes, their possessions, their rights, yet there was no rebellion, no revolt. Once they'd crossed the camp threshold, they seemed to accept their fate and make the best of things, learning the new rules and settling into the routines. Not that they had any choice, she realized. Besides, everyone was frightened; nobody knew what was going to happen to them. They were made to feel ashamed of being Japanese, and blamed for the heinous "yellow peril" attack on America. In response, the internees cooperated fully and followed orders as a way to prove their loyalty to the US. It wasn't just the *issei* either—the older people who spoke Japanese among themselves. Even third- and fourth-generation Japanese like Kay—non-Japanese speakers who had never been out of America—seemed to have somehow inherited this shared passivity. Perhaps it wasn't that exactly. Kay remembered Mrs Ishi sometimes using a Japanese phrase, *shikata ga nai*—it can't be helped. It described the Japanese people's ability to accept circumstances beyond their control and maintain dignity in the face of unavoidable tragedy or injustice. Kay wasn't sure she really got it; perhaps, several generations removed, it had become too diluted in her blood.

She saw how families in the camp clung together, finding solace and stability through the family union; it made her worry about Mrs Ishi, the nearest thing to family she knew. Sooner or later she too would be rounded up and sent to a camp somewhere to face the indignities and hardships alone. Kay couldn't help thinking about the poor woman with the pillowcase over her head; she kept imagining how that could have been Mrs Ishi. It wasn't—she saw the woman's face later in the washroom—but the idea of Mrs Ishi being forced to suffer such humiliation was more than she could bear. *Shikata ga nai* could only go so far.

Kay shook her head. "I've got to get out of here." She was really talking out loud to herself, but a woman sitting on the ground nearby took up the conversation.

"How?"

"I don't know."

"You can't escape. They'll shoot you."

"People come and go all the time."

"You need a pass to get out of here. Anyhow, why would you want to escape? You know how you'll be treated on the outside. It's only going to get worse. At least you're safe here."

"But for how long? We don't know what they have planned for us."

"Where would you go? If you go home, they'll find you. They're gonna find you anyway. And even if you do get out, you're in the middle of the goddamn desert. You'd have to walk for days to get to the nearest town—if there is one. You'd die of thirst. That's why no one tries to escape. There ain't nowhere to hide."

Kay folded her arms determinedly. "I know a place. If I can just get to it."

George sat alone at one of the tables in the Overland Diner. He was there more out of habit than anything else. No Effie or Residents to talk to and, more pertinent to his present needs, no food to eat. The donuts he'd found that morning behind the counter had a powdery coating of green mold on them. As for the coffee—that had all gone even before the last of the Residents had departed, whenever that was; he wasn't entirely sure. On the first day of major hunger, he'd gone scavenging through the town and discovered a bag of peaches that someone had left on the tennis court. Later he found a real can of Hormel Ham among the dummy packaging in the window of Kaiser's drugstore. The ham with the peaches was a surprisingly good combination: the saltiness of the meat, the sweetness of the fruit—he salivated, just thinking of it. The next day, despite promising himself that he wouldn't, he ate both cans of Japanese sardines and the apple left in his fruit bowl at Lakeside Cottage. Now, with his rations all gone, he was running on empty.

The prospect of returning to the world below, even to fetch rations, filled him with dread. His thoughts quickly strayed to the disastrous marriage from which Overland had become such a blessed escape—especially once he'd figured out what was going on. Back then, even with the evidence right under his nose, he had failed to see that Muriel and Gus's roller-skating partnership had strayed beyond the parameters of the rink.

One night in early February, George had come home late after a long day at the studio. Muriel was asleep so he undressed in the dark and slipped between the bedcovers without switching on the light so as not to wake her.

When he turned to put his wristwatch on the nightstand, he noticed a tie clip that did not belong to him lying in the ashtray. He picked it up and studied it in the dim light. It was gold and had an antique-car motif with fake rubies as headlamps. At the time, he assumed that Muriel had bought it for him as a gift and forgotten to hide it. George had regarded the clip as rather vulgar—more Muriel's taste than his own—but he didn't want to spoil her little surprise so the next morning when he got up for work he left it there in the ashtray, pretending not to have noticed it. When he came back from the bathroom five minutes later, Muriel was lying in the same position as when he left her, apparently not having stirred, yet the clip had mysteriously vanished.

He said nothing.

A week later, he happened to spot Gus at the local Texaco station buying a can of Servalube motor oil (for his hair possibly?) and saw that he was wearing an identical tie clip. But instead of putting two and two together, as even the most unsuspecting husband would already have done, George imagined that Muriel had so admired Gus's handsome clip that she had decided to buy him one just like it as a Valentine gift. And all he could think about was how he was going to avoid wearing such a dreadfully tasteless item—further tainted as it now was by Gus's endorsement of it—without hurting her feelings.

He needn't have worried; the gift, of course, never materialized.

Outside the Sheet Metal and Routing building, a crane and a scrap-metal hauler had been brought in to deal with the wrecked tractor carcass discovered earlier that morning. A handful of men stood and watched as the crane's extended arm reached across, its grab claws widening in anticipation of the lift. Lurching to a halt over the desecrated remains, the grab suddenly pounced on the tractor as though afraid it might try to escape, determinedly tightening its grip around the vehicle's chassis before dragging it into the air. Part of the crumpled muffler broke loose and clattered to the ground. Swiveling on its base, the crane arm swung the tractor over the open top of the waiting hauler truck, then released its grip to dump it unceremoniously onto the tangle of scrap already on board.

Pasted onto the vehicle's side were posters urging the American public to donate their salvaged metal for the war effort. One showed a saucepan in mid flight. Underneath, the caption read *Send your pans flying. 5,000 make a fighter. 25,000 make a bomber.*

TWENTY-THREE

It was Kay's fifth day as an internee. She sat on an upturned pail in the shade of one of the huts, observing, as she had on previous days, the movement of traffic in and out of the camp's main entrance. There seemed to be hundreds of new arrivals each day. Buses transported them to the far side of the camp for processing, grading, inoculation and allocation of living quarters. Though there was no gate as such—each vehicle, each person entering and, more specifically, exiting, was carefully checked by the gate guard on duty, overseen by flanking watchtower guards.

She had noticed a workman wearing blue denim coveralls and heavy mud-caked boots who for some time had been crouched over something lying flat on the ground just inside the perimeter fence. It wasn't until he put on a full helmet mask that she guessed what he was doing. A concentrated crackle of white light confirmed it; he was welding.

She watched him for more than an hour, studying his movements, which seemed languid and lazy. At one point he wandered outside the camp to fetch something from the back of his pick-up truck parked a short distance away on the other side of the fence. Neither of the two nearest tower guards seemed to even notice him. He stood there measuring various bits of metal before returning to the job with one of them in his hand.

Sometime around noon, there was a distant sound of clanging from the lunch bell. The welding guy must have heard it because he downed tools, flipped off the current, removed his helmet and set it on the ground. When he turned round, Kay could see that though he had the slight frame and stature of a juvenile, he was probably in his forties. There was something of the Mickey Rooney look about him: a tall tuft of red hair and a face like a bulldog's behind. He headed into the camp along the main drag between the rows of buildings, presumably in search of whatever victuals were on offer. The gatehouse guard, busy with something inside his hut, had seen none of this so was unaware that the welder had left his post. As Kay saw it, a vacancy had opened up. She pushed her hair up into her baseball cap, which she turned back to front so that the peak pointed down her back like the girls in the factory sometimes did. She stood up, lingering in the shadows of the barrack room nearest the gate. It was the perfect opportunity, if she had the courage, but she had to act quickly—take the welder's place before the gate guard spotted that he was missing.

Hardly thinking what she was doing, she sauntered over to the welder's gear and dropped to her knees, quickly donning the helmet and gloves he'd left behind. So impetuously had she acted, it only

now occurred to her that she had not checked first to see if the tower guards were watching. What was she thinking? But after a minute or so when she remained unchallenged, she assumed that no one had noticed the switch. She was similar in stature, same baggy blue denim coveralls, near as damn it—and after all, who looks that closely at a welder? All anyone sees is the big domed head of the helmet and that sizzling splash of light. Besides, she was still inside the perimeter fence; she had not yet overstepped any official boundaries. Why would their suspicions be roused?

She imagined that Mickey Rooney would by now be safely sucking up soup in the staff canteen, but it didn't give her long. She looked down at the job he had been working on, a metal sign for the camp entrance: *Manzanar,* the individual letters fixed within a rectangular steel framework. He'd got as far as the Z.

Fixing the ground return to the frame, she switched on the current. She couldn't get the electrode to spark; it stuck to the work piece and she was forced to tug it free. She adjusted the amperage and tried again. Stroking the tip a few times, the electrode popped to life and continued to sizzle and fizz along the puddle of the welded seam. After a couple of minutes' pointless welding she paused, pretending to inspect one of the letters, turning her body to see what she could make out through her darkened visor window. The gate guard was just a stone's throw away. At first she thought he was looking straight at her until she realized his attention was fixed on an approaching flatbed truck behind her. It entered the camp and pulled up

beside the gatehouse. It was laden with an assortment of suitcases, parcels and wrapped bundles. The guard looked in the back, laughing convivially about something with the driver. They exchanged a few more words, and the guard scribbled a few notes on a clipboard before waving him on into the camp. He watched the truck for a few seconds and then went back inside the gatehouse. He appeared in no way suspicious, but could she be so sure of the tower guards? For all she knew, they may have been watching her every move. Glancing up, she saw that the tower to her left was not manned or the guard was sitting out of sight. The soldier in the tower on the right stood at the far end of his platform looking in the other direction. But what if it was a trap; what if he was only pretending not to have noticed her? Maybe he had watched her change places, knew exactly what she was up to, and was deliberately turning his back to inveigle her into making her escape. The moment she set foot outside the camp he might whip round and raise his rifle. Bang! Shot while attempting to escape. No one would question that. She suspected that all of the guards were just itching to take a potshot and, given a legitimate excuse, would enjoy nothing more than to spend the afternoon picking off Japs one by one like clay ducks in a shooting gallery.

Kay continued welding for a while and then set the electrode grip down on the ground, getting up off her knees. She stood with her hands on her hips looking down at the sign, hoping to appear both nonchalant and masculine. Her heart was racing. She dared not

look up at the watchtowers. She somehow felt that if she didn't look at them, then they wouldn't look at her. After a moment, she picked up a tape measure and strolled out of the camp towards the welder's pick-up.

Resting her elbows on the side of the truck, she flipped up her visor, but made sure to face away from the guards. Not knowing if they were watching her, she pretended to sort through some equipment in the back. She dug out a few offcuts of scrap metal and tossed them to the ground behind the truck, making a conspicuous show of measuring various pieces before sending them clattering onto the pile. Sidling round to the driver door, she saw through the open window that the key was in the ignition. She sneaked a glance up at the tower guard; his back was still to her. In the truck's side mirror, she could see the gate guard checking some paperwork, with no interest in what she was doing, but then beyond him she spotted the approaching figure of the little Mickey Rooney guy on his way back from lunch. The gate guard hadn't seen him yet, but Kay figured she had better make her move before he did. She opened the driver's door of the truck and jumped in behind the wheel.

She cranked up the engine and headed off down the road. Little Mickey slowly realized what was happening and started running after his stolen vehicle. Seeing his reaction, the gate guard put two and two together and turned to see the truck disappearing behind a thick rolling cloud of dust being kicked up from the surface of the road. Panicked, he darted back into the gatehouse and reached for the phone, but then thought better of it and ran out to the foot of one of the towers. He shouted up to the guard, jabbing his finger sharply at the disappearing pick-up, his outstretched arm quivering to emphasize the urgency of the crisis.

Spurred to action, the tower guard raised his rifle and took aim. A shot rang out.

TWENTY-FOUR

At Fort Benning, the staff sergeant was in the middle of roll call. Jimmy stood among a group of twenty rookie soldiers wearing all-in-one flight suits with their pants tucked into high-laced boots. As the sergeant fired off their names from his list, the men responded with a sharp and attentive "Here!" When Jimmy answered, he instinctively raised his hand like he was at school. Some of the others sniggered.

In a darkened barrack room, Jimmy sat among the new recruits watching a movie projected onto a screen. Cigarette smoke picked out the sharp beam of flickering light from the whirring projector behind them.

The film showed a black and white aerial shot of the countryside, a hazy patchwork of contrasting gray fields and roads. The figure of a falling man entered the frame and continued to tumble towards the ground below, growing gradually smaller in the picture. The film had no sound, which lent the sequence an eerie, dreamlike quality. When the man was almost out of sight, a straggly ribbon of white spilled from him, quickly taking the full billowing shape of an open parachute. Jimmy sighed with nervous relief. He tried to catch the eye of the soldier sitting next to him with a view to exchanging genial nods, but he turned away to talk to someone else.

Before he'd had chance to settle in, Jimmy's Overland jump practice was being put to the test. In one of the training hangars, a series of platforms stood at different heights, all of them far higher than the front porch of Shangri-La Cottage. Jimmy watched from the ground as in choreographed succession men jumped confidently down onto coir matting below, immediately rolling forward into a tidy somersault and springing back to attention like performing gymnasts. Later, when it was Jimmy's turn to jump, he lost his nerve, hesitating at the critical moment. He might have remained there on the platform edge for longer had he not felt a firm hand on the small of his back, pushing him over the edge.

Later that day, Jimmy and the other soldiers were gathered round the staff sergeant who was delivering a lesson. A kitted-out soldier, Garcia, stood beside him for demonstration purposes. The sergeant pointed to various parts of Garcia's equipment as he spoke.

"Your kit consists of a main chute and a reserve chute for emergency use only." He unhooked a length of webbing attached to the guy's backpack and passed it to one of the men whilst pointing to where it gathered into a series of bunched folds.

"This is known as your static line. This end attaches to a cable in the aircraft; the other end attaches to the cover of your main chute. When you clear the aircraft, your weight on the line pulls the threads loose holding the cover of your chute, releasing it into the

air. Like this. Brace yourself, Garcia. OK, Eisner."

Garcia turned and hunched forward in readiness like a downhill skier while Eisner obliged the sergeant by taking the static line for a run in the opposite direction. The chute cover was quickly released and, as Eisner continued on, the folded white silk inside tumbled out, stretching longer and longer on the ground behind him until the folded zigzag of lines whipped out and came taut, tugging Garcia over on his rear. The men laughed.

"Right. Fall out to the packing room where we'll show you the most important thing of all: how to pack your chute. A poorly packed chute is the quickest way to suicide."

The soldiers began to head off to another building. Jimmy caught up with Garcia.

"What about the reserve chute?" said Jimmy.

"Huh?"

"The reserve parachute. He didn't tell us how to use it."

"I guess he forgot."

"Forgot? Well, don't you think he should—"

"There's like a handle on the side. You just pull it. Nothing to it."

"Yes, but what if you can't get your hand to it? You panic or you black out? Someone said a lot of the guys get so scared they faint as they jump out the plane."

"Relax. Your main chute will get you down."

"Sure. In theory. But they don't give you a reserve chute for nothing."

"What's up, Shepherd? You chicken?"

Jimmy was indignant. "No, I'm not chicken. I just think we should have proper instruction. I'm thinking of the other guys as much as myself."

Garcia nodded knowingly. "Sure you are."

Later that day, Jimmy was heading back to the barracks from the mess hall. Garcia caught up, falling in step with him.

"A word of advice."

Jimmy turned.

"Whatever you do, do not surrender."

"Surrender? Who to?"

"Who d'you think? The Japs, you dummy. Once we get to the front line and those yellow bastards start coming at you, you'd better pray they shoot you stone dead 'cos if you get taken prisoner then boy, are you in trouble. Especially a pantywaist bed-wetter like you. My advice is to shoot yourself before they get to you. I'm serious."

"Why? What do they do?"

"You don't want to know—but I'll tell you. First off, you gotta understand the Japs are not like us. They're a bunch of sick, sadistic animals, see? They'll torture you just for kicks. You must have heard about the bamboo torture."

"No." Jimmy was not sure he wanted to.

"They tie you in place over the sharpened point of a fast-growing bamboo shoot. That stuff can grow two or three feet in a day. The point punctures and then penetrates your body till it eventually comes out the other side. Most times they shove it up your ass. Man, that's gotta be a painful death, having that thing growing inside you.

Then there's the 'water cure' where they make you drink gallons of water. They pour it down your throat until your stomach is—"

"Stop! I don't want to hear any more."

They entered the barracks; Garcia stayed with him. "I'm just telling you what they do. I'm trying to help you." He continued. "When you're nearly bursting, they kick you round the floor until your stomach splits open like a water balloon."

Jimmy tried to walk away, but Garcia attached himself like a limpet.

"Didn't you know about the Japs? They're inhuman, the goddamn lot of them."

"I can't believe anyone would do such a thing."

To his dismay, Jimmy found one of his squad sitting on his bed. It was Swain, a loud-mouthed jackass who liked to push people around—someone he had taken an instant dislike to on day one. Having overheard the tail end of the conversation, and seeing Jimmy's reaction, Swain seemed keen to crank it up a notch.

"Well, you'd better believe it, buddy boy. And remember to save the last bullet for yourself." Swain pointed under his chin. "Right here. Straight up through the top of your head. That way, you're guaranteed to blow your brains out; even *you* can't miss. But if you find yourself out of ammo, you're going to need your bayonet. Same point of entry. Right under the chin. Get your rifle pointing upwards, hands on top of your head and drop to your knees. Instantaneous death."

Jimmy undid the top button of his tunic. "I need to lie down. I don't feel too good."

"Aw. What's up? Feeling a little dizzy?" Swain's sympathetic tone was mocking. He got up to make way for him. "That's too bad. Now you just sit yourself down. And Garcia here will go fetch you a glass of water. A nice big glass." He laughed raucously and made a series of exaggerated cartoon gulping sounds deep in his throat: "Gurnk, gurnk, gurnk."

Over the course of the day, Jimmy grew increasingly anxious, particularly in open spaces: the cavernous hangars or out on the airfield where he now stood among the new recruits. No longer certain of the ground beneath his feet, he was tormented by a lurching need to clutch at something solid: a pillar, a post or a wall. He tried not to think about the distressing advice he had been given about what to do if captured, but the dreadful image haunted him. Somehow sensing his angst, Swain, who was standing next to him, met Jimmy's troubled eye with a wry smile. He leaned over, poking his index finger under Jimmy's jaw. "Chin up," he said.

Though on terra firma, Jimmy felt as if he was stranded on a tightrope a thousand feet in the air, petrified and with nothing but the wire beneath his feet to hang onto. As the staff sergeant stepped up to address the group, Jimmy had to resist the urge to grab the belt of the man standing in front him.

"Now this is probably the first time most of you will have seen a man jump from a plane. In a few days' time it'll be you up there waiting to jump."

The plane overhead droned by and the men raised their heads to watch a string of men being spat out of the open doorway, like some silvery sea-creature giving birth. A wisp of white spilled from each of their backpacks, billowing out into the full familiar mushroom-cap dome of a parachute. After six textbook deployments, the seventh man's chute seemed slow to fill with air. The staff sergeant was quick to identify the problem.

"The shroud lines are tangled! She's not going to open!"

While the first six men dangled below the safe canopy of their chutes, swaying gently from side to side as they slowly descended to earth, the seventh paratrooper was plummeting helplessly towards the ground. He accelerated at an alarming rate past his companions, a useless thin ribbon of fabric fluttering above his head.

Jimmy watched with horror, praying that some miracle would come in time, but it didn't. Before he had time to look away, the trooper hit the ground with a sickening thud.

Some of the men in the platoon cried out; others covered their faces with their hands.

The staff sergeant calmed them. "Take it easy, take it easy. It's just Oscar, our dummy."

Garcia was confused. "Dummy? You mean he's not real?"

They all breathed freely again; some chuckled with nervous relief. The sergeant beckoned the group. "Come on, I'll show you."

Everyone followed him, but Jimmy couldn't move. Suddenly finding himself alone, he felt horribly adrift. Panicked by the dizzying ocean of open tarmac around him, he instinctively fell to his knees, to make closer contact with the ground. He might have lain down, but he knew how odd that would look—his fear of humiliation for the moment superseding his fear of descending into the abyss. Even now, some of the squad had turned to see what was wrong. Swain seemed tickled at the sight of him kneeling there. "Look out, fellers. Quicksand." He nudged the guy next to him with a gurgling laugh. Others stared with more serious concern.

The sergeant doubled back to check on him.

"What gives, Shepherd? You sick or something?"

Jimmy tried to pull himself together. What must they be thinking? What was wrong with him? What was he doing? Praying? "Sorry, sir. Bit dizzy. I'll be all right in a minute."

The sergeant regarded him dubiously for a moment, glancing at Jimmy's shaking hands. Presently, he jerked his head. "Get yourself over there."

Jimmy somehow got to his feet and joined the rest of the squad who were gathered around the fallen seventh parachutist like mourners at a funeral.

While at the far end of the airfield, the rest of the jump team were landing softly on the ground, Oscar the dummy, still posed expectantly in the prescribed landing position, was lying face down in the dirt.

Jimmy felt Swain's hot breath on his ear. "You pay attention now. That could be you."

Jimmy looked forlornly down at Oscar.

"Pick him up, Shepherd," the sergeant said.

Jimmy did so. Oscar was a scale rubber model of a parachutist, less than two feet tall. The shroud lines trailed from the pack on his back to a parachute no bigger than a tablecloth.

"Hold him up so the others can see."

Jimmy turned Oscar round to face the group.

Garcia adjusted his cap. "Well I'll be. He's just a little feller. He looked life-size from over there."

The sergeant explained: "Oscar here took a dive to impress upon you men the importance of packing your parachute correctly. When the lines get tangled like Oscar's did, your chute won't open. We call that a Roman candle. Now, Oscar's a good soldier but he's dumb. He plum forgot to use his emergency chute."

"What a dummy!" Swain had elected himself as the unit's funny man.

The sergeant pointed at Oscar's reserve chute. "All he had to do was pull on this ripcord and he'd have had a second chance."

But to Jimmy this made no sense. How could Oscar be expected to pull his own emergency ripcord? He was just a dummy. Jimmy tugged at the tiny handle. It failed to budge. He tried again. Nothing. The emergency chute didn't even work. Poor Oscar never stood a chance in hell.

TWENTY-FIVE

Kay headed south on a straight empty road. No cars, no nothing. The rush of air through the open windows added to her sense of liberation. Having checked her rear-view mirror anxiously for the first twenty or thirty miles, now she began to relax a little. The prison guards did not seem to be in pursuit. She took off her hat and shook her hair free. The needle on the fuel-tank gauge was almost at full.

By mid afternoon the terrain had changed and there were more built-up areas, but she was still a long way from home. The fuel-gauge needle was beyond empty now and she had no money for gas. The sun continued to beat down. Somewhere way out in the boondocks the engine finally spluttered and then cut out; the pick-up rolled gently to a halt. Kay got out, slamming the door behind her. She pulled her hair up into a knot on top of her head, and secured it with her baseball cap before setting off on foot.

There was no sidewalk so she was forced to the very edge of the roadside, stepping off onto the dirt siding whenever a car passed. Occasionally one of them would slow and pull in to offer her a ride, then, seeing her face, step quickly back on the gas. To avoid contact with anyone she veered further away from the road and headed across rough scrubland where the hot, breathy hiss of distant traffic faded into the distance.

After walking for several miles, she was parched, weary and a little lost. She trudged across the vacant parking lot of a shop selling tires. A couple of battered hydraulic trolley jacks were sitting out front. There was an old gas pump set into an island of concrete, and a little distance away was a kid with his head under the hood of an Oldsmobile.

She peered into the window of the office. Seeing no one, she pushed the door and went inside, glad to be out of the unrelenting blaze of the sun. On the wall behind a sales counter hung various advertising posters, all depicting tires with sharply emphasized deep-edged grooves, promising positive traction and safe braking in wet weather. In the customer waiting area, there was a scruffy bench seat and next to it, a low table display of well-thumbed magazines.

Seeing a wall payphone, she dipped two fingers into the coin refund slot, hoping to scoop out a rejected nickel or dime, but she was out of luck. On the wall next to it was a Cracker Jack vending machine, but she found nothing there either.

She turned her attention to the water cooler in the corner, looking round furtively before pulling a paper cup from the holder. She filled it from the faucet below, feeling the cool, squishy weight of the water in the thin paper cup. She drank it down in one, the coldness catching her breath, and then refilled it. The cooler gave out a deep gulp as the

air bubbled to the top of the glass bottle. She was halfway through the second cupful when she saw a black and white police cruiser pulling off the road and heading towards the tire shop. Kay froze, the paper cup still in her hand. It hadn't occurred to her that it would be the cops, rather than the army, who would be chasing her down. Well, she did borrow the welder guy's truck, which, she realized, they would probably classify as theft. They must have discovered the abandoned truck and tracked her down. She considered crouching, or at least facing the other way, but instead simply stood, petrified, as the cop car crept slowly past the building. The driver turned to peer in through the window, but didn't seem to make eye contact with her; perhaps the reflection on the glass was too strong for him to see clearly. Whatever the reason, the car drove on by. She edged towards the door, just to make sure it had really gone, and was relieved to see it pulling back out onto the highway. She had all but calmed herself again when she was startled by the sudden appearance of a face at the window. It was an old man, squinting to see beyond the reflection. Catching sight of Kay, he tapped sharply on the glass with something metal: a key or a coin. She didn't know who he was or what he wanted, but she made for the door, hoping to bluster her way past him.

"Top her up, would you, son?" he said, blocking her escape.

Beyond him, she saw an old Ford parked by the gas pump. There was no one else around. The kid working on the Oldsmobile had disappeared, as had the Oldsmobile. Realizing that the man thought she worked there (and that she was a boy), she decided to play along. She studied the pump, unsure exactly how to go about it. Having successfully unhooked the nozzle of the hose she checked the dials. There was a handle on the side; she gave it a turn and the dial reset. She unscrewed the Ford's gas cap, inserted the nozzle and squeezed the trigger. The man leaned against his car's hood, gazing at the highway ahead. He took out a handkerchief to wipe the back of his neck.

Kay watched the dial go round, keeping an eye on the price.

"Get the windshield too, would you, kid?" said the man over his shoulder.

Kay nodded.

She replaced the nozzle, then looked around and saw an upturned soda crate on top of which lay a rag and a spray bottle. She squirted something soapy onto the glass and wiped it off again with the rag, moving round to do the same on the other side.

"How much do I owe you?"

"Ninety-five cents."

The customer took a dollar bill from his billfold.

"Oh. I don't have any change," said Kay.

"Keep it."

"Gee. Thanks."

As the man drove off, Kay stepped back into the office. She laid the bill on the sales desk and began to walk away. She looked back at the money, and then at the Cracker Jack machine with its big red painted price flash: *5 cents*. She hadn't eaten all day.

She peeped gingerly behind the sales desk and spotted a little wooden cash tray with a few coins in it. She plucked a nickel from one of the sections, tweezing it between forefinger and thumb, as if to prove that she was taking no more than she was rightly owed. This was her tip; she had earned it.

She made a beeline for the Cracker Jack machine, laid her nickel in the slot and slid in the lever with her thumb. It sprung back, having accepted her money. She pulled the drawer to claim her reward, but it was stuck. She tugged it hard, repeatedly jerking it towards her, but even using both hands, the drawer remained tight as a vice. She hammered on the front of the machine's metal casing with the heel of her fist, venting her frustration on the smug-faced sailor-boy logo painted on it. The boy waved at her mockingly, a greedy armful of giant Cracker Jack boxes drawn possessively towards him. The caption underneath warned her *The More You Eat The More You Want*.

Walking away from the tire shop, Kay passed two kids playing in a vacant lot: a boy of about seven years old, and a girl maybe a year or two younger. The boy had fashioned himself a rifle from a long, tapering shard of wood and was taking aim at a line of birds perched on a telegraph wire, making gunshot sounds as he imagined picking them off, one by one. *Kheeow! Kheeow! Kheeow!*

When the girl saw Kay, she put her fingers to the outer edges of her eyes and pulled the skin taut. The boy put down his rifle and followed suit, both of them mugging at her, barely able to see through their tightly slitted eyes.

"Sayonara!"
The girl repeated what she had heard the boy say. "Sayonara!"
Kay smirked feebly in half-hearted response.
The boy took up his rifle and aimed it directly at Kay's face. Kay instinctively cowered, raising her hands in surrender. Showing no mercy, the boy pulled the trigger. *Kheeow!*

Something was clearly wrong with Overland's traffic system; vehicles were moving sluggishly and juddering on their tracks. It had taken George some time to locate the problem. One of the roadside trees north of the Overland Diner had fallen diagonally across Providence Street, blocking traffic on the East loop. The tree had been pushed aside by the traffic flow, but part of it had become detached and was caught beneath the wheels of a two-door sedan, which was now struggling to move forward along the track. Consequently, traffic sequencing had been interrupted causing a truck on the West loop to collide with a dawdling taxicab at the Main Street intersection, shoving it off the road and into one of the flower beds in the town-square gardens. Another car in its path had slipped off the track and was now obstructing oncoming vehicles. George had to shut off the power and push the truck back a little way before he could drag the car to one side. Once he had removed the tree branch from under the sedan, he restored the power and things began to move more freely. He noticed, though, that many of the roadside trees were not securely fastened and wondered for how long the system would continue to run without the regular maintenance checks it needed. He realized now how much of the smooth running had been down to the Residents keeping an eye on things. He knew he was supposed to be in Seattle but he was damned if he was going to let Overland fall apart.

Mrs Ishi wrung her hands nervously.

"Quick. Before they catch you."

From the tire shop, Kay had headed south on Tujunga Avenue, an interminably long straight road flanked mostly by light industry, warehouses and small businesses. It was a hot afternoon so very few people were out walking. From time to time she'd pass someone working curbside on a truck, or a group of men chatting in a parking lot, but these people were too caught up in their own lives to worry about the nationality of Kay's ancestors. It was the police and army she had most to fear; they were the ones who would be out looking for her. It was only once she reached North Hollywood, when traffic became heavier, the streets busier, that she became more vigilant. Her best strategy, she realized, was to keep her head down and keep moving; that way no one had time to notice her. She finally made it back to Mrs Ishi's, having walked for several hours without a break. She was exhausted, but knew she couldn't risk staying there for long. She stood at the foot of her bed, wriggling her shoulders free from her coveralls.

"I'm going. I'm going. I just want to get out of this work wear and into normal street clothes."

"Your gray suit is hanging in closet. I pressed for you."

"Thanks, Mrs Ishi, you're a dear, but I need something with more color, something more, you know, American."

Kay crossed the landing into Queenie's room and opened the closet. Mrs Ishi followed, hovering in the doorway. She got the picture.

"Ah. Something trashy, like Queenie would wear?"

Kay reacted, surprised by the slight on her friend, but Mrs Ishi smiled back sweetly. Trashy was just a word she had picked up; it was more of an observation than a criticism.

"When does Queenie get off work?" asked Kay.

"Not until midnight. She is on evening shift."

"Oh. Well I'm sure she won't mind me borrowing something."

"Queenie, she was worried," said Mrs Ishi. "Looking for you everywhere. Someone at factory said they had taken you to camp. Nearly all Japanese have gone now."

Kay nodded. "I know. It's awful."

Though she didn't doubt Queenie's sincerity, Kay was aware of one of the likely reasons for her concern. Not knowing what Queenie had told Mrs Ishi, she broached the subject carefully.

"Mrs Ishi, do you know if Queenie managed to … ? She needed some money …"

"To pay doctor, yes. Bad toothache. He must take out tooth—stop pain. Appointment tomorrow. Very expensive. But she got money. Someone at factory."

"She did? That's swell." Kay had felt bad about having let Queenie down.

Kay moved cautiously to the window and looked out onto the street below, but could see no one there. She returned to her own room carrying the same cotton floral print dress she had borrowed for her job interview at the factory: brazen red, pink and white

flowers on a decorative leafy green background. She put it on and topped the outfit off with the wide-brimmed green hat. It was a stylish and elegant contrast to her greasy coveralls.

Checking her reflection in the dresser mirror she noticed that an old envelope had been propped up against it. Fastened through the back of it was Queenie's shiny enamel Resident pin. Written above it, in Queenie's loopy handwriting, were the words *Go Fish!* Kay took the pin and fastened it to her dress.

In the doorway, Kay hugged Mrs Ishi goodbye. Kay's sunglasses helped to mask her emotions. She held Mrs Ishi's face in her hands, looking searchingly into her eyes. Mrs Ishi blinked and the tears that had been welling up burst free and ran quickly down her cheeks in two straight lines. Kay wiped them away with her thumbs.

"I wish you'd come with me. They'll send you to a camp if you stay here."

Mrs Ishi shook her head dismissively, gently breaking free from the embrace. "No. My brother-in-law, Kiyoshi … he come tomorrow to fetch me in his car. Go live in Chicago with my sister." She took a neatly folded handkerchief from her sleeve, shaking it loose from one corner.

"Chicago? That's a long way," said Kay.

Mrs Ishi nodded, smiling weakly. She dabbed at the damp stains on her cheeks.

"And the bird too?"

"Yes. Mr Green come with me in car. Send for other things later."

"What will happen to the house?"

"My brother-in-law, he take care of it. Lawyers sort everything."

For a moment, Kay was thinking about her own possessions. For now, she would make do with the few things she'd packed in her blue suitcase; she'd have to sneak back to the house when things had died down.

"This secret place where you are going?" said Mrs Ishi. "You will be safe there?"

"Yes. Queenie will know where to find me."

"OK." Mrs Ishi seemed satisfied. "I told Queenie she can stay here till she finds new home."

"That's kind of you, Mrs Ishi." Kay bit her lip. "You're sure you'll be all right?"

Mrs Ishi nodded.

It was time to go. Mrs Ishi looked away, ushering Kay out onto the street. She tried to make light of their farewell, but as Kay headed down the path to the sidewalk, she glanced back and saw Mrs Ishi still standing there on the doorstep, looking sad, lost and alone.

TWENTY-SIX

Queenie stood nervously to attention outside the Landmark movie theater. People passed by: shoppers darting in and out of traffic, workers returning from lunch. Nobody paid her any notice.

Behind her, a poster promoting a Universal Pictures flick, *Back Street,* featured an impassioned Charles Boyer nuzzling up to Margaret Sullavan's ear. Though yielding to his affections, the faraway look in Sullavan's eyes suggested she was troubled by deep inner turmoil.

A recent telephone conversation played in Queenie's head.

Dr Young? I've got the money. Fifty dollars like you said.

Oh, yes. Eleven weeks wasn't it?

And a bit.

Be outside the Landmark theater at two o'clock tomorrow with the money. Don't tell anybody where you're going.

OK. Two o'clock.

I'll be in a black Studebaker Champion.

Queenie glanced up at the clock outside Jay's Jewelry. Ten after two. She checked each passing car until finally a scruffy black Studebaker swung into the curb. She approached the open passenger window, her hand on the door handle.

"Are you Dr Young?"

"Get in the back."

She did so, and he drove off before she barely had the door shut.

"Have you got the money?"

"Yes."

Dr Young took a faded blue and white floral bandana folded into a blindfold and passed it back to her.

"Here. Cover your eyes with this. And sit in the middle of the seat."

Queenie complied, sliding over so that her feet were either side of the central column of the car's drive shaft. There was a slight gap under the blindfold; she could see her own hands resting nervously on her knees.

The car drove round for a while, seemingly making a series of unnecessary turns and doubling back on itself. Queenie tilted her head to increase her field of vision until she could see the back of the driver's head. He wore a gray fedora and he could have used a haircut; thick black hairs sprouted from his neck like iron filings. There was an angry pink pimple just above the collar of his shirt, its pale green pus-filled center just waiting to pop. She nudged the blindfold a little higher with her knuckle hoping to see where she was, but instead caught sight of the driver's eyes in the rear-view mirror, staring back at her sternly. She quickly lowered her head again.

"My name's Queenie."

"I didn't ask, did I?"

*MEANWHILE *Lilium philadelphicum, or something resembling it, was among the blooms attached to a series of nets that had been bundled to form vibrant flower beds in the town square. The profusion of roses, hibiscus, chrysanthemums and begonias, all fashioned from waxed paper and plastic, provided a visual stimulus so strong that when the Residents were around to notice them they frequently commented on their pleasant fragrance. When told that the flowers were not real and therefore had no scent, passers-by had assumed that perfume had been added artificially or was somehow inherent in the plastic or paint. It wasn't, but memory and imagination were sufficiently powerful to trigger a floral fragrance as distinct and as genuine as any they had ever experienced.*

As the wind picked up, some of the flimsier paper petals became detached and were carried like confetti along the gutters of Hope Street.

Queenie would have snapped right back at him with something smart, but she was feeling jumpy and a little off her game so she buttoned it.

The Studebaker turned off the road and pulled up. Dr Young got out and walked around the car to speak to her through the open window.

"You can take that off now. Get inside, quick."

She removed the blindfold, blinking at the light, then opened the car door and slid out. They were parked by the side of an anonymous-looking house. It was modest in size with putty-colored siding in need of a lick of paint. The doctor ushered her quickly forward, looking about nervously. She climbed two steps up to a buckled screen door with a ragged tear in the mesh.

Beyond it was a small steamy kitchen with something cooking on the stove. A woman in her sixties stood over a black pot-bellied saucepan prodding the contents with a short, pointed knife. She looked up as Queenie entered, and dragged the lid on the pot with a clatter as if to keep whatever was in there private. She wiped her hands on her pinafore apron.

"Where's the money?" She was giving Queenie the up and down, but her question was aimed at the doctor, who had followed Queenie inside and was shutting the door behind them.

"She's got it."

There was a moment before Queenie recognized her prompt. She nervously took the money from her purse and handed it over to the woman, who unfolded the bills and counted them quickly before stuffing them into a coffee can on the shelf above the stove.

Dr Young and the woman headed off into the hallway, telling Queenie to wait.

She stood, nervously taking in her surroundings. There was a wooden table covered in patterned oilcloth, held in place by thumb-tacks along its edges. Its surface was laden with pots and pans. A mop and dull gray galvanized steel pail stood in the corner; a damp cloth had been draped over the end of the mop handle to dry. Looking round, Queenie made a mental note of each item as though she had been asked to take an inventory: a blackened kettle sitting on a footstool; two empty milk bottles; a grubby towel hanging from a rail on the back of the door; a calendar featuring the famous Dionne quintuplets, who were pictured standing in a field of daisies, wearing long Bo-Peep-style dresses and matching bonnets in a range of pastel colors. Below it, hanging from a fixture on the wall, was a mangled assortment of well-worn kitchen utensils.

Dr Young appeared in the doorway before she could take note of them all.

"This way," he said.*

Queenie followed him back down the hallway to another room.

He opened the door and snapped on the light. The curtains were drawn and the bare bulb hanging from the ceiling picked out the gloomy contents of the small room. Against one wall there was a large office desk with its drawers missing. A large sheet of waxed paper covered its top. Next to the desk was a table with a pitcher

of water, a bowl and some paper cups. The woman entered and dumped a shallow stack of folded hand towels on the table next to the pitcher. Dr Young got down to business.

"Take your panties off and lie down on the desk with your legs apart."

Startled by the bluntness of his request, Queenie hesitated. The woman saw that Queenie had failed to respond.

"It can't be the first time a man's asked you to do that."

Dr Young chided her. "Ma!"

"Well, she wouldn't be here if she'd learned to keep her knees together."

"I'll deal with this. You get back to the kitchen."

"Don't worry. I'm going. Got better things to do."

Dr Young took off his coat and began to roll up his shirtsleeves. Queenie was feeling apprehensive. "Are you a real doctor?"

"Of course."

"Why don't you have a proper doctor's office?"

"I do, but I can't take you there, can I? Don't worry, it'll all be over in a few minutes."

She quickly removed her underpants and stuffed them in her tartan purse on the side table.

"Will you give me something? To put me to sleep?"

"No need."

"Will it hurt?"

"Now, I just need to explain a few things. Afterwards, you'll bleed quite a bit. That's normal. And you'll feel some discomfort, naturally." He handed her a small bottle of Aspro. "Take two of these if the cramps get too bad. Do you have the number to call me?"

"Yes."

"You have it with you?"

"Yes."

"Let me just check that."

She handed him the card on which she originally noted down Dr Young's number.

"Ah, yes. This number doesn't work any more. Let me give you my new number."

He took a letter from his pants pocket, tore off the triangular envelope flap and wrote something on it. He folded it in half, and then in half again. He opened her handbag and slipped the tiny triangle into her coin purse, then snapped it shut. The sight of the doctor's hands rummaging uninvited in her purse painted a disconcerting picture of what was to come.

"Keep it safe. Don't call unless it's an emergency."

"What kind of emergency? I'll be all right, won't I?"

"Fainting, fits, that sort of thing. They're quite rare."

"How will I know if everything's all right? Afterwards?"

"Be at the Black Cat Cafe tomorrow. She'll stop by to check you're OK." With a gesture of his head, he indicated "she" to be "Ma" in the next room.

"The Black Cat?"

"It's right across the street from the Landmark theater where I picked you up."

"What time?"

"Four o'clock."

Queenie nodded. She took in a deep breath, letting it out in a long anxious sigh.

Ten minutes into the procedure, Dr Young was getting agitated, working some instrument deep inside her while trying to hold her still by pressing hard on her stomach. Queenie was begging him to stop. When he didn't, she tried to pull away, to draw her knees together, but his elbows were forcing them apart.

"Quit moving. I can't do what I need to do with you jumping around."

The pain was like nothing she'd ever felt before: an excruciating, searing pain, intense and tight—a pinching, acid-burning, needle-scraping sting way up in the sharpest, uppermost register. Somewhere lower down, a darker, heavier aching, like a lead weight on a jagged hook dragging out her innards. Something warm and sticky was pooling on the wax paper under her. It threw her in a panic. She screamed.

"Hey! Hey! Pipe down," Dr Young hissed.

Ma ran in the room in a flap. "What the devil are you doing to her? Do you want the neighbors round here?" She glanced between Queenie's legs. "What happened?"

Dr Young was clearly distressed. "I don't know. Something's gone wrong. She wouldn't keep still."

Queenie tried to sit up on her elbows. She caught sight of the doctor's gory hands and a rusty smear up one of his forearms before Ma pushed her firmly back down.

"Just lie still and let the doctor do what he's gotta do."

She couldn't. "Stop. Please stop. Ow! Stop! Stop!"

Ma was getting panicky. "You'll have to give her ether."

"She'll be here for hours if we do. I want her gone from here."

"We've got to shut her up. Someone will send for the cops."

It troubled Queenie that they were talking about her like she wasn't there. She screamed again to prove that she was.

Ma had had enough. She turned to her son. "We have no choice."

She grabbed a medicine bottle of clear liquid from a cake tray, unscrewed the top and spilled a big swig onto a hand towel. Queenie recoiled as the pungent odor caught her. She barely had time to react before Ma clamped the towel to her nose and mouth, turning her own face away from the suffocating fumes. Anxiety rising, Queenie was trying desperately to struggle free, to wrench the cloth from her face, but Dr Young stepped in to secure her flailing wrists while Ma overpowered her.

Queenie widened her eyes, fighting to remain conscious, but it was futile; she felt herself plummeting as the acrid-sweet vapor sent her into oblivion.

TWENTY-SEVEN

George stood with his fists in his pockets, staring hopefully into the middle of the lake. The daylight fell through evening into night, the passing hours seeming like brief seconds, and George was still waiting.

He couldn't get used to the fact that there was no one else around. Even the stragglers had left; he was totally alone. Without its Residents, the days passed without incident. Overland felt strangely empty and depressed—not the place he had designed at all. He had not realized what an essential role they played.

The next morning, he was across the street from the Orpheum movie theater, trying to summon the courage to enter. The Orpheum was the one building that until now he had avoided, knowing it to hold, amongst the assorted props and costumes, the disquieting little portal to the "other" world; a place to which he had become increasingly reluctant to return. Though he was filled with an uneasy dread about embarking on the journey, he feared that if he did not, he would never find Kay.

Inside, he discovered that the trapdoor had been shut tight, presumably bolted from the other side. Looking around the room, he spotted a garden spade—the perfect prop for his needs. He stomped on the shoulder of the blade to wedge its cutting edge into the crack between the trapdoor and the frame, enabling him to lever the hatch free.

It opened with a splintering crack.

With the door now fully folded back, he leaned cautiously over, peering down through the gaping rectangular hole.

Beyond the short ladder, the staircase seemed to extend for a mile underground. Its perspective fell away into the cavernous world below, dimly lit and unforgiving. Noise of industrial commotion rose up: clattering hammers, whining drills and splattering rivet guns against the constant drone of machinery and the furious hiss of compressed air. The occasional flash from a welding torch or a spray of sparks from an angle grinder briefly cast an eerie blue glow onto the space below before it fell back into blackness. To George, it was like looking into the pit of hell.

Down below, the morning shift was in full swing: everywhere brisk efficiency and maximum effort. A pair of metalworkers slid a wobbly sheet of aluminum onto a pattern-cutting bed. A forklift carrying metal parts passed by. Busy workers swarmed round a half-constructed fuselage like insects feeding on an animal carcass. No one noticed George's hesitant climb down the iron staircase to the factory floor.

He found the brutal cacophony of industry unnerving. He looked up at the massive machines, awed by the sheer scale of production. Some were as big as two-story houses, with complex mechanisms and indeterminable functions. Navigating a tentative path around the activity, he ventured into the depths of the factory.

A line of women in bib overalls and protective eyewear worked with single-minded focus at bench lathes, milling and drilling precision parts, their machines dribbling milky white lubricant. Behind them, intricately tooled metal shapes passed by on their conveyor-belt journey to some other part of the factory. One of the women glanced up from her work to take in the stranger, but her concentration remained unbroken. George scrutinized the goggled faces of her co-workers, in the hope of spotting Kay, but she did not appear to be among them.

Further on, George came upon a woman setting flat panel sections under a bench press. She had to position them just right before a huge weight clamped down on them, instantly shaping the two-dimensional sheet into a three-dimensional form. George edged over to her.

He raised his voice above the hissing and whirring. "Hello."

The woman looked up briefly—a little smile. "Hello."

"I'm looking for Kay."

She shrugged, uninterested.

"She works here with another girl, Queenie."

The woman shook her head. "Sorry."

A little further on, he approached an older woman.

"Do you know a girl called Kay? She works here in the factory."

She too shook her head, indicating not so much that she didn't know her, but that he was asking a futile question. "Which department is she in?"

"I don't know."

"You don't know? Gee, mister. There's twenty-five thousand people work here and a third of them are women. She could be anywhere in the factory."

"She must work round here someplace. She's petite. Dark hair. Pretty. As a matter of fact she looks kind of Japanese."

"Well if she's Japanese, or even looks Japanese, she's history."

"History?"

"They came and took all the Japs away."

"Who did?"

"The army. I saw a load of them being rounded last week. Sent to prison camps."

"Whereabouts?"

"Most of them go to what they call assembly centers first. Probably the one in Pomona; they set up a camp there in what used to be the county fairground. Unless she's a 'disloyal,' then she might have gone

straight to one of the big concentration camps, like Manzanar—that's two hundred miles north of here."

A steamer trunk, three suitcases and a birdcage were lined up neatly by the door in Mrs Ishi's hallway. The caged Mr Green edged nervously along his perch. He paused, craning his neck as if trying to identify some distant sound. Mrs Ishi sat on the hall chair beside him. She was wearing a dark two-piece suit with a white lace-edged collar and she had curled her hair in a kind of roll that framed her face. She straightened her necklace and then began fussing with her handkerchief, transferring it first from her sleeve to her purse; and then from one part of her purse to another. Satisfied, she checked her watch against the hall clock.

"We're all set, Mr Green. Going to Chicago."

Mr Green eyed her between the bars of his cage, saying nothing.

"Yes," said Mrs Ishi brightly. "Chicago." Her voice betrayed a note of apprehension. "Kiyoshi will be here anytime now."

Forty minutes later they were still waiting when she heard footsteps on the path, but it was only the mailman. She got up to open the letter he had brought, reading the contents with a troubled look.

Mr Green watched from his cage. "What is it?" he said.

Mrs Ishi turned the page over to finish the letter before answering. The color had drained from her face.

"It's from my sister," she said slowly. "Kiyoshi. He's not coming."

Mr Green took a moment to respond. "Oh, no," he said.

TWENTY-EIGHT

George emerged from one of the factory hangars into a kind of goods yard. Fractured beams of light filtered through the camouflage netting overhead onto parked trucks stacked with pallets of steel rods and aluminum sheeting. After a frustrating twenty minutes looking for the way out of the plant, he found himself on the camouflaged runway: a straight, flat piece of painted tarmac that stretched out before him into the distance.

Being on the ground, and therefore under the jurisdiction of the military, the runway pattern painting had been carried out by Colonel Lund's men as part of the US Army's practical rather than conceptual contribution to the Overland deception. To blend in with the surrounding landscape when viewed from the air, the shape of the landing strip had been interrupted by irregular painted shapes, both on and beyond its surface, to break the perceived visual border. Incorporating ideas already tried and tested in Europe—*trompe l'oeil* patches of black, green, brown, gray, white, and occasionally orange—were contrived to resemble fields, rows of houses, and areas of woodland. Additional roads and paths had been added using lengths of gray tarpaper or by burning strips of existing grass, which intersected the runway at unexpected angles to further confuse the eye. George had played an important part in drawing up the plans, but had never seen the finished effect. At ground level it was hard to picture how this might look from the air.

Imagining a bird's-eye view, George pictured his own tiny figure traversing the obscure two-dimensional reality, corrupting the intended three-dimensional illusion. Having crossed an orange grove by stepping across the treetops, he saw himself walking vertically up the front wall of a farmhouse, over its pitched roof, and onto the building's painted shadow on the other side—all without breaking step. In the harsh sunlight, George's own shadow would look like a length of black velvet attached to his heels, a theatrical effect borrowed from Peter Pan.

George heard the low hum of an engine behind him. He turned, catching the suggestion of something gray looming in the distance. He continued to stare, unable to make out whether what he was seeing was some sort of approaching vehicle or merely the trees on the horizon appearing to shift in the undulating heat-haze from the runway. One second later, he realized it was an airplane coming straight towards him along the runway. Unable at first to gauge its tremendous speed, it was almost upon him before he instinctively dropped onto his haunches and covered his head. There was a deafening roar as the plane's dark mass passed over him and he was dragged off-balance by the pull of the ground air beneath the aircraft.

He extended an arm to steady himself, averting his face from its dusty wake. Once the plane had passed he straightened up to see the familiar silhouette of a P-38 Lightning banking to its right as it climbed steeply into the sky.

The plane seemed to be circling.

George looked up over his shoulder anxiously, as if being pursued by a bird of prey. He'd lost sight of the plane, but the snarl of its engines still rang in his ears. He decided to run for cover, gripped by the same panicky adrenaline rush of fear that, as a kid, would spur him to sudden flight: spooked while walking alone through a dark forest or graveyard, he would imagine he was being chased by some unknown sinister force, and bolt into the night like a pony with its tail on fire.

There was no reason to suspect that the plane had deliberately tried to run him over—his own stupid fault for walking on the runway—or that it was intent now on hunting him down, yet George was still troubled by it.

He left the runway, taking a path off to his left that led towards a gate between two yellow hedges. Were the hedges real or phony? He could no longer tell. Real, they looked real. Their color seemed too bright, but that's nature for you. He made a mental note. He tried the gate, pushing and pulling, but it was either stuck or locked so he vaulted over it, landing clumsily on the other side. He paused to catch his breath for a moment, crouching by the gatepost and peering up at the sky.

Five hundred yards farther on, he came to a winding lane and a gray Buick parked at the curb outside a row of pretty cottages. Beyond the houses, the road disappeared into the shady depths of what looked like a hillside tunnel.

George crossed the road to the car. He recognized it as his own, but he was puzzled to find it parked there since it was not where he remembered leaving it. He delved into his pants pocket and pulled out his car keys. Fumbling to find the right one, he heard the buzzing of engines overhead as they changed direction; he looked up, scanning the skies, but was unable to spot the plane's position. Was it flying away or merely circling? Was it there at all? He tried his key in the car door, but couldn't locate the keyhole. When he pulled the handle, he found the door was unlocked so he opened it and climbed in. Something about the car seemed unfamiliar. He reached for the starter button to discover that the dashboard controls were merely two-dimensional painted images. He ran his fingertips along their surface to test the illusion. The steering wheel was real, but fixed solidly in position; it wouldn't turn an inch. He looked down into the footwell—no pedals. Perplexed, he climbed out of the car and saw that it was an obviously constructed wooden fake, just like the cars in Overland. Furthermore, now that he looked more closely, he realized that the nearby houses were fake too: fabricated from painted construction panels. How come he hadn't noticed all this before? He presumed he must still be on the outskirts of Overland, yet he did not recall building, or even visiting, this part

of town. Had he somehow strayed onto one of the film-studio backlots? Warner Brothers, maybe? No. It was more likely that the cottages and automobile had been put there by the military, adopting George's techniques to enhance the concealment of the runway. Blurring the boundaries from both sides; no wonder he'd been fooled. Even he had failed to spot the tell-tale edge.

The grass at his feet appeared to be genuine. He decided to make sure, bending to pluck a daisy growing amongst the blades of grass. Twirling the stem between finger and thumb, he touched its silky petals to his lip. Satisfied, he threaded the flower's stem through his buttonhole, but he pulled too hard on it and the head fell severed to the ground.

The sound of the circling plane returned. Feeling conspicuous, he ducked for cover under a nearby tree. He peered up through the leaves, but there was no visible sign of it. He had taken it for granted that, like the grass, the tree was real, but when he leaned against its trunk, it toppled and then keeled over, leaving him exposed to view from above.

He ran from the stark sunlight into the cool gloom of the tunnel's mouth, where he felt safer, calmer. He doubted now whether the P-38 had been after him at all. Probably just a test pilot carrying out checks on the latest output from the production line, hence the constant circling. He felt a little foolish about how he had reacted.

The tunnel, he now saw, was more like a tree tunnel, where shimmering light filtered through a more or less continuous canopy of overlapping greenery. He looked down at his chest to see how the dappled sunlight was creating a natural disruption camouflage pattern, just like that printed on soldiers' uniforms, which he imagined would render him indistinguishable from his surroundings. Ideal in combat, but here in the tunnel it occurred to him that any approaching vehicles might not be able to see him. As a safety precaution he stepped to the side of the road and made his way along the bordering grass verge.

Deeper into the tunnel, he found the hedgerows populated by an abundance of rich blooms: red roses, pink and white chrysanthemums, seemingly growing wild amongst the grasses and vibrant green leaves. The flowers looked almost too picture-book perfect, their arrangement too deliberate; George trailed his hand through them to reassure himself that they were real, but found he couldn't tell the difference.

TWENTY-NINE

The others in Jimmy's platoon had begun to decorate the inside of their footlocker lids with pictures. Some had family photos, there were pictures of guys proudly holding big fish, snapshots of automobiles, but the majority were saucy calendar pin-ups or shots of glamorous movie stars—Betty Grable, Veronica Lake, Rita Hayworth—a testament to their healthy male instincts. Jimmy saw an opportunity to create a little shrine of his own. He took an envelope of pictures from the bottom of his locker. One of the guys, Harris, had sold him a length of Scotch tape for a nickel.

His first was a snapshot of his mom posing in the yard. She stared dutifully into the camera, looking awkward and stiff, the long shadow of the unseen photographer prone on the ground like a paper silhouette. After some consideration, Jimmy returned the picture to the envelope; none of the other guys seemed to have pictures of their folks and he didn't want to be seen as a momma's boy. There was a picture of himself sitting astride his recently sold motorcycle. He studied it wistfully for a moment before taking a couple of pieces of tape to stick it up. Next he brought out a small box Brownie photo of his brother in uniform standing at ease in the front yard at home, legs apart with his hands behind his back, his pale face squinting into the sun. It was a picture Jimmy had taken just before Carl went overseas. The image was overexposed and thin, more so than he remembered it. Jimmy touched the picture's surface, rubbing Carl's face, as if the heat from his finger might stimulate the photo chemicals in the paper and bring his features back to life, but nothing happened. There were other pictures of home, which made him feel odd because it wasn't actually his home anymore—not for much longer anyhow. His mom had decided she was selling up and moving back to Iowa to live with Uncle Giff. He guessed that with Carl passing and Jimmy moving out at the same time, she must have been feeling too lonely to live on her own. But where did that leave Jimmy? Homeless. He supposed the army was his home now, though he hated to think it.

Next he brought out Queenie's eight-by-ten photographs, choosing his favorite, the one where she was looking demure. Eisner, who was passing by, happened to see it.

"Who's that? Ginger Rogers?"

"No."

"Barbara Stanwyck?"

"No."

Eisner snapped his fingers. "I know. It's that … what's her name. Carole Lombard. She's dead, isn't she?"

Jimmy sighed. "It's not Carole Lombard and she's not dead. Her name's Queenie if you must know."

"Queenie who?"

"Queenie Meyer."

Eisner was dismissive. "Never heard of her."

"You wouldn't have. Not yet, anyway. She's just getting started in movies."

"So she's a nobody. Not bad though. How come you've got this pin-up?"

"She's my girl. Back home."

"Get outta here. She's not your girl. You just picked up her picture someplace."

"No, I didn't. She gave it to me."

"Horse hockey! If she's your girl, how come she didn't sign it for you, lay a few kisses on it?"

Jimmy studied the picture, stuck for an answer. "I didn't think to ask her."

"No. Because you've never met her. If you're dating that broad, I'm dating Groucho Marx."

Swain walked by, catching wind of the conversation.

"Dating what broad?"

"Romeo here thinks he's dating this movie starlet."

"Let me see."

Jimmy tried to put the picture away, but Swain grabbed the corner between thumb and forefinger and was yanking at it. Rather than let the picture get creased or torn, Jimmy reluctantly let go. Swain studied the picture, nodding.

"Not bad. Not bad. Who is she?"

"She's a nobody," said Eisner.

Swain spotted the other eight-by-tens, snatching them from Jimmy's locker. "Hey, what's all this? Well looky here. Here's the real meat, fellers."

The other men began to cluster.

"Give those back. She's not public property."

"You could've fooled me."

Swain flicked through the pictures: Queenie perched on a button-back couch, pouting coquettishly, her lacy negligee provocatively lowered to expose her bare shoulders and a little cleavage; Queenie looking sultry in a tight swimsuit and high heels, draped along the diving board of a hotel swimming pool; Queenie in a low-cut dress leaning alluringly towards the camera, her hands behind her head and her chest thrust proudly forward; Queenie perched on the hood of an automobile, with the hem of her skirt raised to facilitate the apparent need to adjust her garter.

Swain became increasingly enthusiastic. "Holy jumping catfish."

The other men leaned in, lasciviously ogling the pictures. Swain took his favorite in both hands and held it to his nose, closing his eyes to breathe in deeply. He stuck out his tongue and slowly licked the glossy surface of the photo from bottom to top.

Jimmy was revolted by the degrading assault and snatched the picture from him.

"You dirty, disgusting ..." He was speechless with indignation.

The picture's glazed surface had been dulled and made sticky by Swain's saliva. Jimmy tried to wipe it off with his sleeve, but the fabric dragged on the wetted area. He gathered the pictures into a pile, stowing them in his locker and slamming the lid shut.

Swain laughed at Jimmy's prudish reaction.

"Now don't tell me that's the first good tonguing she's had."

Jimmy was too furious to speak.

Swain turned away, clacking his sticky tongue noisily against the roof of his mouth as he considered the unusual aftertaste.

That night, shortly before lights out, the men were preparing for bed: undressing, combing their hair. Swain sat on his bed in shorts and undershirt, one foot crossed over his knee, enabling him to pick the dirt from between his toes. Jimmy was already tucked up in the next bed, trying to concentrate on the book he was reading while Swain loudly held court over the others.

"Once they know you're gonna be in uniform, fighting overseas, most dames come across with the goods. You say, 'Listen sweetheart, I'm off to fight in the war, serving my country, and I don't know if I'll be back. Give me something special to remember you by.' And before you know it, their panties are off and they're giving you everything they got. You're the big hero, see, and they feel they owe it to you. It's their patriotic duty, right? To comfort you in your hour of need."

Eisner was gazing longingly at a magazine cover portrait of Lana Turner. "My hour of need is right now."

The others sniggered.

"Boy, this one girl I'd been swapping chews with, she was a real slinky piece of homework."

Jimmy turned on his side, trying to shut out Swain's voice.

"She was this bit player in the movies, you know, walk on parts, that kinda stuff. She thought she was really going places. Probably coulda been too if she'd taken the mattress route. Brother, was she stacked! For weeks she'd been getting me all hot in the zipper giving me the 'Oh no, I'm not that kind of a girl' routine. But once she knew I was off to fight … turned out she *was* that kind of a girl after all and, what's more, she couldn't get enough of it. I got so much comfort I nearly fell into a coma." He adopted a silly, mewling feminine voice. *"Oh, baby, give it to me again; I want something to remember you by when you're gone.* Well, I sure did that—with extra sauce on the side. Next thing I know, there's a letter and, naturally, she's got one up the spout. She thinks this means we'll get hitched and live happily ever after. As if. I never wrote back. That little romance fell apart like a two-bit suitcase. I mean, I don't mind stirring the gravy, but I don't want it for breakfast every day."

Jimmy snapped his book shut, unable to remain detached.

"What a beautiful love story."

"What's eating you?"

"A little mean-spirited isn't it? Abandoning your child."

"Keep your breeches on, Snow White. It ain't my kid."

"Well whose 'kid' is it?"

"Hers. I made no promises. She got herself knocked up, that's

her problem. It's not like she's my wife or nothin'. She'll never track me down."

"So that's it, you just give her the brush? Leave her to cope on her own?"

"You got it, buster."

"You know what? You're a bastard, Swain. A genuine twenty-four-carat bastard."

"Hey. Watch your mouth, Fairyboots."

"Ah. What's the use?" Exasperated, Jimmy got out of bed and strode over to the other side of the barracks, feeling rather silly standing there in his undershorts.

Swain threw open his hands in wide-eyed appeal. "What's with him? What did I do?" The guys chuckled, but none of them wanted to get involved. The soldier in the bed near to where Jimmy was standing, a man with whom he'd had little exchange, lit a cigarette.

"Forget about Swain. It's all swagger. He's just a dime-a-dozen chump."

Jimmy was still fuming. "Yeah? Well I hope that girl does track him down and I hope she's got both barrels loaded. Some people are better off dead."

THIRTY

Queenie had been someplace, doing something—she couldn't quite think what—and had come home to find her belongings, or somebody's belongings, piled up at the foot of the stairs. It was not exactly Mrs Ishi's house she was in; it was more like the apartment she lived in before that: the Rosary Hall Residence with that horrible landlady … what was her name? And yet these stairs were somehow different: cast iron with open treads like the staircase at the factory.

Everything had been carefully packed into boxes and crates and there were rugs, lampshades and the like lying on top of them. She was sure someone had decided to chuck all her stuff out and, naturally, she was feeling quite indignant about this. She checked through her possessions, but was unable to find anything to confirm whether or not these were actually her things. Then she saw her red armchair in the corner and that really got her mad because she loved that chair. She had almost forgotten she had it because she'd been forced to leave it at her parents' house when she moved out.

She had bought the chair with her own money, three dollars, from a man in the neighborhood who sold house-clearance furniture. It was small and low with big semicircular arms. The upholstery was dusty and threadbare, but she adored its shape. Once she'd got it home she set about recovering it with some rich red curtain fabric with a tree motif on it that her mother had stashed away. Not knowing quite how to go about it, she had cut a pattern from newspaper and stitched the fabric together on her mother's old Singer, securing it to the chair frame with carpet tacks. There wasn't enough fabric to do the whole chair so she used some other material to cover the seat and back in a similar red, but with a different pattern. The two fabrics contrasted well, and to highlight this she had made a small cushion, no bigger than a phone book, from remnants of the first fabric. The chair looked perfect and she was pleased with what she had achieved; she had never done anything like it before—or since. On nights when she stayed home, she would relax in her room, snuggled into the chair reading magazines or listening to the radio.

But when Queenie looked again, she saw that the chair on the landing was not hers; it was merely similar in design and color. Its shape was not as pleasing, but the condition was good. If someone was throwing it out, she could, perhaps, take it and make a (nearly) matching pair. That would look nice. She was wondering if she needed to check with someone first, when she noticed the small cushion with the unmistakeable tree motif and was sure that this, at least, belonged to her. She picked it up and held it close to her body. Someone—a woman she did not know—came out of one of the apartments and tried to take the cushion from her, telling her that

it was not hers. Queenie was convinced that it was. She held on resolutely, unwilling to surrender what was rightfully hers, but the woman finally managed to wrench it from her grasp.

"Sit up. Sit up."

Queenie was dizzy and confused, still entangled in the dream. She struggled to orient herself.

She was suddenly racked with pain and instinctively doubled up, wincing as the stomach cramps gripped her. She felt sick and instantly vomited. Ma, who must have anticipated this, caught the contents of her stomach in a mixing bowl and set it on the table.

"You'll have to get going. Can you stand?"

Queenie shook her head.

"There's a wad of dressing inside you. Leave it there for a few hours."

On the table was a sanitary belt and a Household Assortment box of Kotex Modess napkins. She noticed the drugstore price sticker: forty-three cents. Ma offered the box like they might be saltine crackers. "Here. Take a couple for later."

Queenie ignored the offer. She swung her legs over the edge of the table. "I don't feel so good. It hurts real bad."

"Barney will take you back. He's waiting in the car."

"Who's Barney?"

"Dr Young."

"Should it be hurting this much?"

"Come on. Up."

She slid herself off the desk and stood cautiously clinging to the table. A wave of pain hit her—a jabbing blow to the solar plexus from a heavyweight. Her body folded to try and absorb it.

"I can't. I just can't."

"You can. Come on." Ma gave the sanitary napkin she was holding a little shake as one might use a toy to attract the attention of a baby.

Out in the kitchen, a nervous-looking girl of about seventeen sat on a straight-backed chair. Queenie entered, fully dressed now, her pallid face shiny with perspiration. She took feeble little steps, holding onto furniture whenever she could to aid her progress. Ma offered no assistance, merely goaded her towards the door. Queenie sucked air between her teeth and winced, barely able to focus on the young girl in the chair. Nevertheless, their eyes met for a second and Queenie realized she'd seen her somewhere before. The audition line at Warner Bros. She was the girl she had seen carrying the fat-legged baby. And now, presumably, with another on the way—for the time being, at least.

Though the girl didn't recognize her, she shifted uncomfortably at the sight of her condition. Ma caught it.

"Pay no mind to her. She's got a migraine, haven't you dear? Nothing to do with the procedure. Come on. Quit making a fuss."

Outside, Dr Young waited impatiently with the engine running and his windshield wipers swishing back and forth, for it had started to rain. Queenie managed to sit and swing her legs into the car. Ma was quick to slam the door after her.

* **MEANWHILE** *The first rain in more than sixteen weeks bounced off the untreated timber roofs on George Street. Water beaded on cables and dripped from the speakers. Flags hung sodden from their poles. Dry clothes that had been hung out on washing lines "to dry" had become wringing wet. Water pooled in the footwells of open-top vehicles as well as, for the first time, in the town square's ornamental pond. At Overland Lake the rain skimmed the drooping blue surface in shallow waves as it gathered and headed for the drainage hole at its center. Though some plastic varieties got a much-needed rinse, flowers generally did not benefit from the downpour: paper and card disintegrated, their once bright pigments ran and merged together into rivulets of dirty brown.*

During the weeks the sun had been shining, no one in Overland seemed to have anticipated that the weather might turn.

Dr Young studied her in the mirror.

"Blindfold. And don't puke in my car."

She took the blue bandana that lay beside her on the seat, but it was all too much for her. "I can't. I don't feel well at all." She slumped down, resting her head on the seat and closing her eyes.

"Fine. Stay like that."

Dr Young backed out onto the street and set off.*

"You said it wouldn't hurt."

"What did you expect?"

"Am I going to be all right?"

"Don't call unless it's an emergency. And if you go to your doctor, don't say nothing about where you've been. Got it? You could go to prison for what you've done."

"So could you."

Dr Young snapped back sharply. "Don't get fancy with me. I don't like being threatened."

Queenie had no fight in her. "I wasn't. I can't afford a doctor anyway."

She felt around in her purse for the aspirin, spilled four out into the palm of her hand and popped them into her mouth, crunching them between her teeth and trying to swallow down the bitter crumbs.

Dr Young watched her in his mirror. "I'll drop you at the Landmark."

"How am I going to get home?"

"How do I know? Get a cab."

"No money."

"Can't you get your boyfriend to pick you up?"

She didn't answer.

Dr Young snorted derisively. "What a heel. Well, I can't help you."

The car swung in to the curbside outside the Landmark. Queenie was still slumped across the back seat. Looking out, Dr Young caught sight of a policeman sheltering from the rain in the doorway of Jay's Jewelry. Though the cop was minding his own business and hadn't yet noticed the car, the doctor felt uneasy. He knew that dumping Queenie on the street now was bound to draw the cop's unwanted attention. He couldn't risk it.

"Where do you live?"

"Burbank. Nine thirteen Lakewood Drive."

"OK. I'll drop you a couple of blocks from there. You'll have to walk the rest."

In Fort Benning, the staff sergeant was on his way through the mess hall when he noticed a puddle of water on the floor under a pair of steps. Looking up he saw that the skylight had been left open and it was raining in. He climbed the steps to close the hatch, squinting against the rain falling on his face. As he grabbed the handle to swing the hatch shut he took a quick look out and saw one of the new recruits standing on the roof in the rain. It was Jimmy—stock-still, staring straight ahead. His uniform was soaked through. Rain dripped from the peak of his cap.

"Shepherd! … Shepherd!"

Jimmy turned, disoriented.

"What are you doing?"

"Nothing sir."

"Nothing? It's pissing rain—in case you hadn't noticed. What are you doing up there?"

"I have to move the sheep."

"Move the sheep?"

"It's my job. Shepherd. Same as my name."

"What the blazes are you talking about? What job? Why are you on the roof?"

Jimmy looked around him as though he was only now becoming aware of his surroundings. It was a good question. Why was he on the roof? And how did he get there? He had no idea. There were no sheep here.

"Oh, no. Sorry, sir. That's someplace else. Not here."

"Shepherd? You're not going loco on me are you? I won't have any crazies in my platoon."

"No sir. I just came up here to get some fresh air."

"Fresh air? You're a damned idiot."

"Yes sir."

"You left the skylight open, you moron. The floor's soaked. Get down here and get it cleaned up."

"Yes, sir."

Queenie was in the bathroom at Mrs Ishi's house, sitting on the toilet. There was blood on the floor, blood on her skirt, blood on her hands—even blood smeared across the tiled wall where she had tried to steady herself. She doubled over in gut-wrenching pain, trying not to cry out.

As night fell, she lay hunched up on her bed, the Aspro bottle empty on her nightstand. The house felt lifeless and still. Mrs Ishi had left already—halfway to Chicago by now, she imagined. With Kay gone too, it no longer felt like home.

At around 3 a.m., she dragged herself to her feet and drew back the curtain to look outside. It felt as though there wasn't another soul in the world. Everything looked damp and heavy from the recent rain. A car rolled slowly by, but there didn't appear to be anyone driving it.

Queenie made it downstairs and was standing in the dark hallway wearing her bloodstained skirt—the color turned rusty brown now like old varnish. She picked up the phone, but the line was dead.

THIRTY-ONE

The tunnel led out into a parking lot full of automobiles. At the exit a man in a little wooden hut was counting dollar bills. He glanced up. George greeted him genially.

"Morning. Another beautiful day."

The attendant nodded apathetically, resumed his counting.

George added a little pep. "What have we done to deserve it, huh?"

The attendant shrugged. He didn't know and he didn't care.

George moved on.

He found himself on the streets of a suburban shopping area. In many ways it was similar to Overland, yet this place had a seedy edge. There were overspilling trashcans on the sidewalk and across the street the offices and storefronts were dominated by a flashy money-to-loan joint and the frowzy frontage of the Kozy Klub Girlesk Revue. Such places did not feature in the Overland townscape. The other difference was that traffic here was busier and more erratic. Cars weaved in and out, passing each other in lurching stop-start bursts and making left and right turns at will, as if there were no regulated system at all.

His attention was caught by the greasy but intoxicating smell of hot meat and fried onions. Just around the corner in a side alley was an old home-made hot-dog stand manned by a guy in a flat cap and a grubby apron. He was selling "red-hot frankfurters" in a milk roll for a nickel. The set-up looked none too hygienic, but George could not resist; he was ravenous. He stepped up and bought two, then stood there on the street devouring them. He made a mental note to introduce similar (though more sanitary) food stands in Overland and wondered why he hadn't thought of it before.

Once he'd finished eating, he stood outside Gam's Stationery wiping his greasy fingers on his handkerchief. Stuck to the inside of the store's window, a poster encouraged customers to *Reach Out to Someone Special with a Gibson Greetings Card*. The woman in the picture had been represented in such a way that her reaching hand was life-size—as if she were placing her palm flat against the surface of the window. George raised his own hand and rested it on the glass, spreading his fingers to mirror the shape. Out of the corner of his eye, he caught a young schoolgirl watching him. He quickly removed his hand and put it in his pocket.

A little farther on, he paused on the street corner looking up and down, trying to figure out how he might get to Camp Pomona. A middle-aged woman in a smart beige twinset and a single row of pearls stopped to offer assistance.

"You look a little lost."

"Where is this?"

"This is Fourteenth Street. Fourteenth and Kenwood Parkway."

"No. The town."

"This is Newtown."

"Newtown? That sounds like a made-up name."

"Yes, I guess it does."

"Where *is* Newtown?"

She was unsure how to answer. "Well it's … here."

"I've never heard of it before." He figured it must be some shopping area in Burbank.

"Can I help you find someplace?"

"Actually, I'm trying to get to the county fairground at Pomona."

"Oh yes. Now, where is that? Heading east, I think. Do you have a car?"

"I do, but the darned thing won't start." He was going to explain why, that it was in fact a fake car with no pedals and a steering wheel that wouldn't turn, but thought better of it.

"Well, you could always take the bus. The depot's just a couple of blocks north."

As George headed towards it his path was blocked by a man who, seemingly oblivious to the warm weather, was dressed in a dark overcoat and had a thick woollen scarf tied round his head. He was holding a hand-painted banner, which hung at shoulder height from a pole, proclaiming *The End of the World is Nigh*. Despite the limited time available, he had made the extra effort to decorate the bottom of his sign with red satin curtain fringe. The man tried to hand George a printed flyer, presumably giving further details, but George sidestepped him and continued along the sidewalk.

On his way home from dropping off Queenie, Dr Young had gotten caught up in traffic, his path blocked by the commotion going on ahead of him outside the bus depot. A soldier waved his hand up and down a few times. Dr Young nodded, though the message was unclear. The soldier came to explain, speaking to Dr Young through his open window.

"It'll be a few minutes sir, just sit tight. We've just gotta get this lot loaded up. You could try backing up."

Dr Young turned and saw that he was blocked in by the cars behind him.

"It's OK. I'll wait."

He turned off his engine and just sat. The rain had stopped and now the air was muggy. Exhaling heavily, he loosened his tie. He took the bandana from the passenger seat and wiped his face with it before stuffing it into his coat pocket. He lit a cigarette and vacantly watched the scene taking place up ahead.

A sprawling crowd of Japanese men, women and children were being corralled onto the sidewalk to make way for an approaching truck. It rolled up with its rear doors already open and folded back. On the side of the van: *Lyon Removal & Storage Co. Let Lyon Guard your Goods.* A couple of guys jumped down. They began slinging suitcases in the back from a mountain of assorted luggage stacked

in the road. Each piece had been tagged with a tie-on label. Japanese people, similarly tagged, stood and watched, timid and confused.

Across the street, lines of Japanese were being boarded onto a series of Greyhound buses, their destination window marked "special." A combination of military police and government officials were supervising the operation. Soldiers lined the street at intervals, ready to round up any strays, stragglers or absconders, or perhaps to protect the Japanese from the taunts and abuse from a crowd of white American bystanders who had stopped by especially to wish them good riddance.

Some of the Japanese were carrying packages and smaller suitcases as hand luggage. They looked apprehensive as they edged forward towards the front of the bus.

A smartly dressed woman carrying a small suitcase and a vivid green conure parakeet in a cage attempted to board. A soldier stopped her, grabbing the cage and setting it down on the ground behind him. The woman was ushered onto the bus without it. Next was a boy of about twelve cradling a black cat. The soldier wagged his finger indicating that pets were not allowed. The boy protectively pulled the cat closer to him. Asserting his authority, the soldier made a grab for it and in the scuffle the cat wriggled free and leapt from the boy's arms. Panicked and confused, the cat crouched low to the ground and darted this way and that, looking for refuge. A woman in the line stooped to grab it, another "helpfully" blocked its path, but the animal was only spooked by such actions and frantically ran

out into the road where it was quickly caught under an oncoming automobile. The car pulled up sharply, but the cat lay motionless between the front and rear wheels. The boy broke from the line to rush to his pet's aid, but the soldier used his rifle to hold him back, pushing him toward the door of the bus.

The soldier, keen to absolve himself of any blame, kept his back to the scene.

Dr Young watched from his car. The cat was on its side, staring expressionless into the ground. There was blood coming from its nose and mouth, which opened intermittently to emit a pathetic spluttering sound as the cat snorted out its last bloody breaths onto the asphalt. The car responsible had stopped, but without getting out, the driver was unable to see what was going on. He eased gingerly forward, unwittingly running over the dying animal's tail with his back tires. There was a slight involuntary movement of its body, but otherwise little reaction to the added assault.

Dr Young jumped from his vehicle and rushed over, screaming as the car crept guiltily away. "You stupid, stupid idiot!"

The cat continued to stare at the ground as though deep in concentration. Dr Young approached slowly. Dropping to his knees, he laid his hand gently on the cat's side and stroked it a couple of times, as though this might offer it some measure of comfort. He winced, racked with sympathy for the poor animal. The cat tried to lick its lips, perhaps attempting to swallow. Another weak slabber of blood.

Dr Young spoke soothingly. "It's OK. It's OK."

He took the blue bandana from his coat pocket and draped it lightly over the cat's head, then got to his feet and returned to his car.

With the cat's face now covered, a couple of the soldiers felt confident enough to venture nearer. Dr Young turned, speaking sharply.

"Don't touch it. I'm a veterinarian."

The soldiers backed off, pocketing their hands.

From inside the bus, the distraught Japanese boy looked on helplessly.

Dr Young opened the trunk of his car and grabbed a battered black leather medical bag and returned to his kneeling place beside the cat. He opened a folding instrument case, took from it a heavy steel syringe and quickly fitted a needle. This he inserted into the neck of a small upturned bottle, drawing back the plunger to fill the shaft with clear liquid.

He set down the bottle, pausing for a moment; his hand rested lightly on the cat's side, stroking it along its length.

"You're a very brave girl. But I can't save you. I'm so sorry."

Dr Young swallowed hard as he pinched the flesh between the cat's shoulders. He inserted the needle and depressed the plunger.

THIRTY-TWO

In Overland a light mist had descended bringing an unexpected chill to the air. The lamps that had been put in place before the evacuation, which at night had previously given the town such a cozy, welcoming glow, now appeared bleak and uninviting. Without the vibrant community to reflect their spirit, the warmth seemed to have gone right out of them. One string of lights adorning the Orpheum theater had fused and burnt out completely. Now, under sombre starless skies, the neglected building loomed, gray and drab.

The only movement in the forsaken town was the traffic system; its idiosyncratic programming, recently restored by George, so far unimpeded by any further natural disasters. The rumble and clatter now took on an eerie quality as the unoccupied vehicles continued on their pointless journey through the night.

Jimmy was sitting up in bed. Barely touched by the moonlight that filtered in through the skylight above him, he stared vacantly into the gloom. All the other men in the barrack room were fast asleep.

Increasingly troubled by compulsive thoughts of violence, Jimmy had become fearful of closing his eyes. During the day, providing he could avoid Swain and the other scaremongers in his platoon, he managed to keep these ideas largely in check by overriding them with more menial and immediate thinking, but at night, the demons resurfaced. The harder he fought to dispel them, the more invasive they became.

He kept going over the words: *killed in action*. Which action? The telegram gave no details. Had Carl been killed in heroic combative action, or through the ill-considered action of raising his curious head above the parapet of his foxhole? How? Bullet? Bayonet? Grenade? Did he die instantly, or was there time to identify his internal organs as they spilled from the gaping wound in his torso: his spleen, his gallbladder, his lungs, his (shortly to cease) beating heart? Would he recognize them from the textbook diagrams of his high-school biology classes? Or had his face already been sliced clean off by a Japanese sword, now lying expressionless in the mud like a rubber carnival mask, his unspoken last words—*Tell my kid brother not to be scared*—still quivering on his lips? Where did the fatal bullet enter? His stomach? His groin? His ear? A bullet lodged in the throat? How would that feel? A sharp tightness of the larynx followed by a sensation similar to heartburn? Jimmy remembered having swallowed a glass marble as a boy. For a few moments, the object had stuck in his

esophagus, hard, cold and choking. Was it anything like that?

How did he face the end? Was he whimpering like a lost child, crying out for Mother? Carl, the big man, a coward after all, just like himself? Or did he die a hero's death like the army would expect of him, sacrificing his own safety to save others in his unit?

Jimmy tried to imagine himself in such a role.

Swain's parachute caught on the tail wing of a Douglas C-47. All of his previous boorish bravado stripped away, he is blubbing like a baby. It's up to Jimmy to rescue him. Selflessly overcoming his fears, he risks his own safety and manages to ease himself along the fuselage, his switchblade held between his teeth. Climbing onto the tail wing, he sees the tangled line and how he might free it. Swain's pathetically pleading face looks up at him.

He takes the knife and, momentarily overcome with hatred, jabs it upwards, thrusting the blade deep into the fleshy area under Swain's chin. Yah!

Jimmy was startled by the unexpected violence of his own thoughts. He could never do anything like that, yet it was a compelling image he could not suppress: Swain's stupefied face with a knife buried in his jaw, clear to the hilt, his filthy drooling tongue permanently pinned to the roof of his mouth.

Before he enlisted, Jimmy had seen motion pictures about guys joining the army. It all looked kind of like fun. As a new recruit he had expected to have to endure certain hardships—getting up at the crack of dawn, being shouted at by a strict drill sergeant, peeling

piles of potatoes—these things had been routinely depicted in most of the movies. The message that came across was that it was tough being a rookie, but they were all in it together making the best of things, and forging lifelong friendships along the way. War was serious business, naturally, but the best of them rose to the challenge and everything came out right in the end. In *You're in the Army Now*, there had been no suggestion that once posted overseas on front-line duty, Phil Silvers and Jimmy Durante might be torn apart by machine-gun fire or die a slow agonizing death at the unscrupulous hands of their Japanese captors. No telegram would be sent to *their* next of kin to say that they had been killed in action.

In *You'll Never Get Rich*, Fred Astaire turned up on Rita Hayworth's doorstep looking neat and fully intact in his smart army uniform ready to tap dance his way to her heart. There was no question that he might be forced to do it with the side of his face missing, or with his intestines spilling out of him like a pile of butcher-shop trimmings.

Jimmy took George's switchblade from under his pillow. He could never imagine using it as a weapon, targeting a person's vital organs—the aim to pierce or to sever something sufficiently to curtail its functioning. He pressed the button to release the blade, snapping it into position. It made a loud clicking noise, but nobody stirred. He looked across at Swain, still sleeping peacefully.

He retracted the blade and slid the knife back under his pillow.

Court was in recess. Jimmy, smartly dressed in his military uniform, was standing around in the lobby distractedly touching the knot in his tie. His gaze fell on nothing at all. When his eyes refocused, he saw Queenie coming towards him.

"Queenie. What are you doing here?"

"I heard you were home. I thought you might want to see me. I wanted to write, but no one knew where you were. I searched in vain."

In vain? Queenie's words sounded like lines read from a movie script. Jimmy found himself playing his part in the stilted dialogue.

"I was behind enemy lines. Communication was forbidden. Besides, I didn't know how you felt about me."

"Truth is, I didn't know myself until you'd gone. I didn't realize how much you mean to me. So now I'm here to stay—if you want me."

"I want you, Queenie. More than anything in the world. But they're trying to pin a tin can to my tail for what I did."

She looked longingly into his eyes. "I don't care."

"Maybe not, but a lot of people will care."

"Listen. You're a hero. Nobody's gonna blame you for what you did to that Swain guy. He had it coming. Whatever verdict they reach in there, it's for both of us—straight down the line. If they took you away from me now, I'd just die. I'd rather go to the chair with you than live without you."

Jimmy went off script. "Wait a minute, wait a minute. Did you say the chair? You mean the electric chair? They're not going to send me to the electric chair, surely? This is just a reprimand. A court martial at worst ... Isn't it?"

* For a moment Jimmy was in heaven. They surrendered to the moment
as their passions rose.

"Oh, hold me, Jeff. Hold me and never let me go."

"Jimmy."

"Huh?"

"Jimmy. You said Jeff."

"Sorry. Hold me, darling. I never knew I could love a guy as much as I love you. We were made for each other. Like James Stewart and Carole Lombard. Even if we had a baby that was dying of pneumonia and a serum has to be flown all the way from Salt Lake City—even through this turmoil our love would never falter, would it?"

"Never, darling."

"I can't wait to start making babies with you."

"Me neither. You're so beautiful."

"Well, let's begin the beguine right now."

"What, here?"

Queenie sat on a desk, her dress hiked up around her waist like in one of her cheesecake photos.

She looked up at him yearningly. "Look, darling. I can't help myself."

He glanced down and saw that she was naked there.

"Oh, my word."

"Come to me darling. Kiss me."

Jimmy stumbled forward; Queenie's legs parted and her arms enveloped him. Her breath was hot against his ear. The tip of her tongue slithered against his neck, making his scalp buzz with pleasure.*

Through the misty euphoria of this blissful union, Jimmy became aware of a middle-aged couple dressed in black, standing at an adjacent table. The man had removed his hat and was nervously clutching the brim. Gradually their faces came into focus. Jimmy called out to them.

"Mom, Dad. I told you to wait in the car."

But they didn't appear to have noticed him. His mother looked pale and distraught. His father, whom Jimmy was somewhat surprised to see since he had been dead for two years, laid a consolatory hand on her shoulder.

Right now he was caught up in the physical urgency of Queenie's writhing pelvis. He stole another look and caught a thrilling glance of petticoat frill and pale flesh.

His mother was edging forward as if to say something. Embarrassed, Jimmy tried to cover their nakedness while attempting an introduction—*Mom this is Queenie. She's my new ...*

But the distraction of the consummation was too much. He screwed up his face, no longer able to conceal the sensations he was experiencing. "Oh God. I can't help myself."

Jimmy woke. He was in bed, lying on his back. For a moment he was still, reorienting himself. The barracks. Dead of night. He swallowed, realizing what had happened. Did he cry out? Everything around him was quiet so he assumed he did not. He breathed in deeply, exhaled slowly and gently cleared his throat. He slid his hand under the bedclothes to confirm his suspicions, slowly raising his knees to form a tent with the blankets over his sticky groin.

THIRTY-THREE

Left unattended, the sheep in Overland's South Pasture had remained in the same position for four consecutive days. By late afternoon the clouds had darkened and the wind began to pick up. Some of the sitting sheep—that is, those without legs—started to quiver on the breeze. A sudden gust sent several of them rolling across the pasture like tumbleweed.

The man at the bus depot was shaking his head.

"The fairground at Pomona's closed, Mac. They're using it as a prison camp for the Japs."

"I know. Is there a bus that goes out there?"

"A bus? No. Well. There is, there's one loading up right now over there." He pointed to the other side of the depot. "But you gotta be Japanese to be on it."

Crossing the depot, George found a line of Japanese laden with suitcases and other bundled goods waiting to board a blue and silver Greyhound. In the road just beyond it he noticed a man easing the edge of a shovel under what appeared to be a contentedly sleeping cat, which was stubbornly refusing to budge. Another man stood by, both hands gripping the open top of a grocery sack. It was only then George realized it must be dead.

George approached the man he assumed was the driver, who wore a peaked cap and breeches tucked into his jackboots with a little black bow tie the same shape and color as his mustache.

"Can you get me a seat on that bus?" asked George.

"Sorry, pal. These are for transporting Japs. You'll have to get a regular bus service."

"Yeah. Trouble is, there isn't one."

The driver shook his head. "Sorry."

"Couldn't I hitch a ride? It's very important that I get to the Japanese assembly center at Pomona."

"How so?"

George was thinking on his feet, but his hesitation seemed to go unnoticed. "I'm working at the camp as an administrator. On the clerical side. I should have been at work an hour ago. My car broke down. My boss is going to have my ass in the grinder."

"Oh. You work for the outfit? You ain't army though?"

"Not exactly. I'm more of a government administrator. You know, for the relocation."

"Well I guess that makes you one of the family." The driver called to his partner who was sitting on a low wall, incinerating ants with the glowing tip of his cigarette. "Hey, Charlie. OK if this feller hops a ride to the center? He works there. His car broke down."

"So long as he don't mind sitting with a load of Japs."

George caught the eye of a young Japanese man in the line.

"No, I don't mind … at all." George looked away awkwardly.

The young man spoke out. "What are you doing, working for these people? We are American citizens. We have constitutional rights. We—"

The driver cut him short. "Hey, hey, hey. Butt out, Toto, while your conk is all in one portion." He turned to George, with a congenial smile. "Come on, buddy. Climb aboard."

The young Japanese man glared at George. "You should be ashamed."

"I'm actually trying to help," said George.

"Yeah. Right. Help yourself."

The driver stepped in. "All right. That's enough."

The young man grudgingly backed off. The guard put his hand on George's shoulder, steering him towards the door of the bus. He

grabbed the collar of a man mounting the steps, yanking him back into the line. "Outta the way. Make way here."

George climbed aboard.

Most of the seats were taken. Japanese Americans of all ages, family groups, some standing, some sitting, all laden down with parcels, and suitcases, were trying to get themselves settled. Eager to avoid further hostility, George scanned the bus for a seat on his own, but there were none available; he was forced to share. A middle-aged woman dragged a small but heavy-looking suitcase onto her knees, leaving the seat beside her vacant. George made a beeline for it.

"Do you mind if I sit here?"

She said nothing, but bowed her head in assent.

"I can put your case up on the rack if you like," said George.

"Thank you. I'm fine."

Out of the corner of his eye George saw a tear roll down her cheek. He tried not to look. The woman ran her hands over the suitcase, feeling its polished surface, its smooth edges. He sensed that this was all she had; everything else had been left behind. She stared straight ahead contemplatively and sighed. After a few moments she spoke.

"You're not Japanese."

George felt apologetic. "No. I'm not."

"Why you sent to prison camp?"

"I'm just hitching a ride. I'm looking for someone. A friend."

"What will happen to us? Where are they sending us?"

"The county fairground in Pomona."

"I don't want to go to a fairground. I don't like fairs."

There was a beat before she spoke again.

"What do they do with the animals?"

George shook his head. He thought she was talking about animals at the fairground, perhaps confusing it with a circus. "Animals? They don't have animals there."

"I know. Pets not allowed for Japanese people. They take away all the pets."

"Oh. I didn't know. That's too bad."

"What happens to them? Do they feed them? Look after them?"

"I really don't know, I'm afraid."

The bus started up. The woman looked out of the window. George tried to think of something to say, but came up blank. After a while, when they were heading through the suburbs, she turned to him.

"You like fish?"

He considered this for a moment, wondering where the question was leading. Slowly, he nodded.

The woman unsnapped the catches on her suitcase and opened it.

George recognized the design on the can immediately, the Japanese lettering, the leaping fish with its goggling eye. He turned to her.

"Do you know a girl called Kay?"

"Yes, of course. She stay in my house since she is fifteen year old. You know Kay?"

George nodded. "And Queenie. From the factory."

"Yes, Queenie in my house also."

"They are my friends. I'm trying to find Kay. She was sent to a detention camp. I believe to the one we're heading for, Pomona."

"No. Kay is not in camp."

"I'm afraid she is. They came to take her from the factory."

"Yes. But she escape."

"Escape?" George looked around conspiratorially, hoping that no one had heard.

The woman lowered her voice. "She is hiding. I tell her, you must go underground. She say, no, not underground, overground."

"Overground? You mean Overland?"

"Secret place. No one will find her. I don't know where. But it has a beautiful lake."

A few minutes later, the bus drew into the side of the road and George leapt out onto the curb.

Though the curfew put her at increased risk, when Kay had left Mrs Ishi's the previous evening, she imagined that traveling on foot under the cover of dusk she could find her way back to the Lockheed plant unnoticed. What she hadn't taken into account was that her journey to and from work had always been via the factory bus and she had never paid much attention to the route it took. Navigation was further hindered by the need to avoid main thoroughfares where she was more likely to have her papers checked. The side streets were generally darker and there was seldom any helpful signage. Consequently, her decisions tended to be based on intuition and erroneous guesswork. Before long she was hopelessly lost.

There were still people on the sidewalks, but she kept her head down, fearful of asking directions. She had all but given up hope when she finally spotted a familiar landmark. In the distance, she could make out the stubby tower and crossed sails of the Van de Kamp Bakery, its characteristic windmill shape silhouetted against the night sky and lit by a blue neon sign. It instantly became a beacon of hope since she knew Van de Kamp's was not far from the factory. She headed towards it through the suburbs with renewed vigor. Though she lost sight of her target for a while when a fenced off railroad track forced her to take a detour, she eventually got there. Only then did she realize it wasn't the Van de Kamp's she was familiar with on San Fernando Road, but another branch in some unknown part of town. She had not realized there was more than one Van de Kamp Bakery. And now, inadvertently, she had taken herself even further off course. It was past midnight. She was frustrated and completely exhausted, having already spent the best part of the day walking in the hot sun. She finally decided to give up—at least until morning.

In a quiet church graveyard, she found a bench with wrought-iron ends and wooden slats shaped into a scroll. She couldn't walk another step. She lay down with her head resting on her suitcase, her hat on her stomach, and fell almost instantly into a deep sleep.

She awoke next morning with a stiff neck, but feeling rejuvenated and more optimistic about getting back to Overland. She still had

* **MEANWHILE** *A meadowlark that had landed in Howard Farmer's field, presumably to investigate the crops, now found itself caught in the netting. It flopped around, flapping its wings trying to free itself, but in doing so one of its claws had become inextricably entangled. The panicked and exhausted bird would rest for a few seconds before making a renewed effort, but each time the struggle was in vain.*

no clue in which direction she should be heading, but she had a hunch that she might be nearer now than she thought.*

Inside the dark carcass of a Douglas C-47, the men were seated side by side on rough benches, fully kitted out in bulky jump gear, their arms folded across their reserve chutes. Towards the rear of the plane, the instructors were at the open doorway in the fuselage making their final checks and calculations. The sound of rushing wind mixed with the incessant rasping drone of the engines.

Jimmy stared at his feet, brooding on his predicament. Even if he got through today, it wasn't going to end there. Before long, he would be forced to parachute into enemy territory and who knew what awaited him there? The jump was only stage one in a series of fatally connected and increasingly terrifying ordeals.

Sitting beside him, Swain, full of boisterous bravado, was oblivious (or just plain insensitive) to Jimmy's mood. He turned his head this way and that, checking out the other men, looking for signs of weakness on which he might prey. He nudged Jimmy, shouting in his ear to make himself heard.

"Don't look so worried. If your chute don't open, just take it back and they'll give you a new one."

Big joke. Jimmy couldn't bring himself to even look at him.

"Stand—up!"—the order from the jumpmaster, yelling at the top of his voice. The words came widely spaced, pronounced with equal emphasis.

The men got to their feet, parroting the command in chorus as they had been trained. Now they were all facing the doorway. Jimmy, last in the line, could see only the backs of the other men silhouetted against the light. He felt trapped.

"Hook—up!"

"Hook—up!" The men hooked their yellow static lines onto the steel anchor cable above their heads, which ran the length of the plane. They took up the slack, as trained, making the folded loop known as a bight, which they dutifully clutched at shoulder height. Jimmy, more than a beat behind the others, stared at the hook in his hand. Once attached, he knew there'd be no going back.

"Check—static—line."

"Check—static—line."

He was still gazing at the hook when the jumpmaster snatched it from him and clamped it firmly onto the anchor, jiggling it to check it was secure. He shot Jimmy a stern look as he went back down the line, checking all the other guys' equipment and scooting them along the cable like shirts in a Chinese laundry. Jimmy reluctantly looped his line into a bight.

"Thirty—seconds!"

"Thirty—seconds!"

It was all going too fast. Jimmy tried to think about something else. He stared ahead, fixating on Swain's chute—the neat lacing and tight zigzag folds of his static line where it attached to his canopy cover. If it hadn't been for Swain's constant taunts while he'd been

at Fort Benning, Jimmy might have found a path through this. But Swain smelled blood from the start and had never let up: goading him, poking him, shoving him—right to the very edge, just for the fun of watching him squirm.

No one heard the click of Jimmy's switchblade over the din of the engines. Swain's static line was only inches away. It would be a cinch to cut one of the loops. The knife was sharp; one swift tug would draw the blade clean through it without Swain feeling a thing. Was Jimmy fully aware of the consequences of such an action? Sure he was. The jumper's weight pulling down on the static line was designed to rip open the threads, release the chute cover and deploy the canopy. Severing that line would cause a serious malfunction: the cover would remain in place and Swain would be wearing his chute all the way down to the ground, like a camper on a backpacking vacation.

But that wasn't the plan. Besides, knowing Swain, he'd probably make it down safely on his reserve chute and then make a big deal about it, establishing himself as the daredevil hero of the day. Jimmy wasn't prepared to let him have that. Better to let him jump and just hope he broke his neck on landing. He wouldn't, of course. Guys like Swain never got what they deserved.

Then came the *Stand in the door* command.

Number one jumper stepped forward to hand his static line to the safety. The men shuffled forward to tighten the grouping. Jimmy felt the ripple of nervous apprehension running through the squad. This was it. Swain, all rubbernecking and edgy, was trying to see

ahead of the guys in front. He was holding his static-line bight high like an Olympic torch.

Jimmy needed to get out of there, away from Swain, away from the army, away from the war. He needed to get home.

He hooked the blade of his knife into the folded loop of his own static line. Pausing for a second, not to think about what he was doing but to check that no one was looking, he sliced through the webbing as easily as if he was cutting himself a piece of apple. With that, he quickly pocketed the switchblade and re-looped the severed line so the jumpmaster wouldn't notice what he had done. He stood holding the two severed ends tightly in his fist, like a magician performing a rope trick.

Now he'd done it. Now he'd really gone and done it. No going back now.

Wait!

Wait!

Ready!

Ready!

Go!

The first man was out, the others were ushered quickly forward, the jumpmaster swiping their static lines to one side before shoving them ungraciously out the door like unwanted nightclub guests.

And before he knew what was happening, Jimmy was gone.

This was how Overland was originally designed to be seen: as if

through the camera lens of someone flying at 3,500 feet. Jimmy had the perfect vantage point to study the topography below: a hazy pattern of fields, roads and buildings. The rushing wind punched up through his nostrils and into the back of his throat. It reminded him of his first time out on his motorcycle, gaining confidence, gathering speed, his eyes streaming, giddily choking on the suffocating rush of air.

Glancing down at his chest, he saw the reserve chute's ripcord handle. He wasn't even tempted. Poor Oscar the para-dummy's reserve was a fake; he never had any choice, but Jimmy's fate was in his own hands now. He was going home. His chance to become a permanent Resident.

Would he be able to spot Overland—find the new patch sewn onto the patchwork quilt below? Adopting the spreadeagle position to reduce his fall rate, he had all the time in the world to search for the identifying edge. The wind flapped vigorously at the loose fabric of his jumpsuit. As per his training, he looked up to check his canopy, reassured to see there was nothing there—nothing but clear blue sky.

When he looked down again, he saw the ground rushing up towards him. He could make out neat rows of red-roofed houses, and a road with a daisy chain of circling cars and buses. There was a church and a tennis court with players in mid rally and, coming quickly into focus, a field of carefully arranged sheep.

THIRTY-FOUR

On a tranquil side street Kay came across an elderly lady tending to the flowers in her garden. She wore a wide-brimmed summer hat similar to Kay's, except that hers was tied with a ribbon under her chin. It was still very early so there was no one else about. With her Chinese-ancestry story at the ready, Kay took a chance and went to talk to her over the picket fence.

"Yes," the woman said. "There *used* to be an aircraft factory I think. Before the war. Quite a big one, but I don't know what happened to it. They rerouted all the traffic in that area, a lot of the roads got closed—some kind of military security, I think. But there's no factory there now. Guess they must have closed it down or moved it someplace else."

"They can't have moved the buildings. It was massive. The runway was maybe a mile long."

"That's right. I remember it. We used to be able to drive by it, but it's not there now."

"Can you point me to where it used to be?"

"I couldn't say, dear. It was round here somewhere. I think there was a tunnel, but I can't recall how you got to it. When they change the roads around, you sort of lose your bearings."

Without Lockheed, Kay had no idea how she might get to Overland. The only point of access she knew was via the factory: through the hole in the tarpaulin lake or up the staircase and through the hatch. Obviously, Kay couldn't risk going back to the factory itself; they would be on the lookout for her and in no time she'd be picked up and sent straight back to Manzanar. But if she could at least figure out where the Lockheed plant was, surely she would be able to find a way to get up to the secret town on the roof. It would be the ideal place to hide out—that perfect little cabin by the lake; she could be very happy there, living as a Resident and no one would ever find her. There had to be an alternative route to it; the equipment and materials to build the trees, the houses, the fields couldn't possibly have been taken up through the tiny factory trapdoor. But nobody around there seemed to know where the Lockheed plant was, or if they did they weren't telling. Military security perhaps—an official directive forbidding local residents to ever speak of it. Was the army worried that Japanese bombers might stop and ask for directions? Or had the camouflage been so effective that in making the factory disappear from everyone's field of vision, they had also managed to erase it from their memories? Out of sight, out of mind.

Newtown was a suburb Kay had never previously visited, but which felt vaguely familiar to her. She was standing in the doorway of a store, wondering which direction to head in, when she found herself drawn

to a poster advert in the window. *Reach Out to Someone Special*, it said. Yes. She would like to do that. Reach out and be touched. Even for a brief moment, just to feel that physical contact, the fleshy warmth of hand against hand, quite apart from any spiritual connection: the palmistry imprint of lifeline, heart line and fate line (or whatever those creases are supposed to represent), one hand echoing the fate of another. Without thinking, she lifted her hand and rested it gently on the glass, spreading her fingers, exactly mirroring the hand shape on the poster. Shifting the focus of her gaze she noticed that inside the store there was a countertop display stand of assorted roadmaps. She withdrew her hand and quickly stepped inside.

Behind the sales counter was an enthusiastic young man with thick greased hair, a hatchet-sharp parting. He was keen to offer the best possible customer service.

"A map of the local area? Why certainly, ma'am." He briskly selected a Standard Oil street map of Burbank from a rack nearby, opening it out on the counter and pressing the folds flat with his hand. "This one's right up-to-date. Shows all the local attractions: parks, movie theaters, shopping areas, that kind of thing. It's fifteen cents."

"Does it have the Lockheed aircraft factory on it?"

"Aircraft factory? Well, I'm not sure where that is, but I guess it will if it's in the Burbank area."

Kay studied the map. "It should be around here someplace."

"I don't know of an aircraft factory."

"You don't, huh?" Kay nodded knowingly.

"No, sorry."

She was still scrutinizing the map when it occurred to her. Of course! They must have taken Lockheed off the map, hidden it as a security measure. That's why it wasn't there. She checked the front and read: *Special notice. In cooperation with the United States military authorities, we have eliminated from this map all airports and military establishments which they have suggested.*

"Do you happen to have an older map?"

"Like an antique?"

"Just a year or so old."

"Hmm. Mr Voss, do we have any of the old stock of the local maps?" Mr Voss was passing through, carrying a stack of calendars.

"Old ones? No, we sent 'em back."

"Darn. Yeah. We sent them back. Sorry, miss."

"Where would I get an old map?"

"Mmm. Could try the library."

Though she felt it had taken her further out of her way, half an hour later Kay was in the reference section, poring over a large map that lay unfolded on one of the tables. Tracing the surface with her finger, she quickly located the Lockheed plant. She stabbed it conclusively with her forefinger, like a dart finding the bullseye.

George was having less success. He stood in front of a public street map, stroking his chin. He tilted his head, trying to establish his

location. There was a big arrow telling him *You Are Here*, but he was none the wiser. The street names meant nothing without some sort of context, and the sign above the map failed to provide one: it merely said *Town Center*.

Ironically, the map was disorienting. But then down here George was finding many things perplexing. He felt his judgement shifting increasingly off kilter. Yesterday, he'd spent the entire day wandering around town, following one unavailing lead after another: a local aircraft enthusiast (who was not at home); a mailman who, he was assured, knew every factory in the area (except, it turned out, this one); and a genuine shepherd who, when described, purportedly looked exactly like Jimmy (but didn't, and wasn't). All of it had come to nothing. It didn't help that at one point George was so addled he couldn't remember the name of the factory. Still, he wondered if, as a security measure, the locals had been instructed to keep quiet about it.

At the end of the day he had wound up in a cheap motel feeling groggy and confused. Did he have a fever or something, he wondered? Heatstroke?

He'd woken that morning, no nearer to locating Overland than he was when he first came here. It felt as though someone kept hitting a reset button. Each time he felt like he might be getting somewhere, he'd be forced to start over, feeling strangely like he was stuck in a dream from which he could not be woken.

To further confuse things, the motel he had stayed at looked disconcertingly like the Rest Haven Motel in Overland. He assumed he must have unconsciously copied the design; perhaps it was typical of all motels. But he noticed the same thing in other parts of the neighborhood—where things looked more like replicas or prototypes of Overland than original features of Newtown, or Burbank, or wherever the heck he was.

It worried him to think of Kay already being back in Overland, wondering where he was. Now all the Residents had gone, she would find the place deserted and would have no idea that he was on his way back to be with her. Would she wait? Without food, she would eventually be forced to leave. However would he find her then?

On the previous afternoon, he had entered the library hoping to find a pre-war map—one that hadn't been censored. He was familiar with the practice known as map masking so he knew that areas of strategic military importance like the Lockheed factory would have been erased from all recently issued maps. But he had high hopes in the library when he found a three-year-old street map—until he unfolded it and discovered that a section of it had been crudely torn from the middle, leaving a large gaping hole. Not only was the aircraft factory missing, but so was the entire surrounding area. Ridiculous. If they were so concerned about security, why not simply remove the map from public access? Wasn't the hole rather drawing attention to itself as having contained something target-worthy? He wondered whether the librarians were acting under instruction or had taken the task upon themselves on behalf of the US Department of Defense.

There was a ray of hope at around lunchtime on the following day when he found himself on a street he thought he recognized. There was a Cooperative Food Mart, outside which stood a six-foot sign announcing a special price of nine cents. He remembered seeing it some weeks ago, wondering to what exactly the nine cents referred. A couple of stores up from the Food Mart was the Doheny Smoke Shop. Yes, hadn't he once stopped there to buy cigarettes? He looked around for more clues. There was the Mermaid Club (open till late), Rite-way dry-cleaners and a tiny antiques emporium with a *For Sale or Lease* sign in the window. It all looked vaguely familiar, but he still couldn't think where he was. A block further on, he saw something that brought it all back with a queasy, sinking dread. Set back from the street behind a large parking lot was the Skateland Roller Rink.

This was where all the trouble started—Muriel getting the part-time job and teaming up with that greasy hunk of ham, Gus Moretti. He no longer cared for Muriel; she and Gus probably deserved each other. But seeing the Roller Rink again and thinking back to that time of demeaning betrayal was a reminder that though this neighborhood sometimes *looked* like Overland, it wasn't. Beneath the surface, everything down here in the underworld was essentially rotten. If he were to stay here he'd be faced with it again and again.

Of *course* he'd been on that street before. He had dropped Muriel off there on numerous occasions, delivered her to the door. He might as well have carried her inside and set her down right in Gus's lap.

He turned away from the Roller Rink to light a cigarette, staring through the window of a Western Union office where folks inside were going about their business. Various placards and posters promoted a range of telegraph services: cablegrams, singing telegrams, holiday and special-occasion telegrams. Everyone pictured here was cheerful and smiling. There was no hint of the darker role Western Union played in sending messages to the folks back home: the ones expressing "deep regret" … Or *the* telegram: the one delivered to him on February 14th last.

What George had never understood was why she had sent it as a Valentine Greetings Telegraph, the envelope promising friendly, even romantic, felicitations within. He liked to think that this had been no more than an unfortunate clerical error: an uncharacteristic example of Western Union getting its wires crossed. The telegram itself had a color illustration panel across the top depicting a jolly tableau in which a smiling middle-aged man was reading a recently delivered telegram while behind him a gay party was in progress. Two young ladies in long dresses wearing red hearts in their hair had taken time out from the festivities to pin a big cardboard heart onto the uniform of the blushing delivery boy who waited, cap tucked under his arm, by the door. The message below it, purple block capitals on hastily pasted ticker strips, had read: *I wanted to tell you this before Valentines so you can cancel the Parkmoor. It's no good anymore George. There's no use pretending. You are always at the studio and it's where you belong. Now I've found where I belong too. I have taken Fuffy as he never really liked you and Gus is more of an animal lover. —Your wife, Muriel.*

Since he had naively been expecting her to present him with the tie clip as a Valentine gift over their planned candlelit dinner at the Parkmoor Supper Club, it would be fair to say that he had not seen this coming; now he kicked himself for being so blind. The line that troubled him most was the one about Gus being "more of an animal lover" and what she may have meant by it. It conjured up unwelcome images of Gus stripped to the waist, beating his big gorilla chest, his brow dripping sweat from the exertion of his lovemaking.

In Overland he had put Muriel to the back of his thoughts. Not going home at night had made this easier. Besides, there was no longer any reason to go home. No Fuffy to feed or take for a walk. She'd even taken his bowl—with the food still in it. He had been left with nothing—nothing but a big stupid cardboard heart pinned to his chest. What a dope.

As Kay was passing a bus station, she saw travellers waiting in line or gathered in groups around clusters of suitcases while buses drew in and out of the allotted spaces.

Tucked round the side of the main building an assortment of boxes and baskets had been stacked against the wall beside a couple of dumpsters. Among them was a bright green bird in a cage. It caught Kay's attention because it reminded her of Mrs Ishi's bird, Mr Green. It was the same kind of cage too. There was no one nearby so she went over to take a closer look, and for a moment she thought it *was* him, even though she knew that by now he was on his way to Chicago. But, this bird's demeanor was different. When she asked the bird what it was doing there, thinking it might answer like Mr Green would have done, it suddenly lunged at the bars, startling her. There was a miaow from one of the baskets and rustling movement in what looked like a rabbit hutch. In a little wire cage, she saw something furry—a hamster or guinea pig—asleep (or dead) amongst the straw. She realized that all the boxes and baskets contained pets of one sort or another. Was anyone going to take care of these animals or had they simply been abandoned? She wanted to ask someone, but had to remind herself that she was incognito and trying not to get herself noticed, especially now that she was so close. She couldn't afford to get involved.

At the corner she opened her purse and took out the tightly folded piece she had torn from the street map in the library. She rotated it to establish her relation to, and distance from, her goal. If she could just find a way through the recently introduced army roadblocks and diversions she'd be there. She remembered there was a tunnel—several tunnels, Queenie had said—all feeding in from different directions to hide the rush-hour traffic flow to and from the factory.

It was as she was cutting through a parking lot that she saw it: a long straight road leading into the freestanding stone archway of a tunnel entrance. At first she thought it might have been the same tunnel that the factory bus took, but inside the mouth of it, she could see that this one was richer with flora and herbaceous

vegetation. The whole thing looked artificial, like an accessory for a child's train set, or something that might have been created as an entrance archway to some fancy public botanical garden. Had she got it wrong? Perhaps it was nothing to do with the Lockheed factory. She continued, just to see, burrowing deeper into a rich, leafy cocoon. Further on, she stopped to admire the profusion of roses and chrysanthemums growing in the hedgerows, interested to note that their colors—red, pink and white—perfectly matched the flower design on her dress. She plucked a rose and discovered that the flowers were artificial, made from plastic. She took one of each color, removed her hat—Queenie's hat—and threaded their stems through the band around the crown. She held it against her skirt to admire the coordinated colors. Pleased with the new adornment, she placed the hat back on her head.

A motorcycle sped along the approach road towards the tunnel entrance. The engine was sounding sweet, like a contented mountain lion. The bike's new owner opened up the throttle to put it through its paces. As he headed into the mouth of the tunnel, sharp sunlight broke through a gap in the clouds.

In the shade, the motorcycle rider struggled to adjust his vision. The sunlight twinkled and flashed as it pierced through gaps in the foliage canopy overhead. The wind swayed the trees, creating stippled shadows that fell across the road ahead. Confused by their movement, the rider squinted and blinked in an attempt to navigate a safe path through the spangled green gloom.

As he approached a hedgerow full of flowers, everything before him seemed to be shifting. A pattern of red, pink and white. For a moment, he thought he could see someone, a woman in a flowery dress, moving in the road up ahead, but unable to make out the outline of anything solid, he put it down to the confusing effect of the creeping shadows.

Kay stood, mesmerized by the effect of dappled light shapes playing across the floral pattern of her dress. The buzzing drone of an engine somewhere in the distance filled her head, growing louder and louder. She turned, surprised to see a motorcycle racing towards her.

Stranded there in the middle of the road, she had only a split second to decide which way to move, to anticipate the direction the rider might swerve to avoid her. But it seemed she and the motorcycle were predestined to occupy the same space at the same precise moment—the collision was inevitable. She made a too-late dash for the hedgerow opposite, inadvertently running into the rider's path. She raised her arm in a futile attempt to block the impact, but with devastating speed came a shattering blow; her elbow, along with every other part of her, smashed by the unstoppable force. The jolt came like an explosion, punching the air from her, jolting her insides as the bike carried her along at equal momentum. She was looking up at her own legs floating in the air, a section of swirling sky, something spinning: her shoe and a piece from the bike. Then her face suddenly slammed into dark asphalt. A series of body-twisting flips followed and then she found herself on her back moving at

tremendous speed along the ground, the road beneath her, gritty and searing hot. Her shredded dress tugged tight at her armpits. As she gasped for breath, she caught sight of the bike on its side, skidding along ahead of her— someone, the rider perhaps, tumbling like an acrobat into the hedgerow. And she was still sliding along the ground, traveling in a perfectly straight line as if she were on a luge sled. She finally came to rest—neck all skewed and tight, a choking bone in her throat. Arms useless. After a drifting spell of dark sleep, a motorcycle boot smelling of freshly grated rubber appeared near her head. Its wearer stood over her, silhouetted against the sun. His face came into focus for a moment as his shadow fell across her. He had a beard and an eyepatch like a pirate. She heard his voice. *Oh Jesus. This is bad. This is bad.*

But it wasn't so bad—was it? If only she could catch her breath, straighten herself out. Deep in her chest she heard a thick fluttering like a caged bird and felt a choking throat full of something warm, like the time she tried to eat tomato soup lying down, the rich tangy taste reminding her of home.

Her eyes were still open, but the light here was quickly fading and in a couple of heartbeats she was transported to—

—Overland. Kay lay on a grassy hillside by the lake, a permanent Resident now. She gazed up into the azure sky, shielding her eyes from the bright sunlight. It was a perfect day, like all the others that were to come. The lazy growl of an airplane overhead reverberated through the atmosphere, but she was unable to pinpoint its position. Abandoning her search, she closed her eyes, let her hands drop to her sides and slipped peacefully away.

THIRTY-FIVE

Queenie entered the Black Cat Cafe and shuffled to a window booth. She looked completely drained of life, no longer recognizable as the vivacious Hollywood starlet, the girl about town with pep in her step. Now she was pallid and shaky with barely the strength to walk. The only trace of color left in her face was lent by sunlight reflecting off her red tartan purse, which she had placed on the table in front of her and from which she now took a cigarette.

The clock on the wall showed five minutes to four.

By four twenty Queenie was growing agitated, checking folks on the street, hoping to spot Ma Young among them.

Four fifty-three, and still no sign of Ma. Queenie nudged her empty coffee cup to one side with her elbow and rested her head in her hands.

One minute to five. She opened up her handbag and took out her coin purse. Getting to her feet, she managed to haul herself to the payphone. The waitress, who had been staring idly out of the window, turned to eye her with uneasy concern.

Queenie called to her. "Watch my handbag, would you, miss?"

The waitress glanced over to the corner booth table where Queenie had left it. She nodded, but was more troubled by Queenie's enfeebled movements.

Queenie took the little triangle of folded paper from her coin purse and opened it up, ready to dial the number. But there was nothing written on it. She turned it over in desperation, but the reverse was blank too. She realized she had been duped. Ma wasn't coming to help her; no one was coming to help her, she was on her own. She staggered back to her seat.

The waitress approached. "Are you OK, sister? You don't look too good."

A stocky man wearing a cowboy hat looked up from his ice-cream sundae.

"She's got anemia."

"Who are you, Dr Kildare?"

"I'm only saying."

Queenie smiled wanly. "I'm just tired."

The waitress touched Queenie's shoulder. "I'll get you some more coffee. Perk you right up."

"Er. No. Just some water. I feel a little dizzy. I'll just sit here for a moment, if you don't mind."

"Iron. That's what she needs."

The waitress snapped back at him. "Pipe down, would you?"

He did so with a huffy little shrug.

Queenie was slipping in and out of consciousness. The scene

outside the window seemed to change each time she blinked her eyes, as though a new shift of extras had been brought in to replace the last. It was becoming increasingly hard to pull herself out of the dark spaces in-between. A nearby voice brought her back.

The waitress set a glass of water down in front of her. "You'll have to move when it gets busy."

"Sure. I'll move. I just need a minute."

Using the Roller Rink as a point of reference, George headed left at the next intersection. It was a one-way street going against the traffic, so wasn't one he would have taken if he'd been driving, but he reckoned it was heading in the general direction of the Lockheed plant. He wasn't used to so much walking. By car he could probably be there in ten minutes, but that would mean taking the freeway and he could hardly do that on foot. The street should have brought him out somewhere near San Fernando Road, but he'd been walking for ages and had not yet come to it. At a Y intersection, he took the right-hand fork and headed towards a big white building he thought he recognized as the Spanish colonial revival church on Vineland only to discover when he got to it that it was a movie theater. He thought he knew all the theaters, but he'd never seen this one before. None of the street names rang any bells either. He stopped and turned around, reviewing the path he had just taken.

A man carrying a sack of groceries stopped to speak.

"Are you lost?"

"I can't seem to get my bearings," said George. "I know it must be round here somewhere. I'm looking for the aircraft plant."

The man frowned, puzzled.

"You know. The big factory that builds airplanes." For some reason George kept forgetting the name of it. Why was that?

He shook his head. "Hmmm. Not round here."

"Why does everyone keep saying that? It's vast. You must know it."

"Don't think so, bud. I'm a resident of this neighborhood and I've never heard of it."

"This *is* Burbank?"

"You're not talking about the movie studios?"

"No, no, an aircraft plant. I think it's near Empire Avenue. Empire Way, something like that. Near San Fernando Boulevard. There's a railroad track …"

The man shook his head. "Sorry, bud."

"Oh, I get it. You said you're a Resident."

"Uh-huh."

"So you're sworn to secrecy."

"Secrecy?"

"Of course!" George nodded sagely. "You think I might be a spy."

"I don't think anything, mister."

"You don't have to worry about me. I'm a Resident too. I work there."

"You work there, but you don't know where it is?"

"I know where it is. I just can't find it."

"There's a factory over on Compton makes machine parts—for tractors, I think."

"No, no, no. The aircraft factory. It covers over a hundred acres of ground. There's like twenty-five thousand people working there."

"No. Definitely not round here."

George leaned in, speaking confidentially. "You can tell me. I designed the whole thing. You know … the place upstairs."

"Upstairs?"

George spoke under his breath. "Over …" He nearly said the name, but decided to swerve. "You know. Over … the top of it."

The man looked back blankly. "You've lost me, mister."

"You said you were a Resident."

"A resident … sure."

"Then where's your Resident's pin?"

"Pin?"

"You're supposed to be wearing a pin."

"No one told me."

"I should report you. Make sure it doesn't happen again."

The man tried to move away. "Well, sorry I can't help."

George fingered the man's sleeve. "You must have seen planes taking off?"

The man looked down at his cuff like something alien had attached itself to it.

"Come again?"

"Planes. Taking off. You must have seen them."

"Oh, sure."

"Where? Where do they take off from?"

The man answered as though it were a quiz. "Er, the airport? Los Angeles airport?"

"No, there's a place right here in Burbank. Manufactures military aircraft. Big bombers. Hey, wait a minute. How do I know you're not a spy?"

"Who would I be spying on?"

George sized the man up. "You don't look like a spy."

"What do spies look like?"

"Same as everybody else, that's the problem. They blend right in."

The man smiled, but was trying to extricate himself from the conversation. "Well, good luck. Sorry I can't help."

"If you really are a Resident, you should know who I am."

"Who are you?"

"I'm the boss. I created the whole place and everything in it. I'm God."

The man nodded, backing away.

"Well, not actually God, but you know what I mean. God as in Godfrey. George Godfrey."

"Well, I gotta get going."

"You're good, I'll give you that. But it doesn't help me none."

"Sorry 'bout that."

"I'll ask someone else."

"You do that."

"I don't even want the factory. I want what's above it."

"Uh-huh."

"Overland."

"Overland?"

George checked himself. He realized he had breached the security protocol. He lowered his voice again. "Overland. You know. A little burlap, a little green paint."

"Green paint? Oh, wait a minute. Overland. Now I got you. I didn't know what you were on about. Overland is right around the corner."

"Well why didn't you say so?"

"You confused me talking about an airplane factory."

"No, it's Overland I want."

"Just around the corner. Go past the library and it's a couple of blocks up on your left. There's a coffee shop on the corner, right across the street from the movie theater." The man was illustrating his directions with hand gestures.

George followed the shapes and patterns, nodding.

"Take a left there and you'll see it. Overland. It's a big place. You can't miss it."

George was relieved. "I don't know why I couldn't find it. Completely lost my bearings. I was expecting it to be on a different level. You know, much higher up than this."

To George's eye, some of the buildings and storefronts were beginning to look distinctly phony, which suggested he was on the verge of crossing, or had already crossed, the threshold into Overland. The border between the real world and the one he had created blended so seamlessly that even he, its creator, was unable to spot the point of transition. He should have been proud, but instead he felt disoriented and uneasy, once more caught up in a shifting no man's land between realities.

A little farther along, these doubts were laid to rest when he saw the familiar architecture of the Overland Public Library with its impressive brass clock hanging outside—the workings of which, he noted, must have recently been mended since it now showed the correct time: two minutes to five.

A workman with a big canister contraption on his back like an aqualung was spraying the grass in front of the library building. George vaguely recognized him as one of the Overland crew. He called out to him.

"Your paint's too thin."

The man turned. "What?"

"Your paint's too thin. There's no color coming out."

The man smirked. "Wise guy."

George smiled weakly, unsure what he meant. His attention shifted to the impressively authentic-looking street lamp at his shoulder. It seemed taller than the ones he had designed for Overland. And now that he looked more closely, the library building was taller too. Much taller.

Nearby, a man was getting into his car. George caught him.

"Am I in the right place? Overland?"

"Overland? Right around the corner."

"Oh. So I'm not there yet?"

"No, not yet. Right around the corner. Take a left at the cafe."

George saw the cafe up ahead on the corner of the block and, across the street, the movie theater mentioned to him as a landmark, which, coincidentally, was actually called the Landmark.

Painted on the window of the Black Cat Cafe was a silhouette of a cat: spine arched and hackles raised. There were signs offering hot wieners or hamburgers for a nickel, and quick lunches at twenty-five, thirty and thirty-five cents. George was hungry, and debating whether to step inside for a snack. He sauntered by, glancing in through the window to check it out.

Inside, a handful of diners, caught between mealtimes in a no man's land of their own, were taking a late lunch—or an early dinner. A fat guy in a cowboy hat, unconcerned about such formalities, was tucking into an ice-cream sundae with a long spoon. In the open doorway, a woman in a white uniform with a little folded paper cap stared out. George assumed she was a waitress, but it occurred to him that in another context, a hospital or a doctor's surgery, the same outfit would squarely identify her as a nurse.

On the table of one of the empty window booths, he noticed someone's purse had been left unattended. Box-shaped and covered in red tartan—he'd seen the bag somewhere before, or one just like it, but couldn't think where.

The cafe looked dead; George decided to wait until he was back in Overland.

THIRTY-SIX

Two blocks from the Black Cat was Kaestner's, a ladies' dress store. Smart red awnings jutted out over each of the windows like scarlet salutes. A sales assistant emerged carrying a broken display mannequin, which she stood out on the sidewalk next to some cardboard boxes—perhaps leaving it there for the garbage truck to collect.

Across the street, George had paused at the corner to get his bearings. By now he was convinced he was back in Overland because a few minutes ago he had spotted the Resident tennis couple, racquets at the ready, no doubt on their way to play a match. Just to be sure it was them, he'd waved and the woman had waved back, albeit a little hesitantly. Then he spotted Kaiser's drugstore with the mannequin standing outside. He was pleased to see that the red awnings he had suggested had been installed, but confused why the name had been repainted. Kaestner's? Wasn't it supposed to be called Kaiser's? Oh well, same difference.

Reassured, he began to relax. Everything now seemed harmonious and serene. Overland as he remembered it, the pedestrians all busily doing nothing as per the Resident program. Many activities seemed well choreographed: street sweeping, taxi driving, window shopping, but others seemed aimless and uncoordinated. Three elderly men sat motionless on a bench. George couldn't help but say something.

"Come on, guys. If you're going to sit there like a set of dummies, we might as well *use* dummies. They're a whole lot cheaper to feed, you know."

The men turned to face him, unsure what he meant.

"Come on. *Do* something. Move around, take a stroll. You've got to keep moving."

Confused, the men got reluctantly to their feet.

Farther along, a man wearing a sandwich board advertising fast service-while-u-wait photos was standing on the corner.

"Well I guess I made it," said George.

The man looked George up and down. "I guess you did at that."

George let out a contented sigh. "Home."

The man repeated the word, savoring the concept with equal relish: "Home." He nodded slowly, letting the idea settle. "You been away for a while?"

"Seems like years," said George.

"Good to be back, I expect?"

"It looks different. I recognized the drugstore right away, but I don't remember any of this—the dry-cleaners and the print shop. Who built those?"

"I don't know, bud. I'm not from round here. Still, things change, I guess. That's progress."

"Well, I must say it's all looking very authentic." George spotted a sign over one of the stores. "Schumacher—that's good. It means shoemaker. I bet that was Jimmy's idea."

The man smiled affably.

"Jimmy Shepherd," George explained.

The man nodded. The name meant nothing to him.

A woman pushing a baby buggy was heading towards them. Was it the woman from Overland? George wasn't sure. What was her name? Gladys? She met his eye and smiled. As she drew nearer, she spoke.

"Another beautiful day."

George smiled. "What have we done to deserve it?"

"Beats me."

"How's the baby today?"

She paused, straightening the baby's cover. "He's fine. Sleeping, thank heavens."

George took a peek in the buggy.

"Oh, he's not so bad. I expected to see … you know, a big ugly mug like Edward G. Robinson."

"Why would you expect that, mister?"

George was wrong-footed. "Sorry, I didn't mean … I thought you said he looked like …"

She was clearly offended. George tried to make amends.

"My mistake. Well … er … congratulations. Beautiful baby."

The woman huffily steered her buggy around him and left.

Further along the street, he paused outside a furniture store, his hand pressed flat against the building's facade. He slapped the stone-work a couple of times, feeling its solid coldness against his palm.

"I can't figure where Burbank ends and Overland begins." He was not addressing anyone in particular, but a passer-by responded.

"You looking for Overland?" she said.

"Isn't this Overland?"

"Almost. It's right behind you."

George turned to see a large hardware store occupying a flat-fronted four-story building. There were two wide display windows at street level, above them, a sign painted in chunky white three-dimensional letters: *OVERLAND & SONS Hardware*.

"No. No. No. That's not what I mean. Not a store. I mean Overland the place."

He turned, but the woman had gone.

He went inside anyway; he wasn't sure why. He'd come to a dead end.

Store clerks wearing matching striped neckties and brown cover-alls with a smart red pocket badge were busy attending to customers from behind glass-fronted display cases. George looked around.

Overland & Sons offered a wide range of home-improvement tools and supplies—everything the professional builder or home handyman might need. Gallon cans of Monad Non-skid Rubberized Spar Varnish had been stacked in a pyramid in the middle of the gleaming wood floor, itself presumably coated with the product. There were rakes, hoes, shovels and other long-handled tools that George recognized

but to which he could not put a name. Hammers, screwdrivers, wrenches of all shapes and sizes were set out in neat rows. On a pegboard wall unit, a family of paintbrushes stood to attention, ranging from the smallest baby brush to the big fat daddy of them all.

Every inch of the Overland store's wall space had been used to display or promote its merchandise. Watering cans and pails hung from a beam above the counter and in the corner there were rolls of linoleum standing on end. Above a display stand featuring a fanned spectrum of color swatches there was a sign: *Paradise Paints.*

A sales clerk approached, rubbing his hands together enthusiastically.

"Welcome to Overland, sir. What can I help you with today?"

George knew it wouldn't get him anywhere, but he needed to have his say. "This isn't what I meant. This isn't what I meant at all. This is just a store. It's not Overland, it's just a store called Overland."

The sales assistant was unsure how to respond.

George exited, frustrated.

To the side of the store was a vacant lot used for parking. George wandered round to study the building from another angle and saw that high up on its side wall, perhaps fifty feet above the ground, was a giant billboard sign bearing a pictorial depiction of Paradise. It was another advertisement, its headline inviting the viewer to *Join the Paradise Club—A Little Piece of Heaven on Earth.* What, or where, the Paradise Club was had not been made clear, but the idyll portrayed in the poster made membership an extremely attractive proposition.

A boardwalk path led the viewer into the picture and out onto a jetty extending into a clear cerulean lake bordered by exotic flowers, luxuriant trees and shrubs. Rare birds sporting implausibly vibrant color combinations perched proudly among the branches.

At the water's edge, a pair of vacant reclining chairs faced the tranquil waters of the lake, offering their prospective occupants the opportunity to relax and reflect on the enormity of their good fortune. A fishing rod had been set up on a makeshift stand at the lake's edge, but the fish here were so eager to be caught that they were leaping high above the surface to offer themselves up to anyone who might show even the slightest interest. The keen look in their eyes seemed to say, *Just show me the basket, my friend, and I'll jump straight in.*

Beyond the lake, winding roads traversed gently rolling hills of Arcadian splendor. These were flanked on one side by distant mountains depicted as a series of craggy shards painted in cool lilac and white. The sky was striped with horizontal ribbons of orange, yellow, pink and turquoise, suggesting a setting sun—the perfect end to a perfect day. George recognized the scene at once as a depiction of the lakeside at Overland—an interpretation, admittedly, somewhat glamorized by the scenic artist, but one with which he could immediately identify.

Accommodation in Paradise, as in Overland, was offered in the form of a white picture-book cottage with a cherry-red roof, which sat on the water's edge with a little rowing boat moored alongside it. A couple of pink flamingos waded in the shallows nearby. Flamingos? Too much? The artist did not think so. He used everything at his disposal to enhance his vision of a perfect world, drenching it in sumptuous

hues: scarlet and coral pink, buttery yellows and zesty greens. Here, even the shadows, depicted in velvety indigos and mauves, were rich with color. It seemed that all of the blackness had been removed from this world, and correspondingly from the color palette used to portray it. As a testament to this, in the picture's foreground were three cans of colored paint with brushes sticking out of them. Their labels proudly proclaimed that they were Paradise Paints.

Responsible for the image of Paradise was a man in white painter's coveralls clinging to a tall, thin ladder that extended all the way up to the surface of the lake, at a height somewhere equivalent to the building's third floor. Here, with paintbrush in hand, he was adding flecks of vermilion to a bird's plumage. He glanced down at George momentarily before returning to the picture. It was a sunny day so the man's shadow, and the shadow from his ladder, fell as heavy black shapes across the billboard, separating him from the picture he was painting—a three-dimensional being, forced by the laws of geometry to exist outside of the two-dimensional world he had created.

But must it be necessarily so? Couldn't there be a way to enter that 2-D world, thereby lending it that third dimension and so bringing it to life? Major Lund, the country's leading expert on this sort of thing, had always insisted that a flat, painted image could be made convincingly three-dimensional so long as the viewer was prepared to bring that extra dimension to it. What was to stop George stepping though the painted surface into the alternative world of Overland? Access might be gained more through faith, a willingness to challenge the constraints of Euclidean geometry and its three-parameters model of the physical universe. Perhaps the painted picture was the portal through which one must pass in order to experience the world of Overland as a three-dimensional space.

George was prepared to make that leap of faith. Besides, it seemed far more than coincidence that the picture was painted on this particular building. The faded letters of the word *Overland* even appeared on the brickwork above the billboard picture. It was, he thought, not just a sign; it was *A Sign*. George waited and watched from the shade of an adjacent store on the other side of the parking lot.

Eventually, the painter began to climb slowly down the ladder. Once on terra firma he began to sort through the paints and brushes scattered on a ground sheet at the base of the ladder. He crouched, pouring the contents from one can into another and stirring the resulting mixture with a short stick. He added a little from a smaller tin, clearly in the process of creating a specifically required color. George kept his distance, slyly observing the alchemist at work.

The painter shook a couple of tins that appeared to be empty and then stood looking round him before finally strolling over to the Overland hardware store, presumably in search of fresh supplies. George anticipated he would be thus occupied for some time and seized his opportunity, heading surreptitiously over to the ladder.

He looked up with trepidation, daunted by the enormous height he must climb. Stepping onto the first rung, he began his ascent.

The sound of an airplane overhead drew Queenie's attention. She was on the street outside the Black Cat looking up at the narrow band of blue sky between the buildings. She shielded her eyes from the bright sun, but was unable to locate the plane's outline. She started to walk, keeping her eyes on the sky rather than on her feet, but when she eventually did look down, she saw that her feet were not moving, as though she were being carried. Before long she found herself in a pretty country town shimmering with quiet bucolic charm.

From a speaker somewhere, the romantic lilt of the Jimmy Dorsey Orchestra with Helen O'Connell singing "Embraceable You" was carried on the breeze, the seductive melody surfing over the smooth foxtrot tempo.

Residents ambled slowly by: a couple in tennis whites, a man carrying a stepladder on his shoulder, a woman riding a bicycle: people leisurely going about their daily business. No one was in too much of a hurry. They looked relaxed, smiling cheerfully in Queenie's direction, fully accepting her as a Resident. She was one of them now.

Finally, she spotted the plane, the sun glinting off its silvery fuselage. She waved up at it. From a hole in its side came first one then a whole stream of parachutists, their chutes quickly filling with air. Hanging like a string of bubbles from a child's soapy wand, the troopers sank slowly towards the ground. Her gaze fixed on one of them who seemed to be steering himself away from the group and directly towards her. As he drew nearer, she could make him out in more detail, his hands gripping the risers above his head, legs slightly bent, knees and feet together. She held her arms aloft in welcome, but at the last minute the wind whipped him off course, carrying him over the roadside fence, where he landed in a field of sheep.

She quickly climbed over the fence to the field where she found her hero lying on his back. The wind flapping at his chute threatened to drag him away from her, but she caught hold of him and lifted him up. He was a dummy, a two-foot rubber replica of a parachutist, yet she didn't seem in the least bit disenchanted.

"Oh, Jimmy. I knew it was you. I knew you'd come back."

She cradled the little man close to her, gazing adoringly at his face. A trail of strings hung from his backpack; the wind fluttered through the shiny silk fabric of the parachute attached to them. The doll's pose remained unchanged, but now its raised arms seem to gesture a complete surrender to her love.

Someone approached, tapping her on the shoulder. It was Dr Young, now wearing military uniform. He gently took the doll from her with a nod of reassurance.

"It's time now."

Queenie looked up at him and reluctantly she released her grip.

The waitress shook Queenie's shoulder, gently at first, then more firmly. Getting no response, she touched Queenie's face, tapping her cheek with the back of her fingers. Then came cold realization; the waitress flinched, quickly withdrawing her hand and tucking it behind her back. She took a moment to compose herself, then gently lifted Queenie's wrist to check her pulse. She acted with calm efficiency now, as if the similarity between her waitress uniform and that of a nurse had allowed her to slide more easily into the role.

After a few seconds she laid Queenie's limp wrist back on the table and headed for the payphone.

"Told you she's anemic." The fat customer had been watching, wanting to have his say.

The waitress glanced at him coldly.

"Not any more, she ain't."

Out on the street, passers-by noticed Queenie slumped against the window of the cafe. They couldn't tell whether she was drunk or merely asleep, but with her face pressed to the glass and her mouth agape, she made a comical picture and some chuckled lightly at the sight as they passed by.

George firmly gripped the top rung of the ladder with both hands. From here the distance between him and the ground below seemed enormous. But now that he was so close, his nose almost touching it, all he could see was a vast expanse of blue. In his peripheral vision he could vaguely make out other colors, but nothing identifiable. He was in the middle of the lake; it was not surprising that all he could see was water. He rested his fingertips on the surface of the picture and was both surprised and reassured to feel that the lake was wet. Calmer now, he released his other hand's grip on the ladder and reached out so that he might plunge both hands into the cool, clear depths.

THIRTY-SEVEN

George found himself in the middle of Overland Lake. He was glad to be there, but his immediate concern was that only the upper part of his body was clear of the surface; his lower half was dangling below the hole. He looked for a way to pull himself up, but he was surrounded by slippery tarpaulin and there was nothing to grab hold of. He was supporting his weight on his straightened arms, his palms flat on the surface of the lake either side of him, but he was quickly beginning to weaken. Under the increasing strain, his arms buckled and he reluctantly lowered himself further into the hole until he was resting on his elbows. He was fading fast and knew he couldn't hold this position for long.

Then he spotted Jimmy standing at the water's edge, calmly looking on. He must have registered the anxiety on George's face, yet did nothing to help, as if he couldn't quite understand what the problem was.

"What are you doing?" he said.

George was growing increasingly frantic. "What's it look like I'm doing?"

"I don't know. Swimming?"

"No, I can't swim."

"Oh. So what are you doing?"

"Drowning."

"Oh." Jimmy considered this for a moment.

"Throw me a rope."

"A rope?" Jimmy seemed half asleep, slow on the uptake.

"Yes! There's one right there on the porch. Hurry, pal. I can't hold on much longer."

The urgency in George's voice seemed to snap Jimmy into action. He made a beeline for the lakeside cottage porch.

George could see nothing of what was below him, and could no longer rationally think about what was physically supporting Overland. For him, it existed, like a child's concept of heaven, as an alternative utopian world hovering independently like an enormous magic carpet high above the surface of the earth. Nevertheless he sensed a dark void beneath him and knew that he could not afford to let himself fall through to it.

Outside the Overland store, a small crowd had gathered at the foot of the sign-painter's ladder. They formed a tight, concerned huddle around a figure lying motionless on the ground. An ambulance with siren and flashing light approached along the main street and was flagged down by a man on the corner who signaled it towards the incident in the parking lot.

For a brief moment, George found himself on the ground looking up. He recognized the perspective as one often used in cinema to show the point of view of a delirious patient waking up to see the caring face of a pretty young nurse looking over him, her features swimming in and out of focus. *Where am I? Lie still. Don't try to talk.* Here, though, the nurse had been replaced by a group of nosey spectators. One of them, a sales clerk from the Overland store, leaned in to offer his diagnosis.

"I think he's coming round. He opened his eyes for a second."

"What happened?" someone asked.

"Darndest thing. I saw him up the ladder. He was kinda pushing himself against the billboard, like he was trying to climb into the picture."

"Is he awake? Uh, no wait. He's going again. Hey buddy. Can you hear me?"

Jimmy slung the rope across the lake. It uncoiled and the end landed on the surface directly in front of George. He made a grab for it with one hand, but in doing so he was forced to relinquish his elbow grip on the tarp and this caused him to slip a little farther down the hole. As Jimmy pulled on his end of it, the rope tautened, but George had lost considerable ground; his head was now barely above the surface.

"I can feel a pulse, but it's weak."

"You're gonna be OK, pal. Ambulance is right here. They'll get you fixed up in no time. That was quite a fall you took. Stay with me, buddy. You gotta just hang on."

"You gotta just hang on."

Encouraged by the voice in his head, George snatched at the rope and, hand over hand, attempted to haul himself up onto the water's surface. He was desperate to reach solid ground. He yelled to Jimmy, spurring him to greater effort.

"Pull me up!"

Jimmy had him secured, equilibrium established between them, but seemed unable to haul him up. The tension on the rope increased, but nothing happened; it was like a deadlock in a tug of war.

Kay suddenly appeared from the lakeside home, wearing an apron and clutching a big spoon. Seeing what was happening, she tossed the spoon to the ground and rushed to George's aid. Taking her position in front of Jimmy, she grabbed the rope and hauled with all her might. The extra effort was enough to tip the balance. Like a newborn baby's emergence from the womb George slithered easily across the surface and was soon safely on dry land where the pain and distress of the delivery was quickly forgotten.

Kay touched his shoulder. "Where have you been?"

"Lost. I couldn't find my way home."

"Well, you're home now. Lunch is almost ready. You'd better wash your hands."

George looked down and saw that his hands were covered in turquoise-blue paint.

The ambulance men were steering their stretcher through the gathered crowd. One of them kneeled beside the reclining figure on the ground to assess the situation. The Overland store clerk pre-empted further investigation.

"Too late, pal," he said, shaking his head woefully. "He's gone."

THIRTY-EIGHT

George and Kay leisurely climbed the steps from their lakeside cottage up to Lake Street. Everything seemed even brighter and cleaner than before. In George's absence, new and unusual color schemes had been introduced and he was wonderstruck by the effect.

A peacock-blue sky swirled with yellow created the perfect backdrop for a salmon-pink bungalow with newly painted orange window frames and a bright vermilion roof. It sat perfectly displayed in the middle of a vibrant green lawn like a delectable confection waiting to be eaten. A man in white pants and candy-striped blazer was tending his azaleas. He paused to remove his hat, using it to fan his hot bald head. He caught sight of George and held the hat aloft in greeting. George didn't recognize him, but responded with a friendly wave.

Horticulture seemed to be a strongly developing neighborhood pastime. Next door in a garden lush with exotic blooms a woman in a sunsuit and white gloves was trimming her hedge. Perhaps fearful of spoiling the perfection she had already achieved, her actions were fussy and tentative, the snipping blades of her shears never quite making contact with the leaves.

Birds warbled as George and Kay sauntered through the suburban idyll. Stacked against a low wall near the church, they found painted wooden boxes overflowing with a bountiful harvest of succulent fruits: pomegranates, plump strawberries, juicy tangerines, lychees, shiny red tomatoes, vibrant pink dragon fruit and strange spiky yellow things too exotic to name—all seemingly chosen to test the properties of Technicolor. It looked like a market stall, but there was no vendor; instead there was a handwritten sign that said *Help Yourself*. A woman dressed as a nurse sailed by on a child's scooter, snatching a rosy red apple from the display as she passed.

George was particularly taken with the stream of clear blue water that wove a meandering path across the landscape as far as the eye could see. A pink footbridge traversed the stream, its color perfectly complemented by the blues and greens of the riverbank. A flotilla of toy sailboats threaded its way steadily downstream, watched from the bridge by a woman in a yellow polka-dot blouse. For an added dash of color, the banks of the stream were adorned with bluebells.

"Why didn't I think of that? Bluebells are my favorite flowers."

Kay smiled sagely; she seemed to already know.

The trees on the sidewalk, he noticed, looked taller and more luxuriant, their leaves glistening as though freshly varnished.

"It all looks wonderful—better than anything I could have imagined."

"Everyone's been busy, trying to make it perfect. Look. Here's Jimmy and Queenie's house."

It was the house whose roof Jimmy once painted brick-red—and

from which he subsequently fell. Apparently undeterred by the mishap, he was up there again brandishing his long-handled paint roller like some quasi rooftop gondolier, but this time he was painting the roof canary yellow.

George and Kay looked on while Jimmy busied himself with the task. He eventually turned and saw them watching him. Looking down at his handiwork, he was a little dazzled himself by the brilliance of the color.

"What do you think?" he said.

"I think it's … very … bright," said George.

"I told Queenie you wouldn't approve."

"It's not a color I'd have chosen, but …"

"I know it doesn't conform to your vision …"

"Well, no, but—"

"Queenie wants everything to be bright and cheerful … like the sunshine."

"—it's actually very beautiful. Besides, I think Queenie should have whatever she wants—so long as it's what you want too."

"Oh, I want what Queenie wants. We see eye to eye on everything. That's the way it is between us."

George smiled, nodding his approval. "She's a good girl, Jimmy."

Jimmy smiled back. "I know," he said.

As he and Kay continued their leisurely stroll, George peeked through the young couple's window, curious to see the world they had created for themselves.

The room was gay with modish simplicity. Facing the picture window, angled slightly towards each other as though in conversation were two cute red armchairs. Though not identical, they at first appeared to be a matching pair, so well did they complement each other. The chair on the left, with its fashionable painted tree motif declared itself daring and modernistic, though George suspected this might be a more conventional chair re-covered to make it appear à la mode. Its partner was more openly traditional, the integrity of its simple lines denoting a timeless elegance. He imagined Queenie and Jimmy sitting side by side in them, arms reaching across, their hands clasped together with fingers interlaced as they watched the world go by.

George and Kay paused at the entrance to the new Overland Golf Club to look out over the fairways. A chestnut horse, sleek and handsome with glossy mane—the equine equivalent of Errol Flynn—greeted them over a neat white picket fence. The horse, perhaps a merry-go-round runaway or a retired display model from a saddle shop, had been cast from some kind of lacquered resin. Beyond it in the middle distance, a golfer in plaid knickers, sleeveless pullover and cap, played a long, driving stroke that was destined to be a hole-in-one.

A woman turned the corner and headed towards them, pushing a splendid new baby buggy. As she drew nearer, George saw that it was Queenie. She was wearing a little bolero jacket over a white summer dress, cinched tight at the waist and decorated with a yellow rose-motif print. Matching accessories, crisp white gloves and a stylish wide-brimmed straw hat completed the look. She was perfect, like

351   UNDER

a model mother from a magazine advertisement.

"Queenie! I'm so glad to see you," he said.

She replied archly. "Well of course you are. Why wouldn't you be, with me looking so radiant?"

George was amused. "I don't know."

"So what happened to you? We've been waiting for you. This place didn't feel quite the same without its creator. Everyone's been saying the same thing: Where the HE-double-hockey-sticks is George, the 'artistic' director?"

"I got lost."

"You got lost? How could you get lost?"

She turned to point at a newly erected street map: a beautifully painted, two-dimensional graphic representation of the town. George had seen one just like it recently, but couldn't remember where; perhaps it was this one. It showed the roads and fields, the lake, buildings and all of Overland's important landmarks. There was a big red arrow pointing to their present location on Main Street.

"See? You never need to get lost again. YOU ARE HERE." She pressed a button and a little indicator bulb on the map lit up.

George conceded with a little chuckle. "I guess I am."

"Listen," said Queenie, "Jimmy said it was OK with him, if it was OK with you, if I played the part of the young bride. It's quite an undertaking, I know, but I think I can handle it."

George was a little thrown. "The young bride? Sure. Remind me how that goes again."

"She falls for this sweet guy who goes away to war while she stays home praying for his safe return. He's a paratrooper dropped behind enemy lines in France or someplace like that, and he's like this big hero, but he gets captured and sent to a prison camp. Well, then she gets a telegram saying he's been killed in action, but he's not, he's alive …"

During her story synopsis, Jimmy pitched up. Queenie took his hand, drawing him possessively to her side before continuing.

"So, anyway, he makes a daring escape and finds his way home. She's waiting for him with open arms and she realizes she loves him twice as much—she had no idea how much until she thought she'd lost him. And he adores her, of course, because she has good legs and a nice figure—in spite of the baby."

"Baby?"

"Oh, yes, there's a baby. Didn't you know?"

She pivoted the buggy around to show him. George warily leaned in to peek under the hood, fearful of what he might see: a scary vent doll or a rotten piece of painted fruit. But to his surprise he saw that there was a real baby—a gently squirming, gurgling pink-faced baby. As if to assure himself that it was real, George cautiously touched the baby's tiny clammy hand, feeling its fingers close around the end of his forefinger. The baby's eyes swam a little, trying to focus on his face.

Kay watched George's reaction. She and Queenie exchanged warm glances. Gushing with pride, Queenie rested her palm on Jimmy's chest. He draped his long arm around her, drawing her close.

"Anyhow, that's the story so far. I haven't seen a full script yet, but

it's bound to have a happy ending; these kinds of stories always do. Happily ever after. That's what the audience wants."

Jimmy agreed. "That's what *everybody* wants."

George nodded ruminatively. "You'll be great, Queenie. But you don't need me to give you the go-ahead. You're a very lucky girl. Leading men don't come any better than Jimmy."

Queenie made light of it. "*He's* the lucky one. He's crazy about me. Do anything for me, wouldn't you, babe?"

Jimmy gazed into her eyes, squeezed her shoulder. "Anything."

Leaving the happy couple at the corner, George and Kay strolled up to Vantage Point, a small promontory high up on one of the slopes that offered a panoramic view of Overland.

George turned to her. "How long have I been away?"

"How long?"

"I mean. Queenie's baby. Is it really hers?"

Kay smiled a smile that suggested some unknowable wisdom. She didn't answer, but he suspected he was asking the wrong questions.

They stopped at a bench and settled down together to look out over the town. Amongst the houses there was parkland, and meadows dotted with tiny wild flowers. Residents, who in the past diligently obeyed the signs telling them to stick to the walkways, now discovered that the netting *would* support their weight; they wandered freely over the previously restricted areas—nonchalant rather than defiant. The ban appeared to have been lifted. Kay breathed in deeply. The air was clean and pure; in the new improved Overland, fire hydrants no longer emitted smoke. She let out a contented sigh.

"I love this special time, when the day melts gently into twilight."

"Twilight?" George was surprised; he had thought it was still mid afternoon.

As if in response to her cue the sun slipped quickly from the sky, like they were seeing it in a speeded-up film. Sinking below the horizon, it cast glowing pink and yellow streamers across the milky lilac-gray clouds. Soon, the sky was suffused with the burning tangerine and gold of sunset. The clouds darkened, like coals amongst the glowing embers of a welcoming fire, everything gradually cooling as the light began to fade.

They continued their stroll. When they came to a stretch of cobbled road, Kay paused.

"What's the matter?" said George.

"I'm afraid these shoes weren't designed for walking over cobbles."

"You'll be fine. They're just painted on. Look." To demonstrate, George ran the toe of his shoe across the surface of the canvas that had been stretched across the road. He carried on walking, but Kay remained at the curbside. After a moment he turned to see her there, apparently stranded.

"Will you carry me?" she said.

"Carry you? What, you mean like a piggyback or something?"

"No, darling not like a piggyback or something; I mean like a groom carries his new bride over the threshold."

THIRTY-NINE

By the time they returned to the main road, it was officially dusk and a new lighting effect was in place. Old-fashioned street lamps had been installed, each throwing a soft pool of lambent light onto the road. A gas station boasted garlands of colored bulbs, and various illuminated advertising signs glowed warmly against the darkening skies.

Kay, for the time being at least, was back on her own two feet on the understanding that should they encounter some other obstacle or if she should twist her ankle, George would be there to carry her again—a proviso to which he readily agreed. In fact, he couldn't wait for the opportunity to sweep her up in his arms again, now that he had proved himself so capable of it. There was really nothing to it. Kay was as light as cotton candy and felt so deliciously perfect in his arms that he felt he could carry her forever.

The traffic floated silently by—perhaps at a more relaxed pace than during the daytime, as though the vehicles themselves were now off duty and taking a leisurely promenade around the town to enjoy it for themselves. All were equipped with headlights and tail lights, some with winking turn signals. Buses oozed buttery soft light from within.

When a particularly splendid red and sky-blue two-tone taxi approached, George stepped forward and opened up the back door. Taking his prompt, Kay climbed inside and slid along the seat while the cab continued to trundle along. He jumped in beside her and off they went, traveling at a vehicle speed equivalent to an easy walking pace.

As they passed along the streets, vignettes of Resident life reflected the soul of a society rich with community spirit. A man carried a small boy aloft on his shoulders so that he might reach the overhanging branches of a tree to which a confectioner had attached clusters of pink marshmallows. An artist in smock and beret, having completed a picturesque oil painting of the sun setting over the little church on the hillside, was packing up for the day. The local fishmonger stepped outside his shop to admire the artist's work; he was clearly taken with the painting. The artist, in a bold gesture of generosity, presented it to him as a gift. The fishmonger was overwhelmed. He thanked the painter profusely, pumping his hand in a hearty handshake. As an afterthought, he dashed back to his stall and grabbed a large and beautiful shining silver fish, which he then proffered to the artist. The artist accepted with reciprocal gratitude. More handshaking.

Sweethearts canoodled on park benches, oblivious to anything but each other. The more senior couples took a leisurely post prandial promenade along charming, tree-lined avenues. A mustachioed street-cleaner stepped aside to let George and Kay's taxi pass. He shouldered his broom, military style, and saluted as they rolled gently by. Many Residents paused to watch the happy couple, as if witnessing a royal

wedding parade; some gave a warmly respectful wave.

The line was growing outside the Orpheum theater.

"Where are all those people going?" said George.

"To see a movie, of course," said Kay. "Jimmy installed a projector and a screen. Queenie's idea. They have screenings every night."

According to the marquee, tonight's showing was *Andy Hardy Gets Spring Fever*.

When their taxi finally arrived at the town square George and Kay disembarked.

The little Overland Diner had been festooned with quaint colored lights and garlands of flowers. It was a balmy summer evening and customers dined al fresco, chatting affably over candlelit food and beverages. A trio of middle-aged musicians—guitar, violin and accordion—had set themselves up in one corner of the garden and were playing a sweet rendition of "The Very Thought of You." A tiny dance floor had been set aside between the tables where a few couples shuffled around to the music.

George held out his hand gallantly; Kay accepted and they headed directly for the dance floor. Once there, his arms enfolded her and she fell into the rhythms of his movements, swaying lightly to the music.

Someone had stepped up to the microphone. A rich, mellifluous female vocal, full of warmth and purity of tone, drifted across the diner. George and Kay turned, curious to know who was singing, and were surprised to see that it was Queenie. She was dressed in an elegant sage-green evening dress, her face a perfect painted picture, her hair done up in a sophisticated swirl and adorned with a diamond clip. More diamonds caressed her throat. Though her glamorous outfit and the quality of her performance were deserving of a large orchestra or dance band, here in the special moment the little trio's charming interpretation seemed the perfect accompaniment. The melody soared, carried by her lovely voice. She was a natural. Discreetly, George and Kay exchanged wide-eyed glances. *Who knew Queenie could sing?*

Queenie was at full melodic tilt. She gently caressed the microphone, making love to it, as though whispering sweet nothings into the ear of her lover. Her eyes locked on a customer at a nearby table: Jimmy. He looked up at her adoringly, knowing that the words of the song were meant just for him. His hand rested lightly on the handle of the baby buggy parked next to his table, rocking it gently back and forth in time to the music.

Having decided to cut out of the party to spend a little time alone, Kay and George strolled arm in arm up the hill, away from the diner. The sound of Queenie's lilting voice carried on the warm evening breeze. They paused to enjoy the tranquility of the moment, looking back at the little twinkling cluster of diner lights in the distance, seen now through the leafy lacework of greenery. Beyond it, Jimmy's grazing sheep were just visible as fluffy white specks in the moonlit fields where Howard Farmer's tractor continued to roll along.

Everything was more wonderful than either of them could ever have imagined. They both knew that they would never have cause to leave Overland again.

At the end of the street, a newsvendor stood at his kiosk. Various magazines hung from a string above his head, but his main line of trade was the stack of newspapers in front of him, which he was keen to promote.

"*Overland News*! Final!"

George and Kay sauntered over.

"Ah, good evening. Newspaper, sir? *Overland News*."

George glanced down at the masthead, delighted to see that his idea for a local newspaper had come to fruition.

"Final edition." The newsvendor urged them to take a copy; this might be their last chance.

George nodded. "Sure."

Seeing a little tin of coins on the counter, George sorted through his pants pockets for change. The vendor raised a halting hand.

"On the house, Mr Godfrey. You've done so much for this community. We're all so grateful just to be a part of it. You've given us a perfect home and we all get a tiny share of it. A little piece of heaven on earth, you might say."

"A little piece of heaven on earth." He mulled this over for a moment. "I guess it is at that. Thanks. That means a lot."

George raised the newspaper and took in the front-page headline. Smiling, he offered it for Kay to read: *Another beautiful day in Overland!* And then, below it, a smaller subheading. *What have we done to deserve it?*

George tucked the newspaper under one arm, slipped the other around Kay's waist and they strolled off together down Overland Main Street.

Music from the diner was channeled now through the town's speakers so that everyone in Overland might find comfort in the honey-cake warmth of the refrain. It was the hauntingly beautiful "Stairway to the Stars"—Queenie's lilting voice, full of optimism tinged with wistful longing, supported now by the big-band richness of a full orchestra. The melody's determined three semitone steps climbed up to a heart-warming surge on the crest of the lyric before settling comfortably back to continue on its gently meandering descent. It was an anthem, brimming with cheery hope, inspiring the Residents down the hill to join together in chorus, their voices soaring high and clear into the night sky.

Basking in the song's uplifting glow, George closed his eyes to savor every lovely moment of the melody, rapt by the romantic sway and swoon of the lyrics and their confident promise of eternal happiness.

A thousand feet above them, Colonel Wagner looked down from the cockpit of his Lockheed P-38, still unable to find what he was searching for.

AFTERWORD

In the wake of the Japanese air attack on Pearl Harbour on December 7th 1941, the War Department ordered Lieutenant General John L. De Witt, head of Western Defense Command, to find a way to protect critical military installations along the Pacific Coast. No one knew where the enemy might strike next, but the vast unprotected, uncamouflaged aviation factories just a few miles inland were obvious targets for a Japanese assault. Among those considered most vulnerable were the Douglas Aircraft plant in Santa Monica, Boeing's B-2 plant in Seattle and the Lockheed Aircraft factory in Burbank, California.

The Lockheed plant, with its subsidiary, Vega, and recently acquired air terminal, was one of the most strategic military facilities in the United States. In early 1942 Lockheed's workforce (90,000 during peak production) was the largest of any US airframe manufacturer, occupying nearly 3.5 million square feet of floor space.

While the army quickly set up barricades to keep out all but company employees from factory areas, windows were painted, electric lights were blacked out or dimmed and the building of bomb shelters began. Key personnel who had gathered at the Lockheed site to plan their broader defense strategy placed an urgent call to Colonel John F. Ohmer, a pioneer in military camouflage, deception and misdirection techniques. Though the USAAF had originally rejected his ideas as too costly, Ohmer, an amateur magician and a photography hobbyist, was now given free rein and a limitless budget to protect the facilities from enemy air attack. His mission was simple: to make the entire Lockheed Aircraft plant disappear.

Using a technique he called "visual misinformation" he combined two-dimensionally painted canvas with foreshortened three-dimensional props to disguise the Lockheed plant as part of the California landscape. When photographed by air reconnaissance, he claimed, it would blend inconspicuously into its surroundings.

With a camouflage engineering battalion under his command Ohmer began recruiting set designers, construction engineers, large-scale scenic painters, carpenters, prop masters and landscape artists from nearby movie studios in Hollywood. Among those offering up their specialists for the camouflage workforce were Warner Brothers, Metro-Goldwyn-Mayer, Walt Disney Studios, 20th Century Fox, Paramount and Universal Pictures.

Hangars and factory buildings were blanketed with acres of chicken wire, netting and painted canvas, transforming them into what to an observer flying at an altitude of 5,000 feet was an innocuous Burbank suburb with residential streets and sidewalks. Hundreds of fake trees and shrubs crafted from wire armatures coated in tar and then dipped in spray-painted chicken feathers gave the area a leafy, three-dimensional appearance. It was an elaborate operation: some army observers remarked that it looked like a Hollywood studio back lot. Buildings of all shapes and sizes – houses, schools and public buildings – were fashioned from timber and canvas. Most of the trees and buildings were not very tall, but appeared normal when viewed as a two-dimensional aerial photograph due to the extremely shallow depth of field.

In case Japanese reconnaissance planes were secretly flying over Southern California, Ohmer's team needed the ersatz neighborhood to show signs of life. Employees from the factory below would periodically emerge through hidden trap doors in the canopy to move the full-size inflated rubber automobiles around to suggest they were regularly being driven and re-parked. Workers hung laundry on clothes lines only to take it down again later the same day.

Though Hollywood and the Pentagon had at first seemed unlikely partners, the movie set designers' expertise proved invaluable in creating the grand illusion. Accustomed to budget and schedule constraints, they worked quickly and efficiently, but more importantly they understood the principles of stagecraft, artifice and visual deception, using their own techniques to fabricate landscapes that would appear realistic from a specified viewpoint, whether from the front row of a movie theater or the bomb bay of a Mitsubishi Ki-21.

The recruits included leading visionaries in the motion picture industry. John S. Detlie, an Oscar-nominated production designer and architect, led the effort to camouflage the vast Boeing aircraft plant in Seattle. Detlie, who was married to movie star Veronica Lake, left MGM in 1942 to manage the Boeing project as a member of the Army Corps of Engineers. Under his direction, the entire twenty-six-acre Plant 2 was canopied with a suburban network of streets adorned with some 300 tar and feather trees, fifty-three homes, twenty-four garages, three greenhouses, a corner store and a gas station. Detlie's bogus town was dubbed "Wonderland" by Boeing employees below.

Warner Brothers, whose movie set designers had been instrumental in hiding the nearby Douglas Aircraft plant in Santa Monica under nearly five million square feet of chicken wire, was forced to give its own sound stages the same camouflage treatment fearing they may be mistaken for aircraft hangars.

In all, some thirty-four air bases along the Pacific Coast were camouflaged, but the elaborate subterfuge was never put to the test; no enemy planes ever flew over and the feared air raids never came.

The disguise of California ceased to be critical when in June 1942 the US Navy dealt a decisive blow to the Imperial Japanese Navy at the Battle of Midway, during which all four of Japan's large aircraft carriers were sunk and Japan's capacity to replace them was crippled by devastating casualties. The threat of a serious attack against the West Coast diminished then gradually vanished.

The camouflage programs that had been so rigorously implemented during 1942 were mostly removed by 1944. Some remained in place, but were largely forgotten. In the final months of the Second World War, Boeing and Douglas staged film and publicity photo shoots in which women from the factories were photographed in faux leisurely pursuits – gardening, sunbathing and picnicking – to show off the mystery villages that had until then remained officially classified. Prior to this, photography of them at ground level had been a criminal offense. The secrecy over the project was now lifted, but even before the photographs were published, crews were moving in to tear the camouflage structures down. Designed *not* to be seen, it was as if by making the fake towns publicly visible, the magic that had enabled them to exist could no longer support them.

Lockheed finally closed the Burbank plant in 1992. After the area was razed, the lot stood vacant for almost a decade, its redevelopment stalled by environmental concerns. The vast triangular plot lay completely flattened and eerily empty, like a mirage that had vanished. On maps and aerial photographs it looked as though it had been purposely blanked out.

Lockheed Air Terminal was renamed Bob Hope Airport in 2003, and the plant itself has since been replaced by the Empire Shopping Center: 900,000 square feet of major tenants, specialty shops and restaurants. Apart from the occasional airplane motif on shopping-mall signage, visitors might never guess that one of the largest aircraft production facilities in the US once occupied the space.

One tangible yet ultimately useless clue to the past remains: winding along the lower slopes of the Verdugo Mountains is a road named Lockheed View Drive. It offers a vantage point from which, ironically, the Lockheed plant can no longer be seen, having once more been made to disappear into Burbank's suburban landscape.

Graham Rawle, September 2017

ACKNOWLEDGEMENTS

Enormous thanks to my wonderful editor Clara Farmer for her unique critical insight and unflagging support all the way through to this, the eleventh draft of Overland; to all the people at Chatto & Windus who have gone out of their way to make the book work; and to my agent Will Francis at Janklow & Nesbit for championing this project from the outset. My thanks also to David Pearson, Mark Duff, Mark Lewis, Mags Swift and Margaret Huber.